The Gorky Adm... slapped a strange crimson square on my shoulder as I stood in the "shower." Then the crimson square was fading, as though the water was washing it off—but the red color was inside my skin!

I knew suddenly he had drugged me, and I stepped from the rain to face him.

"So the noble Lady Kimassu finally condescends to recognize Alexei Gorky?" His lips drew back in a strange smile.

"I recognize you. Now you have what you want." My blood began to race with the effects of the drug. I did not want to be left alone, but I cried, "Leave me!"

He smiled again; he was breathing heavily now, almost panting. "No, Kimassu. It gets much worse.

"In five minutes you'll be screaming for someone, for anyone. And it's going to be me."

JAYGE CARR

LEVIATHAN'S DEEP

For Roger

LEVIATHAN'S DEEP

Published simultaneously in the United States and Canada by Playboy Press Paperbacks, New York, New York. Printed in the United States of America. Library of Congress Catalog Card Number: 80-80984. Reprinted by arrangement with Doubleday & Company, Inc.

ISBN: 0-872-16699-6

First Playboy Press Paperbacks printing August 1980.

Chapter One

MOTTO:

'Twas of a pallid, wicked dwarf,
Full woeful mien had he;
"Were but my dreadful deed undone,
I in my own countree."

—*Ballad of the Boy Freed from the Garrote*

There are many levers to crack open a mind.

Pain. The blade. Sleeplessness. Simples. Long interrogations. Degradation. Hope dangled and then snatched away.

But surest of all is willingness, the door thrown open from within. Second best is obligation, the door opened grudgingly from within.

I've used them all. I'm an expert at opening minds; it's part of my duties, a very important part.

I inspected my latest subject covertly while listening to the report of the guards who had brought him in. There was little in it I didn't already know; I had already spent much time soothing the very wroth Noblelady involved. I knew what he had done; and what was going to be done to him. The question was, could I pry anything useful ou of him *first*. . . .

Unprepossessing even for a Terren, he was. My problem, the Terren. My problem, because he was a Terren, and because I, of all the Consecrates in the House of Equity, had with practice become an expert in Terre ways of thinking—at least, as much an expert as any Delyen can become on those exotic creatures that call themselves Homo sapiens. Homo sapiens: Wise Men. Wise *men!* Look at the *wise man* now, I jeered to myself, quaking between his two guards, the top of his shaven, crestless head scarce higher than their waists.

Gutterrat! The Terre term fitted him. Gutterrats, so I've been told, are the cowardly cousins of the shiprats that plague us so, even in areas far removed from the Enclaves. Shiprats have the courage of cornered animals, they *fight*. But this—*gutterrat*. Begging animal eyes, trembling useless hands, flabby flesh drooping from scrawny frame. The problem in breaking this one would be to keep him from crumbling to uselessness in my hands.

I rose, walked around my work table, and leaned casually against it. Because I was under a roof, I was wearing only my kilt and Sash of Consecration, belt and blade, my daggertooth necklace, an armlet or two, and, as always, my Tear of the Goddess set in my left pinnafin.

"Terren," I spoke his language rather well, "you are in trouble, in very bad trouble." His external genitals made the change that meant he found me desirable. The disgusting animal! No wonder most Delyene can't abide even being in the same room with a Terren. But someone has to do even the most distasteful duties; and where it concerned the Terrene, I was that someone. The "specialist" on the Terrene. Much as I disliked that growing portion of my duties, I couldn't help being proud of all I had accomplished. For example, it was I who discovered the effect stripping and shaving have on the Terrene. Shaving had always been done: the Terre fur tended to harbor parasites. Odd, that the Terrene, who proudly point to themselves as the most advanced species in the universe, treasure their badge of animality. Deprive them of it, and they shrivel in their own minds. As for their clothing—who would have suspected that their gaudy, infinitely variable, meaningless clothing would be so dear to them? They who recognize no tradition, no honor, no Guilds, no Families? They often go naked by choice, but take their clothing away forcibly, during its necessary search—and *don't give it back*. The effect is the same as on the Delyen whose kilt is replaced by the undraped, undyed, unmarked kilt of early development. To a Delyen, this means your Family has denied you, your Guild has rejected you, your honors are as if they had never been, you have neither rights nor obligations nor privileges, you are *nothing!* Take away a Delyen's kilt, and you are halfway to breaking your Delyen. Take away a Terren's clothing, and you are halfway to breaking your Terren.

"I dint mean no reel harm," the Terren whined, staring at me slyly out of weak, pale Terre-blue eyes.

I made an almost imperceptible signal, and the guard on the left rammed his padded club into one of the Terren's most vulnerable points, called the solar plexus. The Terren doubled up, moaning and gasping for breath. I let him writhe and struggle for long seconds, until I decided that he was faking, playing for sympathy. My sympathy. For a *Terren.* Another signal, and the guards hauled him up and held him, a merciless hand under each of his armpits, so that he dangled between them like a gaffed fish.

"Terren," I made my voice stern, "you have broken one of our laws." This was not strictly true. In the first place, we have no laws, in the Terre sense of codified, written-down rules of behavior; instead we have honor, custom, traditions, Family judgments. In the second place, even if we had laws, we would have none against what he had tried to do, for the same reason as we have no custom that prohibits holding one's breath until one dies. Either is physically impossible—for one of us.

"I hadda, I tell ya." His sour voice grated in my ears. "I hadda, I wus *desprit.* The Captain, that—" Even his curses were unimaginative. I tried to make sense of his complaints and justifications. There was some Terre magic called an amadroid that he hadn't been allowed his fair share of.

"The fact remains," I interrupted his repetitious plaints, "that the Noblelady you attacked was of the Dawnglow Family, First Advisers to the Empress herself, long may she reign." (I had to use clumsy Terre equivalents of the proper Delye honorifics, of course.)

"I dint know, I dint know, I dint know!" Of course not, mindblind, stupid Terren that can't interpret a kilt. Sullenly, he mumbled, "Offered t' pay, dint I?" One of the guards growled, low under his breath. They all understand some Terretz. I fixed the growler with my eyes; this particular Terre slime was not—repeat—*not* to be touched. Unless I ordered it. "Anyways," he continued, licking his lips as his bleary gaze wandered below my angry glare, "I dint! So there!" Forgetting or not knowing of the acute Delye hearing, he added, low, "Orange skinhead bitch near broke my arm."

A second signal. I turned away, hearing the muffled thuds as the padded clubs landed, the screams, the pleadings. It was a calculated move. Poor softhearted me distressed by the pain of a fellow being. Arrrrrrrgh! I wanted—how I wanted!—to let them finish the job. It would be easy. So easy. Just . . . wait. Long enough. But that was the coward's way, that was failing in my duty. And disagreeable as it was, I knew my duty.

"That's *enough!*" I whirled toward them. The Terren collapsed in a heap on the packed hard floor and lay there, sobbing and snuffling. He probably thought he was dying. Nonsense! Properly used padded clubs (my boys are well trained) can produce a great deal of pain, but no permanent damage. If not applied to excess, that is.

I knelt beside him, clicking my tongue to make the noise the Terrene use to express sympathy and concern, bending down so I could run my fingers (what will power that took, to touch him!) over the faint pink marks that would fade without leaving brusises. "You hit him too hard," I said loudly, in Terretz. One of the guards defended himself, and we had an angry discussion, shuttling back and forth between Delyetz and Terretz. Under cover of one angry harangue, I whispered to the Terren, "Hush, lie still." He stirred. "Lie still, pretend to be unconscious." I pushed him down. "I can't control them, they're too angry." He was sprawled half on his side, half on his belly, his head slightly twisted so I could see most of his face. One cloudy blue eye stared at me—and slowly shut. He moaned. "I'll help you if I can," I whispered. He started to say something. "Shhhh!" I hissed fiercely. "You're unconscious, you're *hurt.*" I had decided; this one would respond best to his "friend." From now on, anything bad that happened to him would be out of my sight, without my knowledge, and against my express, loudly spoken orders. All good would come from me.

I rose. "There must have been some mistake," I said in Terretz. "This man is a Terren, an important Terren, not a criminal. I'm going to check into this whole matter. Meanwhile, I want him well taken care of. Treat him gently, do you hear me! Any complaints, and I'll send the whole brainless lot of you to pull galley oars." The phrase "pull galley oars" told them what I wanted. The only oar-drawn vessels we Delyene use are Ceremonial Barges, used by the Empress, the Council, the Priestesses. Pulling such is a high honor much striven for. But the Terrene, so I have learned, use oar-drawn craft for much lesser occasions; "galley slave"—I do not understand the insult implicit in slave—is to them a darksome threat. Not that my loyal boys need to be threatened, or punished either; and if either becomes necessary, I certainly wouldn't shame them by administering it in front of a *Terren.*

My boys are good boys. They know what to do. As soon as they are down the corridor and out of hearing, one of them will start kicking and cursing the Terren. The other will stop him, saying, "Remember our orders. Remember what the Kimassu Lady said." Grumbling, the first will stop, glaring at his victim and muttering threats and curses. The Terren will be escorted to a regular cell, smallish and minimally furnished, but not uncomfortable.

Time will pass. Then two different guards will look in on him. "A new one. Say, that's a Terren. What's he doing here?"

"Haven't you heard? He's the one who—" (All in Delyetz, naturally. But gestures and eye-rollings will make the meaning clear.)

"He *did?* Then what's he doing *here?*" A sharp prod with a club. "Come with us, Terren!"

The cell he'll be taken to is a *very* special cell. (Once we used cells up by the roof; they got very hot. But these are better.) A trap door will be lifted, and he will be dropped into the cell, feet-first; the trap door will slam shut. Uneasy, he will feel the wet walls in the darkness. The floor is a square half a fathom on a side, the walls higher than he can reach, but not too high; he won't be hurt by the drop. He may compare it to the box the Terrene used to encase their dead—a coffin. A vertical coffin. He may lean against the wall, he may squat awkwardly.

And then the tide will come in. It comes in very quickly, and it fills the cell to within a hand's breadth of the closed trap door. At some point in his ordeal, he may discover that there are two small outcrops in adjoining walls; if he braces his knees on them, and scrunches over, he can keep his face up out of the water. Or he may simply paddle frantically. For an eternity.

Until another pair of guards fish him out and take him to Draxuus.

I've trained Draxuus IV very well. He looks the part, being very bulky for a male of our race. A black eye patch covering a perfectly good sea-green eye and spatters of dried something on his bared arms and upper torso add villainy. By the time the Terren is brought in, I'll have been able to rehearse him. Not that it's very necessary; Draxuus IV has a flair. (Though he cannot compare with Draxuus I, sweet in memory, my lovesome boy with the topaz eyes!)

The Terren will be dragged in, getting glimpses of terrible, used equipment. Despite his frantic struggles, his wrists will be bound together, the ropes lifted over a ceiling hook, so that he dangles, suspended, helpless. He'll be able to see Draxuus going from table to table, picking up an instrument, looking back at him, musing, perhaps laying it back down, perhaps handing it to an assistant. A hot iron will be brought dangerously close. But Draxuus will touch it, will frown, will order it thrust back into a bed of glowing coals. Assistants will make suggestions; one will crack a whip.

The prisoner will scream, plead, beg, threaten. Uselessly. No one, he will realize, understands a word of Terretz. He will be poked, prodded, pinched. Gloating expressions will tell him how much they hate Terrene.

When Drax thinks he knows what frightens the Terren *most,* he'll saunter slowly toward him, waving whatever-it-is in his hand. Usually it's a hot iron. The Terrene have this thing about hot objects.

Then, just in the nick of time, one of the guards who originally brought the Terren to me will rush in panting. A quick argument in Delyetz. Much excitement. Much worry. Much shaking of heads and furious accusations and denials. Drax will frown, will snarl, will finally, reluctantly, nod agreement. (The Terren will be in no shape to realize that the Delyene do not nod to show agreement, as the Terrene do.)

Drax will speak to the Terren, using the guard as an interpreter. "Terren, bringing you here was a mistake. A bad mistake. Not *my* mistake, but the Kimassu Lady will simpy blame *everyone*. If you complain. If you tell her." The Terren, cut down by sullen assistants, is no doubt rubbing his wrists to get circulation back into them. "Now, you haven't been hurt, and the guard will take you back to the right cell, and we'll all forget this whole affair. A mistake, but no harm done. Of course, you can complain to the Kimassu Lady. If you do, I'll be punished. But . . ." Here he smiles, showing a mouthful of daggertooth-sharp teeth. (A little filing helps.) "But the Kimassu Lady talks a lot meaner than she does. I'll still be here. And—I have friends. And the Kimassu Lady, she's a bit—well, naïve. Thinks everybody is as honest and sweet-natured as she is, bless her. Why, if a guard reported to her that you had *died*—" A long, hard pause after this is translated. Then, "Terrene die here all the time. Our climate is hard on them. She might not even ask to see the body." While this is being translated, he winks. She's squeamish is the unspoken implication. "But if she did," he goes on, "we could show it to her. Without a mark on it, either." By now the Terren is probably protesting volubly that everyone makes mistakes—he wouldn't *think*— "Of course," Drax smiles more broadly, "if she doesn't want to see it personally, just orders it thrown into the sea, well—there are always empty cells here. Not very comfortable, I'm afraid, but then you could come and visit me . . . often . . ." Whatever he is holding is brought close to the Terren, waved threateningly. "I know lots of games, Terren. Amusing games—to me. And I can make a new toy last a long, long time . . ."

This Terren Willis is a coward, he will not complain. The Kimassu Lady can't be everywhere at once, can she?

Only once, long years ago, did one of them have the courage to speak up. He was a ship's officer of some sort, his crime the result of ignorance not malice. (He tried to cross a Ceremonial Procession!) The Priestess-Hierophant was most wrathful, but he had offended without intending to (the Terrene have this custom called a parade) and besides, the Terrene wanted him back. (I suspect the Terrene will cheerfully throw this Willis to the daggerteeth. But arguing with them over him is no part of my duties, thank the Goddess!) When the officer told me, I pretended confusion, upset. I *believed* him, but that my own men could do such a thing. Behind my back. Against my orders. Even by mistake . . .

I sent for Draxuus. (Draxuss I it was, my sweet, faithful boy!) The Terren was hidden behind a screen, but the stench of him flooded the room; Drax didn't need to see me playing with my Tear of the Goddess to know what to say. Of course, it didn't take me long to trip him up; I tangled him in a skein of his own lies until, at my signal, he retreated into a sullen silence. I sent him out and apologized to the officer. I was so upset that he actually ended by comforting me. That my own man should disobey orders (even by mistake); and then lie about it. Poor discipline, he said. Do it differently in the Service. Of course I intended to punish Draxuus! A lecture, loss of all privileges, even confinement to his rooms for a cycle.

He nodded slowly, obviously unsatisfied.

That was when I had my great idea, the one that brought me so much attention.

"I'm so glad you approve," I stammered huskily, not meeting his eyes. (I have never been above using the Terre peculiarities most shamelessly.) "I just *couldn't* . . ."

Naturally, he wanted to know what I just couldn't. So I let him draw out of me that there was a standard punishment for disobedience, but I couldn't order it. I couldn't even *think* about it . . .

I also let it slip that I had obtained this position through my Family (true), that I had only had it a short time (false), and that I was hoping for a change (true, but that hope was later destroyed by my own cleverness) so I wouldn't have to question people or—(whispered) order people *hurt* . . .

He stiffened my spine.

I branded Draxuus.

A most impressive ceremony. There was steam and smoke and stench of burnt flesh, and Draxuus howled most heart-rendingly.

I stood straight as a spear through the whole. Then, dry-eyed and dry-voiced, I escorted the Terren to his cell (Very Important Prisoner-type), saw to his needs, and obviously near the end of my control, begged to be excused to attend to other duties.

He patted me on the shoulder, muttered something, hesitated—and let me go.

I controlled myself—my laughter, that is—until I was out of earshot. Oh, I was proud of myself. Oh, had I fooled him! Stupid Terren, he never even suspected . . .

And after all, it isn't easy to pretend youth and inexperience when you are the taller (though this officer was tall for a Terren, if I remember correctly, almost as tall as I am) and probably the elder. It's difficult to judge age with the Terrene, because of their back-to-youth magic. We Delyene merely age slowly, by our nature. This Terren was in what they call early middle age, and I felt it was his first; but it could as easily have been his twelfth. Except that anyone of such years would have been harder to fool.

But *I* was not fooled, nor so young and inexperienced that I failed to recognize the look in the Terren's eyes. (Though it seemed most unnatural to see it in a male's eyes.) I did not know what had made him hesitate, but I would be most careful to give him no further opportunities.

Draxuus was badly hurt—his feelings, that is. I hurried to see him as soon as I left the Terren.

As soon as I drew aside the doorway drape, he leaped up and fell at my feet, clasping my knees and sobbing. "What did I do wrong, mistress, what did I do wrong?"

I rapped my knuckles sharply against the lovely arched dome of his skull near his pulsing deep orange crest. "Let go of my legs and stand up, you muscular beast," I grumbled, laughter in my voice. "You did *good!*" He was mine, my pet, and though at that time I had not yet an established household, still I had gotten him a room of his own, much nicer than the male dorms. I closed the drape behind me.

"I did good?" His lovely eyes, of rarest pure topaz, begged for reassurance.

"You did perfect." My voice was firm. "You did exactly what I wanted. I knew you could, even without my warning you. None of the others would have been able to guess what I wanted without my telling them. But I knew

I could depend on you; you did perfect, Draxuus. I'm so proud of you."

He tilted his head up to stare in my eyes. "Not sayin' that to make me feel better, mistress?"

I caught his pinna-fins and hauled him to his feet. "You did *good,* Draxuus."

He smiled, finally satisfied. "I pleased you, mistress." He really was quite bright, Draxuus was, for what he was. I had only spoken truth. He was one of the few of my guards who could have played his role properly, with naught but the hints I gave him in my lecture. ". . . and I know this is going to *hurt* you, Draxuus, *hurt* you terribly, but it's for your own good. It'll *hurt,* and you'll remember the *hurt,* and remember why you were *hurt* . . ."

I could have waited and rehearsed him, but why give the Terren time to get suspicious, to ask questions or make idle comments. I knew I could depend on my Draxuus, bless him! (I had also chosen guards that couldn't speak Terretz, so their comments woudn't give the game away. A good thing, too; listening to them *I* had difficulty keeping a straight face.)

Poor dear Drax! Those comments were what was bothering him. But I had finally convinced him. His skin glowed brilliant, deep orange as the life-fluid surged under it. "I did good!" He was beautiful, so very beautiful. My fingers stroked delicately at the base of his crest; I could feel it stiffen, rise, the pulse beat becoming stronger, faster.

"Mistress . . ." He was so *very* beautiful.

"But first," I controlled myself with an effort, "I want to check that burn."

"The burn?" Neither Delyene nor Hardyene worry about burns; we get too many of them. "It's nothing, mistress! Nothing!"

"I know, Draxuus. I wouldn't have ordered it if I thought it might hurt you, damage you, not even for that important Terren." I stroked his other cheek. "You're my best boy, Draxuus, my very best boy. That's why I just want to make sure . . ." Firmly, I raised his head so I could see the cheek he had been protecting with a hunched up shoulder. Very rarely, for no reason we can understand, a burn fails to heal properly. I tweaked his nose in relief; this one had already started the healing process. Oh, it looked hideous, as it had when it was done, fluid under the skin distorting it into a swollen dark angry brand. But underneath I saw the pale gold gleam that meant healing skin was already forming. It had only been a small chance, but the Four-faced One too often played a hand in my game. But not that time. The fluid would gradually be absorbed back into his system, while the healing continued. The outer, wrinkled skin would gradually dry out, until it could be peeled off as easily as peeling a tanna. Within days after that, the sun would color the new skin until it matched the old. The Terrene do not seem to have as effective a healing; also, and this I have difficulty in making my fellow Delyene believe, burning hurts them. The heat does not deaden a Terren's nerves. The Terrene are inefficient, in more ways than one.

"It itches, mistress," Drax said, his eyes wide in the way he thought proved innocence, and I knew meant fib. As if I wouldn't have known, anyway; a burn doesn't start to itch until it's ready to peel. Nonetheless, I stroked it gently, while he closed his eyes and moaned in sheer animal content.

And afterward . . . .

He was, after all, my very best boy.

We'd both earned our reward.

Chapter Two

MOTTO:

It is forbid both great and small,
Unless that they be Pure,
To set their feet in Holy Hall;
Lest pain of death endure.

—*Canons of the Nameless Prophetess*

Willis safely bestowed, I stood without the Elyavaneet Nobelady's undraped door in the Respectful pose, my legs slightly spread, my hands clasped behind my back, my eyes tightly closed, and waited for her to notice and acknowledge me.

"Kimassu, child, come in, come in. I was just thinking to send one of the boys to ask if you could join me for dawnmeal." Once noticed, I could open my eyes and enter. Since the sun was barely two palmwidths above the horizon, the huge woven fiber fan in the center of the room was still, the boy who would pull it during the heat of the day off somewhere asleep. At this season, even a Delyen feels the noon heat. The room itself displayed the Noblelady's rank and taste. There was a small pool with fountain in one corner, and the rest of the floor was padded with a woven covering, patterned in the greens and blues we Delyene prefer. The walls were whitewashed and painted in murals, mostly religious scenes, such as the Infinitely Wise One creating foodfish and placing them in the seas for Her servants to eat.

In a niche next to the entrance, a spray of water fell from a ceiling pipe to collect in a sunken bowl lined with a mosaic of jade and aquamarine and lapis lazuli. I removed my kilt and sash of office (though neither would be harmed by water; I just wanted to feel wet all over) and slipped off belt and blade. One of the Noblelady's boys accepted my accouterments, and I rotated gratefully in the stinging stream, letting it cleanse and refresh me, letting cool wetness trickle into my parched mouth and down my dry throat. Ahhhhhhhh, that was good!

I stepped out, smiling at the boy and wondering for the dozen-dozenth time why it was such a *dry* route to the Elyavaneet's quarters. I shook myself and the boy handed me my things, which I draped over one arm. Besides the Elyavaneet herself, several of her boys were scattered about the room, industrious at their tasks. I thanked the boy, who had reseated himself at his loom. He was new to me, and, curious, I peered over his shoulder at his work. It was worth the compliment I gave him; it wasn't finished enough to judge pattern, but the threads were fine and even, the colors bravely dyed. He flushed bright orange and admitted that he had done both dyeing and spinning. So then I had to refuse the offer of the tapestry from the Elyavaneet herself. We compromised; I was to have his next weaving, this would give me a choice of subject. I must, I made a mental note, decide on a complimentary gift for the dear Noblelady. My Jerbon was particularly skilled in jewelry-making. An armlet—no, better, a pectoral—with the insignia of our Family set with colored stones . . .

She was in the shallow end of the pool, and as I approached she lowered her eyes with a frown to the cords neatly arranged on the work ledge beside her. I slipped quietly in, and waited, not disturbing her frowning concentration. She might have been a carven statue, only her lower body in the water, elbows on the ledge, chin on fists, eyes on the row of cords. Suddenly, she gave a little shake, glanced at me with a rueful air, clapped her hands. "Dear child, how remiss of me. What would you care for?" Tiredly she rubbed the bridge of her nose. That nose was the only flaw in her otherwise regally handsome face; it arched high but was too thick between her eyes. She was short, too, but held herself so erectly that one was seldom aware of it.

"Just juice," I told the boy who came running in answer to her clap.

"Passinfruit, cashelberry, grue, seacream, lilili, or sours," he rattled off.

"Sours," I told him. He made a quick face, an amusing wrinkling of his turned-up stub of a nose, before turning to his mistress.

"My usual, Simsam, dear."

"Yes, mistress. At once, mistress." And he was gone.

With a sigh, the Noblelady lowered herself completely into the pool; she broke the surface, facing me, eyes twinkling with mischief. "Well, child," her voice was gently scolding, "It's been quite some time since I last saw you. Are you neglecting all your old friends, or have I offended you particularly in some way?"

Her teasing went awry. Sheer shock held me frozen for a long heartbeat; then in one smooth motion I was out of the pool and down the steps. On the bottom step I knelt, so that my head was lower than hers. "Noblelady," I gasped, "Revered Noblelady, I never meant—I would not *neglect* . . ." I crouched beside the stone wall of the pool, trembling.

"Dear child, dear child, I was but teasing." Her hand rubbed my bent neck, a caress all the more precious since we Delyene dislike touching one another; I straightened and her hand and her smile urged me up, until I was standing, facing her. A gesture, and I slid gingerly back into the cool water. "I have missed you, child; it has been overlong since last we met."

"Noblelady, the press of my duties . . ."

"Ah, yes." She closed one eye slowly in the Delye sign of agreement, but her aged face remained sad. "Your duties. I've good word about you, child, very good." I shut my own eye in quick acknowledgment, but said nothing. I knew I had done well, but I was never one to boast. "But are you—are you—ah—happy in your work, child?"

"Noblelady?"

"Are you *happy*, child?"

I pulled myself onto one of the sitting ledges below the surface. Then I spoke, choosing my words carefully. "Noblelady, what I do is often not—pleasant. But it needs must be done. And I do it well, this I know. I am —content."

She sighed. "Yes, you do your work well. And you find

contentment in accomplishing a necessity well. But you would do as well in other duties, and this is not the life-work I would have selected for you."

"Someone must do it. Why not I?"

"Why not someone else? You had an opportunity to exchange duties with your sister the Enghadu, and you refused. Why, child?"

I hunched my shoulders uneasily, fixed my eyes on the underwater ripples caused by one idly moving foot; the Elyavaneet had always seen further into a stone than most could see through sunlit air. It was not that I distrusted her; my honor, even, was hers for the asking. But some things can be ill-omened through the barest mention, the saying of a careless confident word. "I would not leave with tasks incomplete."

"Child, child," she chided. "You are overconscientious; for you, no task is ever complete. I should have spoken of this sooner. I fear, child, too long at such duties may leave you hardened. Too much exposure to the evil, the wicked, the morally weak may leave you cynical. And power over others may become an appetite that grows as it feeds."

I thought of the Terren Willis I had examined earlier, the momentary impulse to let the guards beat him to death, to cleanse our blue world of his filthy presence. Yet who was I to be judge, a Family Council rolled into one body? Scum he was, and I knew it; weak, cowardly, cruel, mindless animal filth. Yet the sun warmed his back as mine, a passinfruit tasted as sweet in his mouth as mine, and were not his poor substitutes as dear to him as my higher, more intellectual pleasures were to me?

Pah! Scum is scum!

"I know not, dearest Noblelady." I smiled at Simsam as he handed me my tart sours juice in a tall porcelain goblet the subtle blue-green shade of the fertile sea. "Have I changed? I seem no different to myself, so how can I tell? And if I have or if I do change, could it not as easily be a change for good as ill? I must change, in some manner, everyone must, for growth is change, and we all grow, until the Infinitely Wise One"—at the sound of Her Name, everyone in the room made the Holy Circle and murmured, Blessed be Her Name—"calls us back to Her," I finished.

The Noblelady's usual was sliced lilili and fresh shallowgreen. "How can one tell if one is changing? Are changes for good or ill? Can one stop oneself from changing? Would one wish to?" She hissed loudly, much amused. "All in one breath, too. You always have had the talent, child, for asking the most unanswerable questions."

I hissed, too. "You must admit, it's an advantage in my work."

She chewed thoughtfully on a lilili. "It is that. Child —never stop asking questions."

"Noblelady?"

"There are times, dear child, when clear-sighted question-askers may become—an embarrassment. They might even be encouraged to silence."

"But it is my *duty* to question."

"It may not always be your formal duty. But always remember, child, be true unto yourself. Follow no orders blindly, even from such as I. Ask, and demand answers if you are the slightest touch unsure. This duty you owe yourself." She sighed. "Times are changing, child, whether we will or no, just as people change. And no one can say, this change be for the better—or worse." It's hard to imagine, but she remembers life before the Terrene came, with their magics and their enclaves and their pushy, noisy, enigmatic, obscure selves. My heart skipped a beat. The Elyavaneet spoke almost as a Last Blessing; surely she wasn't that old. Not yet! Goddess, Goddess, not the Elyavaneet!

Yet it is said that those over whom the Hand of the Goddess hovers speak to their friends with the Meaning Tongue.

"I know my duty," I managed to stammer. It was meant to reassure her, but she sighed again.

"Yes, dear child, you know your duty. And you remind me, I have mine." She gestured to the cords laid out on the dry work ledge. "I would others knew their duties as well."

I welcomed the change of subject. "What's amiss?"

"Some of the sea harvests have been poor this year—or so it is claimed. Naturally, then, the twelfths will be scanty. Other years have been generous, so the storehouses will not be dangerously depleted. It's more a nuisance than a problem, still . . ."

We are a sea people. If I have a rare day to spare from my duties, I volunteer to spend it with the shallow-fishing fleet; a few hours, and I take out my own craft, the *Wave-eater*. My guards also; were I to miss anything, they would not, and I would hear of it. "I've seen no evidence of scant harvests, not even in Goddess-frown Cove or the Severed Fingers."

"Nay, not here, our bounty of the Goddess has been most generous. But several of the Outer Isles have complained, the Mirror Isles, the Green Skeleton, the Misties . . ."

I pictured the lay of the Outer Isles in my mind. "Um. And the other islands, those that haven't complained?"

She consulted the cords, one slender finger pushing a couple closer to me. "Average."

"Ummmmm. And those isles that complained, did they also mention an unusually warm dry cycle?"

She stared at me shrewdly, remembering, if she hadn't before, that I had spent several cycles some years back as an apprentice twelfthsmistress on the Farflungs. And the Honorablelady I had been 'prentice to had been old and wise and much given to reminiscences. "Yes," she said, "it is so reported. An unseasonably warm dry cycle, so that land plants fruited poorly, and the shallowgreen and fleshroot could not be found in their usual places."

"Ah, so. The Raliltivan Honorablelady used to speak of what she called the Whims of the Goddess. How for many, many years, lifetimes even, a current of fertile coolth would flow by an island, bringing plants and fish. But then, for no known reason, those currents would alter, and times would be hungry, long-used harbors would need to be abandoned. But, she said, naught is ever lost of the Goddess's bounty. What one isle loses, another may gain. I would check most closely those islands that have reported merely average harvests." I frowned, remembering. "Even the best of times are hard on the far islands. And flesh-hungry folk harvest what they do have poorly . . ."

She blinked agreement. "I follow your thought, child. If you are right, and it is the others that have lied, the storehouses will not suffer, for filling the bellies of hungry islanders. No, the *storehouses* will not suffer . . ."

Simsam took down a gittern and, seating himself on a low stool, began to sing softly one of the ancient ballads, a boisterous tale of rivalry and heroineism and brave deeds and contests of wits. His voice was very sweet.

The Elyavaneet and I continued to chat on various topics, catching up as old friends will. What did I think of my chances of winning the Three-isle Race? Had she heard aught of our sister Mimnetti? What do you think of . . . Have you seen . . . Had I heard that . . ..

Once there was an awkward note.

It began when she asked if I remembered a certain Terren, the Gorky Admiral.

My Terren who had had the courage to complain had been the Gorky Captain. But that had been long ago. And he had left Delyafam soon thereafter.

Could this Gorky Admiral be the Gorky Captain I had known, his honorific changed?

This Admiral, she told me, had in recent years been visiting Delyafam at intervals, in various sectors. It wasn't surprising that I hadn't met him; as long as he didn't trespass, it would have been surprising if I had. He was now very important to the Terrene, and so our honored guest. And he was visiting the Enclave near Swiftfaring, and wanted to meet with the Kimassu Lady, *to talk over old times.*

Talk over old times? Too old! The Noblelady's eyes narrowed when I told her *when* I had known the Gorky Captain. I may not agree with all the Council's rulings, but this one is surely wisdom. One does not embarrass a guest, for one's own honor's sake; nor does one hand power-knowledge to an enemy. (And with the Terrene, who could say what they could use as power-knowledge.)

Wasn't he told the Kimassu Lady is dead? I asked.

He was at Swiftfaring a mere two cycles ago; he asked as though he knew you were alive, as though he had known you then and merely wanted to see you again. The Lady he spoke to didn't know you well, didn't realize when he had known you. She simply put him off, said she'd ask, said she thought you might be on Retreat.

We had three choices. The Gorky Admiral could be

told that the Kimassu Lady, who was, after all, quite old, had died on Retreat. But that might be dangerous; the Terrene are so suspicious. (And for some reason this of the age is a sore point with them. It is as though they were embarrassed, or their honor touched, that their age magics work not on the Delyene. Doubly would they be embarrassed to learn we need them not. Though if we could use them . . . ah, put that from your thoughts, Kimassu, and be content with what you have.) Let the Gorkey Admiral meet then a very, very old Kimassu Lady. Or a young one, a Direct taken a Family name in respect.

The difficulty with the second and third choices was, too many know of the Kimassu Lady. The freak Lady. I had risen by diligence and wit and force of personality, adopted by a Family willing to put merit before appearance, my friends cheerfully blinding themselves to the dreadful truth.

If the Gorky Captain/Admiral hadn't realized when we first met, his many visits to Delyafam would have made him aware of the enormity of my disgrace.

In a world of scorching, merciless sun, I have no pigment in my skin.

In a world where the ideal of beauty is brilliant orange, I alone am pallid, bleached-pale . . . loathsome. (And do I not know why my dear boys, my loyal ones, so often have swellings, sore knuckles, teeth awry. I know. How I know. And I know too that the Kimassu Lady has risen high, may yet rise higher—but there is one thing, one infinitely precious thing that the Kimassu Lady may never have. The Kimassu Lady will never be Chosen. The Kimassu Lady will never be Purified, never be escorted, gleaming in pride, into the Holiest of Holies. The Kimassu Lady will never watch the broodpouches of the Select swell, and know some fraction of that blood is *hers*. The Kimassu Lady will never, ever watch a class of younglings at play, and know that some are hers, that some part of the Kimassu Lady can never die. No matter. I am I! Kimassu!)

So in a world where all may conduct their business under the sun clad only in pride and kilt, the Kimassu Lady must swathe herself in cloths, must protect her tender skin from burning. If there is anything uglier than a cavefish-pale skin, it is that same skin patched with healing skin, itching and peeling and—disgusting!

At least I heal properly. That is some consolation.

But there is no old Lady to play the Kimassu Lady, to mock ageforgetfulness to fool the Gorky Admiral. No old Lady with skin pallid as mine.

The Elyavaneet blinked regretful agreement. Dare we use someone else, someone obviously different, a youngling taking an old name in respect?

"We can't." My voice sounded harsh in my ears. "We dare not. He may already have heard too much. A joke—the Kimassu Lady's skin. A careless comment. Anything."

"My dear child, have I ever reproached you, spoken of you as less than you are—my child?"

"Not you, Noblelady. Never you. But there are discontents among the lumpen, among the houseless boys. It pleasures them to sneer at a Lady. This I *know*. The Gorky Admiral must never see a *normal* Kimassu Lady."

"You *are* normal." The anger in her voice was not directed at me. "You are a Lady of the House of Morningstar. Who says otherwise stains our honor! Your flesh our flesh. Your blood our blood. Your honor—our honor."

Her words were soothing in the ear. But even so, that tiny question thrust deep, deep within me. If this be so, why have I never been Chosen?

"You know," she said thoughtfully, after a pause, "the signs of age for us be none so many. Suppose the Gorky Admiral were to meet the Kimassu Lady in the Serene Gardens, her back bent with age, her self swathed to the eyes in protective clothing, her voice cracked, her gestures slow and hesitant. . . . Do you think you could do it, child?"

"I—I suppose." I had fooled him once; I could do it again. Though there was a peril here that the Noblelady hadn't foreseen: that the pleasure I felt in such trickery was another appetite that grew as it was fed. "If I didn't have to do it for too long. Think you, would it content him?"

"It would must." We went on to pleasanter topics.

The walls were thick, they swallowed sound. We had no warning until the boy burst into the room. I shot out of the water like a flying fish, hand grasping belt and blade hung on the rim. I didn't draw blade from sheath, I grasped the hilt and threw the sheath aside. Only a mindless berserker would dare enter a Noblelady's private quarters in such a manner.

He collapsed at my feet, screaming, "Lady come, Lady come!"

I paused on the downward deathstroke. This was no berserker. The Elyavaneet spoke. "I know this boy. Best see what the trouble is."

"And leave you unguarded?"

She smiled. "At my age, if the Goddess chooses, she has but to stretch out her hand. Go, child." I glanced about. Not a decent guard in the room, only trembling houseboys. Worse than useless. One of them knelt and offered my belt and sheath. I waved it away. Take a cloak, the Noblelady ordered. Luckily, I had taken the upper way (shorter but dry) to these rooms, so my own cloak was hanging by the entrance way. Blade in left hand, cloak thrown over my shoulder by an eager houseboy, I gestured the trembling stranger to lead the way to the trouble.

And the first guard I see, I thought, grimly following the running boy, goes to the Noblelady. We were going up, away from the private rooms, into the main courts, into an Open Court, deep in the heart of the Sacred Complex, used for meditation, for any Pure who would care to enjoy it. But no one was meditating now. It was amazing how many writhing, shouting bodies were packed in there, and more arriving every second.

One near me was wrapped in a guard's simple kilt. I plucked him bodily from the mob. His eyes saw me without seeing; I slapped his face, hard. "Obey me!" He licked dry lips, nodded slowly. "Follow me!" Another guard kilt. "Obey me! Clear these people out. Use the flats of your blades on stubborn heads. Find other guards." I cut through that mob like a net through empty water, my growing force of guards a wedge behind me. I peeled off a half-twelve and sent them to the Noblelady, though the trouble seemed to be localized here. The center of the mob was like a school of spawning plunny—no, like a pack of daggerteeth in a feeding frenzy. I divided my guards into a double wedge, cleaving into the mob and sending them into the corridors and into nearby Ceremony Rooms.

My guards were shouting, "Kneel, kneel for the Lady, kneel!" With the outer fringe dispersed and my guards increasing, the sound finally penetrated into the bestial roar that was the heart of the mob. And they knelt. All but one.

One stood upright, swaying.

I shoved through, in time to catch him as he fell.

I might have known.

A Terren.

Here, of all places.

He was a dead man walking, whether he knew it yet or not.

Chapter Three

MOTTO:

What's brighter than the morn?
What's deeper than the sea?
What's sharper than the thorn?
What lies twixt thee and me?

Love's brighter than the morn,
Thought's deeper than the sea,
Death's sharper than the thorn;
Naught lies twixt thee and me.

—*Riddles Wittily Answered*

"Why did you do it, Terren?" I was genuinely curious. He looked ugly, even for a Terren, his brown skin marred by mottled bruises, souvenirs of the mob that had discovered him where no Terren should ever be. He might almost have made it; he was tall for a Terren, and so short for a Hardyen. Among us, a short individual is sometimes bulky also, so that wasn't too bad. Skin dyed orange, a fake crest, a fisherman's kilt, fake skin to hide his fur, other fakeries. Oh, he passed, in looks, at least. (And I think my guards would have been most pleased to scrub the lying orange off his skin, and if the skin came too, so much the better; but his pouch held several mysterious potions in it, and the second one I gingerly tested took off all fakery with neat efficiency. He awoke during the midst of his cleansing and protested vigorously if somewhat incoherently; but he could see that the guards were for the most part done, so he subsided, grumbling to himself.) But looks alone aren't enough; he must have given himself away in a hundred small ways (his Terre stench alone!) until even the most dull-minded realized; and the riot started.

Two things had saved his repulsive Terre hide. There were no guards near him at the beginning so he was only mauled by fists and kicked by sandaled feet. And he didn't fall and get trampled. (Had someone held him up the better to beat him, and so unwittingly saved his life?) He wasn't trampled, he didn't suffocate, his attackers (once the crush began) couldn't even get enough room to beat him effectively. There he sprawled, living and breathing. Pity. Now he was *my* problem.

He made that deep ground-rumble of a noise the Terrene call a chuckle. It signifies amusement, though what he had to be *amused* about . . . "Because it was there, tall and gorgeous. Because it was there."

I stared at him in stunned, unbelieving silence. Because it was there? What kind of a sun-struck Terren was this? Because it was *there?* A suspicion arose in me. A Terren told me once that among the Terrene one touched by the Goddess in certain ways is not accountable for her actions, no more than a half-dry sprat. Not guilty by reason of insanity, they say. *Well!* If this sun-struck Terren thought to fake his way out of difficulty, he would learn better, and that soon.

He was smiling now, teeth showing Terre-style, moving his head up and down; nodding, the Terre way of indicating agreement. "That's right, long and lovely. It was there. It was forbidden, *verboten,* taboo. It was a lure, the ultimate challenge; and I accepted it." He leaned back on the bench, set too far away for him to relax against the wall. "Haven't you ever wanted to do something just *because* it was forbidden?" *Was* this Terren then a youngling, irresponsible? His mouth twisted. "Well, what do *you* do for kicks?"

"Define kicks." It couldn't mean simply hitting something with one's foot.

He nodded again, as though I'd answered him. "What a waste," he muttered, as though to himself.

I thought so too, though it didn't dawn on me then that we were thinking of two entirely different things. I thought his death would be a waste; because it had taken intelligence and empathy and courage to have gotten as far as he had, even with the aid of Terre magics. I wondered if the females of his own people found him attractive; was there a Terre female somewhere grieving for the loss in her household? His face was too full, too rounded for a Delyen's taste, the lack of a crest made him appear sexless, like a handsome youngling; but his features were cleanly made, boldly wrought. His nose jutted proudly out like the prow of a ship. Very unmasculine, but somehow, not unpleasing. Odd. Was it the intelligence in the deep blue eyes, the twist of humor about his mouth? Then I understood. Were he a Delyen (impossible!) with the excess flesh removed, he/she would be quite handsome, the sort of Delyen one might invite into one's Family, choose as a friend. "Terren," I said, almost gently, because I couldn't help a flash of pity, "do you understand, your situation, what's going to happen to you?"

He moved one shoulder in a careless gesture. "I can't pay a fine, so I guess it's the slammer."

I didn't say anything.

He pursed his lips. "No-oo-oo. Not the slammer, then. What? Don't tell me I'm going to be a sacrifice to the ruddy great Orange Goddess?"

"Blessed be Her Name," I murmured. Then, "We're a bit more civilized than that. But, yes, you're going to die." I don't know why I told him. That pity, I suppose.

He whistled. "When?"

"I don't know. Soon. It depends."

"On what?"

I spread my hands. "Quite soon, if your people demand you back. If they do, if they insist, they'll get you back. In so many pieces even your magics can't put you together."

"And if the Consul General washes his hands of me?"

"Washes his . . ." Terretz is a very unlogical tongue, full of phrases that do not mean what they appear to mean. He made a pushing-away gesture. "Oh, I see. Then you will live somewhat longer. Not much, but some. While we can learn useful knowledge from you."

"And who decides when the ax falls? You?"

"Ax? What do you mean, ax?"

He made a chopping gesture on his neck. "Ugh. We don't chop people's heads off. We use a cord. Quick and sure, in skilled hands." I'd see to the skilled-hands part myself, if need be.

"Garrote," he nodded. "But I didn't ask how, tawny-eyes; I asked who decides *when?*"

"Oh. My"—I searched for the proper Terretz word—"my superiors." Based on my recommendations. And according to whatever omens occurred. Within certain limits, I controlled his fate, but he needn't know that. Yet.

"Would you prefer Delyetz?" he asked, in that tongue.

I shouldn't have been surprised. He spoke a Rainbow accent purer than mine, grammar correct, no fumbling for words. "Terretz will do," I told him. "I need the practice in your tongue more than you need the practice in mine, it appears." Besides, he would talk more freely in his native tongue.

"Terran, my bald but beautiful Valkyrie. The language is Terran, and I'm a Terran, too." I knew what bald meant; his own fur was a color I hadn't seen before on a Terren—no, a Ter*ran*. Pah. Terren. It was an ebony-black, with a sheen that caught the light, and silver strands scattered through it like the coat of a winter-wardel from the cold Farflungs. Curious, I had touched it during his cleansing; it had been crisp yet soft under my fingers, strangely alive feeling. It seemed clean enough, free of parasites, so I ordered it left on him. Freed from its covering of fake skin, it sprang about his head, swaying as he moved, like the fins of the lace-veil fish, except that it was thick instead of filmy. "A Valkyrie, my tawny-eyed Valkyrie," he answered my unspoken question, "is a sword-maiden, one of Odin's messengers. The Valkyries kept vigil over the course of a battle, and from the fallen they chose the bravest of the brave, to fight again in the great Battle at the end of Time, when the Immortals and the Giants contend for the Fate of the Universe itself."

"Is that part of the Terre beliefs?"

"Sort of. An old religion, very old. Mostly tales to amuse youngsters with now, or forgotten entirely, except for a few oddballs like me. But it's what you reminded me of, coming through that mob, head high, sword in hand, white cape billowing behind. A Nordic Watusi, a Valkyrie without a shield."

Well, I thought I understood Terretz. *What* was a Nordic Watusi?

Nordic, he explained, was a name for a very fair (i.e., light-colored) Terren from a particular area on Terrafam. Watusi were a tribe from another area, who were dark, much darker than the Delyene, but tall and slender, as the Delyene were.

So now I understood. The Terrene used different names for different physical types.

No, it wasn't it at all, he told me. Where different peoples had lived for long periods of time, isolated in extreme environments, they had developed into different physical types. The names he had used were simply those peoples' own names for themselves.

Isolated? *Terrene?*

It took a while for him to explain it all to me. I thought I knew the Terrene well, and perhaps I did. The bureaucratic (his words) artificial narrow-brained modern Terrene. The bewigged painted lisping fashionables, and the hurry-scurry ambitious clericals, and the brutal militaries, and, worst of all, the mushy-mouthed do-gooding missionaries.

(Oh, we tolerated the missionaries. It was unworthy to be rude to a guest. Besides, if they got discouraged and left, who knew what worse Terrene would follow? So they always had a few "converts"; some of them might even have been genuine. It kept them happy and working hard for more. Was that wrong of us? Fooling those dedicated Terrene? Or should I say, was it more or less wrong, than the Terrene themselves encouraging and supporting those same missionaries, hoping we would be converted to the Terre way of living (pah!!) as well as the Terre path along the Religion we all share. As the Noblelady has said (many times!) I have a talent for asking hard-to-answer questions.)

We are a very ancient people. Our history is long; it includes interminable lists of genealogies and incredibly old epic ballads, dealing with the time before the First Empress (may her name shine ever brightly!) united our scattered tribes into one people. Talking with my black-furred Terren that day made me see clearly how different it was with the Terrene, how the keynote of their lives is change, which they call progress. As though it were some sort of commendable feat to move ever onward to something new instead of striving to perfect what one has. I believe now, that our beloved First Empress was ashes borne on the wind for many generations when the first Terren curved clumsy fingers around a stone and slew her dinner.

He made me see his world, at last, with his gift of words. A world complex where ours is simple, a world of harsh extremes instead of gentle graduations; a world of huge land masses instead of shallow seas and island chains. A world of (believe this if you can!) wide waterless areas that parched all invaders, of lands that thrust probing fingers into the sky, of wide, deep, islandless oceans, of areas where the water turns to solid the year round. And on that wide, diverse world, Terrene developing, changing, migrating from climate to climate, from land to land, sometimes cut off from their fellows generations uncounted by natural disasters, natural barriers. And those groups of Terrene, adapting, altering, developing, until the changed becomes the norm. Terrene with broad flat noses and cheeks padded with fat to protect them from the cold. Tall, long-limbed Terrene in hot countries. Stunted Terrene in foodpoor wastes. Terrene with skins of white, yellow, gold, pink, bronze, brown, black; with hair of a dozen textures and a dozen-dozen colors, eyes of different shapes and shadings. Limbs long and short, bodies heavy and slender, thick-furred or scanty-bald. (And one fact was clear to me, though he never—was he embarrassed?—spoke it in so many words: the Terrene could not or would not control their breeding; instead they pushed their sisters into lands poorer and poorer.) Terrene who lived by hunting, by farming the land, by harvesting the seas as we do, by simple gathering. Terrene divided into three (four? five?) major groupings and innumerable subgroupings and mixtures. With fascinating anomalies that kept the learned ones who study such happy for generations.

So what happened?

Happened?

"Terrene aren't like that now," I told him. Despite what many Delyene think, all Terrene do *not* look alike; but they aren't *that* different, either.

He smiled, showing white teeth; the two in front overlapped slightly. "Did it ever occur to you, my tawny-eyed Valkyrie, that you've only met *one* kind of Terran up to now? That there are others, plenty of others, you haven't met?"

It hadn't. *He* certainly wasn't like the others. What a depressing idea. Other kinds of Terrene. Dozens of them.

"Technology did two things for us," he continued. "First, it knocked down all those barriers so those different physical and cultural types could meet and rub together and compare and compete. Those must have been exciting times to live in, every day new and fresh. And then, before we could homogenize back into dullness, technology gave us back our barriers. Light-years instead of mountains. Parsecs instead of oceans. We had eaten our world, now we began to eat the universe. Nobody can keep track any more, how many planets we've colonized, including—I'm sorry, tawny-eyes—some that already had their own people. But if we take land and resources, we give our technology in exchange. But your people don't think that's fair, do they, tawny-eyes? They're right, you know. But it won't make any difference, in the long run. Oh, the new worlds have their flavor, their independence—for a time. Until the most important race of Terrans comes. We breed our new breeds, until homo technologus takes over. The military/industrial/bureaucratic complex. And another world is crunched into the mold and comes out copy."

Not here!

"Oh yes, tawny-eyes, here, too! You lucky people are right at the crossing of two major trade routes. And you're near the border with—" He frowned, then went on. "Most definitely here. Frankly, I can't understand how you've managed to hold them off this long. Because they get you coming and going, tawny-eyes. If you resist, they flatten you, and if you don't, they take over, bit by bit."

Not here, they wouldn't!

But he kept talking, and every story he told, every land he reminisced about, rubbed the lesson in harder. They would.

He even recited a ballad to me. A Terre ballad called "The White Man's Burden," by the Rudderkiplin Bard. Her poem sickened me. It was beautiful, the words, the rhythm, but what it *said*. New-caught, sullen peoples, are we? Half devil and half child? Well! Because we don't *want* their magics? Because we prefer our handcrafted to Terre shoddy? Because our values are different? Because *we* are different?

My problem was never getting him to talk. He talked, Goddess, how he talked! To himself, even, if nobody else was around to listen. My problem was absorbing and understanding and picking out the significant from the amorphous mass of knowledge and philosophy he had to impart.

And not letting anything vital slip in return.

I had the advantage. He were merely enjoying companionship, occupying time; I was fighting for everything I valued.

"What's your name?" I asked at one point in that first interview.

He clicked his tongue against his teeth. "No compliment to me, tawny-eyes, that you've taken so long to ask." (I had announced my name and position at the very beginning; nonetheless, he persistently addressed me by nonsensical phrases.)

"We're a backward people," I told him.

He burst out in helpless laughter. "So, Miss Prunes-and-prisms has a sense of humor, has she?"

"Define sense of humor" This sent him off into more paroxysms of mirth. "Enough is cnough, Terren. The stonecutter will need to know."

"St-st-stonecutter," he managed to get out.

"We are a slow people. The stonecutter to carve your tombstone."

His face assumed exaggerated hurt. "No Viking funeral in a blazing boat?"

"If you prefer. I assumed you would want the customs of your people, not mine."

He shrugged. "Valiant Valkyrie, when I'm through with it, what's the difference? You will understand"—his blue, blue eyes were innocently wide—"if I try to delay the inevitable as long as I can?"

I could never tell if he was serious or making, Goddess help me, another obscure Terre joke.

I never liked him, my Terren, my problem, the weight on my back, my source of unpalatable knowledge.

But I—envied him. I, too, would sometimes have liked to cast away duties, responsibilities, and go voyaging off, wherever fancy or the winds might take me.

"I'll order the stonecutter to carve 'Unknown Terren,'" I told him.

"La Belle Dame Sans Merci," he said.

"That's a funny name, even for a Terren."

That set him off again. La Belle Dame is the name of a Lady in another Terre ballad. He recited it for me. It's about a Knight (male Terren) who meets a Lady; she accepts him, but he disappoints her, so she tosses his sandals out. And he remains on the hill where they met, "alone and palely loitering." Typical male behavior.

"Something tells me," he said, "that you don't properly appreciate our immortal bards."

"They're pretty to listen to, but they don't always make sense. If I could meet the Johankeets Lady Bard and discuss it with her . . ."

His face got a funny expression. "John Keats—ah—Lady Bard is dead."

"But you said immortal."

"The works are immortal. Their creators are not."

"Oh."

"My name is Neill," he said suddenly.

"Kneel?" It didn't seem to fit him. Casual, lazy, sprawling, even-tempered; but somehow I couldn't picture this strange Terren kneeling to anyone, even the Goddess herself.

"Neill. N-E-I-L-L. In one of our old languages, it means 'Champion.'"

That I believed.

Chapter Four

MOTTO:

There was a net that had no rope,
There was a Sign that none could Read,
For the hopeless, there was yet some hope,
In darkness, came the blind to lead.

—*Saga of Valeria, She Who Dared*

I crouched behind a stone wharf piling, scarce daring to breathe. This raid would be the culmination of over a cycle of investigation and planning, not only my own, but also three sister Consecrates. Behind me, I heard a blade sliding from its sheath and dropping back. "Tssss!" I hissed gently.

(Ironically, it had not been Neill who had given us the final strand of this net, but that animal Willis. Unknowing, he had described for me the packages he had delivered for "a friend." When. *Where.* Even his pay, two bottles of Terre whiskey. Fair pay, I thought. Poison for delivering poison.)

Another shadowy figure entered the warehouse, which should have been deserted at this late nighttime. I stiffened. That made twelve-and-two through the entrance I was watching. My blade would drink sweet this night, and tomorrow and for many morrows to come, Vlayonna and Draxuus and my sister Consecrates and I would have long and exhausting work.

I had little sympathy for these, who preyed on frailty and weakness. This night would make Delyafam better. This was a new thing, a strange thing for Delyafam, an organization of wickedness, and soon it would be a dead thing. And good riddance.

Oh, there have always been lumpen, and even adopted, who have set up households with more boys than they could possibly earn livings for. And if those boys were exceptionally young and pretty and (just maychance) very well skilled in certain arts, exchanges of favors were not unknown. A Delyen on business on a strange island might well accept hospitality in return for —say—a few bolts of well-woven cloth as a guest-gift. But there is a great ocean of difference between such as they and the sort of demon-nests we would clean up this night, once we had their heads safe and secure. Pretty young lads from remote islands, intercepted as they came to pay homage at the Sacred Courts, or beguiled from the fleets, or more daring, seduced or abducted from Family dorms or even established households; and then held by force or fear or iKlee addiction for the usage of whomever would bring a worthy price.

IKlee was the second strand, that potent simple made from the livers of fish that have eaten of the crimson death. Its effect on males is most powerful. For a few hours they are great, all-conquering heroes, Hlyldar of the Dozen-dozen Hours one and all, rapturous, insatiable, ecstatic. At such times (though this I cannot bear personal witness to) they become more sublime partners. After, they pay the penalty, weakness, mental confusion, acute depression. One dose does little permanent damage. Two or three are not too harmful. But sooner or later, the aftereffects become so unbearable that only another dose can relieve them. The body becomes accustomed, and the doses must be larger, closer together. Still, they have less and less effect; once the addiction is established, iKlee users rarely live out the year. Females are affected differently; they merely become vilely ill, vomiting and purging and desiring, most heartily, to die and end their sufferings. I know because I was once ignorant enough to handle a small lump of iKlee confiscated by my former superior, with my bare hands. (She could have warned me, but she felt certain lessons are best learned by experience.) IKlee is most potent when sucked or sniffed; but it works effectively if slowly through the skin.

IKlee is forbidden, for good reasons, as are other such simples with ill effects. But this—there is no proper

Delyetz word for them—this source of wickedness offered, so it was claimed, simples of any type—for a price. And brash or ignorant or careless youngsters were being enmeshed in the net of evil. There were items missing from the warehouses, even *food* which should be held to be shred in common during seasons of want.

No one else had gone into the empty warehouse for many heartbeats. I worried my lip between my teeth. Were all inside, or were there more yet coming?

There had been other warnings. A rash of duels. Odd accidents. Persons who always had substitutes to do their share of the common work. Scarcities of certain raw materials.

Finally I could wait no longer. I made the low hoo of a ganner calling its mate. I heard my call echoed softly, twice. Then a third time.

"Now," I ordered, and started at a quick trot for my entrance, blade ready in my hand.

They were squeezed into a clump between two thick pillars when I burst through the door, but they scattered like a school of foodfish menaced by a daggertooth.

The warehouse had three exits, two people size, and a third, larger, directly on the wharf, so that ships could be loaded and unloaded from the warehouse itself. There was also a trap door for dumping refuse into the water. Anyone who tried to use it to escape would find herself sliding down a cargo chute and landing in a drawstring net, to be hoisted out from under the wharf and held for my pleasure.

"Lay down your weapons, by order of the Council," I cried.

Behind me, I knew Yassu was pulling the rope we had concealed earlier. My own fear had been a running battle through the maze of cubbies and temporary sheds that filled the back half of the warehouse. When Yassu pulled the rope, a huge cargo net billowed up, cutting the warehouse into two roughly equal areas. I exulted. All the evil was on my side of the net.

The guards streamed in through the two smaller doors. (The cargo door was already shut, bolted, and chained from the outside. And there were guards stationed behind it, just in case someone managed to wriggle through a crack.)

It was an ancient warehouse, the glow-animals on its walls scattered and dim. They had some sort of light on the empty crate they were gathered around, it was bright, a Terre magic. One of them had the sense to out it, and in the dimness, they scattered.

"Lay down your weapons; stand still with your arms high!"

Some obeyed me; others slid behind pillars, gathered into tight knots. Even in the dimness, I could see the pale flash of blades.

I engaged.

I couldn't keep track of the others, my concentration was on my own foes. A tall thin female in a Navigator's Guild kilt, a shorter huskier male in a Deepsea Fisher's kilt, and a cloaked figure that swirled in the background, waiting.

The fight clashed up and down among sturdy old pillars. The male went down with my sword through his ribs, I had barely enough time to jerk it free to parry the female. The shadowy figure was drawn off by one of my guards, another male took the place of the one downed, this one with guard's training.

I fought in cold fury, one opponent, two, three. This stroke for that aged boy with hollow cheeks and haunted eyes who died in my presence two days gone. That for the pitiful wreck thrown on the refuse pile to die. This for an accident that wasn't an accident. That for—

Up and down. We were split into half a dozen little indivudal duels; I had no time or energy to spare for my back. I could only hope my guards were not in any serious difficulty.

Someone grabbed me from behind, pinning my arms to my sides. I went limp reflexively, almost gagged. *Terren.*

Well, I had served the Goddess to the best of my ability.

But she flinched aside as the blade flashed down, and the blow that should have cleaved me, neck to crop—and maychance her behind me as well—swished through empty air.

My captor threw me away from her, and I fell to one knee, twisting to face my enemy—

There was a brilliant flash, brighter than staring at the noon-high sun.

I was blind.

Judging by their cries and screams, so was everyone else.

I clicked, though clicking is not as effective in open air as water, and the nearest door was that way. I scrambled toward it, regardless of who or what was in my way, shouting, "Drax, Drax, don't come in, don't come in, there's blindness in here. *But stop anyone coming out!*"

Someone clutched at me, and not knowing if it were guard or foe, I snapped my hilt up, connecting with a chin. The hands let go, and there was a slithering thud. My eyes were beginning to hurt. I clicked, located the door, charged toward it, yelling again, "Drax, don't come in. But stop everybody coming out!"

"Mistress!" Right by me. That idiot, Draxuus! That loyal idiot.

"Draxuus—can you see?"

"Yes, mistress."

"What's happening?"

"Most of them are falling on the floor, moaning and screaming. Some are crawling out. Two, no, three, are crawling toward the doors." I put out my empty hand, and he caught it. His hand felt oddly slippery; later I discovered that I had gotten a nasty flesh cut on my upper arm; at the time, such was my fury, I hadn't felt a thing. But I certainly felt my eyes; they were watering freely, and the pain was intense and worsening by the heartbeat.

"Lead me out of here, Drax." I got into the cool night and began to organize for this weird disaster. Two guards inside to bind all the evil ones; others to guide or carry our casualties out into the moonlight. A messenger to the House of Healing, for immediate aid; another to my fellow Consecrates, to start the remainder of the night's work; another to Vlayonna, guarding the far door, to come and assist me.

I was sitting, cursing steadily, on a piling when they came from the House of Healing. Twelve-and-ten evil ones had gone into the warehouse; I had counted, with Vlayonna pacing impatiently behind me, twelve-and-nine bodies, brought and lined up on the wharf in a neat, cursing, groaning row. I had seen twelve-and-two go in, Vlayonna, eight. That made twelve-and-ten. Drax guided me down the row, twice, pausing at each one so I could count easier. Twelve-and-nine.

And none of them stunk Terren.

My drawstring net had not been triggered.

Twelve-and-*nine*.

She had escaped. I tried to sort from my memory of cloaked, hooded figures in a dim light. Toward the center, I thought, a short figure. I had had the barest glimpse, as I turned, of a pale face with feral eyes.

(Later, we examined the cargo chute under the trap door and found a circular bite taken out of it, right at the top. The edge of the cut was perfectly smooth, it didn't feel like wood at all; it felt like polished stone, slick and solid instead of grained. I had to give her credit. A formidable opponent who, in that confusion, had looked before she leaped, as the Terre saying advises. Perhaps the cargo net had given her warning. And Terre magic had enabled her to slice through the chute without even a jiggle to warn the guards below. Intelligence and quick thinking, and Terre magic. A sore combination to strive against; I wished we had lost the other twelve-and-nine, rather than her.)

The Noblelady Twimuldina herself came from the House of Healing, with a Reveredlady, and several others. She clucked over my eyes and put soothing salve in that eased the hurt. I had to wear a bandage and the salve for three days, but after that my eyes recovered rapidly. (one of the Ladies bound my arm. It was nothing really, a flesh cut, the bone unharmed; it healed easily.)

None of the guards took any permanent damage either, not from the blindness, that is. We had to hold a Farewell for Zirco; a blade had sliced hilt-deep, from his rib cage down until it had wedged in his hipbone. There was nothing the Noblelady could do; he died that night. He died well. By careful questioning of our prisoners, I discovered which one was responsible. That one I paid very special attention to.

Unfortunately, the Noblelady Twimuldina hadn't enough salve to go around. Naturally, I told her to take care of my guards first. Six of the evil ones were permanently blinded; several others suffered some damage. It made my task easier.

Despite my blindness, I helped lead the raids the rest

of that night and through the next long day. We cleaned up houses and cleaned out storerooms that did not contain what they should have. What simples it was safe to burn, we burned, holding back only the small amount necessary to ease the pains of the worst afflicted. What couldn't be burned, or converted to useful purpose, we either buried in rock cairns or took far out to sea.

Despite my activity, or perhaps because of the bandage, I had plenty of time to think. I had not been mistaken. There had been a Terren there, bartering for things. For drugs, for strange rocks, for the seed of the shiningsnail, for other things. In return, she (Or he. Some of them thought the Terren was a male. I wanted to believe it. Such sly treachery fitted a male's character), the Terren, as I said, had brought other items in exchange: simples, weapons, ornaments, various small objects. Since we do have some trading with the Terrene ourselves (the Council, that is) such items might not be too conspicuous among us.

With so many to question, one fact was clear to me, although I had no real proof. The Terren—Glemmu, they called him, a name for a male or an unadopted female—had organized the whole wickedness, had taken little evils and woven them into a ubiquitous, slimy net. This argued, and the Elyavaneet agreed with me, that the Terrene knew such webs in their homeland.

It would not work again, we were on our guard now. But, oh, my people!

There was one point the Elyavaneet and I did not agree on. She thought the Terre evil one was just that: an evil Terren. But I thought there was more than that. That the Terrene had tried to import their wickedness to Delyafam, just as they tried to import their magics and their religion. That this evil was deliberate policy. The Elyavaneet felt that no one, not even Terrene, could be so depraved. In that we differed. Nothing is too evil for the Terrene. Some Terrene at any rate; I knew I knew only the worst of them.

What to do with our troublemakers once we had squeezed the juice from them was somewhat of a problem. By our customs, if one Delyen harms another, the matter is usually settled between the two concerned. If it cannot be settled so, then the Families or the Guilds take care of it. If the Families or Guilds cannot agree, or one or both is both unadopted and guildless, that is what the House of Equity is for.

As a last resort, anyone may petition the Council for redress.

But this evil was—well—general. So many victims and so many villains that it was impossible to pick and choose, to say this one traded in iKlee so that these many became addicted.

Some levels of guilt were determinable. This one was mindless brawn, acted under orders, keeping the thralls enchained, abusing them as he pleased. That one enticed. And this one plotted and planned and kept her kilt clean.

Our customs forbid us to kill, except in duel. But for the worst, the minds behind the evil, there was an old sea cave, provisioned for a few days. We sealed them in, with rock. The choice was the Goddess'—and theirs. They might survive, by going into Esta-fee—if they could cleanse their souls enough to achieve the proper state of mind. Esta-fee is impossible without a clean conscience, so it is said. These would prove the truth of that. For the others, there were lesser punishments, fitted to what they had done, and agreed to by many, including myself. But I was one of those who physically carried out the punishments.

I had never punished so many in such a short space of time.

Chapter Five

MOTTO:

What hath the Sacred Vessel spake,
What doth the Mouth foretell?
All-knowing, guide the path we take,
Twixt Heaven and dread Hell.

—Prayer to be said at the twilight that divides one cycle from the next, or during any crisis.

Between the evil ones, Willis and Neill, plus my more ordinary duties, I had far more than I could take proper care of. It was time Vlayonna tried her hand anyway. I gave her Willis. Each evening, she and I had a little discussion, she told me her conclusions, and I suggested more lines of questioning.

"Describe the exact relationship between your Captain and the Factor on this planet Flavius you were telling us about . . ."

"Do you know of any planets that have successfully fought off the Terrene . . ."

"Tell us all you can about Terre law . . ."

"What do you know about other worlds in this area . . . especially those not too happy with Terre rule . . ."

"Tell us about cargo ships . . . what makes a trade route *profitable* . . ."

Profit. We have no equivalent word in Delyetz. If times are good, there is more than enough food to fill every belly, and if times are poor, should not want be shared equally? Personal items are just that—*personal.* Everything I wear or use has been made by myself, or earned by myself, or made for me, with love or friendship. How could it be otherwise? Larger things, a fishing ground, the

Sacred Courts, a wharf, a tool house, the usage of these is decided by the appropriate Family or Guild or Council.

Ownership. Profit. My daggertooth necklace is *mine* because I won each tooth. If I give it to someone someday, in love or friendship, then it will be precious to that someone, for that love or friendship. A Terren once offered to "buy" my necklace, and when I didn't understand, brought a necklace of glowing blue beads that shimmered in the light, as a return-gift. She was very angry when I refused, but the beads, though pretty, meant *nothing* to me. We couldn't understand each other. But thanks to Neill I began to understand the Terrene, a little. Oh, we compete among ourselves. Families may maneuver for a better fishing ground, a good island for shallowgreen, a high-status duty; but to despoil another people's world, degrade an ancient way of living, for *profit,* for gain or worse, carelessly—this is foreign to the Delyene, incomprehensible.

"The trouble with your people," said Neill thoughtfully, "is that they're all lotus-eaters."

"Ummmmm," I said sleepily. (Time spent with Neill had to come from somewhere; usually it was my sleeping time. But it needed to be done. I had to learn from Neill what I could, while I could, so—) "What's a lotus, Neill? And if it's good to eat, why not eat it?" We were out on a beach near Southspit, and Neill was teaching me to orange without burning. It was so simple I was ashamed I had never thought of it. The trick was to get a little bit of sun, every day, and to keep the skin carefully oiled. He had a long explanation of why this latter would help. At any rate, between the warmth of the sun, and my own tiredness, and the pleasant pressure of his hands smoothing in the oil, I was in a state of enjoyable lassitude.

"That's part of what I mean, no food prejudices."

There was a bare brown thigh finger-widths away from my face. I lunged.

He was on top. With no inhibitions whatsoever.

I was hissing too hard to hold on, anyway.

He pulled back, making faces and rubbing his thigh. I rolled over on my back, hissing and shaking. The more names he called me, the more helpless I became.

Suddenly he was neither laughing nor angry; without another word, he stalked over, tossed me my cloak, and growled, in a voice quite unlike my insouciant Neill, "You've had enough sun for today; cover yourself."

For a heartbeat, I couldn't understand, what new Terre insanity had I . . . I had eyes, though; I saw.

Because of his intelligence and quickness of mind, I had drifted into treating Neill as a fellow Delyen. But he was no such thing. He was a Terren, a *male* Terren; and somehow—how?—I had triggered that maleness. I froze where I lay and then slowly rose to my feet, the cloak dangling from my hand, the air between us suddenly solid with tension.

Not that I was endangered. Neill talked more freely when we were alone, but I had not been foolish enough to take him someplace where he could kill me and escape. The one climbable path off this beach was well guarded, and not even Neill would be foolish enough to try to swim past the daggertooth net. Not after I took him (and guards, of course) out in a skiff and caught a daggertooth for him to see. All I actually got into the boat was the head, since the school went into a feeding frenzy (a *most* effective lesson), but a look at those teeth made him shudder and comment, "Sharks without the warning fin. Ugh!" But it was the fact that I only knocked out *one* tooth to add to my necklace that made him look thoughtful. He might have looked even more thoughtful had I told him the first tooth must be gotten *in the water,* with a knife, and that swiftly, before the struggle draws the school; and again by tradtion, your first daggertooth must be longer than you are tall.

I hoped that there were daggerteeth beyond the net today.

I should have known what he was. Except that I was blinded by his quasi-Delye good looks, his easy charm (that in itself should have warned me!), his vast knowledge. Only one kind of male could live as he had done, drifting from place to place, from protector to protector.

The—filthy—little—*whore!*

Except for the cape still dangling from my hand, everything I had been wearing was piled in a neat heap next to the remnants of our noon meal. I stared blindly at the pile, then reached down and picked up an armlet of burnished metal—copper, the Terrene call it. It is rare in our world, and so prized, and the armlet had been given to me by—never mind, it was very precious to me. But it was the only thing of mine that would have value to him. I threw it at his feet. "Yours," I choked. "For your time." Then, "Wait here for me."

I dropped the cape on the sand two steps before I hit the shallows, running. As soon as I saw the color change that marked the end of the shallows, I dived, skimming the bottom, and surfaced, swimming strongly, heading for the net, the depths, and the daggerteeth.

I had forgotten that I had left my blade with Draxuus, for safekeeping.

I remembered when I was still short of the net, but I didn't hesitate. Until I heard the commotion *behind* me.

Neill!

Slut or not, he was in *trouble!*

He was floundering in the water not too far behind me, struggling and shouting. Daggerteeth did get through the nets! I swam for him, but he wasn't there. I dived. He broke surface, ten paces to my left, and went under again. I couldn't taste blood in the water, nor click but one figure; I approached quickly but warily, eyes open, ears alert. We were in water perhaps three fathoms deep.

Then I saw what the trouble was; I dived, cursing myself and Neill equally. His legs were tangled in whipweed. Each time he went under, his own frantic threshings enmeshed him that much worse.

And I was bladeless.

He was dying before my eyes. No time to swim ashore and fetch a knife. No time for anything but—I managed to haul his head above water. (Terrene hear poorly underwater.) "Trust me; go limp!"

I dived without waiting to see if he nodded or not; but he was limp enough now. There was blood in the water, too, from the superficial whipweed cuts on his legs. It made it more difficult to see and increased the true danger. Once that blood drifted beyond the nets . . .

I unwrapped methodically, trying to work from above, so as to avoid getting caught myself. The blood, his and mine now, too, clouded the water, but at least he had obeyed me and wasn't trapping himself worse. I risked a quick glance upward. He was completely underwater now, his eyes wide open, his head lolling, an odd, whitish froth issuing from his open mouth.

Goddess, was he dead already?

There seemed an infinite number of strands of whip-weed. Agonizing time passed. I shot to the surface, grasped his shoulders, and heaved upward—and he was free, a sodden, dangling burden. I arranged him so that I could hold his head out of the water and struck out strongly for shore.

I was almost to the shallows when I sensed another figure swimming beside me.

It was Draxuus. Together we carried Neill's inert body through the shallows. I didn't know why he had appeared against orders, but I was too grateful for his help (what Neill weighed!) to complain. We dragged Neill up onto the sand. I felt his chest, his wrist, the place on his neck where any artery should have beat. Nothing.

"What happened, Kimassu?" said a familiar voice. I had known the Hypasha of the Swordshines for a very long time. Perhaps too long. She is short, very short, and brilliant orange; her pinched features could be considered attractive. Her body was childishly undeveloped, but her malice was very mature. "My cloak, Drax," I snapped.

"Tsk, tsk." The Hypasha clicked her tongue against the roof of her mouth in mock solicitude. I rolled Neill onto his stomach, holding his head out of the sand, and pressed down hard on the small of his back with my other hand. A tide of pinkish fluid gushed out of his mouth and nose. "Got too enthusiastic with the poor boy, did you, Kimassu?" Then she understood; she knelt, her hand probed as mine had done. She stood up. "He's *dead.*"

I folded my cloak and laid his head on it.

"He's *dead*. Why did you do it, Kimassu?"

I pressed down on his back, released, pressed down. "Didn't," I panted, as I continued to press rhythmically. "Fool Terren . . . can't swim . . . tangled . . . whip-weed . . . panicked . . . told him . . . stay on sand . . . told him . . . the fool . . ."

"An accident?" She sounded both surprised and displeased.

"Told him . . . told him . . . can't swim . . . can't breathe proper . . . stay ashore . . ."

"An accident." *Very* thoughtful. I felt a shiver of fear, as though the edge of a blade were held delicately against my throat. "Yes, Kimassu; an accident. If you say so." She managed to make it sound as though I had killed Neill deliberately. My jaws ached from clenching them tight on my angry reply. She hissed, lost in her own thoughts. I thought I knew what they were—and I was in bad, bad trouble.

Actually, I didn't know what trouble was.

I pressed down on his back, released, pressed . . .

"Kimassu"—her voice was her best feature, clear and now falsely tender—"did you know that I was bringing you word from the Merwencalla Noblelady?"

"A most . . . important . . . word . . . to track . . . me here." Press and release. Press and release. My head was beginning to swim with effort. But I knew I had to remain clearheaded. Not the Council, word from the Merwencalla. Not a Decision, then, thank the Goddess. I was responsible to the whole Council, and to the heads of my own Family. But the Merwencalla was a Swordshine, not a Morningstar; I might respect a request of hers, but it was up to my own conscience and inclination whether or not I honored such. I had forgotten what else the Merwencalla was, besides head of the Swordshines and member of the Council . . .

"Oh, it was, it was." The Hypasha's hissing had risen to loud and hearty guffaws. "I will tell the Merwencalla that you obeyed her, most precipitously! In fact, before you even heard her words." She howled her amusement now, the sounds echoing back from the rock cliffs surrounding the small beach.

I continued, press and release, press and release, meanwhile thinking furiously. I was for it! My duty had been to keep Neill alive—granted, his death was sure and certain; but at the Council's pleasure, then and only then. And until then . . . I knew the Terrene can't swim properly, I should never have brought him out here. I could never explain that it had made it easier for both of us, that . . . And then I saw the true neatness of the trap. "What word . . . did you . . . bring me . . . from the . . . Merwen . . . calla . . . Noble . . . lady . . . 'Paysha?"

I risked a glance at her face, her gloating face. "Nothing that matters . . . now, Kimassu." I knew then, what I should have realized from the first. The Merwencalla is the Mouth of the Goddess. If she declared that there had been an augury . . . *or if the Hypasha said she had!*

This was a lonely place, no witnesses but a couple of my boys, whose word would count for nothing. I had other boys, on the path above; but so, I was sure, did 'Paysha. But she hadn't needed to use them. Neill was —press and release—an accident, not my fault, but—press and release—

"I would . . . not . . . have obeyed . . . 'Paysha."

"Would you not? Would you disobey the Goddess Herself?" So there it was, out in the open. "Have these Terrene slugs turned you heretic, Kimassu?"

"You said . . . naught . . . of the . . . Goddess . . . 'Paysha," I pointed out reasonably. "You said . . . Merwen . . . calla . . ." For that matter, she hadn't said anything *yet;* just implied. But if Neill were dead, it mattered little; I had failed my duty. A neat trap; whatever I did, I could be accused; heresy on one hand, disobedience on the other.

Press and release. Press and release.

"What *are* you doing?" The Hypasha was pacing around us like a hungry daggertooth circling a school of plunny.

"Terre . . . custom." Press and release; press and release. A lambent haze flowed in front of my eyes; I was hot, then cold, then hot again. Would this work? I didn't know. We are too much water creatures ourselves to—what's the Terretz word?—drown. Die of daggertooth, slaytail, squeezer, leviathan, greenrock, whatever. But not drown. So we had never developed this Terre revival technique. If it would work on him now; if I could work it; if it wasn't already too late. I had found out about it the hard way; I had been teasing him, staying underwater and pinching at his legs. He turned and searched and thrashed, and I dived below him and circled for another attack. And the next thing I knew, I was being towed any which way through the water, flung onto the sand, and Neill was on top of me, squeezing my back rhythmically. The switch from water to air had been too abrupt; and I was choking, all right—on air. Until I could adjust. Only try to breathe with someone trying to shove your rib cage through the sand to the rock beneath. I finally made him understand I was all right, and then, was he ever angry! He thought I'd been trying to make a fool of him, or some such. But he calmed down, and laughed, and showed me the technique. "Just in case." He said there was an even better one, but it depended on some anatomical peculiarity of the Terrene he wasn't sure we shared. Mouth-to-mouth, he called it. Then he showed that one to me—or tried to. I'm afraid I wasn't very cooperative. I wished now I hadn't thought it was so funny.

"I never saw it before." Was she just curious; or suspicious? Either way, it could mean trouble. The Hypasha was only curious about what could be awkward (for someone else); and she was always suspicious.

"Old," I panted. "Not used . . . much . . . any more." True enough. "Local . . . custom." Which might explain why some used it and some did not. Then, a calculated risk. "Draxuus . . . go to . . . the harbor. Get the . . . *Wave-eater*. Add a . . . one-man . . . tow. Fill his upper cargo . . . net with . . . dried stalks. Bring him here."

The Hypasha knew what I was planning. What startled me was her immediate, furious rejection. "Kimassu, you can't give that Terre filth honorable Farewell!"

"Why not? He gave . . . knowledge . . . freely. We . . . I owe him . . . little enough . . . else I can . . . do for him . . . now . . ."

"Let the Terrene take care of their own!"

"Would you . . . like to . . . explain to them . . . how he . . . died?"

"Curse them all!"

Was the smooth back under my hands moving—ever so slightly—of its own accord?

Grudgingly. "You can use the *Lightningshaft*."

I was so surprised I stopped and stared at her. "Hy*pa*sha!"

"You'll *need* the *Wave-eater*. For the Three-isle Race."

I bent back to my task. Press and release.

"I wouldn't ask the *Wave-eater* in exchange."

Press and release.

"You can *have* the *Lightningshaft*. A gift. A death-offering!"

Press and release.

"I've a year's honors wagered on you!"

Press and release.

"Kimassu!"

"Can't race . . . in mourning."

She was shocked speechless (a rare condition, for her). At last she gasped, "For *him?*"

"He has . . . no one else. I go . . . on Retreat . . . this day." Thank the Goddess I thought of Retreat; I need explain nothing to anyone. A call of the Goddess to Retreat took precedence over any duties, any responsibilities, any oaths; *anything.*

"For how long?" The Three-Isle was in eight more days. Even in a borrowed craft, I had a fair chance.

"Until the . . . Goddess . . . gives me leave . . . to go." I let her see a gleam of satisfaction cross my face. I would lose the race if I were still on Retreat, but I would lose no face; to be called on Retreat is an *honor.* The Hypasha was practically dancing up and down in her rage. I had very neatly turned the tables on her—at least temporarily—and she knew it, and I knew it, and she knew I knew. For now, the game was mine. Slyly, I added, "You will stay . . . for the . . . Farewell . . . 'Paysha?"

"Stay! For a Farewell—for *that?* You'll pay for this, Kimassu!"

So would she—a year's honors. Had I been (unthinkable!) a Terren, I would have chuckled. Instead, I hissed through my nose.

It was ironic; she thought she had trapped me so that I could not win, and she could not lose, but I had found the one loophole she had overlooked. Had I been accused of being a heretic, I would, until my case could be heard, have become a non-person; her wager would have been considered never made. Had I been accused of disobedience, I could have raced even with a Council hearing hanging over my head; and it would not have been settled in so short a time, the Council is slow and meticulous in such matters. But to go on Retreat . . .

I could tell when she thought it through completely, I could feel her narrowed eyes boring into my unprotected back, fiercer than the sun. (I would pay, too, for what I was doing; and that quickly. My back . . .) "Stay for the . . . Farewell," I pleaded. "Does the . . . Goddess . . . not preach charity . . . for all . . . her Creation?"

"You're not claiming the Goddess had a hand in *that!*

The Enemy is freezing his anima—if he has one—on a cake of ice right now!"

I was in no mood to argue theology. "Stay for . . . the Farewell. Drax'll be . . . back by sunrest. You can . . . at least . . . Witness." Of course, if she stayed, she would have no chance at all to cover her wager. But if she left now . . .

She knew it, too. "Not I, Kimassu. My chief boy, Hlawwee, can Witness for me. The Goddess watch over you, Kimassu, until next we meet." She made it sound like "watch you."

"And you . . . Hypasha . . . may you . . . receive what you . . . have earned." And if the Goddess needed any help . . .

Hlawwee was a minor enough problem. He was wearing, I saw with genuine gratitude, a short padded cape, the kind guards occasionally wear to protect their upper bodies from being chafed by weapons or shield. A quick order, and he took it off, folded it, and placed it under Neill's head. Then he could cover my shoulders and back (but too late, too late) with my longer one.

Hlawwee watched stolidly as I continued my Terre ritual. Press and release. Press and release. He didn't offer to help; I didn't ask.

To gain a respite, I told Hlawwee to order my own boys back to their quarters; I wouldn't need them. He and I and Draxuus would be enough—for a Terren. As soon as his back went up the trail, I slumped, and Neill drew a deep breath.

"Shhhhhh," I whispered. "For both our lives."

"What . . ." It was the thinnest whisper of sound.

"Later. You're dead!"

"Not with . . . apt pupil . . . *hey! That's enough.*" I had allowed myself the briefest of respites; but at his exclamation I stopped again, panting slightly. One reddened blue eye swung around to blear at me. "Enough, enough, already."

I shrugged slightly; how was I to know how much was enough?

When Hlawwee returned it was with Yassu, my second guard. He wanted to receive his orders in person. Neill was a shapeless cloak-covered bundle on the sand,

and I was resting, kilted and accoutered, in the shade of the rock wall.

If I abbreviated the Farewell considerably, I omitted nothing of import. Goddess, forgive me if I skirted the crime of blasphemy! You, who read our inmost selves, must know that my motives, if not completely unselfish, were good in intent. Hlawwee was a stolid witness, Draxuus a puzzled one.

There was one problem I hadn't anticipated. If I left Drax alone with Hlawwee, had Hlawwee enough initiative (even orders?) to take advantage?

I couldn't allow that.

There were cords in my pouch. Quickly I knotted a message. "I want you to take this to the Elyavaneet Noblelady, Drax. Quickly. I'll give you a ride in the tow, to the point, and you jog the rest of the way."

"Yes, mistress." Since the bay curved sharply inward between this little cover and the point, that should give Drax a safe margin, just in case Hlawwee was nursing a dim idea in what he used for a brain.

I asked the Goddess' blessing on my journey, animated the eyes painted on the *Eater*'s prow by touching them with my own and saying the proper mantra, and tapped the demon-trap on his mast for luck. Then, with Draxuus in the tow and Neill stowed (rather uncomfortably, I was afraid) in the stalk-padded cargo net, I let the wind carry me.

I dropped Drax on the narrow point and then headed out toward the dying sun. It was amazing how far out I could go and still make out tiny figures on the cliff, watching me.

The dying sun made my sails flame red. Precisely as I had planned.

Chapter Six

MOTTO:

Laws were made to be broken,
Standards only to be ignored,
No words there are that cannot be spoken,
What others have done, I can do—and more!

—*Sayings of Neill*

Sunatra was full and riding high, while gentle Anatra had waned into a two-pronged spear; it was the last night of the cycle of the Green Windrider. Both were propitious for me, because green has always been my lucky color, and the Windrider is the second sign of our house. It was light enough for me to see plainly; Neill was crouched in the prow, casting a line while I guided the *Eater* in lazy circles. I hadn't had any food put aboard her (for obvious reasons) and we were both ravenous. I couldn't risk heading into a food-filled bay or cove this close to the inhabited islands, so, perforce, the sea himself would feed us. It had taken all my skill to hold the *Eater* stable while Neill climbed down from the slung cargo net, and to keep him balanced against his clumsy movements.

My plans were simple enough, really. At the *Eater*'s speed, three or so days' sail would take us into a chain of tiny, mostly uninhabited islands. I would drop Neill off on one, chosen at random; though too small to support any kind of permanent village, most of them could easily keep one person. I would make sure that he had food enough, and return to Swiftfaring and make plans with the Elyavaneet Noblelady. Not plans. Plots. Conspiracies. Intrigues. All Terre words, Terre concepts. We had to fight the invader on his own terms; or go under. But it disheartened me to have to plot against my own people, even if it was in self-defense.

"Will you tell me"—Neill's thoughts must have been paralleling mine—"where we are going? And why? And what that touching little scene on the beach was all about?"

"We go where the Goddess directs her winds to take us. How much did you hear, on the beach?"

"Enough to know that—ah—Hypasha is no friend of yours."

"She was my closest friend, once. We were barracks-mates, we shared everything. There was even talk of adopting us into the same Family, but . . ." Was that when the split had started? When she realized that Sword-shines would take her but not me. When we quarreled over a boy? (We *had* quarreled over a boy, but I couldn't remember his name, or what he looked like.) Morningstar would have taken us both. Had she resented that Morningstar would have accepted her for my sake? Had the Elyavaneet recognized the flaw in her (oh, a good comrade, a good friend!) even then? Had ambition made her malice grow, or had it always been there, carefully turned away from me? How could two who had been so close grow so far apart?

Neill snorted. "They're the worst kind, Val, baby, the very worst kind."

"Yes, I know." I explained, as briefly as I could, what had happened on the beach, why I had at first been too busy to tell the Hypasha the truth; and then too wary.

"Let's see if I have this straight. This Hypasha came to tell you there had been an—an augury from your Goddess demanding my death. Right. So by your religion, you should have killed me then and there, right? So why didn't you, especially when all you had to do was stand up and stop respirating me?"

"She laughed. When she thought you were dead, she laughed."

"Doesn't care overmuch for Terrans, does she?"

"Neither do I," I snapped before I thought.

"I could teach you better, if you'd let me."

I didn't say anything. But in a way he already had. Because he had (when?) stopped being a filthy Terren and become somehow, Neill. I said slowly, "Neill, understand this. If the Hypasha had brought me word of an augury that demanded—say—Draxuus' death—then Draxuus would have died. As gently, as skillfully, as lovingly, as I could have devised. But he would have *died.* If the augury had named me, Neill, I wouldn't even have asked for time to say Farewell to those I love. No questions. No protests. No quibbles or delays. But you're different. Not because of any slight fondness I might have developed for you, but because you may be *useful* to my people. Because I can see the pattern of what is coming, and I don't like it. Because you are my responsibility, and . . . But you see, that's the cleverness of it. Had I protested . . . I would have stood accused of heresy."

"Ah-huh. The penalty for that is . . . ?"

"I have friends, a Family. I would have been allowed an honorable death. And a proper Farewell."

"I . . .see."

"Do you? Because if I had killed you, against the strictest ruling of the Council . . ."

"But didn't you say that you *had* to obey this augury? Doesn't that take precedence?" He twisted his head to face me; his deep-set blue eyes seemed dark empty pools in the dim light.

I shifted my body slightly to aim the *Eater* more precisely into the trough of a wave. "If there truly was such an augury."

He whistled. "I see."

"In a judgment, my word against the Hypasha's. And what worth is the word of one who has failed a trust?"

He turned back to his line, and I compensated. How many times did I have to tell him that the *Eater* was a racing hull, a craft trimmed to skeletal dimensions, even his cargo nets the lightest fiber required by custom. He was perfectly balanced, he rode his element lightly, gaily, joyously; by the same token, he responded instantly to the slightest shift of weight. If Neill wasn't careful, he could capsize us.

"Neill, that glowing animal floating there—when I guide us by, scoop it into the boat." I angled the *Eater.* "Now! Fingers under and flip!"

"It slipped out of my hand," he complained. "Anyway, who'd want a jellyfish?"

"Jellyfish? Is that your word for them? We call them Bacqua; it means nightglow. They're delicious!"

"Are they?" He gave a shudder, and the *Eater* quivered.

"Neill!"

"Sorry, Val. Keep forgetting, this is nothing but a surfboard with sails."

"If you want to swim, will you kindly jump overboard first!"

He chuckled. "Odd you haven't developed surfing. Guess it's because you haven't high enough waves for it."

A shift of weight, a twitch on the sail ropes, and the *Eater* crested and swooped. I didn't have to repeat the lesson twice.

"That's enough," he said. "You made your point, Val." In the moonlight, his color seemed odd. Almost green. "I didn't mean not high enough. More like—ah—just the wrong kind." He seemed to be trying to apologize—without actually saying, I'm sorry.

I decided not to throw him in the tow after all.

But I wished he'd caught the Bacqua. Even if he didn't like it. Especially if *he* didn't like it.

He turned back to his lines. He must have forgotten about the Deyle hearing because presently he muttered to himself, "Ate raw fish at the Shogun of New Honshu's palace. But I'll bet even the Shogun drew the line at raw *jellyfish*."

He trolled in silence for a bit, until . . . Was that a darker shadow under the surface over there? I whipped the *Eater* into a quarter turn, furled his sails full; the tow crested behind us like the end girl in a youngling's game of snap the rope. Neill straightened, tipping us slightly. "Whatthehell?"

I concentrated on squeezing the last bit of speed out of the *Eater*.

"Val, what's . . ." He shut up, having gotten a good look at my grim face.

The wind took us, and the *Wave-eater* re-earned his honorable name.

It was quite some time before I felt safe enough to slow down and let Neill resume trolling. Not that I thought he'd have much luck, not with leviathan surface-feeding nearby. A sudden thought, and I asked Neill if he still wanted to swim. He shook his head, grinning. I hissed softly, and we were back in reasonable accord.

"Neill," I said suddenly, the thought of the lost Bacqua reminding me of something he had said earlier, "what's a lotus-eater?"

"What? Oh, I called your people lotus-eaters back on the beach, didn't I?" He chuckled, his grin broadening; yet both chuckle and grin held oddly little of amusement. "And talk about the plasma calling the vacuum thin," he muttered. *"Me* calling *anybody—"* Then, louder, "Lotus-eater, Val, is an old slang expression for someone who's lazy, who drifts aimlessly along, who prefers the easy life to working. Now"—he held up a hand to stop my indignant denial "you people aren't lazy. You're very hard and conscientious workers, mainly. What I meant was, you're not as—as competitive as we are. Oh, you may push and shove among yourselves a bit, but you haven't got the drive to prove yourself top dog, to expand and take and conquer and hold, that we humans seem afflicted with. And if we keep pushing and expanding, sooner or later—if we haven't already—we'll meet somebody bigger or meaner or smarter or just plain more advanced than we are. We'll wind up underneath then. I'm not sure we could take that. In our own history, we have plenty of examples of races that simply died. Fewer and fewer, and then there were none. Race melancholia. Whatever. But one of our oldest books says it best. They who live by the sword, shall perish by the sword."

I thought it quite likely. We mortals may only be able to see a small part of the Goddess' mighty tapestry; but all the yarn forms part of Her pattern.

"You're thinking," he was still smiling, "it couldn't happen to a nicer set of *conquistadores."*

I wouldn't have phrased it *quite* that way.

"We have another saying, Val. Better the devil you know than the devil you don't."

Now that was a thought. Worse than the Terrene? It seemed impossible. And yet . . . Goddess protect us!

"Technically," he was continuing, "the Delyene are very primitive. What you do, you do well. This ship, for example. Beautiful, functional, the ultimate perfection of purpose. But all your industry is hand industry, cottage industry, and you can't—"

"This is our choice," I interrupted. "How can your workers have pride in their creations if all they do is watch a—a machine do their work? I know about your technology, your magic devices that can do the work of uncountable dozens. But how can you appreciate and care for what you haven't created? The *Eater* is *mine,* Neill. I know every cane and fiber in him. I chose and seasoned and carved and fitted and painted and bound. The barkcloth for his sails was gathered by my boys, and dried and woven for *me,* with love and care and devotion. When I die, I'll leave him to someone who'll appreciate him as much as I— Oh!" I had forgotten. The *Eater* must burn. But not quite yet, Goddess, not quite yet!

"You've chosen one path, Val. Whether your people can stay on that path and still fight off change—that I don't know." He rolled over what I was trying to say. "Listen to me, Val. My people evolved in a world where food was scarce and predators many. We had to fight to survive, we had to fight to eat, we had to *fight.* We got our technology, our science, too fast. Underneath, we're still painted savages; we breed and fight and fight and breed. And less aggressive races had better be lucky enough to stay out of our way. Your trouble is, the sea provides you with plenty. Oh, now and then, a little shortage here and there. But by and large, your people have never had to struggle and fight for barest survival. You haven't the memory of thousands of generations of desperate, starving ancestors in the back of your mind. The ones who didn't or couldn't or wouldn't fight got pushed into the badlands or killed outright. We're the end of a long line of fighting survivors, Val. And it shows, how it shows! Whereas your people—oh, you must have had some pressure on you, some time. We've a theory that intelligence evolves because it's *needed.* There's even a theory that intelligence is a result of *intra*species warfare. But, that's neither here nor there. You've gone past that, Val. Tell me, until we came, was there any major change in the lives of your people? Or did things just keep going on, year after year after year, as it was, so it shall be, time without end?"

"I—"

"I'm not talking about minor changes, a new dye, a better net. I mean real major cultural changes, a new technique, a different political system, a new religion . . .?"

"A new religion? Neill, there is only *one* religion!"

"Val, honey, if you can survive, the coming of the Terrans may be the best thing that ever happened to your people." He grinned, but it was a sour expression. "Not even a new prophetess, eh, Val?"

"Neill, that's *blasphemy.* Not to revere the Goddess properly . . ."

"Val, would you believe, that among my people, individuals were tormented and killed, by ones, by tens, by thousands and hundreds of thousands. All for denying or embracing one particular ritual from one of hundreds of religions. On our world, a man could be killed for doing something that he would be killed for *not* doing a hundred kilometers away."

Of course I didn't believe it. That the Terrene might worship the Goddess in a different aspect from the Delyene, might have their own Purifications, might even call her by another name—that yes. We've always known that the Terrene had their own Way, and (unlike them) we've never interfered or tried to guide them onto our path. It made sense that they who are so different from us should have their own path, and that it was not ours. After all, does she who gathers the shallowgreen have the same wants and needs and *prayers* as she who guides one of the fleets? But—to *deny* the Goddess? To have different religions? Impossible. There is only *one* Religion.

"Then there were the Crusades," he was saying. "The Holy Wars. Religion against religion . . ."

"What's a war, Neill?"

He was utterly silent. Then, "If the Delyene have a word for war, I don't know it," he said finally. "What would you call it, when a lot of people fight against each other?"

"A riot."

"If they fought against each other, in teams, for—"

"What's a team?"

"People working together. And what would you call it if that team—those many, many people acting as one—fought against another, similar team, for a long, long time."

"A—a contest."

"And if the winners could do anything they wanted to the losers, even kill them?"

"What kind of a senseless contest is *that?*"

Again the twisted grin distorted his normally smiling mouth. "We'd call it life. Or war. The *human* contest. To the victor belongs the spoils. You call it senseless, and it is. But it's the way most of us live. Big declared wars and little undeclared ones, just to keep in practice. Like you and your 'friend' Hypasha."

We have contests, but always for something that the winner receives, and the loser does not, althouh most often what the winner receives is the satisfaction of winning. We have duels, too, and they can be to the death, if both desire it, though this is very rare. But to live one's entire life in a ceaseless struggle—for what? I couldn't see what they fought *for*. I didn't see how they could stand it. I wouldn't want to live like that, I wasn't sure I could. Yet—there was the Hypasha. How could I undo what she had already done, heal the rift between us. And worse— "Neill?"

"Yes, Val?"

"Those little undeclared wars. Are they something like those intrigues you were telling me about a couple of days ago? Where people maneuver each other to get advantage?"

"I keep forgetting how very bright you are, Val. Yes, that's what I meant. An intrigue is like a small, undeclared war."

"Then"— I was thinking out loud—"I may not have been the intended prey at all. If I were disgraced, the Elyavaneet Noblelady would share that disgrace . . ."

"And someone close to this Hypasha would be advanced," he finished for me.

"Were the Elyavaneet to be silenced," I said slowly, "the Council would pay more heed to the Merwencalla Noblelady."

"Ah-*ha!* And is there some issue that the—ah—the Elvaneet and the Merwencalla don't agree on?"

"The Merwencalla wishes the Line of Dread to be placed about the Terre enclaves. All of them."

"The Line of Dread?"

"The Priestesses proclaim it. Within, all is—is accursed. No Delyen will cross it, lest the Goddess turn aside Her face, lest Her soul be exiled to the Outer Dark and cold."

"And if the Terrans come out?"

"All within be *cursed.* Whatever came out would be a creature of evil and dark, to be destroyed, utterly, by any faithful who sees it."

He whistled. "You know what would happen, if Terrans were killed by your people?"

"Death for death?"

"No. Conquest. Subjugation. It would give the military just the excuse they've been hoping for to crush the Delyene once and for all time. And they could; they have the science to do it. Destroy your people, your culture, until nothing is left but a few scattered, naked primitives, scratching for survival."

"They can't."

"Val, they *can.* Believe me, they can. What does the Elvaneet say?"

"The Elyavaneet. She wants to learn from the Terrene, to absorb the change that they bring, slowly. To continue much as we have been."

"Better, but not much. A slow death instead of a quick one."

"What *can* we do?"

"Nothing. The Delyene, as a people and as a culture, are doomed."

"Never. We'll find a way; I'll find a way."

"I believe you will. If determination alone could do it, Val, you'd be *there.* But you're outmanned, outgunned, and badly outscienced."

"You mean, never," I said, "in that long history you're so proud of, did a determined, outnumbered people drive away invaders? In all those many, many wars, the bigger, stronger side always came in first?"

"Sometimes, Val, you frighten me. But you're right. Sometimes raw determination can make the difference. If your people can find it in themselves . . . let me tell you about a man named Ho Chi Minh . . . but, Val, things will still change. You can never go back, not ever. But still, there's a chance . . ."

Ho Chi Minh . . . Joan of Arc . . . Moshe Dayan . . . Mohandas Gandhi . . . William Tell. . . Robin Hood . . . Lawrence of Arabia . . . Judas Maccabee . . . the Alamo . . . Thermopylae . . . Agincourt . . .

It was a long sail—but not a dull one.

Chapter Seven

MOTTO:

There's none as crosses Consort's Bane
Without they leave a penance;
Either ring so bright or cloak so gay—
Or else their innocence.

—*Pre-Imperial folklore, origins obscure*

I found him a *good* island. Three separate coves, all loaded with shallowgreen. A practically daggerteeth-proof reef around two of them, too. On the shore, lilili *and* sours trees. A tiny rill of *fresh* water (and such is rare). And far enough from any other island and the normal fishing routes that I could be reasonably certain that he'd still be there when I returned.

"I'll be back in a dozen or so days," I told him.

"That's a long time."

"You've plenty of food. And there's nothing here can hurt you if you take reasonable care."

"Man does not live by bread alone."

"If you're bored, meditate."

"Val, Val, I want you."

"I'll be back," I said, kindly. "Don't worry."

He clamped his teeth together so hard that I could hear a gritty, grinding noise. "VAL!"

"I am not taking you with me, and that's final." I tried to put kind reason in my tones.

"Val, I *want* you."

Overgrown sprat! "I'll be *back,* I *told* you."

"I want you *now*."

The sun was high overhead. I hated to sail through the noon heat anyway. I might make just as good time resting and waiting until it got cooler, and then sailing through the night. "All right, Neill. if it will make you feel more secure, I'll wait and go this evening. Would you like to explore some more while we wait, before it gets too hot?"

He made that grinding noise again. His face was red under the brown. Goddess, was he coming down with one of the Terre sicknesses? He was breathing in short, shallow pants, his skin gleamed wetly. But these were Terre reactions to the heat. "That isn't what I meant," he managed to get out.

"Come over here, in the shade of this rock," I coaxed. Then, to reassure him, I added, "This island is perfectly safe, Neill, but if it will make you feel better, I'll be glad to give it another . . ."

He literally howled. "Holy Hell, Val, is there no female in you at all?"

I backhanded him. I won't take that kind of insult from anyone, especially not bought-and-paid-for goods like him.

It caught him by surprise. He flipped head over arse and rolled to a crumpled stop. (The Terrene are often startled at what we can do; we cannot lift near what they can, with their thick muscles, and so they think of us as weak. But long limbs give *leverage,* as Terrene sometimes discover, to their acute discomfort.) He knelt where he landed, for a minute, shaking his head slightly, as though to clear it. He fingered his mouth gingerly, it had split open somewhere, and some of his blood was dribbling out.

"If you ever call me unfeminine again"—I was still furious—"I will forget that you are a mere male and *slice your liver out!*" If a Delyen had insulted me so, there was the Arena. But Neill, effeminate as he was in so many ways, was no Delyen.

He hefted himself slowly to his feet. The sand made beige streaks on his arms and legs and coated the fur on his chest. His plain kilt was stained with sand and turning-brown blood. "Val . . ." It was no apology; there was anger and some emotion I couldn't define deepening and slurring that single word. "Val . . ." He took a step toward me and then another. I thought I knew what he intended. If he knelt and begged my forgiveness, I supposed I would have to grant it. One must never forget that the male is, after all, the Goddess' weaker vessel.

He advanced slowly, step by tep—and equally slowly, took off his kilt. So that was how he intended to apoloize. Well, thank you, Neill, but no thank you! Even if I'd been in the mood, I never touched whores. I didn't even like Temple Duty . . .

A memory . . .

The Hypasha and I, very young; unadopted, still Kimsu and Paysha. Not our first visit to the Temple Courts, but one of the first, so that it was an adventure still, instead of the Duty it became (for me at least).

We ambled through the arbors and exquisite cul-de-sacs, babbling excited comments to each other, as younglings will. I had my eye on one already, a tall, older male, lush deep orange skin and knowing eyes, which he carefully kept hooded, an almost smile playing about well-cut lips.

"That one for me, Pay'." I indicated my choice with the barest flicker of an eyelid.

"Too old," she sniffed. "Younger ones have more staying power."

We circled around my choice with elaborate slowness and unconcern, Paysha giving each seated figure the searching eye as we passed. "Older males," I said, softly, "have more"—I fumbled for the right word—"finesse."

He stretched casually, as though completely unaware of my attention. Beautifully muscled body, lovely face; oh, he was confident, he was, the little hussy.

And he was right. I wanted him. But I wanted Paysha to have her fun, too. "Picked yours yet, Pay'?"

"I think—that big one, over there." I followed her eyes and grimaced inwardly. Quantity instead of quality, big and overmuscled and probably as clumsy as the Limping Servitor Himself. I shrugged to myself: her choice. "And then, I think," she was continuing, "the green-eyed one by the siral shell grotto. And then—"

I turned away as though idly looking to hide my amusement from Paysha. I felt rather sorry for them, her choices. No matter how fine a performance, all they'd get from her would be a single shell; and by the end of the afternoon, she'd have emptied her pouch. I preferred to choose more carefully; my partner would get what he earned—and earn what he got. I seldom had to make a second choice; and surprisingly enough, it was often Paysha who waited impatiently for me to finish.

I caught the eye of my choice, smiled slightly (with my lips closed, as we Delyene always smile); he dropped his eyes, but raised them in time to see my left eye shut. He dropped his eyes again, but his lips curved into an almost imperceptible smile. It was agreed.

Paysha and I were about to split up, when one of the seated males on our path rose and stood in front of us, blocking our way.

"Mistresses," he begged, "please. Please!"

Paysha reacted quicker than I. Her hand lashed out and he crumpled, sobbing, to the ground. Through his sobs, I could hear the please, please, please, over and over. "You hot-pronged slut," Paysha snarled, "I ought to report you to the Priestess-Hierophant."

If he had been good-looking, she probably would have laughed and led him into the nearest grotto, but he wasn't. Which made his action all the odder; a pretty slut might just get away with that sort of behavior, if he tickled the right female's fancy. But this poor clot was plain and worse than plain. Not truly ugly, but ill-favored, badly proportioned, awkward, smallish, clumsy, with his skin coarsened by a skin reaction we sometimes get, harmless but unappealing. For him it was the last krill that burst the cargo net; a fresh, glowing skin makes up for so many other flaws. He lay where he fell, sobbing desperately, and I could see from the way his pouch flapped that it was empty.

His eyes had been desperate, too. So that was it. Poor clot. Passed over and passed over and *passed over* . . .

Paysha was cursing him viciously, ordering him back to his bench, and enforcing that order with threats and kicks. Slowly, whimpering, he crawled on hands and knees back to his seat and hauled himself up. (All the nearby occupants of the Courts had found something absolutely fascinating to engross their attention—in any direction but ours.)

I shouldn't have interfered with Paysha; but I felt sorry for him.

"Boy," I said slowly.

He looked at me, and I saw his eyes for the first time;

no better than the rest of him, and ugly with weeping. Not just the last few minutes either; it took hours and hours of crying to mess up eyes to that extent; poor little clot! Passed over and passed over and . . .

"Come, boy . . ."

"Kim," Paysha exploded, "you're not going to let this diseased little slut . . ."

"My choice," I said softly. "*My* choice, Pay'. And you're about to lose yours." Sure enough, Bigmuscles was being circled, with an elaborate casualness that fooled nobody, by an elderly Minorlady from the Noonheats.

Paysha hesitated. If she stayed to tear this miserable whelp to shreds properly, or called for a Priestess to stop me, then she'd lose her chance at Bigmuscles at least for a while. Paysha never could stand to lose anything she considered hers.

I grinned at her back as she scurried over to assert her rights.

"Mistress," he said hesitantly, "did you—did you *really* mean it?"

"Yes," I said firmly. "Come with me." I couldn't destroy him by saying that I was only scaring Paysha off. I was well and truly for it, now. Well, I had plenty of shells in my pouch, the barracks-mistress had been most generous. I could take care of this poor little clot quickly, and come back and pleasure myself. My lovely-bodied hussy would no doubt be long gone, but there would be others.

He was trembling so hard that I could hear his teeth clattering together. "Would you like," I said, "to sit here and talk quietly for a little while, until you have recovered somewhat?"

"I—" He was frightened again. Had I changed my mind? Would I leave him after we talked? "As—as my mistress pleases," he muttered, head hanging and eyes directed downward.

I felt suddenly as old as the Sea Himself. I tilted up his chin, his eyes dropped. "No." I made my voice as gentle as I could. "As *you* please." I pinched his chin lightly. "I can wait or not, but you fell badly." And there went any small chance at my lovely hussy. A glance told me that Paysha was already well occupied. "Now, shall we sit here quietly until your aches have eased, or shall we go directly to a grotto?"

"You—you're very kind, mistress."

"No, very selfish." I stroked his cheek gently with the pads of my fingers. "What kind of pleasure can you give me with a paining ankle, hey?"

"Mistress—he took my hand and laid it on his chest—"I'll give you the best you ever had, the very best." And then, head hanging again, "It's my shoulder that aches."

He was oddly nervous for a boy who'd been chosen. We seated ourselves on his bench, a single slab of stone that had been split on a grain line and polished smooth and shining in the half-shadows.

I tried to put him more at ease. "I see by your kilt that you're a net-mender. That must take a great deal of skill."

"Oh yes, mistress. A lot of people think it must be very simple, just tying in new strands any old way. But it isn't. You have to match the strength of the new strands very carefully to the old ones, allowing for a little give in the new when they get wet and pulled on; otherwise your new fibers will pull out as soon as the net is cast, and you have to . . ."

I kept him talking, until he was more at ease. By the time we stood up, I knew what was the matter. The poor little clot was a virgin! Oh, Goddess, I thought, a virgin. I had never had any but experienced males; and now, no way out, I was going to have to breech my first virgin.

Plenty of Delyene won't touch a virgin. And there are others, I'm ashamed to admit, who take a sadistic pleasure in hotting a virgin up, almost but not quite enough, and then leaving him hanging, moaning and writhing, his imprisoned prong beating futilely against the tough membrane.

Even then, I had heard stories . . .

Unfortunately, having investigated many cases in my official duties, I now know that all of those stories are true, have happened over and over, time after time after time.

Virgins are sadly vulnerable. A deliberate flaw in the Goddess' creation, maychance?

No matter how you go about it, breeching a virgin is a terrible responsibility. After all, this is his first experience; it will color the rest of his sexual life. If you're clumsy or cruel or force him too fast or hot him too slow or frighten him or demand more than he can give or mess it up in any of a dozen ways, he'll bear emotional scars for the rest of his life. And if you really mess it up, he can be physically damaged.

I didn't want the responsibility; I was too young myself, too inexperienced.

Poor little boob, what would it do to him if I cast him aside *now?*

Besides, better someone like me, inexperienced or no, who was willing to take time and care, than someone more casual, or worse, someone with a mean glint in her eye. (I wasn't *really* thinking of Paysha.)

Of course, I was careful not to let him even get a hint of what I was thinking.

I'd calmed him down (I thought) very well, but when we stood up, he started shaking. I patted his shoulder as comfortingly as I couuld.

"It doesn't hurt near as much as they say," I told him. "And anyway, what comes after makes it worth it."

"Oh, you—you know."

I shut one eye in agreement.

"I—it—it doesn't matter?"

"No." I put my arm around his shoulder and squeezed a little.

"I—I know I should have told you, right away. You—you aren't angry, are you, mistress? You won't change your mind?"

"No. I wish it weren't so, for your sake. But I'll do my best. You'll see. In an hour, we'll both be laughing."

Very low. "If you say so, mistress."

"I say so, because it's true. Now come along." Before you have time to get frightened—more frightened, that is.

I was amused to see Paysha and Bigmuscles, very active, in the nearest grotto.

I was less amused to see the elderly Noonheat with my lovely hussy, cursing him vigorously because he was having difficulty. With her, the old seacow, who wouldn't! My little charge flinched at the stream of abuse issuing from the grotto.

"I know a grotto," I said softly, "that's so completely perfect, you'll think you're Hlyldar of the Dozen-dozen Hours."

It was then and still is, my favorite grotto. It is set under a ragged waterfall, so that you enter through a curtain of stinging spray (which I find marvelously exciting). Inside, the walls are lined with mother-of-pearl and lapis and carnelian, so that lights and color and glow seem to float in the air. Like all the grottos, it has a table with refreshments, a soft couch, a deep pool.

I had taken off my cloak and hung it outside, so that I could enjoy the spray on my skin. Also it would serve as a warning, since it was difficult to see through the spray.

Was one of the reasons I liked the grotto the privacy it gave, that none could see and stare at my freakish nudity? I had forgotten, until I saw him wide-eyed, that many of the females who frequented the Courts wore cloaks like mine to preserve anonymity. With my face shadowed by the hood, he would not have known, until I took the cloak off to go through the spray . . .

I had been holding his hand to draw him with me through the spray; now I dropped it. But it didn't drop, it rose, his fingers touched my bared upper arm. "Your skin," he said, "your *skin* . . ."

It disgusted him, I could see. I'd give him a shell for his time and send him off.

His hand moved up and down my arm, moved to my back. "Your skin, it's not paint, it's . . ."

"Always been that color," I finished for him, grimly.

". . . so soft, so soft," he finished, as though I hadn't spoken, putting his other hand on my other arm at the same time. "Oh, mistress, your skin is so *soft*." Eyes bright with awe, voice soft with reverence.

Sometimes, virtue is its own reward; and sometimes . . .

I left him finally, sleeping deeply, a contented satiated, snoring male who had crossed the threshold into maturity almost without realizing it. He had a pouch filled with shells, more than enough to fulfill his honorarium to the Goddess, and he had well and truly earned them. I was rather content and satiated myself. And proud, too; that one would never be bothered by his Temple Duty again. Frankly, he had surprised me. I was too young then to have realized how deceptive appearances can be in certain situations. But it was a most *pleasant* surprise.

"It's about time," Paysha grumbled. "I've been waiting *ages* for you."

It was close enough to dusk that I didn't truly need my cloak, and I draped it over my arm, instead of putting it on. Paysha's eyes opened wide. I had always covered myself, my pallid ugliness, day *or* night. Perhaps that ugly little net-mender had done as much for me as I for him.

"We're going to be late getting back," Paysha accused, "and you know what that means."

"It was worth it," I told her.

It had been. We have a saying about good deeds being triply rewarded. I had had my first reward, and delicious it was too, a generous payment for a momentary pity. But I had learned an important lesson, too. Not that I forgot my ugliness, or ceased to be sensitive about it; but I came to terms with it somewhat, began to put it in perspective, so to speak. There were times and places—very important ones—when it became of no true importance, no real signficance.

My third reward came some cycles later. I was on the docks, just having come in, with my barracksmates, from a moderately successful day on the inner banks.

"Mistress!" I looked about me. I am most conspicuous on the docks, no one there wears more than she must. He was sitting on one of the piles, the net he was mending draped on and around him. I recognized him immediately and froze. One does not ever, for fear of the Goddess' wrath, acknowledge someone that one has encountered in the Courts. "Was it a successful voyage, mistress? Did the Goddess smile?" His face was bent again to his work; his fingers twined fibers busily. His voice, his questions, were so impersonal that I couldn't take offense.

"The Goddess smiled most graciously," I said, rather stiffly.

"The Goddess favors the worthy." He seemed to give the old truism hidden meanings. His eyes flickered slyly about, to see if anyone seemed interested, if anyone saw more than two strangers exchanging idle conversation. I would have replied, "Blessed ever be Her Name," and walked on, for I was deeply, physically exhausted, and whatever game he thought he was playing, I wanted no part of. But his voice stopped me. "Mistress!" Low yet urgent. I sighed; he hadn't seemed the type, but if this slut wanted to arrange an assignation, he had picked the wrong Delyen!

"Net-mender?" I could already see him in a cage, for soliciting.

"Tomorrow, in the Courts . . ."

In the Courts? Oh, Goddess! An assignation, *in the Courts!* "Ye-ess, net-mender?"

"A boy goes to pay his first duty."

"His first? Not you, then?" My voice was sharper than I intended.

He seemed to dwindle in size. "Me? Oh no, mistress. I'd never dare—" He was trembling now, his eyes glistening in the sunrest with unshed tears. "Mistress, I never meant—you didn't think I meant—mistress!" He gulped. "I just thought—hoped—you were so kind to me, and it's his *first*—" He was crying now, openly; it was my turn to look about, to hope we weren't attracting attention. "If you could—could just—kind—I—he's so *young*, mistress, so young!" And so ugly, like you, I thought. Still, I had to admire his unmasculine courage: Whoremongering is much more hardly punished than simple soliciting. And arranging an assignation in the *Courts*, Goddess preserve us! No one should ever go to the Courts, *knowing . . .*

I almost didn't go.

And if I'd known what he didn't tell me, what had driven him to the extreme of approaching me: his friend had had the temerity to refuse a very generous offer from a highly Revered Noblelady with an unspeakable reputation for ill-treatment of her boys; and the said Noblelady had pulled strings and arranged a reception for him —as I said, virgins are—vulnerable . . .

But I did go, more from curiosity and pity than anything else; and unknowingly, I went early enough to foil completely Her Revered Meanness.

Once I had met him, had him, I would have fought the Empress herself for him.

He was beautiful, my Draxuus, my doll, my first real love.

Chapter Eight

MOTTO:

Oh, land is land and sea is sea, and the shore between them moored,
Till the Goddess orders Her playthings back, to hear Her Final Word;
But there is neither land nor sea, planet nor sex nor race,
When two strong wills clash heart to heart, though they come from the far ends of space.

—Song of Neill, original attributed to Rudderkiplin Lady Bard, of Terrafam

Even when I was young and hot and had no household of my own, I used sluts only as a last resort, and never, ever, whores.

"That's all right, Neill." I gave his hip one gentle but firm dismissing pat. "I forgive you."

He struggled to get it out. "F-forgive me?" In the harsh sunglare, his pupils had shrunk to pinpoints; surrounded by irises of unbelievably deep clear blue, bluer even than Sparklingwater Bay.

"For what you said." I was glad to have the matter settled. "Now put your kilt back on, there's a good boy. I'm not really offended, I know you don't really understand all our customs yet, and anyway, I never take advantage." He was getting redder and redder under the brown; his breathing was in a hoarse shudders. "Neill, are you well? Do you want to go in the water and cool off a bit?"

"Cool off?" He produced a thin rasping sound, a chuckle yet somehow not sounding at all amused. He frowned. "What do you mean, take advantage?"

"Well, isn't it obvious? I mean, we're here, the two of us, alone, and you do have an obligation to me. I suppose a Terre female wouldn't hesitate, not at all, or some Delyene either, for that matter. But I'm not like that, Neill. There's no need to talk of pay between us. You're my responsibility, and I'll take care of you, whatever is needed. As for what you said, I don't believe in humbling a boy for a minor mistake; just say you'se sorry, that's enough."

"Pay—I'm to pay—how?"

I pointed to his prong, already hot and ready without my even touching him, the slut! "How else"—and could I help the dry contempt in my voice—"does a boy with no skills earn his keep?"

His eyes widened, the red under his brown faded and was replaced by a sullen ashy-gray. His mouth opened and shut, but no humble 'I'm sorry' emerged. Instead he turned in his tracks and stalked into the water.

I watched, startled and puzzled. Was this some new whorish ploy? But I knew how poorly he swam (if indeed, his unco-ordinated thrashing could be dignified as swimming at all). And there was something about the set of his body, the purposeful stride, the grim look on his face before he turned . . .

"Neill! Neill, come back here!"

I might as well have saved my breath.

"Neill!"

There wasn't anything else to do; I went in after him.

It was very confusing. I managed to haul him back into shallower water easily enough; *I* can swim. But after that everything went wrong. He turned on me. And he won. Not because he was stronger than I, because in the water I am more skillful; but because he knew some sort of sneaky-fighting. Somehow, he flipped me over his hip, so that I landed with a great splash, on my side.

That infuriated me but it was no fluke. Whether I hurled myself at him, or he, his mouth stretched in a teeth-showing grimace, attacked me; the end was the same: I went sailing over his shoulder or hip, to land hard, sputtering and floundering and throwing water in all directions.

The more furiously I attacked, the more easily he threw me.

At some point my blade went spinning out of my hand, to lie half-buried in the sand.

His chuckles echoed over the waves.

Until I was lying on my back, panting, while he knelt over me, his knees pinning my arms. The waves barely lapped at us.

I wasn't afraid of him; just *thoroughly* humiliated.

"If you kill me, Neill," I managed to get out, "you'll rot on this island."

"Kill you, Val?" It seemed to amuse him. "No, I've a worse fate in mind for you, me proud beauty." He showed his teeth in a grimace, his finger sketching a crescent on each side of his upper lip (a Terre custom or religious observance, I thought). Then he pushed my kilt up.

I didn't believe it. Even while he persisted and persisted, I didn't believe it.

Neither did he.

I had to give him high marks for sheer stubbornness.

"It isn't possible," he kept muttering. And, "There's gotta be a *way*."

When he finally sat back on his heels, his prong must have been one great aching sore. (I was fine, naturally; when you bang your head against a stone wall, it's your head and not the wall that gets hurt. At least a Delye head; I was beginning to wonder about the Terre skulls. They couldn't really be solid rock. Could they?) Neill's face was a study in mixed emotions; I propped myself up on my elbows, the better to see, squinting slightly against the sunglare. (And I was just starting to heal from the last time, too. Itchy, itchy, peel!) The finger-width or so of water soothed about my elbows and body.

He broke the silence. "It's your choice." He sounded almost accusing. "Isn't it? Truly, physically, your choice?"

How else could it be? But he sounded—amazed. Astounded. As though it had never occurred to him that such things could be. Yet he obviously wasn't a virgin. My mind raced. Were female Terrene so weak-minded that being knocked down intimidated them into giving their males a ride? Impossible! But— What kind of freaks were these Terrene?

But! *Neill had expected to have his way*. HIS *way*.

I tried to wriggle away from him, the *freak!* But he

caught and held me, 'Val, listen. With your people, your own kind, do you—ah—enjoy—" He gestured downward unable to remember the Delye word.

"What kind of a freak do you think I am?" I snarled. Like your females, maychance? "I'm a perfectly normal Delyen, but that doesn't mean I'm desperate enough to ride whores!" I really hadn't meant to say that, at least not so brutally, but it slipped out in my anger.

"Oh, so that's it," he said. "Not gigolo, whore. So that's it." Gigolo? The Terretz word meant nothing to me; I tried again to wriggle away from him and froze. Could it possibly be—that among the Terrene—no wonder we had never understood them!

It must have showed on my face, because he nodded, slowly and I was used enough to Terrene by then to understand what nodding meant. "You're beginning to see. Oh, every now and then, we have an Equality for Women movement, but they usually peter out, sooner or later, because of physical reality. Man is the natural provider, the master"—those blue, blue eyes stared into mine—"the sexual commander," he finished slowly.

Sickening!

It meant—I was beginning to see implications—those early male envoys had not been meant as deliberate insults. They had changed quickly enough, when they saw we wouldn't treat with mere males, hadn't they? And, it also meant—that such as Neill and the Gorky Admiral were not Terre male geniuses, but simply Terre male normal; such as Willis were subnorm, culls. Did that also mean that Terre males were actually smarter (by and large) than Terre females? It seemed impossible, yet what kind of intelligent female would allow herself to be provided for instead of doing the providing as she properly ought? What kind of female would—would allow herself to live on (what else) her male's prong?

It washed over me like a Servitor-called wave. Dozen-dozen-dozen-*dozen's* of generations of Terre females, subservient to their *males,* beckoned to on their males' whim, humble, obedient under the threat of physisical force, vulnerable, always and completely *vulnerable . . .*

The chosen, not the choosers.

The ordered, not the orderers.

The guided, not the guiders.

The forced, not the forcers.

My stomach heaved, and I managed to roll over in time. I don't know how long I was preoccupied with my outraged bodily reaction. I heaved until my stomach was empty, until my whole insides ached, until I was too weak to do more than lie limply and shudder.

I was dimly aware of being supported through the worst spasms, of being wrapped finally in my sopping wet cloak, of being carried.

I must have slept then, for when I awoke, it was night. Sunatra was full, and Anatra had disappeared completely. That meant the start of a new cycle, and one, moreover, that neatly fitted my mood: the Crimson Leviathan. (But perhaps I should have remembered that all omens of the Leviathan cycles can be read two ways; for just as the Leviathan is Mistress of Death, so also is she the terrible essence of life.)

I was lying, still wrapped in my cloak, a pace or so away from the tiny rill of sweet-water. My mouth tasted like a cliff-bird isle. I untangled an arm and got a scoop of water.

"Feeling a bit better," said the reminder of unspeakable horror.

He had retrieved my blade, but he had taken it with him to cut some sours off with; that saved his life. My lack of a blade, and his sneaky-fighting.

"Val, Val," he panted, "whatever you're thinking, it's not that bad, it's . . ." Over and over. Then, exasperated, "Use your brains, woman. Look at this from my point of view, it's just as bad . . ."

It didn't do him any good. I wanted to wipe him, his entire obscene race, from my life, my world, my universe.

If I hadn't been so weakened, I'd have splattered the island with him.

As it was, despite my fury, I wound up with vines binding my hands and feet, a helpless raging torrent of futility, with an interested witness to my wrath.

But the vines were strong, and I eventually ran out of wind and energy, if not anger.

"Are you going to listen to me now?"

I managed to drum up a defiant wheeze.

He waited.

I snarled and spat insults.

Finally, he squatted and propped me into a sitting position; then he offered me a sour. Did he really think I would accept food of his choosing? I was too dry to spit, but he got the idea, all right. "Feisty Amazon, are you?" was all he said.

I lay quietly, and (finally!) began to think instead of react. First, I had to convince him to cut me loose. (And how else was he going to get off this island?) Then, I had to get my blade back. Then . . . I had regained enough sanity to realize that I couldn't kill him. I needed him to display before the Council—or the Goddess' Throne, as the events dictated. More accurately, I needed *most* of him. Arms, legs, tongue, eyes. But there was one item that was definitely superfluous—for appearing before the Council.

He ate the sour himself, the juice dribbling down his chin; he used sweet-water (what a waste, with good clean sand available) to clean his besmeared front.

I wasn't hungry, but I was thirsty. I had lost what could be a dangerous amount of fluid during my sickness. But with my hands behind my back and my feet useless, I couldn't drink from the rill without crawling on my belly. In front of him. I decided I could get thirstier.

Then, after eyeing me thoughtfully, and making one or two false starts at saying something, he left. Either to gather more food or (I had noticed this odd prudery in him before) to eliminate in privacy.

Oh, that water tasted good.

He got back too soon.

"Val, why didn't you tell me you were thirsty!" He rolled me on my side and used the sweet-water to clean dirt out of a nasty-looking but superficial gouge on my hip.

"Judging from your reaction," he said thoughtfully, "you must treat your males worse than I thought. Crack the whip. Toe the line. Shades of Uncle Tom and all that."

"That's not true! I've *never* . . ."

"What, never? No, never. What, *never?* We-ell, hardly ever!"

"May your anima freeze eternally!"

"Tsk, tsk, Val, me girl. Temper, temper. I'll admit that

you are the kindest sweetest most understanding ruler a man could hope for; if you'll admit that a man could do far worse. Your friend with the sicky-sweet voice, for example."

"May your an—" He put his hand over my mouth.

"Tsk, tsk, *tsk*. The trouble is, Val-me-gal, that you are such a deliciously tasty morsel of woman-flesh, it does get difficult to concentrate on—heh, heh!—*pure* logic . . ."

Goddess, did the Terrene *eat* human flesh?

"Hoo, girl, if you could see your face. Gramma, what big eyes you've got! Now, the point I was beginning to make, when I was so crudely interrupted, is that whenever you have one person's comfort and happiness dependent on someone else, then that other person's personality, his—or *her*—conscientiousness and empathy, these will determine the first, the dependent person's, happiness to a large extent. Right? Right! Some good, some not so good, and some—like your friend. Right? Right!" His eyes narrowed. "At least, we've tried. Some of us, anyway, have tried. I wonder . . . have you Delyene ever done anything but grind your males under your heels?"

My boys stay with me because they're loyal. Any of them is free to go, at any time, and I'll see that he's taken care of, and they all know it!

He took his hand away. "May you cringe in the eternal dark and—"

"Will you kindly admit to yourself"—there was definitely an exasperated note in his voice now—"that, with —ah—conditions reversed, because of economics or body structure or whatever, that a male can be just as—as generous and kind and so forth as you, you witch! That a female can be loyal to a male, that . . . Oh, blast! Think about it, Val. You've brains, I know that. Use them."

I tried. I really tried. I tried to imagine myself subservient, humble, obedient, to a male. Draxuus, say. Grateful for food, protection, guidance.

Pah! In a cycle, I'd be running him.

What Neill was leaving out, or simply didn't want to admit, was that males need to be guided. They're not as intelligent, they're not as responsible, they're not . . .

Did that explain why the Terrene were so aggressive, so violent, so uncontrolled? Idiot males on a rampage, escaped somehow from their natural governors? But why? What had happened? Were the Terre females simply evading their responsibilities? Letting their males loose on an unprotected universe of more sensible races? Males never grow up properly, they need a firm guiding hand, or they're destructive, like half-developed sprats. Or had the males somehow—how?—revolted, thrown off their tiller ropes and run wild?

And then I realized that while I struggled and strained to turn my world upside down, *he* had managed it easily. Perhaps not easily, but he had managed it. So was he my inferior—or my superior???

"What's the matter, now, Val?" I turned my face away; he had another sour, and he simply couldn't eat it without dribbling.

"You—on your world, worlds—have the males always been the—the rulers?"

"Father Freud, no. I imagine we've come a lot closer to true equality than you have, with that structured society of yours. We've had such a *variety,* you know. In any group, from two to a world, somebody has to have the final say, or nothing'll ever get done. With us, usually, that somebody is a male. But we've had our women, too, from Semiramis to Premier Elizaveta Novosad III. Two people, mutually contributing, mutually caring for each other, loving each other, doing for each other—"

"Two," I interrupted, having seen the glaring flaw in his idyllic picture, "just *two?* Can you Terre males actually keep a female satisfied, one of you, all by himself?"

He chuckled. "We like to think so. I've never had any complaints, I . . ." He frowned. "I suppose you think a male who wants—who has the gall to want—hmmmm. One who needs a lot of—satisfying. You think he's a . . ."

I turned it around. "And you Terrene think a female who—ah—wants . . ." I didn't have to go any further; he was nodding.

We were silent.

He put his hand, very lightly on my hip just above the band of my kilt. "I think, Val, that this Terran male, if you'll let him, can keep this Delyen female very, very satisfied." His fingers moved in slow strokes on my bare skin.

He wasn't a whore, or a slut, not by Terre standards, anyway.

He was Neill, whom I'd thought of as my friend.

"We won't talk about pay," he said, his fingers continuing to move, oh, so slowly. "That's foolish, between equals. We won't talk about bosses, or rulers, or who wants it and who doesn't. I don't know how you manage with *your* males"—he grinned—"but you can't order me and you can't force me; and obviously, if you're not interested, I can't force you, so-ooo . . ."

I am, as I told him, a normal Delyen, and between my work and Neill's near-disaster and several day's sail, it had been quite—a—while.

Several days back, too.

A male is a male, after all. And this one was most definitely willing.

I shut my eyes. "I could force you, if I wanted to bother," I drawled.

"Who's talking about force, if we both want to," he countered.

I assessed him, not as a problem, or a responsibility, or a Terren, or even as a male—but as a person, a potential . . . partner.

At the same time, because I couldn't help being aware of it, he had a rippling-muscled body, squat by our standards but balanced, proportioned; his brown skin was smooth and not really so different from a dark orange; his too-Delye face, when I stopped judging it by our male standards, was not unattractive. Not at all. I just might bother.

He stretched his mouth in that Terre smile so like our own anger grimace, showing square, slightly uneven teeth. "Is that a promise?" So I must have spoken that last aloud.

"A promise?" I stretched lazily. Those vines were most uncomfortable; but I didn't think I'd have them on much longer.

"If I cut you loose, will you force po-oo-or helpless male me?"

After all, this was a unique combination of circumstances; it might never reoccur. A rare opportunity to learn more about this basic aspect of Terre psychology/physiology. The Delyene had always avoided the Terrene except for short, impersonal encounters. (There were exceptions, like Willis. But Delyene can take care of themselves; there was one case of five drunk Terrene . . . we returned them to the Enclave. Gelded, of course. There had been suspicious disappearances also—but we hadn't been able to prove the Terrene responsible.) As I have mentioned, most Delyene can't abide Terrene. I had, by my work, become accustomed. And I had been around Neill long enough to grow past simple prejudice and see him, not just as a Terre freak, but as a—well—possibility.

Besides, it had been *quite* a while.

"If you cut me loose, I'll give you six heartbeats' head start."

He chuckled. "I've seen how fast you can run, longlegs. Make it ten."

I'd seen how fast he could run, too. It could have been six dozen, or a dozen-dozen, and made no difference.

Neill was going to get the ride of his life.

And afterward . . .

I still hadn't made up my mind, about afterward . . .

Chapter Nine

MOTTO:

The female of the species is more everything *than the male!*

—*Sayings of Neill*

He looked rather amusing, standing on the beach shaking his fist at me, as the *Eater* (bless him!) skimmed around the reef.

Oh, I had meant to run him into exhaustion, force him into submission, and ride him into quivering mindlessness.

I thought better of it.

Duty called.

And how would Draxuus and my other boys feel, if they knew?

Water carries sound well enough, but I couldn't understand him at all, he was using so many words I didn't know.

"I'll be back," I shouted. I might even resume the aborted chase when I returned, too. It certainly deserved some sober consideration. The trouble was Neill's unmasculine behavior, it put me off.

I had good luck returning. Fair winds, and one day I didn't have to noon because a storm hit. I scurried before it, close-hauled, ah, it was glorious, the wind, the rain, the *Eater* and I, joined into one magnificent whole.

I wasn't worried about Neill, he could take care of himself for a few days. And he was smart enough (I hoped) not to try to swim for it.

Luckily, I remembered before I sailed him boldly into Swiftfaring Harbor, that I had "burned" the *Eater*. After a bit of thinking, I decided on an underwater cave not far from Swiftfaring that I had explored a couple of times. It seemed as good a place as any to stash the *Eater;* the island it was on was barren, seldom visited. The entrance was above the water level at low tide (which was how I spotted it originally). I unshipped the *Eater*'s mast and towed him in myself. Inside the water was limpid in the dim light, phosphorescent bubbles trailing from the tiniest disturbance. The cave itself was deceptive. To someone swimming in the entrance, it appeared to be a simple small hollow. The entrance to the main cave was concealed inside, between two jagged rocks. I cursed as I maneuvered the *Eater* between them. Sweet sailor as he was, he was balky to scull. I finally got out and pushed and pulled him in, despite the slimy walls that gave little purchase for hand or foot. I moored him to an outcrop of rock above the waterline, with plenty of slack. I caught my noonmeal and ate it in the cave. Then I slept one last time aboard the *Eater,* rocked by gentle waves and lulled by the peaceful lap of water.

The sun was blinding as I emerged, and after the sweet responsiveness of the *Eater,* sculling that crude tow was a penance of no mean degree. I beached the tow an easy walk from Swiftfaring. Who'd bother it, a common tow, empty but obviously left for a purpose.

I wanted, badly, to see the Elyavaneet Noblelady, but I was "on Retreat" and that was too useful to jeopardize. But who would notice a cloaked figure going to or from the Pleasure Courts? And the Elyavaneet's rooms were none so far from the Courts. There were numerous houseboys moving about on various duties near the area of the Courts; I sent her a knotted message by one.

Then, I waited impatiently and (curse it!) alone in my favorite grotto for her answer.

It seemed forever, but she came herself instead of arranging a later meeting. She left her escort outside the grotto, I could see dim outlines through the sheet of spray. (I could even see them approached several times. Once one of them refused so loudly that I could hear even through the noise of the waterfall: "My Lady told me to wait for her. I'm *next.")*

I told her everything that had happened, Neill's near-dying (Terrene cannot breathe water), the Hypasha's sudden appearance, what she had said, what I had done, culminating in my secreting away of Neill. I left out only one item of import, though I meant to get to it later: my relationship (or lack thereof) with Neill.

Then I asked the all-important question. "Has the Merwençalla Noblelady proclaimed an augury concerning the Terren, Neill?"

"Nay, she has *not!*"

I relaxed against the seat. There had always been the possibility, small but there, that there had indeed been an augury, and that I had damned myself for eternity by disobeying it. But if the Hypasha's words had been (as I suspected) a trap . . .

"I am not sure, child, that I appreciate the expression on your face. What is on your mind?"

"I sent you a knotted message, in front of one of the Hypasha Lady's boys. In it, I simply told you I was going unexpectedly on Retreat, and asked you to please take care of my boys, especially Draxuus."

"I had done that without your asking, child."

"I know, dearest Noblelady. Truth it is, I feared for Draxuus. When mistresses quarrel, their boys may catch the fever; I liked not the look in the eye of the Hypasha's chief boy, standing near. Sending you a message was a mere excuse to get Draxuus away."

"My child, a boy has his pride; you should not have prevented him from expressing his loyality."

"Dear Drax, he may express his loyalty at decent odds. But he was alone, and there were six more of 'Paysha's boys within call."

The Noblelady smiled and preened herself slightly. "He has. By rare good fortune, I heard of the quarrel"—I sniffed; the corners of her mouth twitched—"heard of the quarrel, and intervened. But only"—she lifted a warning finger—"to ensure that the odds were even. Also, since the—source—of the fight was a jostle in the bazaar I forbade blades. Nonetheless—" She stopped, and I caught my breath. Had Drax been hurt? A broken neck, a cracked skull? "Nonetheless, the Hypasha Lady is most displeased. A broken arm, two sets of cracked ribs, and a concussion, I believe. Still, the fights were fair, I saw to that, and I declared that honor had been served. As for your boys"—was there sly amusement in her smile?—"your Draxuus—is growing a new tooth—or is it two?" I let out breath in a long sigh. Noblelady, that was cruel! "Another has a sprained ankle. I ordered him abed until it mends. None of them look particularly pretty, but they are all strutting about most pridefully. Have you a message for them?"

"You may tell them that I am most displeased by this unseemly brawling," I said sternly.

"And are you displeased?"

"I certainly am. That I wasn't there to see. But don't you tell them *that.*"

"I won't then, child. But you are rather severe with them."

I said nothing.

"As you wish." (But I learned later that she told Chukker, her chief boy, what I had said. And she neglected to tell him not to tell Draxuus. Ah, well.)

I returned to the main subject. "That message I sent. It was trivial, as you said. But suppose it hadn't been. Suppose I had said that Neill had died, by accident. Suppose I said that I was worried about the Council, but that it would be all right, because the Merwencalla Noblelady had sent to tell me of an augury condemning him . . ."

"But—"

"I know I didn't, but I could have, couldn't I? I should have in fact, but how could I put my vague suspicions in such a message? So all I told you was that I was going on Retreat. But suppose, suppose, Noblelady, that I had sent you such a message, Neill's death and the augury; now how would you be feeling, as the days pass and no such augury is proclaimed?"

"Worried, of course. Worried for your sake. Disobedience to a direct Council decision is a serious matter, you might be—" She stopped. "Go on."

"Yes, you would be worried. More and more worried as the days passed. You would approach the Merwencalla, privately. You wouldn't come right out and ask—suppose you had misunderstood the message—but you would hint. Wouldn't you?"

"Yes, I might, but . . ."

"Then, one of several things might happen. The Merwencalla Noblelady will confirm that such an augury has occurred, but she didn't proclaim it because the

Hypasha told her that Neill was already dead. Or she will say that no such augury has been made. Or she will say that there has been an augury concerning the Terren, but she is still seeking enlightenment. Whatever, you demand that either the augury be proclaimed publicly, whether or not it can be clearly interpreted, or that she proclaim that the Goddess renounces all claim to the Terren, for now. That should bother her somewhat."

Despite the opalescent light of the grotto, the Noblelady was pale. "Kimassu, you are all but accusing the Merwencalla Noblelady of falsifying aguries!"

"Not falsifying. I'm sure she doesn't consider it falsifying. Just taking the most favorable interpretation—for her."

"Humph!" The Noblelady gave that sophistry the contempt it deserved.

"Noblelady," I coaxed softly. "Make the effort. Tell me what she says."

"There is another matter. The Gorky Admiral."

"He's a whore," I snorted. "All Terrene are whores."

"My dear child, what an unkind thing to say."

"True, though. All of them. Even Neill." I couldn't sit still, somehow. Rude though it was, I rose aand began to pace back and forth in the small grotto.

"So-oooo. That's what's bothering you."

"Bothering me? What are you talking about? I feel nothing for Neill, nothing. How can I? He's a filthy slut, like all the Terrene."

"You're young, child, your standards are high. Perhaps a little too high. You haven't learned to make allowances for human nature, frailty."

"Frailty? Frailty! Noblelady, *he offered himself to me!*"

"So? You had not, unconsciously perhaps, encouraged him? You had not favored him, spent more time than needed with him. You gave him no reason to believe that his offering would be graciously accepted? You—"

"Noblelady!"

"You cannot judge him by your own rigid code, child. Remember, he is alone, lost among strangers. He has the weakness of all males, overready to lean on the first strong, kindly female they encounter. He likely made his simple offering, all he had to offer, in a spirit of gratitude. He may have thought our customs demanded it. He may simply have been unable to help himself . . ."

I shut one eye in agreement, but slowly. "That may be part of it; he's used to his own females, and they—" I couldn't tell her. I still couldn't believe it myself. "They've let their males get entirely out of hand," I said instead. "With the results you'd expect. The males run wild, and the females—they're the ones I can't understand. How could they have allowed matters to deteriorate so badly?"

She put a gentle hand on my shoulder. "I don't know. But it certainly explains many inconsistencies about them. How they can be so powerful, so physically advanced; and at the same time, so primitive, so lacking in honor and decency and all the other feminine virtues."

I slammed my open hand against the crystal wall. "And now what?"

"I must think. Later, when I have thought, I may accidentally encounter the Merwencalla in the course of my duties." I hoped she had the necessary—I rejected the word guile and substituted subtlety—the necessary subtlety to accomplish successfully what I knew *must* be accomplished. The Elyavaneet might ignore the spirit and obey the letter of someone's request, when she thought it for that someone's good. She might speak of frailty, weakness. But she had not met, as I had, deliberate evil. Nor could she see it in the actions of her old comrade, the Merwencalla. As I had difficulty seeing it in the actions of the Hypasha. "In any case," she was saying, "I shall meet you. Where, since you are supposedly on Retreat? Or would you come openly with me now?"

"No. I would not"—have the Merwencalla know I'm here, I finished the thought silently. "That is," I hurried on, "I would be here quietly, privately. Shall I meet you here tomorrow, at the end of noonrest?" I smiled. "Unless you fear for your reputation. The Courts, two days running.

"My dear child. At my age, such a compliment. Here will be fine. However, speaking of my reputation, I find I do not need all my escort. I shall leave one guard with you. Until tomorrow, then."

I couldn't protest, she had already raised her hand for the Blessing. Inwardly seething, I knelt. I didn't want to be hampered by a big, clumsy shadow. And she slipped through the water before I could rise and offer her my arm. I was hurt at that, deeply hurt. And then I saw the second form coming through the watery curtain.

Well!

She had sent him *in* to me.

I wasn't that desperate. To use one of hers.

And then I saw his face. Draxuus. *My* Draxuus. One eye swollen half-shut, but to me he had never looked lovelier. My dear darling Drax . . .

Wise, wise noblelady!

Chapter Ten

MOTTO:

Who weaves a snare for her enemy must take great care, lest she entangle her own feet.

—Wisdoms of Laimelina

It would be gratifying to report that the Gorky Admiral looked older, but in truth, thanks to that unnatural magic of theirs, which they call technology, he looked younger. When I knew him before, he had been tallish (for a Terren) and big-boned (Goddess, what wrists!) but gaunted. It was as though something (his intensity? striving?) had burned away the flesh between skin and bone, leaving only driving fanatical energy. I kept expecting his cheekbones (or his knobby wrists) to burst through his stretched taut skin. The effect had been not un-Delye, except for the broadness of his shoulders, the hugeness of wrists and knees and feet. But now—I watched him out of the corner of my eye as my fingers idly unraveled the fringe on my cuff. He approached me through the maze of the Gardens with an easy stride that was almost a lope. He had put on the flesh his bones seemed built for; it made him grossly huge by our standards, but he carried it easily, almost gaily. He was wearing one of those Terre costumes they call uniforms; it covered him, though much more tightly than my cloak did me, from thick neck to high shiny gold boots. The material was fine enough (what splendid weaving the Terrene do) and fitted enough that one could watch the muscles moving easily beneath. I wondered how such clothing would look on one of our males (if they could stand being so covered in the heat). Draxuus, say. Enticing. Suggestive. The Gorky Admiral's muscular waist was emphasized by a wide gold belt, with all sorts of Terre oddities attached or hanging. There were amulets and charms on his chest and neck and shoulders and on the front of the gleaming gold helmet.

He stopped, the first hesitation he had shown, about two paces from the bench I was seated on (carefully chosen so that I was in shadow from a pair of sweet-scented shrubs and an ornamental latticework wall).

I pretended I didn't see him, athough the clear sunlight he stood in made the emerald of his costume shimmer like a sparkling sea.

"Kimassu? Lady Kimassu?"

Why had I let the Noblelady talk me into this masquerade?

"How kind of you to come visit me," I quavered.

He bowed, removing his helmet so that the sun flashed over his glittering silver fur. I suppressed amusement; so we were even. If he couldn't see me clearly in my shadow, I saw little but flashing brightness. "How kind of you to invite me," he replied.

I focused on a point about six paces to his right. "I didn't have to invite you in the old days, did I, Bozyu. Those were the days, weren't they, when we shared a barracks room together. Weren't they, Boz, he-he-he? D'you remember the times we snuck out together after curfew? And the time we got caught? Worth everything the mistress handed us, eh, Boz? He-he-he!"

"Lady Kimassu, don't you remember me? I'm Alexei Gorky, I . . ."

I continued to talk to the mythical Bozyu. "And that lovely boy we shared, what was his name, Bozyu? These young ones nowadays, they aren't like the boys we had, are they, Boz? I saw one in the bazaar yesterday, soliciting, *soliciting* mind you, bold as you please. And he was cross-eyed. Cross-eyed, and he squinted, too. Can you imagine, bold as you please, and . . ."

I could find pity for the Gorky Admiral. I don't know what he had expected, but I continued to ramble on to Bozyu, not even looking at him, a disconnected monologue on every subject of possible interest to two elderly ladies. His face got very red as I discussed, explicitly, some problems I had been having with my bowels, copied word for word from an old barracks-mistress of mine. My audience varied after a bit. Bozyu was replaced by Hypponda, by a boy I snapped orders to, by Bozyu again. Sometimes I talked perfectly rationally, sometimes I wandered, sometimes I changed abruptly in mid-syllable. For me, the garden was well peopled; I didn't make the mistake of ignoring him. I looked at him and spoke and even answered him; he was doubly disconcerted when he realized, from what I said, that I saw someone entirely different instead of him.

Once he took my cloak-shrouded face gently between his hands and turned me so that we stared directly into each other's faces. Despite blinking and fluttering and rolling my eyes, I studied him carefully. I saw little I recognized, except for the tilted eyes. His face was as full as his body, gone were the hollow cheeks; now they were rounded, the lower halves cut by two deep vertical lines. His skin was fresh, healthy, glowing, smooth except for two lines of fur above his eyes, which drew together as he frowned. "Who are—I don't know you." I let my voice get very high and thin.

"I'm Alexei Gorky." His voice was deep and firm.

"I don't know any Lexigorky—you look strange, Lexigorky, you look like no Delyen I ever—guard! guard! guard!"

He rose angrily and replaced his helmet, adjusting a sliding piece until his upper face was covered with polished metal reflecting the sun, so that his entire face was camouflaged by metal and glare.

I could hear running footsteps. "Guards! To me!"

"I regret, Lady Kimassu . . ." The guards came hurrying up. "I'm not ready to go yet."

"The Lady called," panted one of the guards.

"She got a little confused. Misunderstood something I said. Old ladies sometimes get confused, misunderstand." The Gorky Admiral handed him something; I only hoped it wasn't another one of their ever-sharp metal blades. I was talking querulously about modern-day standards, let just anyone into a private garden, what was the world coming to . . .

"Lady," said the guard. "Lady, the—ah—Noble wishes to talk to you a little longer. He means no harm."

"The Goddess smiled on us this day, Megma," I said. "See, we brought back heavy cargo nets."

The guard shrugged. Someone had primed him well. "One of her good days," he said to the Gorky Admiral. "Just be careful what you say, try not to upset her again. After all, there's no real harm done, and the Elyavaneet Noblelady herself approved this visit."

Was I going to have a word with the Elyavaneet, I thought. Enough was enough! But the guards were moving away; the Gorky Admiral stared after them for a few heartbeats, his shoulders sagging slightly. I sang a very good ballad that had been popular when I was younger; of course, I had to stop every few seconds to take another breath.

How I wished he had left with the guards! I was rapidly running out of invention.

He knelt in front of my bench. "Lady, I would like you to accept this—in repayment of past generosities and kindnesses."

"Past generosities—but I know you not, stranger."

He caught my hand. "Poor Kimassu. You don't remember . . ."

Indignantly, I snatched my hand away. "Remember? I remember, if there were aught to remember. Who says different lies. My memory is as good as it ever was. Look you, stranger, who says I don't remember . . ."

"Not, I, Lady Kimassu. Not I. What I meant was, sometimes something that may seem a small thing to one, a little kindness, given casually, of no great import and quickly forgot; sometimes that may have much more significance to the other, the recipient of the deed. And that one remembers. Do you understand me, Lady Kimassu?"

"Good deeds linger long in the memory. The Goddess says, in the Tenth Canto of the Book of the Unveiling, that the scent of such is most sweet in Her nostrils." I looked at him with the innocent pride of one who had managed to remember a difficult lesson correctly. Actually, it was the Twelfth Canto of the Book of Laimelina. It was unnecessary subtlety; he merely looked blank. "One should always trod the Way, the Goddess has ordained it," I said righteously.

"Ah—yes, of course. As I was saying, this—ah—good deed . . ."

"Ah." I smiled broadly. "You've done a good deed, and you've come to me for a Blessing. How sweet."

"But, Lady Kimassu—"

"Ah, ah—" I raised a warning finger. "Mustn't tell me, my boy, that would spoil it. As the Goddess says, through the mouth of Her vessel Laimelina, there are six degrees of holy charity, of which the simplest is the helping hand, aid freely rendered . . ." He heard me, with ill-concealed impatience, through all six, and (I was beginning to enjoy myself again) through a shameless steal of Klatmandu's famous commentary on that verse. Only I didn't finish it; I switched in mid-phrase to Rhyandre's interpretation of the passage in the Book of the Dead concerning the weighing of the animas against the Breath of Truth. Except I stopped in the middle of a sentence, smiled broadly again (already my jaws were beginning to ache), blinked twice, let the silence stretch out, and then said politely, "Of course, I agree with you wholeheartedly."

He groaned low, under his breath. Then, grimly, "Lady Kimassu!"

"I am the Kimassu Lady. Have you a message for me, my child?"

During my sermon, he had pulled himself onto the low ornamental rock nearest my bench and stared into my face. Now he ground his teeth together with a crunching noise; suddenly his face smoothed, got a sly look. Again he knelt. "Not a message, Lady Kimassu, a gift." He fumbled at his belt. "I have a gift for you, in memory of past deeds." He held it in his two hands, an armlet, mayhap a wristlet, of shiny white metal, set with jade and lapis lazuli. It was hand-made, not skillfully. I had no wish for it.

"A gift, boy? From which of my friends, so I may thank them."

"From one who owes you much, far more than this little token can repay."

I drew back.

"Lady, it is *owed* to you."

I hesitated. He had, knowingly or not, touched a chord. One must accept payment of a debt of honor. I had ill-treated and fooled him, but he didn't know that. From his point of view, he had to give me this. I, on the other hand, could not accept it. A pretty dilemma. I touched the largest chunk of jade. "This one overbalances the others."

His face was red and shiny with sweat. "I made it myself. They were as good a match as I could get."

"You need not be ashamed," I said gently. I couldn't take it. I couldn't *not* take it. "I had a boy could beat metal once," I said dreamily. "As though he could see a picture of what he wanted before he started. He'd lay out a group of stones on his workbench, and set them, never hesitating a second. A dear, sweet lad he was, loving and faithful. He could—he could—" I wound down, sat, staring into distance.

He clasped the armlet about my wrist. I was glad we had thought to coarsen my hands and lower arms with rock grit as well as my face. I could feel his bare hands against my skin, and I knew he was feeling the age-coarseness of mine.

"For a girl, who was once kind to the stranger within her gates," he said softly, his eyes turned inward, so that I knew he, too, was remembering. "For a girl who had the courage to do what was right, though it hurt her deeply. And for a boy who loved and walked away, the one unselfish act in his whole selfish life, because he was inspired by that courage. Because"—his lip curled—"he couldn't admit his courage was less than hers. Because it was the one gift he had to give her, then."

"I know not who you speak of, stranger." And I didn't understand.

"It doesn't matter. They're dead, that boy and that girl. Long dead. But you and I—"

"They all died, you know." I addressed the remorseless, uncaring sky. "All dead, all of them, my pretty ones." I dropped my hands and the armlet slipped off to lie in a bed of fallen flowers. There was enough truth in what I said that I heard genuine sadness and regret in my voice, that he heard it, too.

Ah, Draxuus, the topaz-eyed, lithe and loving!

Carefully, he retrieved the armlet, plucked a fragile mauve petal caught between two stones, and replaced the unwanted thing on me, pushing it high on my arm, so it would set firm. "For auld lang syne," he smiled, a charming smile, and suddenly I saw the stiff, intense young Terren beneath the assured, full-fleshed stranger. The tilted, shadow-darkened eyes twinkled through their shining shield. There was a heartbeat's wait, and the smile broadened, just slightly. "May the Goddess"—he rose to his feet—"smile on you, Lady Kimassu."

'But you've just arrived, Bozyu," I quavered. "How can you go so soon?"

"I—" He didn't know how to respond. I had ignored him, lectured him, called for guards to throw him out; now I insisted he stay. Then he realized that it really didn't matter. "Duty calls, Lady Kimassu. Perhaps another time . . ."

"It was always duty with you, Boz, wasn't it? But I forgive you this time. If you promise to come again soon."

"I—I can't make that promise, Lady Kimassu."

"Promise. Promise. Promise!"

"I—Kimassu, I—Kali and Siva, I should never have come!"

I agreed. With any luck, he wouldn't want any repetitions of this little visit.

I kept up my incoherent monologue to his retreating back.

I kept it up until a guard came and told me he was gone, truly gone.

Then I just sat, while the shadows lengthened and lengthened.

Chapter Eleven

MOTTO:

Oh, what a tangled net we weave,
Ourselves more than others to deceive.

—*Sayings of Neill, original attributed to the Walterscot Lady Bard, of Terrafam*

"He had the impertinence to give you a gift, Kimassu." The Noble-lady had come herself, finally, and whisked me away from the deepening darkness into the cheerful closeness of her private quarters. "I regret I gave him permission. I apologize; had I guessed that this was his intent . . ."

"No, Noblelady." I dandled the armlet up and down my arm, so that it flashed in the light of the glow-animals on the wall. "The Terrene view such things differently."

"You cannot mean to keep it. If you can't bear to see it destroyed, the Morningstar barracks-mistress may use it for a prize in the next games."

"No, I will keep it. As a reminder."

"A reminder. Of a Terren?"

"No, of . . . Noblelady, I abused than man. I laughed at him, I tricked him, I fooled him, I made a game of him. I laughed at how easily I fooled him. I *enjoyed* fooling him."

"It was your duty."

"My duty. My duty. Yes, it *was* my duty. But, was it my duty to *enjoy* my duty?"

"I see." A pause. "You are right. Wear it always, then. A reminder."

I paced up and down the room in silence. More and

more, I had found myself doing that whenever I was within walls. Pacing back and forth, up and down, as though my feet were measuring out something. But what? Confines? Restraints? Limits? What?

At last I had to ask it. "The augury, Noblelady?"

"I bring sorry tidings. I fear you are correct about the motives of my colleague the Merwencalla. Tomorrow the augury will be publicly proclaimed."

"Tomorrow? Then there is an augury?"

"Yes." She drew a deep breath. "There is, indeed, an augury."

"And it will say?" My doom, what else?

"That the Terren presently held in the House of Equity shall be brought before the Goddess on Her Throne to bear the weight of Her judgment."

"That's all? Just to be brought before Her Throne?"

"That is all." Death sentence for Neill then, not me. But I meant what I had said to him: better it were me.

Another thought struck me. "Noblelady, *when?* When is he to be presented?"

"I'm sorry, Kimassu. The Ninth day of the Cycle of the Crimson Leviathan."

So the omens were for death, after all. Given even four or five days, I might have managed it. But never— "Tomorrow? The very day of the Proclamation?"

"The very day."

"But I am on Retreat, surely I can give him when . . ."

"No, your Family speaks for you, Kimassu. He must be presented tomorrow."

I had outwitted myself. "I can't possibly bring him back."

"I know. And if he is not produced . . ."

"I have disobeyed the goddess. I am outcast, fish bait, heretic. And if I claim he is dead—the Hypasha Lady saw him 'dead'—she thinks . . ."

"The Council will deny you."

Neither of us said it. The Merwencalla wanted her blood; and she was going to get it. I remembered a Terre tale Neill told me, about a Terren who had had a debt of honor to another Terren, and when she could not repay, offered a measure of her own flesh instead. It sounded right, the sort of act a Delyen might commit, if the scales balanced not and honor were unsatisfied. But Neill saw it differently. Because the first Terren, she who owed, *qualified* her offer, by saying flesh but not a drop of blood! And Neill approved of this sophistry! And the second Terren, she who was owed *to,* instead of spitting on the first Terren as an honor-lost woman, begged the first Terren (*she who owed!*) to forgive her, the second Terren (she who was owed to). And the first Terren graciously condescended to forgive the second Terren, who gave her a generous gift in gratitude, for not ruining her! No wonder we have difficulty understanding them! But this story proved to me that the Terrene value sly hypocrisy far above honor—if, indeed, they value honor at all. Which led to another question: when dealing with those, such as the Terrene, lacking the most elementary concept of honor, must one treat them with honor, for one's own honor's sake?

Had we treated the Terrene with honor?

Yes. And also, on occasion, no.

Had they treated with us with honor?

Emphatically, definitely not. They couldn't; honor wasn't in them.

I would willingly give my life for the potential Neill represented. But, oh, my honor. Not, please, my honor.

"There must be a way out." I paced up and down, up and down, while the Elyavaneet watched. "I'm too close to understanding them, I can't give up Neill, I can't allow myself to be destroyed!" Up and down. "Yet—my honor is my honor. Can the Goddess speak truth through a cracked vessel?"

"Sleep, child, you are exhausted. It has been a trying day for you. Perchance, if the Goddess will, morn will bring wiser council."

"No, now, while my mind is a-fever. The Terrene. And the Merwencalla. They are honor-lost. And she, by promoting divisiveness among us, when we needs must be united, is she not as honor-lost as they?"

"That I should live to hear you say such!"

"Is she not as honor-lost as they?"

"Perchance—mayhap—she feels that she is in the right—that what she believes should be done, *must* be done, at any cost, any sacrifice, even the smearing of her own honor."

I snorted, most rudely. "The Terrene have a saying like that. The goals justify the methods."

"Simsam," she snapped. He had been sitting curled in a corner, idly strumming a five-stringed lute. "Go."

"Yes, mistress. Will you require anything else, mistress?"

Her voice gentled. "No, not tonight, dear. Go and amuse yourself, if you're not sleepy yet; just *try* not to lose your new kilt this time."

He nodded, giggling, and with a quick Blessing and an affectionate pat on the rump she speeded him away.

"Do you know what Neill says will happen if we place the Line of Dread around the Terrene enclaves?"

"Kimassu, you didn't tell him about—"

"I did. I wanted to know his reaction. And he says the Terrene will ignore it, walk past it as though it weren't there at all."

"No. No, I cannot believe they are so lost to the Sight of the Goddess."

"Lost to the Goddess?" I laughed. "The Terrene worship a dozen-dozen gods and goddesses, a dozen dozen-dozen. With their mouths. But Neill says, in their hearts, they worship only the great god Mammon. They worship *things*, Noblelady. Material possessions, wealth, arrogance. They are divided among themselves, more so than we, but when the first Terren crosses the Line of Dread, and is destroyed, for the heretical, cursed creation that they all are; then the Terrene will unite to destroy us. And they have the power to do it, too."

"Yes," she winked agreement. "We've known, almost from the beginning, from the first Landing, that they had that ability. I, myself, have often wondered, in view of their recognized bloodthirst and savagery, why they have refrained for so long."

"Their power is *too* great. They don't want to kill all of us, all of our world. Besides, it's expensive."

"Expensive. That's a Terre word, isn't it? What does it mean?"

"I'll tell you. What they really want, what they're still looking for, is some equivalent of smallpox or the buffalo."

"Smallpox? The buffalo?"

"Smallpox is an old Terre disease. Often fatal. Among

one group of Terrene, it had been common for generations, those suspectible to it had gradually been bred out. But when the immune group exposed another group, one that had never had the disease, the other group died and died and died."

"How horrible for them. What a tragic accident. Their guilt, how desolated they must have been."

"Accident? They did it deliberately, Noblelady. Gave the Indians, that was the name of the other group, clothing and blankets that had belonged to those who had died of the disease."

"They could never have known . . ."

"They *knew*. They did it over and over, deliberately, one tribe after another, for generations, until the Indians were scattered, helpless remnants."

"That cannot be true. Even the Terrene could not be such monsters."

"No? Noblelady, they have words for that which we cannot even conceive. Death camps. Genocide. Racial purity. Half-breed. The only good Indian is a dead Indian. The only good Delyen . . . They wanted the land the Indians lived on, you see. The Indians were willing to share, but that wasn't good enough for their conquerors. The Indians lived simply, hunting most of their food, gathering and farming, too. Not unlike ourselves. The buffalo were their main foodfish. And the Terrene killed them. I don't know how, but Neill says where once multitudes of the buffalo grazed, like a sea of backs, there are only a few carefully preserved specimens now. The Indians depended on the buffalo; when the buffalo died, they died, too. But the Terrene did worse. They destroyed the Indian's way of living, their pride in their accomplishments, until the pitiable remainders had the choice of becoming imitation Terrene, like their conquerors, or dying out. And if they'd do that to their own kind—the Indians were a subgroup of Terrene—what would they do to us? They who neither recognize nor respect honor and courtesy and gratitude. A disease by itself wouldn't destroy us. We're too scattered, and far too disciplined. There would be survivors; and since we can—excuse me, Noblelady—*breed* as rapidly as they if we wished to, there would be resistant survivors. Enough to present a problem, to destroy their excuse for taking our world.

And those survivors would *know*. The coming of the Terrene; and a new disease. They may try yet, a last resort, if all else fails. But what they really want is plenty of thralls to do their musclework for them. The destruction of the best of us, and the rest left, the subservient, the easily frightened, to be controlled by them and only by them."

"How unspeakable. Yet what you are saying echoes one point I have made for years. That we cannot attack them openly, that our wisest course is to resist subtly. Never, ever, dare we provoke them into using their power against us."

I stopped pacing, stared at her openmouthed. "That's it!"

"That's what, child?"

Up and down again, faster and faster, as the thoughts chased themselves about in my head. "That's it. Never openly. But make it uneconomic for them. Make them pay. Not in big bites, but little blood-lettings here and there. Secretly. Sly. Underhanded. Their own techniques, turned on them. They want to fish our seas; *let* them. And if a few venomfish get mixed up in the nets . . . or if they want to fish after a crimson tide—they were very angry last year, when we told them not to, weren't they?—let them! Let accidents happen to Terrene, mayhap even encourage them. If a few keystones in a dam were loosened the night before a big storm, why the storm damaged it, it was an old dam, wasn't it? This is our world, let our world work for us. Shift our villages toward the hotter islands; we can migrate during the hottest season, we did it regularly once. If they follow us, the heat will get them, and if they try to go it alone—they still haven't learned enough, despite their magics. Especially if we help matters along here and there. Delay. Obstruct. Quibble. But always with a smile and helpful murmurs. Keep them in the Enclaves and isolate the Enclaves, shrink them. Frustrate them. Agree and agree and agree and then . . ."

"Kimassu, this is not honorable."

"Noblelady, they are not honorable."

"Nonetheless . . ."

"They are not *honorable!* The Terre word, uneconomic, do you know what it means?"

"I do not, and I fail to see how a Terre word affects this matter."

"Because it *is* this matter, Noblelady. Where you or I or any Delyen would judge a course of action by, is it honorable, a Terren would ask is it economic, is it profitable? And do you know what they mean by these? They mean, what will I gain from this, what good will it do me." The Elyavaneet's face was pale and set; I knew she would never disbelieve me, but she distrusted my source—Neill and the other Terrene I had questioned. "I told you, they worship wealth. What they consider wealth. Not a healthy body or a clean conscience or a shining, unstained honor, but what things, what inanimate, machine-produced shoddy things they can collect. They come here because it is cheaper, less uneconomic, more profitable, because their flying ships can land here and suck up our water and spew out their poison so that we've had to change our fishing patterns again and again, and in return they give us that machine shoddy they're so fond of. It means nothing to us, but our honor won't let us allow a *guest* to leave unfed or in need, so for them foodfish and metals, leaving raw holes on our green islands, but our *honor*, our honor demands it. But if a guest forces herself upon you, is she still a guest? Or is she a sucker-fish, draining your blood, to be detached as quickly as possible, even at the risk of damage to yourself?"

"I say, our honor is more important."

"More important? More important than what? Our lives? Yes, if only our lives were at risk, I would agree with you. But, Noblelady, would you live to see our sprats grow us as they?" The ultimate obscenity. And I had said it aloud, deliberately, in the face of my sponsor, my warden, she who had guided my steps since I had been adopted into my Family. I repeated the offense. "The sprats. Think of them, Noblelady. Think of what they will be like, what their lives, if indeed they have lives at all, what their lives will be like under the thumb of the Terrene!"

"And what would you have, Kimassu? What would your way do?"

"At least, my way holds a chance. Use their own weapons against them, consistently, relentlessly. Use guile and lies and deceitful smiles and, yes, Noblelady, dishonor. Fight them, in every way we can, but never openly, always secretly. Make agreements, and carry out what is favorable to us; and ignore the rest. Claim the land the Enclaves are built on . . ."

"But we don't want . . ."

"But they do. We can afford to give up an island, islands. Draw the Line of Dread about a whole island, but tell the Terrene first, warn them, allow them time to move out. And then, burn the island to the bare rock. Say it's something that has to be done every so many megacycles, and burn everything. We can start anew in our skins; they can't."

"They'd never believe such a tale," she objected.

"They used to do it themselves. Or a group called the Mayanene did, anyway. Neill told me so."

"You put a deal too much reliance on what your Neill tells you, I think."

"I've never caught him in a lie. Everything he says that I can check, with what I know of Terrene, with what I can find out, is purest truth."

"But why should he tell you these things, why shoud he?"

"Why?" I hissed, and then laughed aloud. "For the sake of my pretty blue eyes, he says."

"Blue? Pretty blue? His eyes are blue, not yours. I don't understand this Neill of yours, not at all, Kimassu."

"Neither do I. But he hates where I hate, Noblelady. And if he be not our friend, at least he be the enemy of our enemy."

"That is absurd."

"That is *truth*." I knelt before her. I couldn't bring myself to touch her, but in my intense anguish I clasped my hands in front of me, trembling. "Don't you see, this is the way it *must* be. If we are to have any chance at all, this is the way it *must* be."

"But." She looked aged for once, aged and troubled and uncertain. "But your way, Kimassu. You mentioned —you spoke of—" She lost color, but couldn't bring herself to say the word.

"They," I said emphatically, to show I understood. "Yes, *they*. What would their lives be like? You would be teaching them, by example, to be dishonorable. Is that not a worser evil?"

"It is a risk, yes, I admit it. A risk. But the other is a certainty. What will the Terrene teach them, by example, if they gain what they wish?"

She sighed. "I am—too old, to change myself, Kimassu."

"It must be you. I have no time, no time left. Tomorrow, at sunrest— I have honor still, for my own people, even for such as the Merwencalla. Or say rather for Her whose Mouth the Merwencalla claims to be. She may do with me as she pleases, though I know well what she pleases. But she shall *not* have Neill!"

"Honor—or pride. Is he worth your life, Kimassu?"

"Mine, yours, Draxuus'; whatever and whomever I hold dear. He is our chance, Noblelady."

"No, you are our chance. I meant not to speak of this; but do you think it chance that you are today what you are: our one who knows the Terrene best. Think it *chance* that I chose you, from among so many? I have led our people long and overlong; I have well earned my rest. But I could not rest; I cannot rest; until my successor is ready. You were not—quite—ready. So I kept silence. Sometimes, no matter what the care or the skill, sometimes a pot has an inner flaw that is revealed only in the firing. You have, oh, not true flaws, Kimassu. Faults, slight imperfections that can be amended with time and care. You are too impetuous, too rash; you drive for your goals too intensely. But perhaps that very single-mindedness, that rash, wholehearted drive will yet be our salvation. For now, you are still too unseasoned, too unready. If you defy the Merwencalla . . ."

"I must." I laid my head on her lap, felt gentle hands stroke my bowed back. "Neill must not be—" I stiffened, remembering. "Noblelady, the augury." I was so excited I stuttered. "The augury. How does it identify he whom the Goddess demands?"

"Why, the Terren held in the House of Equity. He who diminished the Goddess' mana."

I fell backward, holding my sides and laughing. "Well, then, the Goddess may have the Terren held in the House of Equity. He who diminished the Goddess' mana."

"Child, you cannot escape so easily. Just because your Neill will not be in the House of Equity the very day the augury is to be Proclaimed . . ."

"Noblelady, I am amazed at *you*. Think you I intend to cheat the Goddess? The Goddess desires the Terren held in the House of Equity; and She shall have him." She stared at me as though I had lost my wits. "His name is Willis." I smiled broadly. "His profane hands touched the Most Revered, the Vlayfoxpillat Noblelady. Can you think of a worse sacrilege? I can't. Except, maychance, an unsanctified one entering the sacred precincts."

"I had forgotten," she frowned. "You did tell me of another Terren."

"The Merwencalla has forgot, too; or perhaps she never knew. They haven't asked for him back; perhaps the Captain of his ship never sent word he missed the launching. The Terrene are careless that way. The Most Revered is not likely to talk about it, she was most annoyed. I've held him close in the House of Equity since his offense; and the Merwencalla may do as she—or the Goddess—chooses with him. Make fish bait of him; or geld him; or return him to his Terre mistresses. I care not. Though they might not be overpleased to receive him back; evil is evil, and I'm sure that he has broken their laws just as he ignored our customs. Criminal, is their word. Willis is a criminal."

"Kimassu! There is another Terren in the House of Equity *now?*"

"Willis. His name is Willis. I was going to penance him and give him to the Temple anyway when I had all I wanted from him. But if the Goddess wants him now, She may have him, and welcome."

"Kimassu, you have learned well, from the Terrene and your Neill. I am not sure I appreciate what you have learned."

"You wished me to learn well, and I have, have I not? And think you on this: You told me of the words of the Terren who asked for Neill back. You reported his words; now tell me, in truth. Did he genuinely wish Neill returned; or did he seem most happy at Neill's plight?"

"I think he was not too sorrowed at our refusal."

I blinked agreement. "Truth. There is much I do not

understand concerning relations between Neill and his own people. But I think they are not sorry to see us take care of their problem for them. So then. The Merwencalla thinks she is asking for a dead man. But perchance she is only the vessel, and the Goddess truly wants Willis. Who am I to deny this? What made the Merwencalla ask merely for the Terren in the House of Equity? Eh? That is what she asked for, and that is what you will give her, tomorrow, in full regalia and ceremony. And my honor is bright, dearest Noblelady, bright!"

"And you?"

"I am on Retreat. I shall stay quietly on Retreat."

"And when you return?"

"The war begins. Fret not, Noblelady. The Terrene know what war is, even if you do not."

Chapter Twelve

MOTTO:

Hark, in the hovering darkness,
A whisper of wave on the shore,
Or flap of a sail where no boat should be—
The Four-faced One meddles once more!

—*Saga of Three Adopted Together*

I was singing as I scrambled down the rough rock path at far too fast a pace for safety, but I was euphoric. Every time I thought of the Merwencalla's face when she was presented with Willis, I laughed again. She'd have to take him, too. And 'Paysha would lose her wager, because a person on Retreat would officially be in the race, at least in spirit. But a spirit, naturally, cannot be seen; so it comes in last.

"Yo, ho, crest of the wave," I caroled.

Of course, 'Paysha could try to kill me. An accident, maychance. But I didn't think 'Paysha would sink that far. A manufactured challenge, more like; after I came back from "Retreat."

I flipped myself in a somersault onto the soft sand; my laughter echoed and re-echoed from the surrounding rocks.

I had watched the train leaving the House of Equity, each member dressed in his or her best. (My assistant, Vlayonna, was overpale and trembling. A youngster of great potential, I would have to move her on and that soon. She was overtender for our duty; and I would not have her anima scarred. Once I had this affair of Neill straightened out . . .) They need not have gone into the sun at all, of course. All the major Houses lie in the center of Swiftfaring, between the docks and storehouses and the Temple and Sacred Courts. Over the years they have grown and grown together, so that instead of many separate Houses, there is one huge interconnected maze of rooms and additions, airways and waterways, winding passages and abrupt level changes. The Elyavaneet could easily have gone from the House of Equity to the Temple of the Goddess without once stepping into the sun, had she desired it. Instead, the entire train issued from the House of Equity, passed down the First Empress' Triumphal Avenue, and turned onto the Sacred Way. It took time, that short journey, paced by the solemn beat of the drum, the rattle of sistrum, the harsh wail of the reeds.

She planned to arrive exactly at sunrest.

The ceremony of reception had not taken long. The platoon of guards returned in the last dying light, tuglennas already starting to glow in their left hands, to claim Willis and take him to the Goddess.

I left at full dark, slipping out full-cloaked from the Pleasure Courts. The walk to where the tow was beached was nothing; I was bursting with energy and high spirits.

I would return to Neill and learn more from him and start our war. Our undeclared but oh so vital war. Was this how Terrene felt, going into battle? This strange exhilaration, this feeling the world was at your feet, this heady surety of ultimate triumph.

I had come close to disaster, and I was lighthearted and lightheaded.

"Neill," I shouted, and heard the echoes of the rocks. Neill-neill-neill . . .

Wavelets played about my sandaled feet.

"Neill! Let the waves carry my voice! I'm coming. Neill! Be ready!" I laughed and in sheer excess of energy began running madly up and down the beach. I splashed into the water and made great swaths of footprints in the soft sand. My cloak went flying, to lay half in, half out of the water.

"Neill!" Neill-neill-neill . . .

"I'm coming, Neill. Ready yourself!" Self-elf-elf . . .

The moonlight was bright on the sand; with gay laughter I made pattern after pattern of dark footprints, finishing with a complex Eye-of-the-Goddess.

But at last flesh and breath could do no more, and I stood, panting and hissing, by the beached tow. "Wallowing old tub," I addressed it. (Unfairly; for what it was, it sailed well enough.) "It's a good thing for poor Neill's patience, that I don't have to sail you all the way." And that sail jury-rigged, and likely to come off in the first decent wind. "You'd take forever. For-ev-er. Well, sooner launched, sooner ported." I pushed and hauled. "Ugh, you clumsy scow. You weigh twice what you did when I beached you. I'll be glad when I can get rid of *you.*"

It was a malignant conspiracy to hold me back. The tow hung up on every minute shell and bone on the beach. I pushed and pulled and tugged and cursed. I had the balky thing in thigh-high water, its long keel barely clearing the bottom, when I remembered my cloak.

Oh, curse!

I looked about but could see no sign of the cloak. Well, it's undyed color was not so different from the pale beige of the sand.

Double curse!

It was a double tide, Anatra and Sunatra lined up in the same sector of the sky. I shoved the tow back onto the beach, my euphoric mood distinctly soured.

I found the cloak finally, by splashing slowly through the shallow water, dragging my feet. By then I was vilely angry and more than ready to take my anger out on whoever or whatever crossed my path first.

Whatever was the armlet the Gorky Admiral had forced on me. It caught on my cloak as I was dragging it out of the water, and I heard a thin r-r-rip-pppp.

Now, that cloak had been made for me by Dawnee, one of my own lads, and a sweet faithful boy he was. Oh, the tear could be fixed, the darn hidden by embroidery; but it angered me that an unwanted gift from an unliked Terren had spoiled a love offering.

Why was I wearing the thrice-accursed thing, anyway?"

Because *my* honor demanded it.

But hadn't I said that we could never drive out the Terrene if we insisted on maintaining full honor?

So I had said; but how had I acted?

I had accepted his gift, because he walked away and

left it, but I wore it as a penance. A penance for a wrong done a *Terren?* Had I gone sun-struck? But on a person-to-person level, I *had* wronged him, though he knew it not; in return he had made an offering for me. But he was a Terren.

And Draxuus? Draxuus hadn't been hurt, and it had amused me to fool the Terren.

Just as it would amuse me to fool Terrene in the cycles to come.

Without debating the matter further, I ripped the armlet off my wrist and hurled it as far away from myself as I could. I heard it fall among the rocks at the cliff base with a hollow clatter and a noise of falling pebbles.

Odd. I hadn't felt it at the time, but the thing had scratched me. As I watched, a drop of dark fluid welled up from my wrist. Clumsy, skill-less Terren, couldn't even properly polish a bit of metal.

I shambled down the beach toward the tow, the exercise I had taken, the energy I had freely expended, finally demanding their price. My feet grew heavier and heavier, my arms flopped limply. It would be work to launch the tow again. This beach was usually deserted; perhaps if I rested a bit. The sand was soft and warm and inviting; besides, I was so—something was wrong, this tiredness was too deep, unnaturally deep. I forced myself to keep staggering down the beach; my limbs seemed so heavy, so clumsy, I couldn't direct them properly. What was wrong with me?

I fell, lay helplessly a moment; then, instinctively, I tried to drag myself closer to the water. Closer, closer; like a giant sand worm I struggled toward the boundary between water and land. Closer. Closer. Slower. Slow—I lay helpless, sand grinding into my skin, wavelets lapping about my outstretched fingers, beckoning, tantalizing; promising. The tide would change, and I would be safe. Safe? In the water, and helpless; not a muscle mine to command? Perhaps it would wear off; but I knew this was no natural exhaustion. Death? To come in such a mode, and I still young. Yet if I hadn't recovered by the turn of the tide . . .

And then I heard it and knew it was worse than I thought. Voices. Deep, Terre voices.

I couldn't see them; I was lying on my side, with my

back to what I heard. First there had been a whirring sound, like a honeysucker, only immensely louder. It had started so small I could scarcely hear it, but within heartbeats it had grown until it pained my ears; and abruptly stopped. Next, while my ears still throbbed, there was a soft whump; and then a softer, slower hum, which slowly died down, until I could hear the voices over it. How close they were I couldn't tell, water carries sound so well.

"How close are we?" one of them said.

"Close enough. I couldn't set her down in that hodgepodge of rocks."

"In that? We'll never find her in that! It's a rock jungle!"

"Her"? I didn't like the sound of that at all. What "her"?

The voices continued to argue and discuss (and complain). What was a regulation, anyway; and how did you break it? Goddess, did I want them to find me—helpless—or not? They were looking for someone; or something. They kept referring to a "her" and an "it."

I tried to pick voices apart. Four, at least, mayhap as many as seven or eight. They were climbing about on the cliff now, I could hear them fumbling and half-falling and cursing. Once I heard a large crash, but it was only a rock falling. From the comments, none of them was hurt. Too bad! One of them was directing the others. "A little to your left, Sven. Jorge, you're too low, try to get higher."

"*Madre de Dios,* have I then the wings of the blessed angels?"

"Clem, are you sure the screen isn't giving you a ghost? There's no one here!"

"Keep looking, keep looking. My screen's accurate."

The line of beach curved inward from where I judged them to be. I didn't think I was in their line of sight; the beach was narrow, and the rock cliffs jagged and high. The waves were lapping higher now, covering my hands, my lower arms, nibbling away at the rest of me.

Then—"Sven, blast it, you're standing right on her!"

"May you be plasmaed, Clem! I ain't. I'd know—wait, there's a crack here. Maybe it gets wider higher up and—"

"Here, Jorge, I think I can give you a boost. Take my hand."

"There's a ledge here, Sven. I'll work my way toward you."

"You do that, Piers. She must be between us, somehow."

"Here, Mahmood, I'll lend you a hand with Jorge."

"Aieeeee—"

"Get him!"

"Mahmood!"

"Madre de Dios!"

Shouts, confusion, falling sounds, but I couldn't *see.*

He wasn't killed, wasn't even (judging by the strength of his curses) badly hurt. The Clem examined him, proclaimed all injuries superficial, and ordered him back to the search. The Mahmood protested, but the tone of his protests was whining; he would go.

One of the others interrupted the argument. "Clem, I found the tattletale."

"Good man, good man. Bring her down."

"I said, I found the *tattletale.*"

"Well, look around. She can't be too far away."

"Look around, blast it, what else have we been doing! She isn't here, I tell you."

"Oh, for—the Old Man'll have our hides for a blanket. Try a little higher, maybe the tattletale fell when she collapsed." When she collapsed. So!

The waves covered my arms, were caressing my face.

"Clem, come see for yourself. There's a sheer face up here."

"She isn't here, Clem." It was a chorus.

"Maybe the sting didn't activate."

"Maybe it wasn't quick enough, maybe . . ."

"Or maybe . . ."

"Be quiet. Piers, check the tattletale. Did the sting activate?"

Reluctantly, "Yes, it did."

"Does it record contact?"

"Ye-ess, it does."

Then keep looking! She's there somewhere. Find her!"

"But, Clem, she ain't here! Suppose somebody was with her and carried her away!"

"Nobody was with her; we'd have heard, you idiot!"

"She kept talking to someone named Neill; ain't he the agent the Old Man's gonna—"

"She wasn't talking to him, she was talking to *herself*. This Neill's somewhere else, plasma it! And if he or anyone came and got her, we'd have *heard*. She's there, somewhere—so find her!"

Sunatra, Anatra—*pull!* Bring the friendly, covering water.

It is said that the worst curse is to have your wish granted. On the beige sand my pallid skin, like the cloak, was well camouflaged. But against the night-dark water—

"Clem, she's on the beach!"

"What . . . where? I don't see anyone."

"Down, way down. Around a curve, sort of; I can see someone, way, way down. Lying half in the water. Look, Piers, there—see!"

"No, I don't—yes, yes, now I do. He's hard to spot because—Clem, it ain't her, it's a Terran. He's too pale to be—"

"Terran or not, get the poor beggar before he drowns, he's half under water now." And then running footsteps.

The water covered my face. I breathed in and couldn't change and, head toward the waves as I was, there wasn't enough water over me to force change. Then somebody hauled me up and I was choking. Except I was flung back on the sand and someone was squeezing my ribs and the water was spurting back out, except what I had swallowed.

"She gonna be O.K.?"

"How'd she get this far?"

"She the one the Old Man wanted? Never saw a native this color. Looks almost human, don't she?"

"The voice of the Clem was confident. "You don't drown on one mouthful of water."

"Maybe she ain't a native. Maybe she's a renegade."

"Ooooo-eeee. If that's it, glad I ain't in her shoes. Only thing the Old Man hates worse'n a Lobsterback is a renegade."

Shiny high boots, sand grinding into exposed skin, my fate discussed as though I couldn't hear; or as though my thoughts, opinions, actions, were of no possible consequence.

Goddess, the way those Terrene talked!

I was rolled onto my back and lifted and placed on some sort of platform.

"*Madre de Dios,* look at those legs!"

"Legs, nothing, look at—feel that skin, like synthi—haven't had a native here, amadroids ain't the same—Whaddya say, Clem—look what's goin' to waste—Come'n, Clem, be a sport—it's a long ride back to the Base— Come'n, Clem—come'n—"

The platform rose; I could see them, pieces of them, at any rate. All male, all Terene, all dressed alike in off-green clothing with various amulets sewn on it, and shiny helmets.

"Hi, girlie, I'm Sven." Young and eager, white-toothed grin.

'I'm Jorge and this is Piers and that's Mahmood." The Mahmood had an ugly swollen discoloration down the side of his face; his lips were full and pouting. "And that"—a careless gesture—"that's Alec, playing work-horse." He was a line of shadow and muscular back. The platform moved smoothly. It moved too evenly to be a sledge (unless the Terren Alec were supernaturally strong) and the ride was too smooth to be on rollers, either. I filed it away, another item of Terre magic.

I couldn't help wondering if the armlet poison would wear off, or if I was doomed to be a permanent cripple.

They had beached their boat. I couldn't see much of it until we were right under it, and then all I could make out was high, smooth, gleaming shadow. The proportions seemed all wrong. It was way too high.

There was a grinding sound, a metal scrape, and a shadow covered me. I was maneuvered a bit more, and the Terrene crowded about my platform. Suddenly we began to rise. If I could have shut my eyes, I would have. Whatever was hauling us up had no walls I could see. I hoped the Terrene were as good with a cargo winch as they seemed to be with their other magics.

We stopped, and I was maneuvered into a doorway with rounded edges, and through something, but all I could see was pale green ceiling and walls. Finally, I was placed on a waist-high padded platform, that seemed to be one of several running around the edge of a room. The ceiling glowed brightly (although I could see no animals on it) and automatically my inner eyelids closed.

"Lady Kimassu." The voice was the Clem. He leaned over me. His face was long and sparely fleshed, almost Delye. His eyes were so light that the irises were barely darker than the pinkish "whites." His skin was paler than mine, a cavefish white, dead and unhealthy-looking. His head fur, clipped short, was a few shades darker, a pale beige. "I regret if you have taken any harm. We are taking you to our base, where our doctors can care for you." He paused. If he was waiting for me to answer, he was out of luck. The poison was still effective; otherwise I would have told him exactly what I thought of this outrageous, obviously deliberate abduction. He switched to badly accented Delyetz. "We want you to help, Lady. We go to help."

If he was trying to convince me that he and his little band of smiling cutthroats (ugh, all those shining teeth!) had had nothing to do with my present physical condition and had found me by merest chance—and didn't he know that I had heard every word that he and his minions had been shouting back and forth at each other?—he spoiled it completely with that Kimassu. How did he know who I was, unless he had been looking for me, specifically, for the Kimassu Lady.

He shut my outer eyelids. Though his touch was unquestionably gentle, I flinched (mentally) under it. It was the same reaction I have to certain slimy crawlers. Ugh! "Try to sleep, Lady. We have a long journey ahead of us."

Unfortunately, I could hear what the others were saying. Whatever a whack at her was, I didn't think I'd like it.

"I have to fly this bird," said the Clem. A chorus of sardonic comments followed. "Put'r on auto an' join the fun," was the loudest.

"I have to fly this bird," he repeated loudly and emphatically. "I can give you orders, but what I can't see, I can't prevent. But consider this: the Old Man was very anxious to get his hands on this girl. Well, that's happened before, and we all know what it means. But this time he was willing to give up an agent for this mopsy. An *agent*. Remember what he said: She was to lead us to the agent, but if she didn't, if she pulled off the tattletale and it looked like we were going to lose her, we were to pick her up, even if it meant losing the chance at the agent. Has he ever set it up that way before? Has he *ever* risked losing an agent for a girl before? Must want this girl awfully bad, right? Odd-looking native, too, isn't she; has the lightest color skin of any *native* I've ever seen. Makes her look almost human, doesn't it? And the Old Man's been here, off and on, for quite a while, hasn't he?" There was a short, loaded silence. Clem chuckled. "And we all know what a"—a phrase I didn't understand—"the Old Man is, right? So until we know just *why* the Old Man wants this mopsy—a word to the wise, eh, boys?"

(It took me quite some time to figure out what he was inplying I was—oh, *obscene!* It was *impossible,* and anyway, I had been named and Adopted before the Gorky Admiral first set foot on our world. And even if it were possible, which it couldn't be, the Elders would never, ever have sanctioned it. However, the paralysis prevented me from telling the Terrene what I thought of the whole Servitor-inspired idea.)

Chapter Thirteen

MOTTO:

O Terre wight, so full of might,
Tell me, is your dwelling far?
Not far, my fair, for we'll be there
In the twinkling of a star.

—*Ballad of the Betrayed Consecrate*

I awoke slowly, with a grinding pain in my head, as though the top half of my skull were slowly rotating. My mouth had a nasty taste and felt like it was coated with dried seafiber fluff. I was lying, naked and clean (even the ground-in sand was gone) on one of those padded Terre platforms, whose purpose I was unsure of. (They were too low for a Delyen to sit on comfortably, but Terre legs were shorter.) I wondered why, since I had been asleep or unconscious, I hadn't been put in a hammock.

I couldn't suppress a moan as I stretched and my muscles (mine again, thank you, Goddess) protested vigorously. Not quite naked, I noticed with a frown. I was wearing a pair of wristlets. I felt one of them. Perfectly plain and smooth, a dull olive green in color, not tight, yet fitted to my wrists so snugly that it took a great deal of effort to rotate them. If I had rotated them, they were so featureless, I wasn't sure. There was no join or catch or clasp on them that I could feel. Unlike the Gorky Admiral's other "gift"—what a blind fool I'd been!—these would not come off unless someone else took them off. Some Terren with filthy Terre magics.

I was actually wearing four of the odd things, I saw with surprise. Besides the pair on my wrists, I had one on each ankle, too. So light I hadn't noticed them until I started to sit up and glanced down, yet, like the wristlets, tightly fitted, with no visible joint or seam.

Someone was watching me. No use trying to pretend sleep, he must have seen me, stretching, feeling those odd bands. It was the dark, sullen-mouthed one. Ahh—Mahmood. I sat up.

Silently, he handed me a container of clear liquid.

Did he really think I would accept something from one of his kind?

"Take it or leave it," he shrugged, when I ignored it and him. "It's only water." He sat it on a table, and then, with another shrug, moved slightly away.

I drank thirstily. If they wanted to poison me again, they had four servants to do it for them. It was sweetwater, bland and flavorless. He was watching me with almost the attitude of a Delye put into a pool with a circling daggertooth. And then I remembered what happened in the Terre boat after the Clem left to "fly this bird."

No wonder Mahmood was eyeing me so suspiciously. Had I really tried to rape all five of them?

As I stared at Mahmood, a deep red stain grew under his lovely dark skin. He needn't have worried. Terrene appeal to me only when my mind is affected by Terre poison. Odd, that I've never been one to indulge in even such mild simples as sweetsmoke or strong-waters or the twisted vine. Yet as the Terre paralysis wore off, it was as if I had had all three together. I had been frightened at first, when I realized that the boat was *lifting*. I knew that the Terre magics flew, of course, but I never dreamed that one might fly with me, Kimassu, inside. I was pressed slightly into the platform, and then, and *then—I could feel the air push lessening*. I wanted to scream, but couldn't. *The air push was lessening!* I had never realized that the glands at the base of my skull that could tell me how deep I was in water by detecting the increase in push could work both ways. But they could. I was feeling the lessening in air push. Then, it stopped changing, and the Terrene got up and moved casually about.

It was some while later that I began to have some control over myself again, and by then I was somewhat used to it. I staggered up, and they helped me—rather gingerly—to a huge window. Oh, we were high. I was frightened again, terrified; what was keeping us *up?* Why weren't we falling? (*They* didn't seem worried.) But the Terre magic held; and we were going fast, so fast; I could tell by the way the specks of islands zipped by below us.

We were *flying*. I, Kimassu, was flying.

The window was actually the back third of the room, a flattened quarter sphere of some clear substance that swept around what would have been back wall and parts of side wall, ceiling, and floor. It was fitted into the room so that one could sit on a curved, padded seat and look out and up and *down* . . .

They spoke politely to me, but I paid them little heed. The Goddess must have felt somewhat like this, when She surveyed the world She made . . .

And that was when I went sun-struck. I tried to go *through* the window and swim in the white clouds I saw below us, like great soft waves. I really thought I could. I was furious at the Terrene for daring to hinder me. I was amazed that what appeared to be open air was solid; and then I tried to break it, the Terrene struggling with me. We landed on the soft floor behind the padded area, a writhing mass of bodies.

Abruptly I stopped and went limp, and announced loudly (in Delyetz, since I had temporarily lost my Terretz) that I was willing to go out the window *later*.

Gratefully, they untangled themselves. I made another announcement in Delyetz. They didn't understand. But none of them misunderstood when I pointed at the darkest one, and said, "You! Come here!"

One of the others protested, and I backhanded him. His turn would come, the hot-pronged Terre slut.

But I wanted *that* one *first*.

He didn't start to take his clothes off quickly enough to suit me, so I knocked him to the floor (uncivilized behavior I never would be guilty of in my right mind) and began ripping his clothes off.

He started screaming.

I would have raped all five of them, but someone else —Clem?—came in through the doorway and hit me on the back of the head. I felt the blow; and then nothing.

Until now.

I eyed Mahmood thoughtfully, and he literally flinched backward. Ugh, crestless, furry *animal.* Squat, too.

I lay back on the platform, one hand under my throbbing head, to *think.*

I looked up at the sound of footsteps, in time to see Mahmood going *through* what I had thought was a solid door.

I was off the platform in a heartbeat to investigate. It wasn't a door, it wasn't solid at all. Seen close up, it had no true boundary, just a hazy border. I probed gingerly with a finger; the finger went *in.* I couldn't see it, but it felt all right. The door was a shadow, a shadow I couldn't see into, but my finger went in, went in and felt nothing. I pushed my whole hand further in; it slid in easily.

Up to the wrist.

Not the wrist. The wristlet. The Terre band. None of the bands would go through the solid shadow. But my head would. Much good it did me. All I saw was a long passageway, painted a uniform dullish olive, with what might be other doorways at regular intervals, and here and there things that stuck out, or were a different color. There were no glow-animals on the walls, but there was plenty of light.

There were no glow-animals in my room either. And no windows or other openings I could see, except the one shadow door.

The platform had no support I could see, above or beneath; but I couldn't get it off the wall. The walls weren't smooth; but I wasn't going to touch the Terre magics I saw sticking out, either. On the other hand, the light had to be coming from somewhere. I got on the platform, and bounced, tentatively, and then harder. I sailed up to where the walls met the ceiling; they did meet the ceiling. (Where was the light coming from?)

I didn't think we were in one of the Enclaves. The air push was still wrong. All the Enclaves feel right—or do they? Did the Terrene magic the air in the Enclaves, for reasons of their own? I didn't know. Hmmmmm. I sat down to think. Water push increases as you go down and decreases as you come back up. And we had gone up, and I had felt a decrease in the air push, along with the lifting feeling. But air isn't water. Suppose the change in air push had nothing to do with the flying. Air push didn't vary, after all. Or did it? Suppose air push varied, but much more slowly than water push. We can dive far deeper than the highest cliffs. Neill talked of heights (mountains?) a dozen-dozen-dozen fathoms high, but it could have been mere boasting. I had never heard of a height on Delyafam more than a dozen-dozen fathoms high. But now the air push was greater again. Too great. How could the air push be greater than what it should be. Less, perhaps, if the push lessened as we went up. But greater? Impossible. But it was. Were we somehow underground? In a deep cave? Would that make air push greater? Or had the Terrene changed it with their magics?

Or was I on the Terre world? On a different world, would the air itself be different?

Goddess, where was I? And how could I get home?

"Come—with— me." It was Mahmood. There was a change in his attitude; the wariness was still there, but to it had been added, a contempt, a disdain.

I stared over his head and waited.

"I said," he snarled in Terretz, *"come with me."*

I spoke not to him, but to the wall. In Delyetz, since I was hoping my knowledge of Terretz was still unknown. "I am the Kimassu Lady of the House of Morningstar, Consecrate of the Flail and the Blade, protégé of the Elyavaneet Noblelady, most Revered and most Honored. I have invited neither peer nor underling to join me; I recognize no superior." I turned my back, waited for him to realize his mistake and leave.

Instead, he grabbed at my shoulder. "I said, come with me!"

"Profane me not!" I backhanded him on the turn. If I had had a blade I would have wetted it with his heart's blood; a shortstick, and I would have beaten him into a shapeless pulp. But I couldn't sully myself by *touching* him again. He was a good head and a half shorter than I, though he must have weighed half again as much. But long limbs give leverage. He flipped and skidded on his back, to lie, momentarily stunned, near the doorway, his mouth and nose streaming blood. One is not profaned by *stepping* on garbage, although the more fastidious avoid it. I wasn't feeling particularly fastidious. I landed on crotch, rib cage (did something crack?), face, and outflung wrist. The door was no longer a barrier.

I had my freedom—until someone saw and stopped me. What should I do with it?

1) Get as far away from where I was thought to be as possible.

2) Kill Terrene.

3) Destroy Terre things.

I was about five dozen running paces down the dull corridor when I thought, Why am I leaving Mahmood, undead? To report my escape?

I wasn't truly a warrior yet. Theory and brave words are all very well, but execution—literally execution—is another matter. Mahmood was simply not a worthy opponent, not one I could honorably meet in the Arena. And here there were no guards to do my work for me.

Think of it as smashing a scuttler. A Black Stinger, say.

Or remember all your fine words to the Elyavaneet.

"Hey, what'r ya doin' out by yourself? Where's Mahmood?" It was one of those from the flying boat. Piers or Alec, I wasn't sure which, all Terrene look much alike. He must have come out of one of the shadow doors, because he stood between me and where I had left Mahmood.

I wasn't fooled by his being so much shorter than I. His grotesquely broad shoulders were thick with muscles; they rippled under his thin clothing as he moved. "Well, girlie, what's up? You're supposed to be with Mahmood. So where is he?"

Run or fight? I knew I could easily outrun him, but how easily in turn could he raise the hue and cry in front of me? Besides, I just couldn't bring myself to run—from a Terren.

I stalked toward him, hands outspread slightly. Smash a Black Stinger, remember, Kimassu?

He backed three paces rapidly before he could stop himself. Then he pulled something off his belt and pointed it at me, "Don't you come any nearer, girlie. Not one step." It was little, and it looked vaguely like a blowpipe; I could see a hole aimed at me, with a handgrip below and a sight above. But it was nowhere near his mouth. "Not one step, girlie! One more step and I fire!" It still wasn't near his mouth, though. I kept coming. "I mean it, girlie! Stop right there!" His voice was high-pitched, sharp with naked fear. All the more dangerous. He raised the blowpipe—and I dived for his knees. Something made a thin crackling noise and I felt heat sear down my back from shoulders to buttocks. And then I hit him. Out of the corner of my eye, I saw the blowpipe, *spewing crimson light.* He was swinging it down, trying to bathe me in the crimson light, but then he was off balance and screaming in pain. I had aimed for his knees, but he was short, and my shoulder had rammed his genitals. (Point to remember when fighting Terrene: not only are their genitals external and unprotected, but they are also extremely sensitive. Mayhap the Hypasha is correct, and the Terrene *are* the work of the Limping Servitor. Such carelessness in one of Her Creations is most unlike the Goddess. Though perchance it serves some purpose that mortal eyes cannot fathom.) I slammed the side of my hand against his wrist, but it was unnecessary, he had already dropped the blowpipe. I smashed his chest with my closed fist, but it was a mistake, it only made him madder. He got his hands around my neck and squeezed. It hurt. I rammed two stiffened fingers into his left eye. His face was so close to mine, reddened and contorted with emotion; his breath was sour. He defended his face, and I hit him again in the chest. I think I hurt myself more than him. Suddenly he heaved, and we rolled, and I was under him. Goddess, the *weight* of him! One of his hands was scrabbling on the floor, the other had my wrist; I hit him again in the chest (pure fury, it obviously wasn't hurting him). Then he had the blowpipe and was swinging it around; I knew that whatever it was, he didn't need to *blow* into it.

I clamped my hand over his desperately, and we swayed and rolled some more, the weapon swinging now toward me, now toward him.

He was the stronger; I knew it was only a matter of time.

And suddenly he bellowed, a gurgling scream of ultimate agony that trailed off into a rattly moan. I didn't stop to think, just swung the weapon to point behind him, squeezing his hand as hard as I could.

And there was another scream.

The weight on me was a dead weight. Literally. I shifted slightly, and it started to slide off. I wrapped my free arm around its back, to hold it as a shield—

Oh, Holy Goddess! It hadn't a back! I could feel no blood on a smooth firm surface—but—but—the Terren was—thinner. I could feel bones under the surface—but! They curved—they curved the wrong way. I was feeling the back of his chest bones, not the proper curve of back.

And the *stench.*

And the *screams!*

Not the one lying on me. *He* was quiet enough. The other one.

Cautiously I peeked out from behind my dead shield. I could see only one other person, collapsed a few paces down the corridor, writhing and screaming; Goddess, was he screaming!

"Turn that plasmaed Tridio down." The harsh growl of yet another Terren was barely audible through the piercing screams. "Ain't you fellows got no consid—"

I didn't really mean to hurt him. But I turned toward the sound of his voice, and the weapon was in my hand, and I must have started it again, somehow.

And the crimson light flared out of the horror, the weapon, and he was in it, and then he—wasn't. Just a blackened shapeless hulk. No screams, because he had nothing to scream with.

The other one was still screaming

"Can't a guy sleep? Shut that thing—" A fourth; he looked down and saw what was left of the other Terren and the screaming one and then he saw me, under my body-shield—with the weapon still in my hand. "I didn't mean—" But he was pulling at something on his belt, and if it wasn't the same as the others had, it was some kind of filthy Terre weapon. So I squeezed the weapon I was holding again, since that seemed to be how one made it go; something moved under my fingers.

And I didn't have to worry about the new one, either.

I waited, scarce breathing under my shield, but no one else came. Cautiously, I slipped out, checked each doorway in the corridor. Most that I could get into were obviously storage, but some were living quarters, similar to the room I had awakened in, but with more furniture and strewn with personal items. In one of the rooms was a pair of transparent leggings, pale lilac in shade. I picked it up and tested it; yes, it would do nicely. It gave somewhat as I pulled on it, but it would serve—my purpose.

The screamer was Mahmood. That thick Terre skull; I must only have stunned him. And the Four-faced One had led him out . . . Already his cries had weakened to pitiful whimpers.

He saw me. "He-help me!"

"I will." There was only one thing I could do for him. He was damaged beyond any possible healing. But I could ease his passage. "No, please." he gasped, and then I had the garrote around his throat. "No more pain, soon," I soothed. "I will swear to your Family, honorable death in combat." His eyes were closing, his weak struggles ceased.

"Stop it, Kimassu!"

I twisted tighter. "He is in pain."

And abruptly, my hands were pulled away, held outstretched at full arm's length. But there was no one there! I fought fruitlessly. And then—not my hands, it was my wrists, so that it was scramble awkwardly to my feet or dangle ignominiously on unseen ropes. Once I was standing, they dropped and joined—most uncomfortably!—behind my back. I writhed; and stopped. They were no longer pulling me; but I couldn't separate my hands, either.

"One, two, three, four. You've started your war with a vengeance, eh, Kimassu?"

Chapter Fourteen

MOTTO:

All kilted and sandaled
And jeweled sailed she;
To port drifted her sweet ship—
But never came she.

"My sails all unfurled
My nets all are dry;
My Goddess unserved;
My duties just lie."

—Ballad of Marsinu of the Noonheats

I had often wondered, in rare idle moments, what it was like to be on the wrong side of the Flail of Justice. Now I knew. Clem, fueled by the death of his comrades, wielded the Flail most heartily.

He had neither skill nor assistants; but Terre magics made up the lack. I envied him two tools in particular, the metal bands which could be controlled individually as though they were on a myriad invisible ropes; and a hand-held tube he called a stim, which gave pain, a large area of mild ache or a small point of intense agony. Had I such tools, I could have long since broken whom I pleased. But, like so many of the Terre magics, the usage of such precludes the development of skill. Clem was a fool, a crude, clumsy fool.

I am I, Kimassu!

I had never realized it before, but what was happening between us, Clem and I, was a form of duel. Will against will instead of blade against blade. For this, I was none so ill-prepared. I had, even, weapons, though they were not tangible, they could not be held in the hand, like a blade. I had my purpose, my strength of mind, my hatred of the Terrene and all they represented. And in Clem, too, was that which I could use. He had a poorly controlled fury, almost a frenzy. With luck, he could be goaded by my continued contemptuous silence into using the bands to tear me apart. I doubted not they were capable of it; they had come perilously close once or twice already. And if he killed me, without my breaking silence, then I would have won our duel, and served the Goddess to the last of my abilities. But there was a worser flaw in Clem. I would never have chosen such a tool, a sharp-edged tool that could turn too easily in the hand and savage its user. Clem enjoyed inflicting pain; Clem enjoyed tormenting the helpless. The stim, which (as far as I could tell) left no ill aftereffects, was too impersonal to suit him. The whip he preferred left him physically exhausted; and gave me needed respite.

Also: he hadn't thought to offer me food. Not that I would have taken aught from him. But a Delyen will die from lack of nourishment in a few short days, unless she can go into Esta-fee. Except that takes a clear mind; my conscience was clear enough, but my shoulders and back ached. I tossed restlessly on the bare floor in the bare room, trying to find a least uncomfortable position. Little danger, I thought grimly, of drifting into Esta-fee in a too deep sleep. Soon, very soon, there would be no turning back. Neill told me once that his people could go without food for many days. If true, it was another of the many differences between us I had always fed my responsibilities most carefully. (I had decided that the lack of food was mere Terre carelessness; deliberate deprival was even beyond Terre capabilities.) Besides, he must know about us. We live, as Neill remarked, on a world where food is plentiful. Deprive us of it, and our bodies rebel and alter—and we die. In the rare times when food is truly scarce, as many as possible go into Esta-fee, the slow sleep, and the rest care for those until times become easier. I could already see the subtle changes beginning. Better a quick death than this ugly slow one, which I wasn't sure could yet be stopped or not.

The room was bright-lit from nowhere, and the light reflected and reflected off the gleaming white walls, ceiling, and floor. There was no escape from that light, and no comfort on the unyielding floor. No hammock, either. I wasn't even sure if the Terrene used hammocks. A piece with the rest; mayhap they preferred the floor; or mayhap they slept sitting up, on those padded sitting platforms of theirs. Yet Neill had seemed content enough with his hammock. And why not, I thought peevishly, as I shifted about, if this was his alternative.

I was jerked into an awkward, half-kneeling position; my body dangling from stretched-up arms.

Clem again. My respite was over. I carefully looked over the top of his head, but out of the corner of my eye, I saw—

Yes, this was going to be my last session. Clem was in a fury before he even started. There was a look in his eyes, a glazed, shining look.

"You——, this is it!" His voice was a high half-scream. The wristlets jerked me higher, and I stared past his face. Even when he grabbed my pinna-fins and forced me to face him, I refused to *see* him. He slapped me; *but he was not there!* I neither saw him, nor felt him, nor heard his threats.

"All right, Kimassu, *Lady* Kimassu," he snarled finally. "This is *it*. You're gonna *learn!* I'm the boss, the boss, *your* boss, understand!"

Clem had even less mind than I'd given him credit for; he was actually drooling as he spoke, drops of spittle spraying my face so close to his. And suddenly he was laughing, laughing and saying, "Your boss, Kimassu. You'll find out, I'm your *boss.*" Over and over he said it. Then I was being pulled, he gave me the chance to get my feet under me, and then he was pulling me at a fast walk, out of the cell, down the corridor, around a turn, into another cell which seemed to be exactly the same as the first, except that the walls were a dull green with many strange markings, and the light wasn't so fierce. Then my wrists were twisted behind my back together, and raised, so that I dangled, my weight painfully and awkwardly suspended from my shoulders. It was a new trick, and most unpleasant. I shut my lips tightly If it hurt, it hurt; and if I screamed, I screamed. No shame in that. But no use letting him know sooner than I had to how much it hurt. Then he pulled me up and down slightly.

Slowly, up and down, so that my toes scarce brushed the floor and then higher, so I dangled again. Every twitch, every adjustment sent fresh waves of agony through my wrists, arms, shoulders, back. I think I screamed. Up and down, up and down, as if he were measuring some thing. And all the time he was talking.

"Ol' Ling, he had this monkey, this Slattery's monkey from Tau Ceti. They look like a man, a short, ugly, hairy man. But they ain't. They been judged animal. But they're smart, yeah, they're *smart*. Almost as smart as a man. Al-most. And that monkey, it didn't want to go with ol' Ling. It scratched and fought and struggled and bit. But ol' Ling, he banded it, the way I banded you. He fed it when it was good, and he punished it when it was bad. And by an' by, he took the bands off, but by then it didn't matter, because it was *his* monkey. His thing, his toy, his possession. *His*. He taught it all kinds of funny tricks, funny to watch, that is. Oh, it was funny, it was, that monkey of Ling's. Well"— he shook the wristlets slightly—"you're going to be *my* monkey, Kimassu. When I get through with you, you'll do tricks, too. On my command. Any tricks, whatever I say. Because you're *mine*, my monkey, my Dolyen monkey. You'll sing for me, too, real pretty you'll sing, when I tell you to. And you'll do other things, whatever I say, my monkey. My lithe lovely monkey."

He'd eaten of the Twisted Vine!

Suddenly, he did something to the green wall, and a whole section of the ceiling slid back. "There's an emergency exit from this level, Kimassu, my lovely monkey, it's lucky I remembered it, because it's going to be just *perfect*. I've already checked; it's only an empty storage room above, and I've locked it. Just in case. Now, u-u-u-up you go." And, indeed, up I went. Dragged by those thrice accursed bands. Above was only another room, similar to that below, dimly lit, filled with hulking, looming shapes, unmoving. I went all the way up, until my wrists were mashed against the ceiling in that upper room.

Then, with no warning, I dropped. Down, down, into the light below. I hadn't time to gasp a breath, when I was stopped with a jerk, all the weight and fall taken in my outstretched, pulled-behind arms. My toes flailed, instinctively trying to relieve that dreadful jolt, finding nothing. Both my armbones snapped from their shoulder sockets, wrists and elbow joints gave. I screamed and mercifully fainted.

I awoke, dripping water. All my senses were hazed with that incredible, impossible pain. A face that might have been Clem's floated vaguely before me. A voice echoed hollowly in my ears.

Goddess, the pain! Goddess, help me! *Goddess!*

He was holding my face so that his own filled my vision, was all my world. "Say it, Kimassu. Say it." Each word carefully enunciated. "Say it. You're the boss, Clem. I'll do anything you say. Say it, Kimassu!"

I couldn't have said a word to save my anima from the outer dark.

He seemed to realize that. "Nod, then, Kimassu. Nod your head, lift it up and down. Nod. I'm your boss, Kimassu, I'm your master. Nod."

I hung, limp, a mindless mass of agony.

He circled behind me. "I'll help, Kimassu, my monkey, my precious toy. I'll help. See." He lifted my head, he had to maneuver between my pulled back arms, his body pressed against mine, moving against mine. Even in my mindlessness, my pain, I *knew,* my body recognized what he was and what kind of tricks he wanted me to play. His hands lifted my head; and I held it high, despite waves of pain, despite sure and certain knowledge of pain to come.

I am I, Kimassu!

He stepped out from between my arms and the bands jerked, and fresh sheets of tearing, incredible agony—Goddess, how much can a body take without going mad? without merciful death? My head lolled, and slowly, with teeth-clenched determination, I raised it again. I could see nothing, there was nothing in my world but blinding pain; and a neck that I had to hold up though it bore the weight of the world.

"All right, Kimassu." He jerked the bands again. Oh, Goddess! "If you want to be stubborn, we can give you another taste of the strap." His voice was thick with suppressed emotion, but every word was spat out clearly. He came out from behind me, and I saw him, a flickering glimpse out of the corner of my eye. And I knew.

And would have cursed my stupidity in not seeing it before, had I thought to spare myself in that agony. Clem-Glemmu. Glemmu-Clem. "But let me tell you something, first." He faced me again, so close I nearly retched at his fetid breath.

"Listen to me, Kimassu, don't faint on me. The strap is an old non-com trick, to bring rebellious recruits in line. One ride on the strap, and there's nothing wrong a little medicking can't cure. But after the first? Minor damage. Permanent damage. Crippling. A major medical effort to save the victim. Nobody's ever survived five, Kimassu, not sane, anyway. There's some things medics can't fix. So, which is it to be, Kimassu? A good little monkey, learn your tricks, answer a few simple questions, be fed and medicked, and go to sleep? Or a bad little monkey that has to keep riding the strap until it's too late?"

I stared straight ahead, my neck stiff, my head high.

I am I, Kimassu.

The second "ride" was worse, impossible as that seemed.

I drifted in and out of consciousness, on waves of pain that lifted—and overwhelmed me. Nothing was real, nothing of import, except that pain. Could I escape into Esta-fee? The floating of the pain, it was not unlike the clear soft rocking of Esta-fee, the floating-on-a-calm-sea feeling. But better death, and not have this to face again. I was ready to seize any means of escape—except one. Clem could maltreat me as he chose; but the gates would never open until I *willed* them so. Surely, surely, no one could survive this abuse long?

Goddess, help me, take me. *I can't stand this!*

I awoke yet again, sprawled face down on the cold floor. "All right, all right, you——! Last chance, Kimassu. You know what I want!"

I knew nothing but pain. But, yet, I knew what he wanted.

I—am I! Kimassu!

"Kimassu!" His voice echoed my thoughts. In that one word was frustration, anger, desperation. Had he then tried already, and found that my unconsciousness would not give him what he wanted? It didn't matter; *nothing* mattered.

That time—was it the fourth? the fifth?—he lifted me

very, very slowly. And held me, my wrists forced against that smooth ceiling that had no mark of fingers smoothing it, for heartbeats that stretched out longer and longer.

His voice came from below, a meaningless, booming noise. Was he pleading? Threatening? I didn't know, didn't care. Another drop would finish me, and I knew it, and I wanted it to come.

Neill would starve to death, or die of loneliness, or try to swim for it. The Elyavaneet would puzzle and mourn, and Draxuus and the other boys would wait and hope, until hope faded, and then they would go—where? To the Elyavaneet, I hoped, or to households she chose for them. I had no debts of honor to pay. There was, of course, the Merwencalla, and my old barracksmate the Hypasha. But I knew I could trust the Elyavaneet to take care, most exquisite care, of both of them. Once the full story of Willis was known about, and the Elyavaneet would see to that, the Merwencalla would have no influence at all in the Council. She had used and degraded her sacred office, and the Ball would choose another at the next Festival and mayhap (though this were against tradition) not even a Swordshine this time.

I was only sorry that I would have a mere four torchbearers along the dark, cold way. Four common guards for a Lady was no fair exchange. But there was naught I could do to alter it. Pity one of the four hadn't been the Gorky Admiral. Or his evil tool, Clem. But maychance we would yet meet in the Goddess' higher realm . . . and if we did . . .

But these were not proper thoughts to take into Her holy Presence . . .

Goddess, Thou who sees our innermost thoughts.

Goddess, Thy will be done.

Goddess . . . Goddess . . . Goddess . . .

Chapter Fifteen

MOTTO:

Oh, fare thee well my lovesome boy,
Fare thee well my laddie gay;
Until our paths do twine again,
On golden sands far, far away.

—Ballad of the Two Untimely Parted

I waited for, prayed for, the final drop.

It didn't come.

Instead, suddenly, some of the weight was taken off my arms; I was being carefully balanced, the bands on my ankles partially supporting me. Was this some new and fiendish trick of Clem's? It mattered not, my life-force ebbed lower and lower. I was sliding away . . . my torch-bearers awaited me. I could see them, clearer and clearer through the mists, waiting patiently for me to catch up to them. Mahmood and Piers, Alec and Jorge. One need not be ashamed of such an honor guard. They were kilted and sandaled and armed. I, too, was kilted, a kilt so white it seemed to glow from its own light. Around my waist was a short sword; I raised it high in salute and each of them saluted in return with his spear.

I sheathed my weapon and we marched forward, along a path of softest golden sand. The mists began to clear, and the ocean lay before us, a sapphire sweep of infinite vastness.

Somewhere, behind us, in an unimportant room on an unimportant world, the broken body that had once housed the spirit of she who named herself Kimassu was being slowly and carefully lowered into waiting arms.

The beach stretched out as far as eye could see, a

glorious playground. Here and there a tiny inlet snaked to the base of cliffs, good, high cliffs, prime cliffs for climbing or diving. The water beneath was a deep clear blue; even as we marched, an orange body arrowed down and splashed into the crystal blue.

Orange. And I was orange, too, the deep and gorgeous shade of browned orange a Delyen gets under the strongest sun. And—where were the twin scars on my left forearm? The slight shortness and crookedness where a broken leg had mended poorly? The marks of (what had been the Terren's name?)—the marks of the whip?

No matter. I wasn't close enough—yet—to see *who* was on the beach; except that they were Delyene. Or were they? My escort was growing more and more orange by the heartbeat. Even as I noticed that, Alec put his hand to his head and brushed the reddish-brown fur off, to reveal a gleaming orange skull. And could that shadow along the centerline be the beginning of a proper crest?

"Too itchy in this climate, eh, mistress," he said. Bits of fur from other parts of him were falling off, too, but they never reached the sand to mar its smooth golden surface.

"You look handsomer and more comfortable," I told him. They all did.

"Newcomer," someone shouted. "Newcomer! Newcomer! Newcomer!" The calls echoed down the beach, a mingling of voices. They came out of the water, out of unseen hollows in the sand, out of nowhere it seemed, a scattered few, and then almost before one could snap one's fingers, a crowd that thickened visibly.

Surely I knew those faces. Old friends, old comrades . . . old enemies.

"Mistress." It was a low-voiced warning from Mahmood, his hand gripping his spear tightly, its point lowered to guard me.

"Wait," I ordered.

"Kimassu." A figure shoving through the crowd, advancing in openhanded welcome.

"Vlaytarru! By the Goddess Herself, Vlaytarru the ganner-eyed!" And then I hesitated. Her far-seeing ganner eyes had not saved the Vlaytarru when a storm drove her vessel into the path of Leviathan. Remembering my sorrow, I had a moment of doubt. "Vlaytarru? It is you, Vlaytarru?"

She hissed politely through her nose. "Even I, Kimassu. I who seconded you in the challenge to the Lorlienn when the Hypasha refused. I who helped you sneak back into the barracks the night you took too much of the strong-water and serenaded the Second Favorite Consort until the Empress' guards . . ."

"Enough, Vlaytarru!" We embraced the quick Delyen hug and withdraw. She eyed my escort approvingly.

"A gallant crew, Kimassu. High-couraged, they look."

"High-couraged they be, indeed, Vlaytarru."

"Stalwart, too, I'd wager, eh, Kimassu." She poked me in the ribs with a hand that had all six fingers on it.

"Aye, that, too, Vlaytarru." The crowd, and there were many familiar faces in it, laughed at a joke I couldn't quite understand.

"Perchance you might care to loan me one of your gallants, Kimassu, to escort me in a stroll down the beach." She smiled, and somewhat puzzled, I caught the eyes of my escort. She was a splendid specimen of lithe young Delyen, the Vlaytarru, her long bronze legs gleaming in the brilliant sunlight, an emerald kilt draped about svelte muscular hips. Not just a spectacular looker, though; I knew that the Vlaytarru would take excellent care of any boy that pleased her.

"My escort are all freeboys," I said slowly, "though most welcome in my household. I would put no barrier should any of them aspire to the honor of joining your escort." Piers shifted his weight forward slightly. "Piers," I said gently.

"Mistress." He licked his lips. "Mistress, I—I would shine your honor by finding favor in the sight of the Lady, your comrade. If it pleases you." His eyes seemed somewhat puzzled, as though what he said was not what he had meant to say.

"If you please the Vlaytarru Lady. A gift, Vlaytarru, a free-gift, for old friendship's sake."

"We'll call him a loan, instead." She smiled at Piers, and hesitantly, and then more confidently, he smiled back. "A winsome loan, indeed." She put out a hand, and he took it. "A most winsome loan, Kimassu. But I cannot leave you, newcome here, with diminished escort.

Perchance"—her eyes scanned the crowd—"perchance I can recommend you a replacement." Again the laughter.

And the crowd shifted and parted, and there he stood, my Draxuus, my first, dearest love, my vibrant boy with the topaz eyes. Not old, not aged as he had been, but *young*, a lovesome male in his prime.

"Draxuus!"

"Mistress!"

I swung him joyously, triumphantly. My Draxuus! *Ah, Draxuus, I named others after you, and they were sweet and faithful; but they were never you!*

And then—"Ware! The Beast!" The crowd scattered along the beach. Swords, knives, spears flashed in the sunrest. All turned and faced the sea, waiting. A few swimmers were piling onto the beach, flinging themselves furiously shoreward.

"Vlaytarru, what . . ."

"Guard, Kimassu. The Beast comes!" she snapped.

"My sword mates yours, comrade."

She barked quick orders, a guard formation facing out toward the sea, a thin line against no danger I could see, except—was that a wake, far out to sea?

"Kimassu," came the Vlaytarru's horrified shout. "You're still tied, to that other world. Look!"

I twisted and looked behind me, and she was right, there were hundreds of fine, shining threads flowing from my body, twisting together to make a long, heavy tie, leading back, fading into misty obscurity. So that I was still tied, still bound to that broken, dying thing that lay —did it yet breathe?—somewhere far, far away. I raised my sword to cut that last remaining link; and the Vlaytarru stayed my hand.

"*Her* Will, Kimassu."

"It will fade, then," I said confidently. But I wasn't sure. It seemed to me, even in that short glance, that the tie was getting heavier, the strands increasing in number, not weakening and thinning as they should have been.

I turned again, and saw out in the sea, ahead of the huge, the unbelievable wake, a great crimson head with eyes a fathom across, black deadly eyes, and a cruel toothed mouth. Could it be a many-arm? Huge even as Leviathan herself? But Leviathan would never dare her bulk so near a shore, and this, indeed, it did appear like unto a many-arm, was coming closer at an alarming rate.

"Ware the tips of the arms, Kimassu," warned the Vlaytarru. "They have sharp, paralyzing spines."

I nodded. "Anything else?"

"It's strong, Kimassu, stronger even than its size warrants. Don't let it get an arm above you without a spear braced protecting your head, or it'll smash you into the sand. Don't underestimate it; it's intelligent enough. And hungry. I'll toast you after"—she smiled—*"comrade!"*

It was a battle for bards to sing of, to tell and retell after feastings. How many was the Beast fighting? I knew not, nor whether it was winning or losing, with us, or with the others. I only knew that the sky was red with crimson arms, that they struck with fiendish malevolence, that our brave, thin line drew together, and again. Ah, it was a splendid combat, a fierce, joyous contest. I cut and hacked and thrust, until our little patch of sand was slippery with blood.

"I think," the Vlaytarru panted, "it's tiring."

"None too soon," I gasped.

"Don't relax your guard—*Kimassu!"* Her warning was too late. Someone had been dragged past me; I couldn't even tell who, a limp body with face obscured by muck. But all that mattered was that it was one of *ours;* and maychance not yet dead. I ran, sliding in that muck, until I could straddle the arm, greater than my waist, and brace, hacking wildly at the arm between my legs. The body slammed into my legs and I was pulled along, still slashing with full might at the arm, my feet making two parallel furrows. I could hear shouts and running feet, and I thrust and hacked with desperate fervor. The place looked like a shambles, and smelled like one, too. Slash! Slice!

I never saw the arm above me.

Chapter Sixteen

MOTTO:

In the end was yet the beginning, in the beginning was always the end; and the end was *the beginning; but before the end and the beginning, and above them, and always, is the* WORD.

—*The Book of the Dead*

"I could be bounded in a snail shell," Neill told me once, "and count myself king of infinite space. Were it not that I had bad dreams."

I had bad dreams.

Worse. I wasn't sure they *were* dreams. What was reality, what truth, what sick disordered fancy? Where was Kimassu? Drifting rudderless through featureless gray mists? Enclosed like a nautilus in a shell of strange device? Helpless prey to the Beast? Where was I? My own Delyafam? On that golden beach? With the Terrene? Or some further choice of the Goddess?

A tiny, hairy Kimassu danced on the end of a chain for a circle of hulking formless laughers.

An orange Kimassu, her head bandaged, drank laughing toasts about a roaring campfire on a shadowy beach.

An unbreathing yet living Kimassu lay, sliced open like a plunny ready to be filleted, in a metal shell, while strange tools cut and probed and manipulated.

A naked Kimassu knelt before a statue of the Goddess, silently pleading. And the statue grew and grew, glowing with its own radiance, and a hand stretched out. A great voice rumbled, echoing and re-echoing. "Not yet, daughter."

Not yet—not yet—not yet . . .

Not yet.

Not—yet.

Chapter Seventeen

MOTTO:

The best-laid plans of Delyene and men—
Are the ones most *likely to "gang a-gley!"*

—Sayings of Neill

I awoke.

I knew where I was immediately before I opened my eyes. Or rather, I knew where I was *not*. I was not on Delyafam, nor on that golden beach that was like unto Delyafam. The air push was that little, little bit too great. Like that Terre place of metal rooms and corridors.

That thrice accursed Terre magic! It had drawn me back somehow.

Which made what I saw when I opened my eyes that much worse a shock.

I seemed to be in the House of Debate, where the Council meets to make major decisions. In one of the private rooms, that is; those for individual rest and refreshment. This was—I even recognized it—this was the Room of Valeria. On the wall opposite me was the ancient but beautifully executed mural telling of the Voyages of Valeria. The scattered furniture was old, worn, comfortable. The floor was dirt packed to rock hardness and smoothness by many feet. There was the scent of seasalt in the air, a hint of incense. On other walls were banners, ceremonial weapons. (I was most careful not to touch the latter.) I was half sitting, half lying on a bench, fully clothed and accoutered, as though I had fallen asleep while conversing, and someone had kindly thrown a cover over me.

I sat up, brushing my hand against the wall. There were no mortar dents beneath the plaster and paint, marking where dressed stoneware had been fitted together.

A copy, then. Most definitely copy. Some of the colors weren't quite right, either. But still, the brushstrokes; fantastic. More Terre magic, I supposed.

And myself; yes, that too was copy. Cloths made of too fine thread, too evenly woven. My cloak—where was the tear I made on that thrice accursed gift of the Gorky Admiral? The other things, my daggertooth necklace, my Eye-of-the-Goddess, my armlets, my pectoral, my Tear, even the sandals I was wearing, all had subtle wrongnesses; none of them were mine.

And I? I stretched. Was I somehow copy too?

I shrugged my shoulders gingerly, working them around. No traces of the damage that must have occurred; unless Clem was an ill-dream, too. I walked up and down, cautiously, and then boldly. I seemed in perfect health; the scars on my forearm were there, the knot on my shinbone. But whip marks, torn flesh, ruined muscle and ligament, dislocated bones: all damage, all abuse, as if it had never been.

It meant they could do it to me again, and again, and again, as they chose.

Had the Gorkey Admiral walked in at that moment of dreadful realization, he would have had what he wanted, because I would have promised whatever he wanted, done whatever he commanded. Whatever.

But I was left alone (deliberate policy, no doubt) and I regained my courage and resolution and began to prowl. They had reproduced, not the single room, but an interconnected suite of five rooms.

Hadn't there been times during the early treatings when Terrene had been guested in rooms in the House of Debate? If so, this suite's original could have been one of those set aside for their usage.

By the time I reached the fifth room, I was beginning to wonder just how free or how captive I truly was. This was a strangely elaborate prison—for one alone. How far could I go before I was stopped?

I wasn't alone. There was someone curled up in a cloak in the corner of the fifth room I entered.

He leaped to his feet at the muffled sound of my footsteps. "Mistress, what is your wish?" Then, worried,

"You didn't call, did you, mistress? I would have heard if you had called. Wouldn't I? I didn't miss hearing you, mistress?" He dropped to his knees as I stared at him suspiciously. His Delyetz was flawless; but Neill's was, too. He was a brilliant orange, dressed—correctly!—in a kilt one of my own servitors would wear, my insignia quartered with the emblem of Morningstar. He looked his part perfectly, as Neill had. His youthful crest was the barest suggestion of a darker umber hump along the centerline of his skull. He acted his part, too; could he possibly be as he appeared?

"Oh, mistress." Fluid appeared in his eyes as I kept silent. He slumped lower, his face almost touching his bent knees.

"Easy, boy, greet not. I did not call. Up with you; you're none of my household."

He straightened up, to stare at me out of shining, reddened eyes. (Flaw the first: they should not have reddened. And I would wager my daggertooth necklace to a sours leaf, the fluid in them was Terre water, not honest Delve oil!) "Mistress, never say you're turning me away. What have I done? I'll never sleep on duty again, I swear it! Mistress please give me another chance! Mistress!"

I put my hand under his chin, tilting his head so that I could stare into his face. The tip of my index finger dug gently into that spot at the base of the neck where we have a sense organ and the Terrene do not. It senses the push of water (or air, as I had discovered); it is also *very* sensitive to touch. I felt the membrane-over-thick-fluid I should have felt, but he didn't flinch or jump. I dug my finger in slightly, and his eyes got a puzzled expression. I turned the dig into a caress, a gentle pat, and removed my hand, satisfied. A Terren. A player in a private pageant, for an audience of one. But why?

Two could play at pageantry.

"Boy, run you to Draxuus, my captain of guards. Tell him I want an escort of six, in full panoply, as soon as they can properly accouter themselves." A smile. "Then you may catch up on your sleep, naughty one. I know well why your eyes are full of sand. I will spend many hours with the Elyavaneet Noblelady, and need you not."

"Yes, mistress, as you order." Then, he broke out of his pretense. No boy would ever question a direct order.

"But were you not promised to treat with the Terren this day?"

So *that* was it. "I have no memory of such," I said coolly.

"Yes, mistress, it's truth. You are to receive the Terren here, in these very rooms, soon after break-fast."

"Not I, boy. I go to the Noblelady." He stood. Was it coincidence that he was between me and the door?

"Nay, mistress, consider. You would not be forsworn."

"I will not be forsworn. Since I have sworn never to treat with any of the Terrene on any matter, I would indeed be forsworn if I now received this spawn of the Outer Dark. So now, boy, do as you're bid."

"Can I not bring you something? You're not angry with me, mistress, are you?" He was young and softly unformed; his eyes pleaded.

"I will be angry with you only if you fail to do my bidding. Or am I to go to the guard's room myself?"

"Oh no, mistress. Let me serve you."

"Boy, do you not know what happens to disobedient boys?"

"Mis-*tress!*"

"You may find out, ere you are much older. Step from my path, boy!" I saw the logic of using this fresh-faced lad as a gaoler. He was so young, so innocent-appearing, so defenseless. It was difficult to see him as enemy.

But I did.

He spread his empty hands. "Mistress, please. I don't understand you."

I was tiring of this game. I could have killed him, but you just don't kill still damp younglings. Terren or no.

Someone must have counted on that. Logic said that a Terren, armed with those terrible coward's weapons I had seen used, was a most formidable foe. But millions of years of instinctive behavior said, "Sprat! Protect!"

I stepped back, laid my hand on the hilt of the blade at my side. "Boy," I said, *very* softly, "step from my path."

He was frightened, confused, resolute. "Mistress, please. You'll feel better once you've eaten." Was there something concealed in his hand?

I didn't thrust. I brought the hilt up under his chin and caught him as he fell. Something dropped from his limp fingers and rolled a few paces away. I left it where it lay. I draped him over my shoulders like a cloak, and not much weightier, either, and marched out the door.

Except I couldn't. It was not like the other barrier, where anything went through except the metal bands. (Which I was not wearing now.) This was a barricade, a feeble, smooth, slightly yielding, vaguely translucent barrier. I set the boy down (his hand wouldn't go through, either), and examined it further. It was real, there, a door made out of some smooth material unknown to me. I peered out through it. Though the other side was dark —deliberately so?—I thought I saw another metal corridor on the other side. It only confirmed early suspicions. I was still in the Terre place.

Not that it mattered where in the Terre place I was. I couldn't get home and I knew it. It only remained to play the game as favorably as possible.

The boy stirred and moaned. I hadn't hit him very hard. Quickly I bound his hands behind him with one of my sandal thongs. Then I sat on a backless seat with carved arms—and waited.

I didn't have to wait long.

He sat up and stared at me, his long legs folded every which way beneath him.

"Boy, do you know the penalties for lying and disobedience!" I snapped. My blade lay across my knees, catching and reflecting the light that was harsher than glow-animal's light truly is.

"Liars," I went on more softly, while I held his fear-filled eyes, "lose the fruits of their lying. You, I judge, should lose that lying—orange—skin." I smiled. Although the Terrene smile to show a different emotion, approval, he didn't misinterpret my showing of teeth. He gulped and tried to say something, but couldn't. "And disobedient boys," I paused, "are not allowed to father other disobedient boys." His eyes got very wide, but there wasn't enough fear in them. So there was some protection for him, some sneaky Terre magic shielded him. "I am Consecrate to the Flail—and Blade." I rose. "There is no reason to delay."

"Mistress—please—what are you—please—*don't*—" he babbled as I bent over him. I flipped him, despite desperate writhings, onto his back, so that his arms were pinned beneath his own weight. He was wearing a crude pectoral, a pair of wind-riders with wings outspread. I flipped it over his face and unwrapped his kilt. And blinked to myself in satisfaction. The disguise had not been completely carried out: he was Terren.

My blade was too sharp for the lesson I had in mind, but one of the armlets I was wearing had rounded shell dangles. While I was waiting, I had played with the armlet as though idly, and now one of the dangles was worked off and concealed in my hand. It had enough of an edge to administer a sharp lesson to this youngling. I flashed the blade before his eyes; his pleas rose. I knelt on him, pinning his upper legs; he twisted and began to scream in earnest. "You've less faith in your master than I, my boy," I murmured as I used my free hand to pin his squirming trunk. I was holding the blade at what might have appeared an awkward angle, but that was because I also had thc shell edge protruding from between my fingers. It was the shell that made a faint pink mark down the length of his belly. He screamed and convulsed. Had I been permitted, I would have continued down and "gelded" him with my vicious shell. A most memorable lesson.

But I wasn't permitted. My deadly weapon had just reached the dent in his belly when a pale scarlet light played over me; and I slumped over helpless. The blade scratched him then, lightly, as it slipped from my nerveless fingers.

He sobbed brokenly.

Heavy footsteps. "Get up, Charlie. You're not hurt." Gleaming white boots finger-widths from my face. A figure bending down. A surprised chuckle. "Well, I'll be plasmaed!" And, to my surprise, a pale amber light gave me my muscles back. I rose warily, to face the Gorky Admiral. He had my blade in one hand, the shell in the other.

"Admiral, Admiral, keep her away from me! She was g-g-gonna . . ."

"I would say"—there was amusement in that gravelly voice, and he glanced slyly down at the shell in his hand—"that she succeeded."

"No, she dint. But she was *gonna.*"

Having lured the Gorky Admiral out of hiding, I was

satisfied. I strolled away, into one of the other rooms, and sat down. I could hear the Admiral impatiently reassuring the boy, and the boy, finally, tearfully, looking down to see himself unmarred, except for that last, slight scratch. I hissed softly to myself. I had almost thought for a heartbeat there, that he would be willing to sacrifice—or what he thought was sacrifice—the boy.

"How long did you know, Kimassu?" The Gorky Admiral's voice came from the doorway. I hadn't recognized him; I didn't intend to. I had just wanted to *know*. I was tired of playing the Gorky Admiral's games. The sandal whose thong I had used to tie the boy was still in the other room. I untied the second one and dropped it on the floor, and sat, contemplating the amusing patterns a sandal thong can make.

I wondered when he was going to call Clem back.

"Kimassu?" That husky, speaking-through-pebbles voice was closer. I didn't look up.

"All right." His voice was back in the doorway. "We'll play by your rules. Will the noble Lady Kimassu condescend to recognize Admiral Alexei Gorky, Commander of the United Planets of Terra Tenth Fleet and Accredited Ambassador to the peoples of Delyafam?"

I spread my toes, seriously examining the webbing pattern between them. Despite the fact that I had been (as far as I knew) out of water for some length of time, the webbing between them, sensitive as it was, was not at all dried out, was, in fact, soft and pliable.

"Perhaps Lady Kimassu forgets that the previous meeting between her noble self and Admiral Gorky was approved by no less a personage than the Most Noble Lady Elyavaneet?"

The Kimassu Lady hadn't forgotten. The Kimasu Lady hadn't forgotten what came of that meeting, either.

"Admiral, Admiral, I think she knew all 'long."

"What, Charlie?"

"She knew. All along, she knew. Knew when she came into the room I was in. It wasn't like you said it was going to be, not at all. She *wasn't* confused. She *knew*. Ast me to go for the guard just to see what I'd do."

"What makes you so sure, Charlie?"

"I—lots of things, sir. Way she acted at the Shield, like. She hit me and I went down, but I wasn't out, not all the way, sir. I could sort of half see her, you know. And she walked into the Shield, and that surprised her. She felt at it, as though she dint know what a Shield was. But she wasn't surprised that *something* was there, you see, sir."

"I think I do. Go on, Charlie."

"Well, she felt it, and she tried to go through, and couldn't. And she sort of, well, nodded to herself, without actually nodding. If you follow me, sir."

I had underestimated Charlie. I should have slit his throat when I had the opportunity.

"Then she looked through it. She knew what she was seeing; you can see through a Shield if you're close enough, and she was. She looked and she saw, and she knew what she was seeing. 'N she *expected* to see it." I stood up and began taking off the armlets, letting them drop to the floor with smothered thuds. "I mean . . ." Charlie's voice slowed; his attention divided between what he was saying, and what I was doing, which was removing the fakery I had been bedecked with. All of it. Piece by piece. "She was supposed to think this was her place, her rooms; but she dint. 'Cause if she had she wouldda been surprised when she found out different. And she wasn't. Not when she saw the corridor, not when she—*Admiral, she ain't got no navel!*"

The Admiral chuckled. "None of them do, Charlie. The physiology boys aren't sure how they work it all yet, but they do have a broodpouch and some equivalent of a placenta—but the connection to the embryo is through the lowest gill openings, and you can't see them now. The gills themselves are protected in an internal sack, and the openings shut tight when she's out of the water."

What else would they do, I thought, irritated. Without a minimum of water in them, my gills could collapse and be damaged. But the Terrene must have some degenerate form of gills themselves, for they have the same glands on their chests as we do, to excrete excess salt. In water, as any sprat knows, the salt is excreted into the water flowing through the gills and out. On land, that salt would collect and concentrate to intolerable levels, had we not this other way of getting rid of it. (I remember one of my instructors explaining, when I was a youngling, how this way we rid ourselves of the salt without losing too much water in the process. It seemed rather complicated to me, but this, she said, is how our bodies adjust, to sea water, brackish, the rare sweet-water, or air. Other animals can get rid of salts with their bodies' waste water more efficiently than we, or use another method, or are confined to one environment. All are part of our Lady's grand design.)

Charlie muttered something about a waste.

The Admiral chuckled again. "Oh, she's built like a human woman, boy, where it counts." He elbowed the younger man in the ribs. "But get this, Charlie—" A snort. "It's the *men* that have the broodpouches."

(We had long since noted that the Terre males are deficient in that respect, as in so much else.)

I stretched, glad to be free of the Terre shoddy.

"Ad-miral?" Charlie seemed to be asking something.

"Try it, Charlie, and she won't bother with a knife, she'll rip it off!"

I sauntered into another room. Knowledge is a weapon in itself. These rooms looked like those in the House of Debate, but that likeness was, so to speak, only skin deep. But what was on the walls . . . Hmmmm . . . I wouldn't be allowed near the *obvious* weapons; but some weapons aren't at all obvious . . .

I knew quite well what would happen *afterward;* but a Terre Admiral for a Lady seemed fair enough exchange.

On a small table was an assortment of various decorative objects, carven figures, polished shells. One of them was a greendeath. A second look, while ostentatiously examining a carved statue of a flyingfish, told me that all the spines had been carefully broken off. I sighed. Pity.

It was a bit too bright for what I had in mind, but when I stroked one of the glow-animals on the wall, to make it go to sleep and stop glowing, nothing happened. I looked at it a little closer; it wasn't a glow-animal at all. None of them were.

"Over here, Kimassu." I didn't look, but all the "glow-animals" in the room dimmed and brightened again.

I didn't think any more delay would serve my purpose. I clicked softly to locate the Gorky Admiral as precisely as I could, without looking. He was . . . *there.* I threw a stool and ran the two steps to the wall to a handsome two-sided throwing ax. I got my fingers on it . . .

"You little devil!"

My fingers on it . . . and it was fake, too! Part of the wall. I spent two precious, futile heartbeats tugging, and he laughed. He laughed. "You vicious little savage. It won't work, Kimassu. They're all fake. And even if you could throw something at me, I'm wearing a small personal shield. You wouldn't hurt me." I sneaked a look out of the corner of my eye. That stool should have at least split his scalp, but his hair wasn't even mussed. "You're a fool, Kimassu," he went on. "I'm the best friend you've got, if only you'd open your mind and see it."

I strolled to the room nearest the Shield, the one I thought of as the outer room. It should have held a waterflow, or at the very least a foot basin, but it didn't. I immediately felt dry. I prowled around the door, and then around the doors of each of the rooms in turn. In the third room, I found a shell, set into the wall for a foot basin, but it was dry, too.

"I should have thought of that, Kimassu. Come in here."

When the ice in the Outer Dark melts will I obey you, Gorky Admiral.

But then I heard the sound of running water. Sweet and *wet.*

I drifted idly toward the ambrosial sound.

"In here, Kimassu." I hesitated. But, ah, that *water* . . .

An entire section of the wall had vanished, and there was a doorway-sized hole right in the middle of Valeria's Third Voyage. Inside . . . I entered, and gasped. Inside was a place of shiny miracles; a dozen distorted figures stared at me from walls of silver, palest pink, amber, turquoise. And things whose usage I knew not, gleaming smooth objects that were neither metal nor pottery but some magic, slick, smooth stuff painted in fantastic shapes somehow inside the surfaces. And in one corner, a water flow, from a round metal thing no bigger than my palm.

I walked around the Gorky Admiral and into the water. *Ahhhhhhh* . . .

His hand came in past me. "Here, Kimassu. Off." His finger pushed in something. The water stopped. "Here. On." Another protrusion. The water back on. "Turn this way, for hotter." And it got—believe this!—*it got hotter!* "Other way, for cooler." And he twisted, and it did get cooler. "Now, the rest of it, *watch me, Kimassu!*" Well, really: I wasn't going to touch any of these strange objects. Goddess knew what they did. But, ahh, this water . . .

"Relieve yourself in the seat here," he was saying. I watched one of his images thoughtfully. "Here, pull down here for a chemcleanser. Toss it here when you're clean. Push this when you're through, for dispose." Whatever dispose was. He went through the whole thing a second time. When I felt the need, I was going to use the handiest corner. After all, I had seen in that seat as I went by. No water, no water at all. The sort of thing I might have expected from the Terrene. Maybe they had no sense of smell.

I think he sensed my attitude. "Now, Kimassu," he coaxed. "You're the one who's going to be bothered by the smell and have to step over, well. I know you can hear me, and I don't want any childishness out of you. I'm not going to order you; I'll leave the matter to your common sense . . ."

He kept talking. All the advantages if I would only co-operate. What a good friend, a useful ally he could be. How sorry he was about Clem . . . "What he did was against my direct orders, Kimassu. He could have killed you; he almost did. I won't deny, that if he'd—well—induced a more co-operative attitude in you . . . success is success, Kimassu. You understand that. I wouldn't have punished him, for disobeying me. If he'd been right. If he succeeded. As it is—" He chuckled. "Clem is a very, very sorry man right now." That I believed. Clem's crime wasn't what he did to me; his crime was failure. I stopped listening. Did he think I wouldn't recognize my very own trick? *I* never ordered anything bad, either. If I squeezed into the farthest corner of the waterfall, the roar drowned out his voice almost completely. Ummmmmmmm . . .

"Kali and Siva, woman! Listen to me!" he roared over the waterfall. I squeezed a little further back. The water cut off. I could have turned it back on, I had seen what magic he had activated, but turning it back on would be an acknowledgment that I had seen him. So I sat cross-legged in the water that was rapidly draining out, shut my eyes, and waited. Either he would turn the water back on, or not. Either he would stay or he would leave.

He didn't turn the water back on, and he didn't leave. Instead he continued to talk. However, with my eyes shut, his voice had the easy regularity, the drone of flowing water. I let myself flow along with it . . .

"Blwfwbbb?" the brook babbled after a bit.

The sun was warm on my bare back, and I was somewhere far, far away.

"Mmphblww?"

Soon I would have to go back to my ship for the afternoon's catch, but it was still too hot, so for a few more precious moments, I could sit quietly and be lazy.

"KIMASSU!"

Funny, I thought a brook spoke my name. How odd. How silly. Brooks can't speak. Or breathe loudly in one's ear, either.

"You asked for this, Kimassu," spat in my ear, while a slap on shoulder made sure I lost, for the nonce, that warm and sunny rock by the secluded bay. Still half in my self-induced trance, I couldn't react quickly to his touching me. After all, his Terre rank, were one to recognize Terre rank, was somewhat the equivalent to my own. I lazily opened my eyes and rose to my feet—and he turned the water back on. I rotated so that I could see one of his images, an Admiral-sized blur, in a shiny wall; he was silent. Watching me. Could it have been an accident, part of turning the water back on? I rotated slowly, thinking.

It couldn't have been meant as a challenge; I hadn't recognized him.

So, then. Accident? Or Terre custom.

One of my own images caught my eye—it looked wrong, somehow. A crimson blotch on my shoulder, about where the Admiral had slapped. I looked down. There was a crimson square there. I felt, and it was some thin, Terre stuff, not cloth. I engaged suckers, but it wouldn't come off, no matter how hard I tugged. I shrugged. If the Admiral wanted to decorate me with colored Terre magic stuffs, he was welcome to.

I relished the warm flow of life-giving water.

Odd. A downward glance told me that the crimson

square was fading. As though the water was washing it off—but there was no trace of red on my arm. Odd. I felt it again. There was nothing to feel—as though the pinkish red color I could still see was in my skin instead of on it.

What an odd people the Terrene are.

But, oh, that *lovely* water. Like a dozen-dozen-dozen tiny fingers—stroking . . .

I knew suddenly what he had done. We have our simples, too, even powerful ones that work through the skin—though none so speedy as this one.

I stepped from the rain, to face him.

"So the noble Lady Kimassu finally condescends to recognize Alexei Gorky?" His lips were stretched wide, showing his teeth. It was not what the Terrene would name a smile, I thought; but I recognized the expression.

"I recognize you, Gorky Admiral. Now go. Leave me."

He shook his head slowly. "No, Kimassu." His tongue came out and ran over his lower lip, fuller and pinker than I remembered, and very, very shiny.

"I said, leave me!"

He was breathing deeply, almost panting. "It gets much worse, Kimassu. Even if you think you want me to leave—now—in five minutes you'll be screaming for someone, for anyone. But it's going to be me."

I didn't want to be left alone *now*. But—*him?* "Gorky Admiral, I recognize you. I will continue to recognize you. You have what you want. Now—*GO!*"

He continued to shake his head slowly. "No, Kimassu. I don't have all I want." His wet, gleaming pink mouth stretched wider. "Not all I want. Not yet."

If he was old, it didn't show. If he was unattractive, by my standards, it didn't matter. All that mattered, as he said, was that he was *there*.

I accepted the inevitable.

Chapter Eighteen

MOTTO:

Give her sea shells all gay, wand'rer,
Give her sea shells all bright;
Give her scarlet and gold, wand'rer,
Give her green, blue, and white.

—*Ballad of She Found and Lost*

I stretched luxuriously. The Gorky Admiral's methods of suasion were infinitely preferable to Clem's. Not that the Gorky Admiral's performance was anything to brag about to one's friends; but it was nothing to be ashamed of either. Especially, matched as it was to a simple-induced frenzy. Had the Gorky Admiral a *talent*—weaving, say—I might even have considered adding him to my household, in a minor capacity. But I had all the guards I needed, and I would never replace any of my faithful with a Terren.

Had he been one of my own people, a met-by-chance at the Courts, a courtesy loaned by one of my own rank, I would have dismissed him with a pat on the rump, sweet words, and an appropriate offering.

As it was, it had lasted overlong, until we both fell into exhausted sleep. He lay beside me, making a hoarse noise through his nose, one arm flung possessively over my body, as though for reassurance I hadn't left him. We were lying on a crumpled blanket, in one of the rooms that was not in the House of Debate. I was altogether too cool. I managed to sit up, wriggle away from where he had me pinned against the wall, and slide away from him entirely. He sighed and stirred and made a low moan, but didn't waken.

I went into the room where it rained and stood under the water for long minutes, refreshing and regenerating. I even dared to open my mouth and drink. It was *sweet*-water, bland and tasteless.

I wandered back into the room where the Gorky Admiral slept, to think.

He was as bulky without clothes as with, his massive bones covered with layers and layers of flesh; I could scarce have spanned his thigh with my two hands. Much of it was muscle; he was fantastically strong, even for a Terren. But there was flab, too, and the beginnings of a paunch. Then I re-evaluated; by Terre standards, he might be big, big enough to have "presence"; but not abnormally big. I decided that he would have presence even if he had been as short and illy-fleshed as the unlamented (but, oh, so useful!) Willis. His head fur gleamed metallically, but his plentiful body fur ("I need another depilation," he had said, rubbing his pelted chest with noticeable pride) was a dull orangish-brown.

It was his mind, his attitude I couldn't fathom.

Did he really believe, having done as he wished under compulsion of his simple, that I would continue to do his bidding of my own free will?

Surely he couldn't be that naïve!

And yet . . . and yet . . .

"You're mine, now, Kimassu," he had said. "Mine." Over and over, he had said it.

"I'll kill the man who tries to take you away from me." He had said that, too. Because you're *mine*, implied so strongly even I couldn't miss it, unfamiliar as I was to Terre ways of thinking.

Even now, his arm curved possessively over where my body had lain.

Possessively. That was the core of the matter.

Mine.

Clem had had the same strange notion. That I would be *his*, his toy, his plaything, could he but tear some acknowledgment from me. As though word taken by force could have any meaning. It was mere pride, perhaps foolish pride, that had stiffened my neck, made me refuse to give him that word, that meaningless word.

There was this knowledge in me, too. That once one starts to talk, it is very difficult to stop. I have found this over and over in my duties. That a prisoner will talk, thinking to bore me down, to talk of anything and everything insignificant, irrelevant; but sooner or later, the truth comes out, the significant, the relevant. Or I find an inconsistency and pick away at it. Or a little, little something slips, and I make it grow into a bigger something. No, I knew I couldn't answer questions, that it was dangerous to talk on the most commonplace level, to answer the simplest greetings.

But there was this to ponder. Had I, from pain or weariness or a simple need for a respite, given Clem what he wanted, what difference would it have made? What advantage would he have gained, save the assuaging of his own desires? I would have been humiliated to some small degree, yes, to be used (if what I suspected about Clem was accurate) as only the youngest, most skill-less, stupidest excess males are sometimes used, by other, usually older males. Yes, to be *used.* I would have felt humiliated—but no more. I would not have obeyed him to avoid a repetition; a repetition which would doubtless have occurred, regardless of what I did. So what connection was there, in the Terre mind, between meaningless humiliation and obedience?

And *why* should the Gorky Admiral think I was "his" because we had performed what must surely be the most natural act in both our worlds together?

Did he consider himself "mine"? Surely this odd relationship must run both ways. Shouldn't it? Did he expect me to offer him a permanent position in my household? He had cockles in his thick Terre skull if he did.

He woke and stood up, all in one easy motion. His tilted dusk-gray eyes searched. "Kimassu . . . where . . . oh, there you are, darling."

Yes, here I was. What's a darling?

But I had other things to worry about. He strode to me, wrapped his arms about my waist, and pulled me to my feet, forcing my body against the hard length of his and pressing our mouths together, his tongue probing urgently inside my mouth.

Sheer shock made me a limp weight in his arms, but that didn't seem to bother him. He held me tighter and ran his hands up and down my back, stroking and caressing, forcing me closer, fitting our bodies together. Then his touch changed, became lighter, gentler, more teasing. But always—possessive.

Mine.

How *dare* he!

It was my fury that saved me. I was literally insane with rage; helpless in the grip of a blind, unthinking anger such as I'd never known.

And then I understood. Of course. The missing factor. I thought coolly and rapidly. This was why the Terre males were as they were; because their females were as they were. Terre females are *flawed*. Whether the flaw was physical or merely mental, I neither knew nor cared. But it was there; it explained that which had long puzzled us. Once a Terre female coupled with a male, *he* was *her* master; she *had* to obey him, be subservient to him. That was what Neill had been trying to tell me, and I hadn't understood. The female *had* to obey her male.

That was it! That was it!

And the Gorky Admiral thought—

How could I turn this to my advantage?

If I could play this strange role properly, I could buy, at least, time. Perhaps, even—oh, joy!—be sent home! If he trusted me . . .

Goddess, I might yet win free!

Gingerly, I let my body go even limper, let him support more and more of my weight. Timidly, I returned his caresses. (Surely a Terre female would do so much? No one of heat and blood could be completely passive.)

Evidently, what I did was right, because he redoubled his efforts, lifting his head only long enough to moan, "Oh, Kimassu!"

There is a natural rhythm to all things, and before long, I, too, was caught up in it. But it seemed strange to be the passive partner, to be guided and not guider, to go at my partner's speed, not to accommodate him, but because *he* willed it so.

It was unnatural.

And yet. Suppose, suppose, it were mutual desire, each partner pleasuring the other, true partners truly joined, body and mind, *equals* . . .

But my own people, my own males, the Hardyene, they could never be my equals. They were boys, always and forever more, immature, undeveloped mentally. Was it the other way with the Terrene? All their female girls, never mature, never equal to their males—

But those who had negotiated with our leaders had been intelligent enough.

Puppets? Manipulated by their (disgusting!) masters?

Suppose I could find a congenial Terren, unruined by his mastery. Assuming, of course, that I had not been ruined by my mistressing. A Terren who—but I knew a Terren like that. Neill. Oh, he had tried to force his way. But in a fit of temper. I might have done the same to him, under similar circumstances. Had he avoided physical contact (until forced by need) because he wished to protect me from the fate that would have befallen one of his own weak-willed females? Had what I had seen as an easy, sexless relationship between two friends, had it been completely different for him? A growing attraction held back by force of will? A desire for me; and a desire to—protect me?

Not so the Gorky Admiral.

He wanted me subservient.

Not Kimassu. *Mine.*

And—he thought he had succeeded!

Far be it from me to disillusion him!

He picked me up in his arms and carried me back to the crumpled blanket.

I carefully waited to take my cues from him; I don't think I fluffed any of them.

Besides, I enjoyed it.

I enjoyed fooling him, too.

"I don't know about you, darling," he said at last, "but I'm starved."

"Ummmmm," I murmured. I didn't want to touch *his* food; on the other hand, he was responsible for my being in this Terre place, for my being removed from my own world, where I needn't depend on anyone but myself for food; therefore, he *owed* me food. I decided to look at it that way. Besides, I, too, was "starving."

He patted my flank happily. "Stay here, darling. I'll take care of it."

Had I a choice?

He stood in front of one of the walls and did something, and a piece of it slid back underneath the next section, revealing a gray square with rounded corners and a vertical row of colored buttons. He pushed and turned some of the knobs (I watched closely, sitting up to see better. Knowledge is power!) and—Charlie's face, yawning, appeared in the gray square. It was a window to another room. Only, I knew the room on the other side of that wall; and the wall that showed behind Charlie was different, a conch-shell pink deepening to violet.

As if idly, I rose and strolled through two doorways to look in the other room. Charlie wasn't there. Charlie was someplace else.

Was Charlie so far away that the Gorky Admiral couldn't walk to see him?

No, because Charlie arrived, only a couple of minutes later; a vague shape calling, "It's me, Charlie," through the Shield.

Perhaps the Gorky Admiral simply hadn't wanted to leave me alone.

But the easy availability of the magic square was, I felt, significant.

Then I learned another reason for his—the Gorky Admiral's use of the square instead of taking me with him to wherever the food was stored.

Noill had been right. Trying to understand the Terrene on the basis of those struggling on our land, in our society, was as difficult as trying to predict the life of a depths-dweller by watching it expire on a beach.

The *differences* between us.

The Gorky Admiral didn't want Charlie to see me—naked.

He meant it, too.

When I didn't understand his first, rather jovial speech, he frowned, slapped me on the buttock hard enough to sting, and literally pushed me through an inner doorway, drawing the drape closed behind me.

"Almost forgot"—he stuck his head in through a crack in the drape—"got a bit of business with Charlie. Won't be but a minute, and then we'll eat." I didn't say anything. "Here." He reached a hand in, and there was the most awful cacophony of noise. Bang-boom-crashity-*bang*. "There you go," he grinned. "How do you like that? Absolute latest from Tau Ceti. The Internal Triangle playing 'Baby, What You Do to Me!' " And head and arm disappeared. It didn't sound like playing. It sounded like they were hitting each other. All those crashes. And moans, too. Boom-crash-moooooooan.

Then another section of wall slid back to reveal another one of those gray squares. Except this one had people in it. Terrene; but little. No, some little, some right size; but never little and big together.

They weren't fighting.

I sat down to watch, since that was what I was supposed to do. But I stopped listening to the noise, so I could hear what the Gorky Admiral and Charlie were saying, on the other side of the closed drape.

"Come on in, Charlie."

"Mornin', Admiral." Charlie's voice was richly jovial. "Have a good night"—a long heartbeat—" 's sleep?"

"Careful, Charlie." There were both amusement and warning in the rough voice.

"Brought you double portions, Admiral. Figured you'd need'm."

"I do, Charlie, I do." I recognized the tone of voice they were using. I'd heard it often, used it myself; when I snaffled a boy another woman wanted, I might speak so. And hear pride of achievement in my voice, and sly admiration—or perhaps envy—in the other.

"And the other stuff I wanted?" There was a funny slick-slick noise.

"Right here, Admiral."

"Ummm-yes. The orders for the Jaguar-Action Squadron?"

"Here, just as you told me. Have them orbit—hey, she can't hear us, can she?"

"No, I have her stashed inside listening to a tridi. Turn on the spy and we'll check, though." A pause. "Good as gold, that one."

"Is she, sir?"

"Charlie, that would be telling. Now, O.K., orbit around Hotasell. Can't keep it up too long, taxpayers'll scream. But the incident should come off any day, now, and we'll be asked in. Neat. Is the Eco report on Langara I wanted in yet? I don't see it here."

"No, sir. The technies say . . ."

"Plasma those gutless technies! Who's in charge of that group? Numurta? I'll give him a buzz later and goose him into action."

"Ahhh, sir. Ah-hem."
"Yes, Charlie?"
"I wouldn't do that, sir. If I were you."
"Why not?"
"Because if you do, you'll get a flat. No. Numurta thinks that dam you want will upset the balance on the whole south continent. I was talking to his exec, and . . ."
"Go on, Charlie. What's the grapevine saying?"
"That Numurta's still stewing over that mess on Cadwallader and—"
"We followed the rec's!"
"Yeah, well. He's saying now that the rec's were incomplete, you didn't wait for the final report, and—He's just itching for the chance to do you one, sir."
"Um. Well, Charlie, we'll just have to do him one first. Two bad Eco reports should just about do it. That exec who likes to talk, Charlie. Cultivate him. Find out his weaknesses, besides talking too much. Is he ambitious? Maybe he'd like to head his own mission, hmmmm?"
I listened to them plotting the downfall of the hapless Numurta, and other business, and watched the square. It was rather dull, really. I had to admit that the Terrene were rather inventive. Ingenious, even. But it was watching, and not doing.
Then, "Ahhhhh, sir. About Clem."
"No, Charlie. I know he was your chum. And the devil knows where I can get a replacement out here. But my order stands."
"But, sir. *Calvin*, sir. Clem won't last a month on Calvin."
"He will. If he learns to control himself. Sorry, Charlie. But he's already en route. There was a troopship warped out for the Relidge Circuit last night. Clem's on it. And, Charlie: Profit by Clem's downfall. Don't go nosing after what isn't yours."
"Yes . . . sir."
"Charlie!"
"I heard you . . . sir."
"What I don't understand," the Gorky Admiral's voice was lowered, as though he were thinking aloud, "is why Clem did it. I thought she was safe enough with him. The rest of you, randy bucks looking for a score, no. But Clem I thought he couldn't stand women. I thought . . . well,

she's a gorgeous piece, with those legs that never know when to stop, but I didn't think it'd hit Clem, I never thought he'd be willing to throw over everything like that . . ."

"Sir . . ."

"What is it?"

"Sir—on Clem's homeworld—he's not service-bred, you know . . ."

"Yes. I knew he was from one of the Digger colonies . . ."

"On his homeworld, adolescent boys shave their heads, until they get married and become citizens. He used to make me wear a skinwig . . . sir." He continued over loud curses. "She is pretty narrowhipped, and that height, and slenderness, and those long legs . . . And she killed Piers and Jorge and Mahmood and Alec; that made him mad. They was his chums, too, you see, and . . ."

"Mad is right." The voice was tired and slow. "Mad enough to lose us the best chance we've had in a hundred years to get a real toehold on Siren'ssong . . ."

"But, sir, didn't you . . ."

"You'd better believe it, Charlie. But I don't know; they look like us on the outside, more than any other humanoid race we've encountered. But inside, the way they think . . . Do you know they're the only ones, the only ones, who haven't come to us begging for the anti-death drugs! Can you believe it? Everywhere else, every other planet, we tell them the same, the drugs work on us and only on us, and everywhere else, sooner or later, they come begging, pleading, offering anything, anything for that extra life. And we make them pay, and pay, and pay. And when they're dependent on the drugs, they're *ours*. Forevermore ours with the Damocles-threat of no more drugs hanging over them. But not these Sirens, no, not them. It didn't make sense, it wasn't natural. And this world is too plasmaed close to the border to take chances with; just our luck we found them first. But then I found out about her, living so long, and thought the Gyrodden were infiltrating, offering their drugs. But when she was hurt, and medicked, there were no traces in her body, no chemicals. She's been in contact with the agent—but only recently. She's just a freak, that's all, a long-lived freak."

"Maybe they all are, sir; maybe that's why they're not interested."

"No, we got a load of specimens early in the game. Survivors of a storm-wrecked ship. But despite the medics best care, none of them, even the immature ones, lasted longer than ten or so standard years. No, their life-span is naturally shorter than ours. Twenty-five, thirty years at the most."

(I didn't understand that—and then I did. Their "specimens"—what a vile word, what a vile Terre concept!—must all have been male. Our Hardyene males are far, far shorter lived than we Delyene. Part of Her plan it must be. But a great sorrow to we Delyene, too, that we must watch our dear boys wither and die. But, oh, the irony of it! We believed them when they said their age magics would work not on us. We believed them! And so thwarted their evil before it could strangle us. Had we been tempted . . . even I . . . Draxuus the topaz-eyed, lithe and sweet and now ashes on the wind! What would I have paid to have him at my side yet, strong and loving?)

"So alien on the inside, Charlie, we've never understood them, but on the outside—physically . . . they're beautiful, inhumanly beautiful, the women anyway, except for the baldness, and even that, somehow . . . And not a one of them, in all these years, ever looked twice at any of us, not a one in all those years . . ." There was a sound, as of impatient fingers drumming against a hard surface. And then, very softly, so that I had to strain to hear, "She makes other women look like hags. And she *moves* . . ."

"Sir, what are you always telling me? Slow and steady does it . . . sir."

The Gorky Admiral chuckled, his dark mood thrown off. It was a very confident sound, and I trembled, hearing it, whether with anger or fear, I couldn't have said. So! That was what I was to these Terrene: a long pair of legs, a pleasant partner for a night's pleasure.

And a path to betray my people.

But, Kimassu, haven't you judged males so? Their practical worth to you? Their talents. A pleasant hour's diversion, an amusing toy for a while, or good enough to be loaned to brighten your reputation.

Like Draxuus. A toy, a thing to the Noblelady you rescued him from—but to you . . .

Draxuus was different.

To *you.*

Draxuus was different!

I couldn't *stand* it. Penned in, helpless, dependent, captive, toy, slave, *plaything!*

You are what you think you are.

There was no place to run to, no hiding place.

But, always and forever, I am I, Kimassu!

I held myself together with an effort, waited patiently.

He was clothed, clothing the deep colorlessness of the sea depths, yet glittering, catching the light as he moved. His amulets glittered, too, rainbow jewels, lit from within. I could see the play of muscles beneath the thin stuff, and wondered, not for the first time, if the enticing effect were deliberate or accidental.

He was carrying, no, guiding—the tray floated itself—a tray, and he urged it onto a table inlaid with a delicate mosaic of polished shell. "Hungry, Kimassu, love? Here's a feast fit for your Empress herself." In his other hand was a length of cloth, amber, no, pale yellow, no transparent in patches and palest green in others, no . . . it changed, in color, in pattern, from heartbeat to heartbeat. "Here," he said, "I thought you might be a little chilly, I brought you this." He draped it around my shoulders, guided my arms into long swathings that came to my wrists, pressed down a piece that wrapped around my hips to another piece beneath—and it held. I was dressed, or, more accurately, warmer. I was certainly not covered, not by a Terre magic cloth that could be seen through, at least part of the time.

"There, now." He sighed in satisfaction. A grin. "Want to see how it looks on you?"

I looked down at myself.

"No, here." He half-turned me, drew me to another wall, pushed a button—and I saw another Gorky Admiral, in front of me, beside another Delyen! I took a step forward and raised my hand in greeting, and so did she.

"Sister, how come you here, I—"

The Gorky Admiral started laughing. "That's you, Kimassu." I slammed into a smooth, hard surface. Another magic, and she on the other side . . . "That's you,

"Kimassu. It's a mirror, a reflection." I hit the smoothing hard stuff, and her fist joined mine on the other side. "Kimassu, that's you. A reflection, a picture, *you!*" I had once or twice seen a blurred seeming of myself in still water, in polished metal. But they were not as this. I stared. But he was right. Another Delyen with skin as mine, with twin scars on her forearm, with, I looked down and moved and the clothing changed again, became completely transparent all over, like a silver gray mist, a Delyen with a small knot on one shin, if you knew where to look. So it was I. I stared unashamedly. So that was what I looked like. A good Delye face. Curiousity satisfied, I turned to the table. With a puzzled frown, he sat opposite me, began to serve us.

The clothing kept tangling in my legs as I sat, so I pulled it aside, and finally, irritated, sat on it, leaving my legs free. He made a stifled, sputtering noise. I was too busy with my food to pay attention to him, though.

Hunger satisfied, I sat back, replete. So did he, except he got a small white stick out of a container on the tray, and stuck it in his mouth, suckling it with every evidence of enjoyment. A curl of smoke came out of his nostrils. I had seen Terrens with such before, so I said nothing.

Suddenly he snapped his fingers. "Almost forgot. Here you go, Kimassu." He reached into his pocket, brought out a finely woven silver net, with long strings of colored beads dangling from it. He handed it to me, and I stared at it. "Go on, darling," he urged, "put it on."

Where?

"On your head, darling, on your head."

Nonsense. It was too small, and how could I see? But he stood up, and sooner than having him jam it on, I slapped it on top of my head myself. It stretched slightly and clung, the beads clinking softly as I moved.

"It's not on straight," he said. "Don't you want to see how you look?"

"But I saw how I looked a few minutes ago," I said. "Thank you; I've always wondered."

He made another smothered sound. "I mean, how you look with the cap on."

"The cap?" He pointed. "Oh, that. But I saw what that looked like when you handed it to me."

He laughed and then frowned. "Slow and steady," he

muttered to himself, "slow and steady." Louder, "Well, I left the mirror lit. You might take a look when you pass it. The cap does look very pretty on you. And it makes you look prettier, too." (I did take a look, later. It may or may not have made me prettier, whatever that meant to him; it certainly made me look more Terre. The strings of beads stood out away from my head, and they somewhat resembled the fur I didn't have.)

He didn't say any more; he seemed content to sit and suck on his stick, and occasionally sip a dark liquid.

He broke the silence. A minor victory for me. "Kimassu?"

"Yes, Gorky Admiral?"

"Kali and Siva, girl. Under the circumstances, you can call me by my first name!"

I could feel my eyes widening. "Your First Name?"

"Yes, my first name. Alexei. Lexi, if you prefer."

His First Name. I hadn't guessed, there had been no hint, not the slightest. I made Ritual Obeisance.

"What the plasma was that all about," he exploded.

I completed the Ritual, and stood, head bowed, waiting for him to recognize me. If I'd only *known* . . .

He paced around me, darting quick, bright glances that slid off my tranquil surface. Underneath, I was seething. *Why* hadn't he said earlier . . .

"Kimassu?"

"Sir?"

"Kimassu, what's all this about?" I could hear anger in his voice.

"Sir," I said formally, "if I have in any way offended, I crave pardon. I can only plead grossest ignorance . . ."

"Stop calling me sir!"

My head jerked up at that; it was the honorific Charlie had used. Quickly I bowed it back to the proper angle. "As you wish, Gorky Admiral *Lexi*."

He muttered something under his breath. Then I felt ungentle fingers under my chin, forcing my face up, until my eyes met his. Quickly, I shut my eyes. "Open your eyes," he ordered. "Look at me, Kimassu." His eyes were so close to mine; they were really a light color, a misty gray; they seemed darker because the stiff fur that surrounded them shadowed them. "Now, Kimassu. I don't know what superstition or religious quirk I trig-ered off in you; but I'm the same man I was an hour ago; a night ago. Listen to me, Kimassu. *Our customs are not yours!"*

His arm caught me around the shoulders so that I didn't fall. I felt a complete fool! Where would a Select be, except in a Temple, where all his wants could be catered to? Would a Select be wandering about with no honor guard? Besides, as I should have remembered, the Terrene take their Family name (or what they call their Family, I am not sure of the precise relationships) as well as a sprat name. But if one had two names, one might call one of them the first name and mean no more than that by it. So then he *wasn't*—but their customs were different. Perhaps he *was* . . . I could feel blood heating my skin. How could I ask?

"I'm a fool," he muttered, catching me to him with eager hands. "I gave you that flaming aphro; yet I can't take advantage of this. I'm not, Kimassu. Whatever you're thinking, I'm not."

I took him at his word and pushed him away. "Take me home!"

"I can't do that." His answer was quick. Too quick.

"Then let me go. I'll find my own way home."

"You can't, Kimassu. You can't—ah—sail one of our ships. And you can't walk home from here, Kimassu. It's impossible." I could hear truth in his voice.

"Then you take me. Take me home and let me go. You owe it to me." I hadn't meant to say any such thing; the double shock had made it pop out. But having said it, I wanted to finish it. He knew how I felt; best he knew how deeply I felt.

He shook his head. "Kimassu, I can't. Even if I wanted to. The transmatter isn't in synch. Oh, Kali and Siva! My—my magic only works at certain times. Do you understand me?" Everyone knows that magic only works when all the influences are correct. But I didn't *believe* him. I knew lie when I heard it. "Look, darling, I'll make a deal with you. A bargain. You be a good girl, and in, oh, three or four days, when the trans is back in synch, if you still want to go . . . What have you got to lose, Kimassu? A little vacation, call it, courtesy of the United Planets. Rest, relax, enjoy yourself. A few days off, nothing to do, no responsibilities." He put his hand on the side of my neck, stroked delicately all the soft, hidden, sensitive spots. "I thought you enjoyed . . . but I won't lay a finger on you, if you don't want. The choice is yours darling. There are plenty of other men on this station who'd jump at the chance to entertain you; any way you want. Or you could just stay here quietly, alone if that's the way you want it. Just rest . . ."

I said nothing, waited quietly under his hand. How much of what he said could I trust?

"I thought"—his voice dropped to deeper huskiness—"I thought we made a good team, Kimassu. I admit I shouldn't have given you that aphro; but I lost my temper. I'm not sorry, either. I *enjoyed* it; and I think you did, too. But if not . . ."

Lie, again. He gave me the simple out of policy, deliberately; why else have it ready to hand? But he had enjoyed it; so had I. I still didn't understand much, but . . .

"I will wait, then. And I would prefer that you leave your—what do you call those things on your feet?"

"Boots," he supplied.

"Your boots by my sleeping blanket when you're not wearing them." After all, I had enjoyed it. "For now." So he wouldn't get overconfident.

He grinned widely, thinking he had won. Poor fool. Did he think that three or four days of what he could supply, no worse but no better than any other male, would addle me into becoming his dupe?

No, he had one real chance—and muffed it. If he had returned me, as I had asked, to my own people, I just might have been better disposed to him . . .

As it was . . .

War to the death, even if he didn't know it—yet.

I would take and use and *enjoy* my few days respite; until someone's patience ran out.

Chapter Nineteen

MOTTO:

She who invites the Four-faced Slut to stand behind her had best count her fingers at every opportunity.

—Pre-Imperial folklore, origins obscure

"Well, Kimassu, I think it's time we stopped playing games." His fingers drummed nervously on the surface of the work area he called his console. My cage had been enlarged by the addition of several rooms, including this one he called office, with its magic screens, its blinking lights, its seats that came out of the wall at a touch and went back when you stood up. He had let me sit quietly, listening to him "work"; talk to people, make the blinking lights do this and that, put funny things *in* his ear and watch the screens.

I sighed. It had lasted longer than I had expected; the Gorky Admiral had more patience than I gave him credit for. At least I had this interlude. I was fed, and rested, and my sense of purpose was strengthened. Wordlessly, I rose, and held out my arms for him to put the wristlets back on.

He blinked, a sign of puzzlement, and then, as I watched, fascinated, a tide of color rose under his brown skin, until one could imagine a fire burning beneath his face. "No, Kimassu. I said we wouldn't play games. I'm not a fool like Clem. You don't have to worry about that." His mouth twisted. "Besides, it wouldn't work on you, would it?"

"The choice is yours," I said evenly. But I let my hands drop.

"If the choice were mine," he said, equally evenly,

"I would keep things as they have been, and slip you another jolt of aphro whenever you get restless."

I was startled to hear truth in that. I had been sitting quietly, so as not to "disturb him"; now I got up and began to pace back and forth, the long drapery I was wearing (he called it a skirt) swirling around my legs. Impatiently, I twisted so that my legs were entirely free through a long slit down the center.

"That's what I mean." His voice was strangely gentle. "No, don't stop, darling. I like to watch you." I continued to pace, the gauzy green and blue material swishing as I moved, molding to my legs, swirling and clinging.

We had come closest to arguments on the subject of clothing. My clothing. I needed something, in the coolth that the Terrene lived in; but I didn't like to drape myself in meaningless cloth, and what he seemed to like was silly-looking, and got in my way as I moved. What emerged was compromise. An overall covering of thin, soft material that moved with me. Long "skirts" that were strips of material attached to elaborate belts that rode my hips. Soft sandals decorated with tiny gleaming jewels. Amulets, collars, wristlets, anklets. And odd flat-topped, swept-back helmets that were based on a statuette head he showed me; a queen, he said, that had ruled a place called Egypt a long, long time ago. I reminded him of her. And it was true, I did look like her—or she like me. But her eyes were serene, her mouth smiled. She had never to make hard choices, never devote herself to duty, never had to struggle and endure and watch her world slowly destroyed and try to hold back the tide with her fingers. Nefertiti her name was; it sounded almost Delyen.

"Have you ever," he spoke persuasively, "considered really considered, Kimassu, the advantages of honestly throwing in with us?" So I hadn't fooled him; not at all. "I'm not talking about the obvious ones, either. Our technology that can at least make sure you live out *all* your natural life-span and maybe more."

I was surprised; not at what he had said, for I had understood ab[illegible]rre age magic drugs since I had overheard his talk with Charlie—but that he dared to admit it to me[illegible]hat one surprise might pass for the other. I turned my face away, because nothing could hide the knowledge in my eyes. That he would only have dared to tell me if he knew I was never to have an opportunity to pass it on.

He let me consider for long heartbeats, then muttered to himself. "Talk about serendipity. I thought she'd been subverted, because of her long life—and it was natural, after all. But there *was* an agent—trying. When I get my hands on him . . . [Louder, to me.] Kimassu—are there other Delyens like you?"

It took me a heartbeat to understand him. "Yes. Rarely."

"Um—*hum.* At any rate, Kimassu, that life could be so much easier. Our technology protects us, feeds us, takes care of us. But that's not what I'm talking about. Our technology has given us a universe, Kimassu, a variety of worlds beyond imagining. You could make your wildest dreams reality. You want a world of water sports, we have them. Primitive or advanced. Democracies or autocracies or technocracies. Ah, Kimassu, you stand out among your people because of the color of your skin—don't flinch, darling, it's beautiful, silken soft, and lovely . . ."

I *hated* him then.

"We have a special name for people like you, did you know that? Flavistic. Fair but not completely colorless, like an albino." He grinned. "And how could we have the name if we didn't have the type. In our worlds they're *envied,* Kimassu. Do blonds have more fun? We're much more varied than you can imagine, Kimassu, because we've always chosen, as much as possible, our agents to be your physical type. But on our other worlds—variety rules. If you want a world of such mixtures and extremes that you would be lost in the crowds, that's easy. Do you want a world where you'd be worshiped, literally worshiped, because of the color of your skin? Kimassu, darling, love, don't you see? You don't have to be the odd one, the different one, any more!"

There was only one world I wanted, odd or different as I was there.

"You don't have to worry about what you'll live on, either," he was saying. "The Compact requires all local governments to supply their citizens with a Basic Allowance. It's more generous on some worlds than others, and some worlds require that you sign up for rotating labor, but there are plenty of words mechanized enough that you needn't lift a finger if you don't want. Just a life of ease and luxury and sophisticated entertainment. And if you want extras, there are universities—places of learning and knowledge, Kimassu—that would pay you to come and lecture there—just talk, darling—so that their students would understand your world better."

Ah-ha! I thought.

"Not because they are interested in your world itself, but because what they learn about your world will help them to deal with other worlds like yours in the future."

Double ah-ha!

His voice dropped. "Or you could have them all. Stay with me, Kimassu!" Then, lower, almost to himself. "Ironic, isn't it? The trapper trapped. The biter bit. Kimassu . . ." I understood and felt a flash of pity. Because I could walk away from him without a backward glance, indeed, with a happy relief. No, that is untrue. I had become mildly fond of him. Under the right circumstances, I might even have considered braving ridicule to add him to my household. He continued, coaxing, pleading, spreading out a universe of delights (all but one!) for my delectation. And then, "There are ranks above Admiral, Kimassu. A wise man, a shrewd man, a strong man, with the Fleet behind him; it's been done before, Kimassu. Time after time. A loose alliance into an Empire." He pulled me into his lap, kissed the palms of my hands. "An Empire. And you at my side, Kimassu. Mistress of the Galaxy! Mother of a Dynasty! Your children and mine, to rule a thousand—what's the matter? Kimassu? Darling? Kimassu!"

I had pulled away from him. "Liar!" I managed to choke through my rage.

He seemed to enlarge, like the dread Gruesome in the old tale, Grimalda and the three Weirds. His rage made mine seem as naught. "I offer you," he gritted out, "the *universe*. And you call me liar to my teeth! So be it, Kimassu! We have other drugs, besides the aphros, to make you more amenable. Of course, you won't—be—*Kimassu*—any longer. But still useful, darling. Very useul."

"You would have, no matter what I said," I spat at him. "Lie in one thing, lie in all. Liar! Who can trust a liar. I no longer recognize you, Gorky Admiral." I turned my back on him.

"Arrrrgh!" An animal growl of rage and—what? His hands gripped my shoulders, tight enough to cause pain; I allowed myself to show no sign. I couldn't prevent his turning me to face him; I could prevent my *seeing* him.

"Kali and Siva, you turn a man's blood to plasma . . ."

I didn't see him; he didn't exist.

"Kimassu . . ." His strength was so much greater than mine; it was futile and undignified to struggle, weaponless, against him. He forced my body against his, and I bent where his arms crushed. But I still stood stiffly against him.

He released me, and I straightened, to stare through him.

"Kimassu . . ." he repeated, and the rage-dark died from his eyes; they became a thoughtful glinting gray. "The problem is, Kimassu, my savage darling, that I want *you.* I find I don't want a docile puppet I control, delicious as that might be. I'm greedy, Kimassu; I admit it. I want it all. *All* of you, my fiery, difficult pagan. All. Sooooo . . ." His lips pursed. "What was I saying . . ." he murmured, his mouth tightening even more, like a net gathered in. "What did you misunderstand . . . what was I *saying* . . ." Then his face smoothed out. "Kimassu, Kimassu, we can do so much! What made you think we couldn't do *that!* Kali and Siva, darling, you've no idea of the tricks our medics can pull. Not the slightest conception!" He chuckled at that, though I didn't understand Terretz well enough then to see the double meaning. All I knew was what he had *said.*

No one had ever said anything outright, but I had always known I would never be Chosen. I knew better than to nurse the slightest hope in the innermost depths of my mind. *I would never be Chosen.*

And this male, this Terren, offered . . .

Could it possibly, possibly be true?

I was limp, marrowless, shocked half-senseless; I hadn't realized how bone-deep, soul-deep I had wanted what I knew I could never have.

What I could never have—*on Delyafam.*

I don't know if my knees gave way, or if he swooped first; but I was lifted in his arms; lifted and held tightly as he spun, round and round, a primitive dance of triumph. Round and round, until, weak and dizzy and helpless, I could only cling to him, eyes shut and trembling.

And he talked, how he talked, the words spurting out of him, a wild paean to his victory. "We'll start the dynasty with twins, eh, Kimassu! Boy and girl. You'll have to help me choose what they'll be like. Her like you, tall and lithe and limber and moving like a willow in the wind. And blond, I think. I must have blond recessives somewhere. Long blond hair and those lioness eyes of yours and that synthasilk snowy skin. And the boy—dark like me, say. Strong and dark. Shall we make him a hairy, too, or a smoothie Delyen?" One hand reached up to rub his chin, crushing me closer to his barrel chest. "Maybe before we decide, I ought to grow a beard—" His chuckles filled the small room, echoing and re-echoing. "I'll bet you've never seen a beard, Kimassu. They say being kissed by a beard is a whole new cxperience. How about it, Kimassu darling? Shall I grow a beard, so we can see if our sons"—oh, merciful Goddess!—"should have them?" His mouth moved against my neck, his breath was hot against my deathly chill, his voice suddenly low, so that I was straining to hear. "Our sons. Our children. It'll be fun watching them grow up, eh, Kimassu. Do your people mature at about the same rate as we do? So many things we still don't know, for all the years since we discovered your planet. We'll find them out together, my barbarian, my magnificent savage . . . Kimassu?"

"I recognize you, Gorky Admiral." But can I believe you? Oh, Goddess! Could I have . . . sprats? If I did, would they be accepted by the Terrene? (No need even to consider the Delyene!) Merciful Goddess, didn't the Terrene control their (I blushed even at the thought) breeding?

Even super-Delve strength has its limits. He collapsed, shaking with laughter, into one of those pop-out-from-the-wall seats. I, perforce, fell into his lap. He held me, stroking and petting, until I regained control of myself and began to pull away.

"You must believe me, Kimassu," he said simply. "How can I make you believe me?"

"You can't." I had seen too much Terre magic. And Terre fakery and hypocrisy. Better I didn't believe. Because if I did—the Limping Servitor Himself could devise no subtler torment.

"Suppose—suppose I prove to you that one thing I said was truth, pure truth. Would you be willing to take the rest on faith, at least for a while?"

"I don't understand."

"You will." Once again I went through the walkways of this strange Terre place. This time I walked (and rode a moving room) by myself, escorted by a single Terren, and wrapped in a voluminous cloak that hid me from the top of my head to the toes of my sandals.

I hadn't time for details as he hurried me along, just merest glimpses of strangely dressed and embellished people and almost people, of closed doors, of weird and wondrous Terre magics. The Gorky Admiral said nothing beyond directions and drummed his fingers impatiently when we sat on padded seats and the room moved instead of us.

We might have been back in the same corridor we started from, for all I could judge, when he placed his hand on the wall and a door opened and he gestured me in.

Charlie was within, dressed in strange, heavy silvery clothing that covered him from neck to heavy boots and thick gloves.

Another Terren, with fur an upswept torchflame of blue and silver, took one look at me and exclaimed, "Malthus, sir, I can't fit *her!*"

"It doesn't have to be a work-suit, Higgs," said the Admiral. "All I want is for her to be able to be outside for a few minutes. She isn't going to do anything, I just want her to be protected."

"Well-lll-ll." His face twisted into a ferocious scowl. "I guess—hmmmm . . ."

A few minutes later I was uncomfortably accoutered in a "suit" similar to Charlie's. Except that my knees were bent to fit in the short legs, and my arms not in the sleeves at all. Then the blue-furred Terren clapped a transparent vessel over my head. I jerked back, tried to get my hands squeezed up above the neck ring, to get the thing *off* before I suffocated.

"It's all right, Kimassu." I froze; the Gorky Admiral's voice, right in my ear, as though he were somehow inside the Terre clothing with me. "It's all right, all right, Kimassu." I shoved harder at the neck ring, managed to get the tips of my fingers past it.

"Kimassu, it's all right! Do you hear me, Kimassu?"

"I hear you Gorky Admiral."

"The suit holds air, those tanks—the things on your back, Kimassu, hold air, you've plenty and to spare." I relaxed. "If you could have seen your face!" he chuckled but there was relief in his voice. "My fault, I should have thought to warn you, but you take technology in stride, I didn't think . . . Now, listen, Kimassu, I want you to do what I say, exactly, no more and no less. I'm going to take you outside, Charlie and I are. To start with, you're not to touch anything inside your suit—you sure you've deadmanned it, Higgs?"

"Yessir." The other voice echoed oddly. "Everything's externalized or cut off completely. All she can do is walk and breathe."

"You hear that, Kimassu? You follow me; Charlie'll be behind you. Don't touch anything, inside or out of your suit—well, I guess you can't, but don't try. Walk carefully, keep your balance. These suits are right at their limit. If you fall in the ice, you could get a bad freezeburn before we could haul you out."

"I understand what you are saying, but not why."

"You will. Just move slow and careful. Charlie'll be right behind you, just in case. All set, Charlie?"

"Ready, sir."

"Follow me, then." Single file, we walked through a heavy door and into a small featureless room. Then we waited, I knew not for what, and then we went on through another, even thicker opening. It was darker in the new place, and I stumbled. A harsh light from behind lit my feet, and a hand gripped my arm long enough to steady me. And I looked about me. And I *saw*.

Once in Delyafam, I was in an underground cavern, and the light from my tuglenna reflected from myriad tiny glittering surfaces, uncountable jewel flashings. This surface was like that, light reflecting and sparkling. Beyond this strange stuff under our feet was a sea of dimness.

"Look *up*, Kimassu." I planted my feet firmly on this slightly slick stu hat must have been more Terre magic, and tilted my head up. And knew, then, why he had brought me here. This was a world, and it wasn't my world. The air push within was different, because this world was different. The sky above—wasn't my sky. The stars, so many, so bright, that in some places they merged into great glowing swaths of light.

And to my left—I turned to see it all. A great curved shape, a rainbow-banded giant that filled the sky and lit the horizon with a soft tammuz-shell radiance. It was *in the sky*—and it was monstrous.

I would not demean myself by asking—would it fall?

I couldn't tell how big it was, or how far away, or even if it were some new form of Terre magic. But it didn't belong in my sky!

"Kimassu."

"Yes, Gorky Admiral?"

"Do you know where you are?"

"I am a fathom away from you, Gorky Admiral." A snicker that must have been Charlie (though who could tell, with voices coming from within the suit I wore instead of properly, from their owners). I ignored it and went on. "Other than that, no, I don't know this place."

"Can you walk home from here, Kimassu?"

"No, Gorky Admiral." I could not suppress the amusement in my voice; he did not need to state the obvious. "I do not think I could walk home from here."

"Do you know what would happen if you tried, Kimassu?"

"I would die. Do people live at all in this place, Gorky Admiral?"

"No, Kimassu. Our base here is completely artificial; a little island of safety in a sterile, dead sea. There is nothing to support life here, not air nor water nor anything to eat outside the base and ourselves."

"I understand."

"Do you? If you walked away now, you'd be lost as soon as you couldn't see the lights from the base—and then you could keep on walking until your air gave out, and you died."

"Would you let me do that, Gorky Admiral?"

"Would you if I let you?" he countered.

"I thought perhaps that was why you brought me here."

He was made even huger by the loose, bulky suit, a formless shadow, a thing of menace. Featureless, so I couldn't read emotion except in his deep, husky voice.

"I brought you out here for two reasons. First, to convince you, thoroughly, completely that I spoke truth. You can't go home. You-can't-go-home!"

"I can't walk home. But you could take me, the same way you had me brought here."

He didn't bother to deny the accusation. "I won't. Don't torment yourself with futile hope, Kimassu. I *won't*. Your world is *lost* to you, you are lost to your people." He put a hand on my shoulder and I could feel heat burning through two layers of strange Terre cloth. "This is your choice, Kimassu. You can co-operate with me voluntarily, or I will have your mind ripped apart by drugs and probes and take what I want, anyway." The area under his hand was feeling hotter and hotter. Charlie murmured something I didn't understand and the Admiral snatched his hand away. Then he took a deep breath and continued. "And, no, Kimassu, I won't let you kill yourself or make yourself useless to me. I said I brought you out here for two reasons, but they're really one. I wanted you to know that I hadn't lied, and I wanted you to know how helpless, how dependent you are. You can't get yourself home, and you can't live unless I choose, or die, either, Kimassu. Even now, I control your suit. Try to run, and I'll just kill the servos in your legs and Charlie and I will carry you back into the base. All you'll get is a painful freeze-burn. Do you understand me, Kimassu? Do you believe me now?"

"The one thing I do not think you are, Gorky Admiral, is a fool." I spoke casually, to lull him. "And I really did not think you would offer me honorable death. What choice have I then? *Except the Four-faced Slut!*" As I spit the last out, I did two things: I eased my fingers above the neck ring, to try to force the fastenings apart, and I threw myself sideways, rolling into the sharp-edged darkness. The Gorky Admiral himself had checked the fastening of that headpiece twice after the other had put it on, so I knew it was important. And there was always the chance the Four-faced One would hazard a throw in this game.

Did I hear, echoing soundlessly in my ears, distant laughter?

Predictably, the Admiral was correct on all counts. I did not get away, they found me quite quickly; before I could loosen whatever held the helmet on. And I got the oddest burn of my life. It *hurt* and continued to hurt, and showed no signs of proper healing.

Also predictably, he was greatly enraged.

Charlie was cursing softly as he and the blue-furred one removed the stretchy Terre clothing from my back. It was no easy task; it was sticking. I sat stiffly, trying not to scream or faint; after my first horrified look, I had stared resolutely forward. The pain didn't upset me as much as the way my body seemed to be reacting to the queer burn—or rather, not reacting. I couldn't see how deep the damage went, but I had lost circulation, and there was an ominous green tint forming in the damaged area.

The Admiral was cursing, not softly.

Charlie muttered something, and the Admiral snapped, "I hope the flaming plasma it hurts!"

Since I didn't understand myself why this burn acted so oddly, I wasn't sure if the Terre magic could cure it. If the Gorky Admiral delayed long enough . . .

He didn't. In the middle of a complex curse he broke off with a gasp, sucked in a long breath, and howled something about warm up that flaming medic! He pulled me along. I struggled against three men's strength, until someone hit me right in the center of my back, and I passed out.

Not completely unconscious, but close enough.

They bundled me onto one of those wheeled padded platforms and into a hole in a wall. Inside was a rounded lid that clamped onto my table. I struggled up, and something took all my muscles away from me, so that I was helpless. Padded fingers arranged me and other tools poked and snipped and felt.

I had been here before, in a dream that perchance was no dream.

I was lying on my stomach, with my head turned to one side, and a reflecting surface came down and settled itself so that I could see my back.

So that I could see what was being done to my back.

There was no pain, and I didn't lose consciousness, until all the tools were sucked into the wall and I smelt a strange sweetish odor, and went into a deep healing sleep. When I awoke and staggered out, I was weak but whole, not even a scar to show.

Chapter Twenty

MOTTO:

But when the shell was broke,
Naught but emptiness lay within.

—*Lay of the Lady Minstrel*

It was the Gorky Admiral who guided me into a comfortable seat, wrapped clothing about me against the coolth, and placed a container of liquid in one shaking hand and supported it to my mouth. I sipped and felt strength flowing back into my muscles.

We were alone in this room with shiny walls and round faces with red darts moving in circles. I glanced around, straightening because I needed his support no longer. He moved away and stood, leaning against a chair, one booted foot resting on its seat. "Well, Kimassu . . ."

I wanted no misunderstandings. His hands were playing with something I could only get glimpses of, a cylinder with crowded-together Terre runes, striped red and black body. "You have a custom, Gorky Admiral," I said firmly, "a last cigarette, I believe it's called."

He sighed. "I can't trust you, Kimassu. You're too bright, you learn too quick, you're too determined. Sooner or later . . . you'd succeed, either in escaping or killing yourself. I can't allow that. I'm not going to kill you, Kimassu. That's the last thing I want to happen."

I set the empty container on the broad flat arm of the chair. "Aren't you?" My voice was gentle. "You disappoint me, Gorky Admiral. Am I to go free, then?"

"Kali and Siva, no!"

"Well, then. I would prefer my last cigarette now, if you don't mind."

He got red, and growled, sullenly. "You don't smoke."

"I enjoy other small pleasures." I looked him up and down, my glance lingering to make my meaning plain. "I would like one last—enjoyment—before I can no longer appreciate such things." He got redder, but said nothing, his hands continuing to juggle the ominous Terre magic. I shrugged. "So be it, then. Do what you will, Gorky Admiral. I will never willingly betray my people."

"You are a stubborn, thick-skulled, willful . . ." There was a persistent itch in the small of my back, and I scratched idly for it. His invective showed a certain amount of imagination, I thought, considering that Terretz was a rather dry tongue, unsuited to truly creative malisons.

Eventually he ran down. "The funny thing is, I think you meant it."

"I did mean it. I will never betray my people."

"Not that. The other. The last—cigarette."

"Oh yes, I meant that. I still do." I paused hopefully; he shook his head. I hissed. "If I hadn't a healthy respect for whatever Terre weapons you have—I said you were no fool, didn't I?—I'd try to rape you, Gorky Admiral."

He seemed obscurely pleased. "Despite what I've done for you, what I might yet do?"

"Oh, well." I shrugged. "I'd much rather you were one of my own boys, you know. But they're not here and you are." That he didn't like as well. I went on slowly. "I'm going to die. Not my body, perhaps, unless you're clumsy or careless, but I, the essential I, Kimassu, will cease to exist. And I want to *live*, to know I'm alive, to experience life in its most potent sense one last time." I let my voice deepen. "I know you, know your potential. And you know me. You're attracted to me, aren't you, Gorky Admiral—Lexi. It's not me you're fighting, it's yourself. You remember what pleasures we've had together and you wonder, can you risk one last time? Why not, Gorky Admiral, why not, Lexi, why not . . ." I spoke slower and slower, moved closer and closer. If I could just keep him distracted for those few vital seconds, I could flip him on his back, pin his arms, and have my "last cigarette"—will he, nill he. After, of course, would come *after*.

He shouldn't have refused me.

I almost made it.

"Kali and Siva," he exploded, jerking back. "Ahhhh—*would* you!"

I hesitated that fatal fraction, jumped anyway. But he was ready. We rolled about on the floor, but I couldn't pin his arms, couldn't get a knee between his legs, couldn't even (Goddess, he was strong!) hold him down for long.

He pulled away, got to hands and knees. "You—little—devil!"

I made a threatening lunge, but *something* appeared in his hand, so I subsided. It had been a good try.

"Well," I hissed, "you can't blame a Delyen for trying, now can you?" He scowled. "You can't say I didn't ask politely, first," I pointed out reasonably. He didn't seem to like that, either. "Buck up, male," I said impatiently. "It's a *compliment.*"

Suddenly, he saw something funny in it and started laughing. "You know, Kimassu," he managed to choke out, "I didn't quite believe you. You see, if a Terran woman had asked what you did, it would really be a plea for mercy, a sort of bribe, a way of getting me to change my mind. But you, you delightfully selfish witch, you meant it. You weren't thinking of me at all, you were thinking purely and simply of *yourself.*"

"Why should I be thinking of *you?*" I was genuinely perplexed. "Nothing's going to happen to you. As for changing your mind, aren't you a male of your word? What difference would a little pleasuring make? Except to me. I'd enjoy it."

He stopped laughing. "I believe you would," he said slowly. "Kimassu, if I were a—a male of your people, someone you'd met, how would you regard me?"

My back itched again, and I scratched more vigorously.

"You haven't answered me."

"That bracelet you gave me in the arbor, did you really make it yourself?"

"No."

"Can you make things at all, have you a talent, do you sing or play a gittern or lute, can you weave or dye or spin or knot a net? Can you—"

"Is *that* how you judge a man?"

"Well, I already know the other part of it. Your capabilities, as a male." When he didn't say anything, I went on. "Talents, looks, virility. They're all important, to me, at any rate. I know some Delyen who only care for a pretty face and a sturdy set of muscles, and some who wouldn't have a boy who wasn't skilled in some household duty, and some who swear that only *one* thing is important." I looked at him, judicially, and saw red rise beneath his brown skin. "You're not attractive, by our standards—" How could I tell him that lack of a crest made him seem sexless, despite evidence I had that he was anything but. "You've no talent or skill that I can see, no useful one on Delyafam, that is," I hurried on. "Well, you might be trainable as a guard, but— You're skilled and vigorous in your primary male function, but I've known better." He was so angry at that his mouth opened and shut, but all he could get out was a growl. I laughed loudly. "Don't you see. You're all wrong for my world, Gorky Admiral," I sobered. "Just as I'm ill-fitted for yours. The difference is, I'm in your world, not you in mine."

"No," he said softly, between his teeth. "The difference between us is that you're flaming attractive, despite that skinhead . . ."

I frowned. "And yet, you wouldn't submit to me . . ." As soon as I said it, I understood. I wouldn't submit to him, either . . .

Stalemate. No, he held all the weapons.

Not that it mattered. Soon, nothing would matter—to Kimassu.

Red and black, with runes of silver. There is a many-armed deeps-dweller, striped red and black so, whose sting is deadly. I doubted not, this one's sting was also deadly.

"Kimassu, would you accept a compromise?"

I hissed softly. One does not compromise with Leviathan.

"Listen, Kimassu, no questions, no secrets, you won't have to betray your people, not the tiniest bit."

I felt my eyes widening. He had what he wanted. I could not fight his simples, not deny him whatever he chose to take. "What *do* you want?"

"Two things." His lips stretched into a predatory grin. "You, for a start. All of you. Willing. In my bed, by my side. Mothering our children."

Still harping on our children. Ah, Goddess, this is torment! "Your simples . . ."

"Will force neither loyalty nor love. Don't worry, darling, I don't demand your love. Just time and opportunity to earn it." Something in his voice gloated; he had no doubts on that score, despite what I had said earlier. "What I want, Kimassu, is what I was talking about before. I want to be able to take you about with me, not to have to keep you penned here. I want you free, I want—there's a whole universe out there, Kimassu. One word, and I know you keep your word, it's one of the traits I admire most in you. One word, darling, and you can see it all. Thousands of wonders you can't imagine, you can't even dream exist. One word, Kimassu. Your word. That you won't try to escape, that you won't try to run away, or hurt yourself, that you'll be mine, stay with me, stay willingly with me."

"This willingness—this is so important to you that you'd leave me mindfree in return?" Ah, I was tempted. Dying is hard, hard. Especially the horror of minddeath.

He nodded. "In a way. I must be sure of you, Kimassu. Sure. If I drug you, hold your mind, then, yes, I'd be sure, as long as the drug lasted. But—I wouldn't have *you.* But if I could be sure of you without mindchains . . . if I could have *you* . . . if I could *have* you . . ."

It would be a favorable bargain for me. My loyalty—as long as it didn't conflict with my loyalty to my people. A small enough price to pay, in truth, for *myself.* My freedom, that was lost, he had convinced me of that. I was never going to escape this terrible Terre place by myself, he would never even permit me honorable death. So what remained, but make the best terms I could. This was naught but changing one prison for another, but, oh, to be out of tiny, enclosed rooms, to walk under the sky, to breathe salt air . . .

And the other that I couldn't even say to myself, the spr—the *children.*

I paced, and he watched as my feet measured out this small room's boundaries.

Until I remembered and stopped in front of him. "The other condition?"

"Do you agree to the first?"

"What moots it, do I or do I not, if I cannot fulfill the second," I snapped.

His lips stretched again into what I thought of as his predator grin. "I want someone."

I didn't hesitate. "No."

The grin stretched wider. "Not one of your people. I want the Gyrodden agent."

"The—*what?*"

"The Gyrodden agent. The one who's been filling your head full of stories. The one you call Neill."

"Neill? But Neill's one of your people, Neill's a Terren!"

"He's 'the enemy of my enemy,' you said it yourself, Kimassu. He's a traitor to his people, the flaming renegade, and I don't leave enemies or traitorous renegades running around loose. When I get my hands on him . . ."

I was startled into truth. "But I *can't.*" For a dozen reasons, from the fact that Neill was the Council's—and the *Goddess'*—to pure physical reality.

He exploded. "You mean you won't! Soooooo! The filthy scum! Was he—*good,* Kimassu? Lusty in your arms? You enjoyed him, didn't you! The filthy, foul, low, slimy *renegade* . . ."

The death in his hands came toward me, and I didn't struggle. I welcomed it. Better this way. Better than—the other. Goddess!

It didn't hurt, just the tiniest prick, like a nip of a winged nuisance. I didn't fall, didn't feel any strangeness, any loss in myself. He jerked it away, his face set. I tried to feel anger, but that was gone, too, only a wistful sadness, an exhaustion so great it was almost relief. So this was the end, and a fine fight I had made of it, but there is no dishonor in losing to overheavy odds. I had done my utmost, and that was all I could do.

"Kimassu." His face was gentle now, as though he too had passed through that struggle into peace.

"I hear you, Gorky Admiral."

"Why don't you sit down, make yourself comfortable?"

I obeyed. Why not? Why shouldn't my last few heartbeats—how long did this simple take to work?—be comfortable?

The chair was soft, and I seemed to sink into it. Yet

at the same time, I seemed to be floating, floating above it, rocking gently, as though I were on an almost calm sea, floating and rocking. Floating and rocking . . .

Tired, I was so tired, why not go to sleep, just drift off to sleep . . .

Floating . . .

Kimassu . . .

Floating . . .

Kimassu!

I split in two, part of me locked tight, floating on that placid sea, soothed and calm, the other, mindless, will-less, spoke, acknowledged. "I am Kimassu." (In that placid floating, a final, tiny flair of rebellion. *Be silent! This is betrayal!* And that rebellion itself silenced, sucked into that unnatural calm, the anima, the will, the very being of Kimassu held willing/unwilling in that soft, inexorable grip.)

Mumbles. Then, harsh, but not harsh enough to destroy that strange peaceful cocoon: You know the Gyrodden agent, the one you call Neill?

"I know Neill."

You know where he is now?

"No, I do not." (I didn't know; if Neill's patience hadn't lasted, he wouldn't be where I left him.)

Do you know where he will be any time soon?

"No."

Isn't he to meet you somewhere?

"No."

(More mutterings.) Kimassu, you must know where he is!

"I must know where he is."

(More mutterings.) Kimassu Lady, do you know where Neill is likely to be? (This voice was lighter, higher than the other.)

"Yes."

(The deeper voice.) Where is Neill?

"Neill is where he is."

Kimassu Lady, where is Neill most likely to be?

"He is most likely to be still on the island."

What island is Neill likely to be on?

"The island where I left him."

On and on, the questions went, until they had extracted bit by bit, that Neill was on an island, that I had left him on the island, that he would stay there until I fetched him or he got too impatient, that I had intended to return him to Swiftfaring as soon as it was safe.

When will it be safe? the deep voice asked.

"When he is no longer in danger from the Merwencalla Noblelady."

He is in danger from the—the Merwencalla?

"Yes."

But he is in danger no longer, you can get him. Where is he?

"On the island."

What island?

"The island he is on."

Has it a name?

"No, it is too small, it is nameless."

How do you get there?

"I will sail the *Eater*."

Over and over, the same questions. And always the same answer. I will sail the *Eater* to Neill. Neill is on the island. The island has no name.

(Another voice, then, thin but precise.) Who are you?

"I am the Kimassu Lady of the House of Morningstar."

How old are you?

"I was named when the cycle of the Orange Ganner coincided with the epicycle of the Emerald Nightghost."

What is your job?

(I was silent; I was unsure of the meaning of the Terretz word.) What are your duties, your responsibilities?

"I am Flail Consecrate of the House of Equity. I stand in the First Chorus at all major ceremonies." I continued to list minor duties until the voice stopped me.

Are you married?

(Again the Terretz word; this time I knew the Delye equivalent.) "I have a household."

What is your husband's name?

(Again I was silent.)

Who is your—your male companion?

"The Gorky Admiral." (More mumbling, a suppressed snicker.)

In your household, who is your male companion?

"Whoever is available, or has pleased me especially."

(Another discussion.) Name the members of your household.

I listed them, starting with Draxuus.
Which of these are male, which female?
"I have no wards at present."
(More discussion.) Name the male members of your household.
It was the same list as before.
She's making game of us!
No, Admiral, it's the cultural difference. She knows what the words mean, but they don't mean the same to *her*. She hasn't a job, she has duties. Ask her how old she is, she tells you when her nameday was. She isn't married, she has a household. Let's try something a little different. Kimassu Lady, do you know your numbers?
"Yes."
Let me hear them. Count for me.
"One, two, three . . ."
No, count in Delyetz. Tell me the numbers in Delyetz.
"Ima, dru, hee, pov . . ." I finished with *xax*, which means twelve.
And higher than *xax?*
"Figgu."
Which means, in Terretz?
"Many."
And higher than *figgu*, very high?
"Presh."
Which means?
"Uncountable."
You see, Admiral, anything higher than twelve is many or uncountable. So, you see. Kimassu Lady, how far is it from the Sacred Courts to the First Spaceport Enclave?
"Many days' sail."
How many?
(The question was meaningless; I said nothing.)
How many, all conditions most favorable?
(All conditions are never favorable.)
How many days' sail, deeper voice growled, to the island Neill is on?
"Not many."
How many, thinner voice asked, assuming a strong favorable wind?
"Four, perhaps five."
That's a great help!

Patience, Admiral. Now let's try direction.

But there they stuck. I can't tell direction without looking at the sky, without seeing the sun, and its angled light, or the night sky with Sunatra and Anatra and Kifa, the fixed star. I could, and they made me, give sailing directions, starting, assuming Sunatra is in the third quarter and Anatra is full and it is the second night of the cycle of the Azure Guilesinger . . .

My throat began to hurt, but they didn't stop until my voice thickened almost into unintelligibility, and then it was only a pause while something I was made to drink soothed my throat.

But finally there were no more questions and a voice said, "Sleep, Kimassu, sleep now, my darling." And I did.

A finger stroked my cheek, and a hoarse voice said, "How are you feeling?" I opened my eyes to the Gorky Admiral's face, so close I could see tiny red traceries in the whites of his eyes.

"I—I don't—" I stammered before I realized that the compulsion to answer was no longer on me. But such was my need I finished the sentence. *"Hungry!"* He propped me up and held something to my mouth and I drank greedily, a rich meaty broth that warmed my aching throat and filled my belly.

When the mug was empty I sat up, looked around. We were in the same room, the room with the medic and the round faces on the wall and the odd noises. And, miracle of miracles, I was still I, myself, Kimassu. Or was I? I remembered the sting that had made me will-less, the questions, the answers. Was I still Kimassu? Or the Gorky Admiral's toy, held on a long string until he decided to pull me in?

"Don't worry, Kimassu," he said. "All I gave you was a light dose, enough to make you talk. A little babbledose, that's all. I admit I couldn't be sure what the effect on you would be. It was a risk, and I took it. [I couldn't help smiling. A risk, he had said. A risk to whom?] Repeated treatments, I won't lie, Kimassu, repeated treatments could wipe your mind out. But I don't intend to repeat them. Unless . . ."

I turned the smile on him. I remembered the questions —and my answers. "Stymied, are you, Gorky Admiral? I can't tell you what you want to know. And you haven't much time, either, because I wouldn't want to guess how much longer Neill's patience will last. And once he tries to swim for it . . ." I twisted one shoulder, tightened my hand around my throat in a universal gesture. "But you don't want him dead, do you?" I went on shrewdly. "Or you'd just keep me here and *let* Neill commit suicide by trying to swim for it." A Delyen would have made it; but Neill was no Delyen. Still, he was brave and ingenious. He *might* make it. "Or are you just determined to make sure of him?"

"I am, I am." He grinned back at me, enjoying a joke I couldn't see.

"At least, you believe me now. I *can't* tell you."

"No, you can't tell me, Kimassu. But you can take me."

I said nothing.

"You can *take* me."

Chapter Twenty-one

MOTTO:

O furl for me the scarlet sail,
Or furl the black, the gray;
O furl for me the swiftest sail,
To reach Calamity Bay.

—Variations of this verse present in many ballads and sagas

He was a much better sailor than Neill. Perhaps it was instinctive; he told me he had never sailed in a small boat before. And I—I was ecstatic! I sailed that clumsy tow with its jury-rigged mast like the *Eater* himself. Not even the ominous wristlet on my left wrist could dampen my enthusiasm. I was home! Home!

He laughed loudly at my so obvious pleasure, and I sang, that high triumphant trill which is the Delyc way of showing joy.

"Wish I'd thought to bring along a 'corder," he said suddenly. "I'd like to keep you like this always, your cloak billowing out behind, my mistress of wind and wave."

I trilled again. "Be there a better world than this, of all your many, Gorky Admiral?"

He shook his head. "Not at the moment."

"Then why not stay? There are many isles here where two could live in ease. Why not let both our worlds struggle along without us?"

His teeth gleamed white in the bronze face. "You tempt me, darling. You really do. You'd almost be worth it, giving up a universe for. Almost." He chuckled gently "But not quite. Besides, why should I? I'm going to have both!" His voice sobered. "You're not getting cold feet, are you, Kimassu?"

"Cold feet?" I looked down, and he laughed.

"You've still a little fondness for your Neill?"

"Oh, more than a little," I admitted, "although he angered me more and oftener than anyone I've ever known—except, perhaps . . ." My voice trailed away.

He only laughed again, and said that made us even.

He was a good passenger. He had brought food, odd little blocks that he called concentrates, which tasted like eating nothing, but filled you up after a few bites, and a water jug that he called a purifier, which could be filled from the sea and then shook, and the water that poured out was sweet.

He asked many questions, but they were innocuous enough. Is that good to eat; what is the name of that bird; does it get much hotter here?

I answered, I can eat it, but other Terrene have gotten stomach cramps; that bird is a ganner; yes, it gets hotter, but we usually rest during the noonheat unless it's a real emergency.

We nooned on a small island, swimming, eating, lazily making love and sleeping through the worst of the heat.

He took my word on what was safe to eat, but if I honestly said I didn't know, he had a device called a tester that he placed small scraps in, and then ate or not, according to the color of a light that flashed. One nooning he let me play with it, and I put various tiny scraps into it, much interested to see which were accepted and which rejected.

Slyly I put in a bit of dead webbing from between my toes. It was acceptable, just as I had suspected.

But he had seen me do it. He bit a fragment of skin off the end of his own finger, too. "You see, darling, it doesn't tell me what I should eat, just what won't make me sick." Another grin. "Nice to know that neither of us is poisonous, isn't it?"

On the third day, I saw what I had been hoping for, a Tribe of Wild Cousins. I had, indeed, been beginning to worry. At this season, I should have seen them sooner, taking a deep-water route as I had—unless the Terrene had poured something out and ruined the schools in this area.

"What are those?" the Gorky Admiral gasped, seeing the huge backs higher than the waves.

"They will not harm us, Gorky Admiral," I soothed him.

"Harm? They'll capsize us if they get too close!"

"No, they won't. The Wild Cousins are friends; they'll be careful." I trilled greetings and heard a chorus of answering hoots, slow and mournful.

"Foghorns," the Gorky Admiral muttered, looking gray under his tan.

It was not a Tribe I knew; nonetheless, I trilled again, steering the tow, despite muttered curses from my passenger, closer to the Tribe.

Suddenly a pair of long-arms came aboard, childishly slender, and accompanied by a very young treble hoot.

"No," I snapped, seeing a weapon appear in his hand. "It's a youngling, never seen a Delyen before. She's just curious!" I went to the side of the boat, showing myself to the youngling, whose oval amber eyes were no larger than my head. Just then one of the elders rushed up, hooting rapidly. I trilled back, and allowed the tip of the long-arm to fondle my body.

"The suckers on that thing," he muttered.

"Easy," I warned, while trilling to the adult.

I made the Cousin repeat back to me. I wanted to be sure she understood—and was willing. She was, although much perplexed at my strange request.

A third long-arm slid aboard. The Gorky Admiral was watching the youngling so suspiciously he hardly noticed what her elder was doing, until it was far too late.

The long-arm took me and we dove. Down, down, far faster than I could have swum myself, so fast that red light was gone in a blink. Down into a blue-green world and deeper, into a velvet darkness. Her arms were firm but not tight.

And still we went down, until the sides of the Cousin began to glow with their own soft light, a warning to the deeps-dwellers that the Queen of the seas was paying them the honor of a royal procession. And Queen indeed she was, the Wild Cousin, second only to the Empress of the deeps, Leviathan herself, mistress of Death and Life.

It was almost amusing to see the stir we made, in

her sea-gem light. Stilt-walkers scrabbled desperately along the bottom ooze, flatwings heaved themselves out of concealment and flapped ponderously along the rough bottom, their great slow beats blowing up clouds of bottom muck, fouling the crystal water. Lure-fish, their lighted bait a mass of glowing wriggling wormlike palps in front of maws lined with stiletto fangs fled away as quickly as placid sieve-mouths, with the fringe of feelers around mouths filled with thin, flexible cartilege spines.

Some were not quick enough. The Cousin Lady was not going to have her dive just for my convenience. As we skimmed along the bottom, all but one of her two dozen arms were at work. Nor was her passenger neglected. I was offered a claw as long and thick as one of my own legs. The pattern on the shell was strange, but the meat within was sweet and juicy. I ate rapidly but carefully, not knowing when the wristlet would sting me, not knowing how long I would remain helpless, not knowing how long I had of freedom . . .

So many ifs . . . if the Wild Cousin could remember everything . . . if the Terre magics could be confused by the same depth oddnesses that confused our click sense . . . if the wristlet didn't carry death instead of sleep . . . if . . . if . . . if . . .

He did none of the things I expected. The wristlet did not sting me into helplessness. Nor was I drawn back to him by some invisible chain. (Perhaps he feared I would be torn in two between such and the strength of the Wild Cousin.) Nor was I left free, the wristlet a guide to fool me into betraying Neill.

He came after me himself. I was amazed. I knew how clumsy Neill was in the water; I had expected the Gorky Admiral to be about the same. I hadn't allowed for Terre magic. I saw the light first, coming from above, harsh and white, instantly recognizable as unnatural. The Cousin was busily feeding, but a couple of clicks told me the light-bearer was Delye-sized, and coming down *fast*.

There was only one thing to do, and I did it. I clicked the one code even the Cousins respect: *Leviathan!* For a dreadful heartbeat I thought she would drag me along (Death from Leviathan would have been quicker—and kinder) but then I was rolling free, caught in the backwash of her panic flight, twisting along the bottom, half-choked by the muck she stirred up. I was flung toward a monster two-shell, its back thick-crusted with a myriad of tiny relations, all sharp and jagged. A frantic effort, and I was swimming free, out of the ooze, higher into clearer, deep blue water, dark except for the lights of occasional swimmers.

It was too deep, I couldn't see; I couldn't trust clicking, there were anomalies in my returning clicks that could have hid Leviathan herself. I swam upward, into the shadow zone, hoping to be below most surface predators and above the bottom walkers.

I didn't make it. He had a device that shot him through the water far faster than I could swim and the wristlet for his guide. To my surprise, he dragged me back down to the depths, and we hung there, despite my futile, incredulous fury, until it pleased him allow us to swim higher and repeat the whole nonsensical performance.

I struggled the fiercer for knowing that I had already been down in the cool depths for some time and too long in the coolth can be dangerous. But somehow—his magics again—the water around us was warm, and I stopped worrying—about the coolth.

When we got back to the surface finally, the tow was nowhere in sight or click.

"Well, Kimassu"—he spat water from his mouth and pushed the face-shield up onto his forehead—"where did your friends take the boat?"

I didn't say anything. I had told the Tribe to swim away, fast, as soon as I went over the side of the tow. Hopefully, they had. But the tow had drifted while we had been underwater; for that matter, so had we. I sighed. Even a Delyen has her limits. We were a good day's sail from the nearest land, a scattered group of small islets called the Consort's Seed; they were small and separated enough that we could swim through them without realizing it.

He repeated his question.

"The Goddess alone knows," I said, "where Her currents have taken it. I hope you feel like swimming." I pushed myself away from him and studied the sky, hoping to get my bearings.

He was looking at one of those magics of his. "I acquit

you of one thing," he said. "Your large friends are nowhere near the boat."

If that piece of arrant nonsense was his idea of a peace offering, I wasn't interested. "If we don't get started, we'll never reach land."

"Land? The boat's much closer."

"Yes, I'm sure it is, but I know where the land *is*."

"And I know where the boat is." I searched his face with care; that nonsense of coming up slowly . . . could he have gotten sunstruck? His idea of where the boat was, I decided, had better coincide with my idea of where land was.

But I couldn't outswim him; I couldn't dive and hide from him. It would have been an interesting struggle between us, except that with a grin, he took one of his magics from the wide belt and tossed it a little away from us. Goddess! I dove, thinking only to put clean water between myself and *that!* He hauled me back, though my desperate struggles made us surface some distance away from where an amber body now rested quietly in the trough of a wave.

"It's only a—blummph!" One of my elbows caught him in the mouth, bringing him to a spluttered stop. I thrust out and swam away; whatever that golden terror was, it wasn't eating *me*.

He grabbed again, but he didn't have enough arms to hold me and guide us toward the Monster. As soon as I wriggled free, I swam away again. I wasn't sure what a safe distance was, but if he wanted to play games with a Monster, he could play them and welcome. Alone.

It was humiliating that he could pace me so easily, but I didn't care, as long as we were heading in the right direction. That is, away.

"Boat, Kimassu!" About the third time he shouted the same message, it penetrated. Boat? From where? How could . . . Terre magic, again! I hesitated, risked a quick click back. It wasn't chasing us, just lying quiet. I angled so that I could twist my head and see it. A boat? It really wasn't as big as it had seemed in that first horrified glance, when it was thrashing about and swelling larger and larger like a sun-struck blowfish.

It *was* a boat, though like none I had ever seen. It was made all in one piece of some thin gold substance that was rigid in places and somewhat flexible in others. The prow was pointed, but the stern was squared off; the seats were humps in the flat bottom of the hull. It took (I must admit) some time for him to coax me into the thing, and by then the sun was down and the night sky darkening—and I was scanning the nearby water hungrily.

A small, clawed stalk-eyes in molt floated by, and I dived for it.

"Kimassu," he was shouting, as I began swimming back to the Golden Horror with my frantically struggling prize. "Kali and—watch out!" I tossed it into the boat before hauling myself in, and he hadn't known enough to dodge. I pulled myself in just in time to see him jerk it off his calf, along with a generous gobbet of flesh, and throw it back into the water. I turned to go after it, and he yanked me roughly back onto the bottom of the boat.

"Curse you, that was mine!"

"It bit me!"

"More fool you, for letting it!" No use trying again for it, it was long gone. As I said, we Delyene need to eat a lot.

He slapped me, hard enough to knock me sprawling into the space between the seats.

For long heartbeats, I lay stunned, then I reached up and felt blood. Now this was something I could understand. All his talk of worlds and empires—and sprats, that was that. Talk. But a slap, that was real. I was too angered to care about formalities, to care about the near obscenity of dueling with a male on his own behalf, instead of as some Lady's champion. "Accepted," I gritted. "Land or water?"

Puzzlement drove anger from his eyes. "Land . . ."

I blinked acknowledgment. "Land it is, then." For the first time I remembered that I had been allowed no weapon. "And I choose Open." And if he had a shred of honor, he'd either give me back my knife or throw his own away. And if he didn't, I was going to kill him *anyway.*

"Open? Open *what?*"

I turned my back on him. "I'll speak to you again, at the proper time, on the field."

"Field? What field? Where?"

Ignorant male! "You chose land. The closest land is that way." I pointed.

"I said, we're going back to your boat."

The chances of currents joining the two craft were small; we were far more likely to drift toward land. I didn't see anything resembling oars or oarlocks, or a sail. So it wasn't worth arguing over; the Goddess would send us where She willed.

Except suddenly we were moving, slowly at first, and then fast, and then faster than the freshest wind could bear us. I turned. He was seated on the back bench, his hand resting on a slender rod extending back over the stern. I moved carefully back, to peer over the stern. Naught to see but wave and froth. He said something that I didn't understand. He wasn't heading for the nearest land, but it mattered little. At this speed, we would get *somewhere* very soon.

Truth to tell, I was becoming bored with Terre magics. And I was tired, too. I curled up between two of the benches. Despite the spray splashing into the boat, it was uncomfortably dry.

"Kimassu . . ." His voice was close. I opened my eyes; he was bending over the bench, his face a bare palm-width from mine. So who was steering this Golden Impossibility? Answer: It didn't need to be steered. Corollary: This was the secret of the Terre enigma. Too much magic made life dull; they were simply *bored.*

Content, I shut my eyes.

"Kimassu, I'm sorry."

I couldn't have heard him correctly. I opened my eyes, stared. His finger stroked my swollen, tender lip. "I'm sorry, I never meant to—I always have had a rotten temper. I am sorry, Kimassu; it won't happen again. I promise."

I could feel my lip curling. He was apologizing. He was afraid. Not of punishment; there was no way I could enforce normal punishment for disobedience, and he knew it. He was afraid to meet me in honor. . . . Under such circumstances, I had no wish to stain a clean blade on him. "The fault was entirely mine," I assured him. And it was. I should never, no matter what the provocation, have recognized him, given him status. It is always a mistake to advance any being beyond her capacities, and the Gorky Admiral (Pah! That meaningless Terre honorific!) was, after all, merely a male. I should simply have used him, slaked my simple forced need, and gone on. I should never have encouraged him, in any way. I had fired his ambition: the fault was, indeed, entirely mine.

". . . clawed thing came flying at me . . ." he was saying, and then, the meaning of what I had said penetrating, he stopped his harangue. "What did you say?"

To oblige him, poor limited creature, I repeated, "The fault was mine."

He blinked. "Well, yes, you shouldn't have thrown that thing at me, but that doesn't give me the right to haul off and slam you like that, I mean . . ."

"You make much over little. The fault was mine, I have acknowledged it. The matter is closed." Creatures act according to their natures. If you thrust your foot into a daggertooth's maw, you have no one but yourself to blame for what you draw back.

Animals have no concept of honor—or responsibility.

"I have the funniest feeling," he was talking aloud, to himself, not to me, "that I have just made the worst mistake . . . and I don't even understand . . ." His voice trailed into nothingness.

I looked out over the pointed bow. If he wanted to hold conversations with himself, I was willing to indulge him.

"Kimassu, look, darling, please understand. I wish it hadn't happened, I—would you wipe it out, make it like it never happened. I'm *sorry* it happened, do you understand?"

"I understand you perfectly." Of course he regretted it. He had never meant to challenge me, or rather, he had meant to, and then lost his nerve. Poor weak creature. Ambition, aspiration, had driven him beyond his capacity. And I—I was at fault, for encouraging him to think himself my equal. Which he never was and never could be. But my recognition of him had been a goad, urging him on . . . I patted him on the shoulder. "Content yourself, Gorky Admiral." He still seemed unsure, distrait. "Can this craft of yours that grew from naught steer itself with no sure hand on the helm?"

"Oh, sure, it's locked onto a homer on your boat. Won't be long now."

"Long?"

"Before we reach your boat."

"Oh? With this magic craft of yours, need we it?"

His lips stretched. "The whole purpose of this jaunt was for you to sail me. Can you navigate with this boat?"

"I—I don't know. It goes so fast. Can you slow it to normal sail?"

His shoulders moved in a shrug. "Probably. But all our supplies are in your boat. We can get mighty hungry and thirsty in this heat."

Well, *you* can, I thought. Especially if you throw away perfectly good food. I, on the other hand, can live off the sea. And drink out of it, too. But perhaps the Gorky Admiral merely *preferred* sweetwater . . .

Chapter Twenty-two

MOTTO:

"Fair" is the dirtiest four-letter word I know.

—Sayings of Neill

"You know," the Gorky Admiral said, searching carelessly among the lilili for the pale pink ovals he liked best, "I'm rather glad you tried to escape yesterday."

I said nothing. The sun was high, and the only tree on this little island gave piteous little shade. I had draped my cloak in the lowest branches, but I was still scrunched up most uncomfortably. I envied him his brown skin, shimmering in the clear hot light. He was stretched out on a thin cover, as though to absorb all the sun he could. When one got accustomed to it, brown was as handsome a shade as orange, and his warm smooth skin covered a generous amount of hard muscle.

"For two reasons," he went on. "First, because I knew you'd try; you wouldn't have been you if you hadn't. So now I can stop anticipating it. And you know you can't get away with it, and I can stop worying about it."

He popped a small oval in his mouth and chewed juicily.

"When I was but new adopted," I said, "I served as a 'prentice to a revered Noblelady, and I spent many seasons on a far, cold isle. And one day I found a ganner—a bird—on the rocky shore, its wing broken and useless. It was dying. I picked it up, and it clawed at me, its eyes flashing red flames. But it was still a handsome thing, brave and gallant and—free. I'd seen them often enough, riding the wind. Couriers of the Goddess, the old legends call them, and other things, besides. I took this one back with me, and mended its wing, and cared for it. Many the night I spent wakeful, caring for it, and I fed it bit by bit, hour after hour, day after day."

"And," he prompted when my voice trailed off.

"It almost died, but then slowly, its spirit drew back from the path, and it began to thrive. And then, one day, I found it battering blindly against the walls. It flew at me and savaged me. I managed to catch it in my cloak, and I ran with it, struggling frantically against my breast, until I was out-of-doors and could let it go. It flew away, never once looking back."

Again the silence, broken only by the muted roar of the surf and the sad keening of an unseen lizard.

"The Noblelady scolded me for my sorrow. 'What are you to the ganner, now that it's healed,' she said. 'Had it stayed with you, it would no longer have been a ganner. Did you really want that?' "

He laughed, a harsh sound. "Perhaps the tamed ganner would have been improved, better. Perhaps you you would have gloried in your prize. Perhaps you set it free too soon; perhaps it would have grown accustomed to you, even learned to love you. You didn't give it a proper chance, Kimassu."

"*Perhaps*—" I showed my teeth. "I prized the wild, handsome creature in its own element. Besides, it would have flown away, sooner or later, anyway."

"Not if you clipped its wings."

If you clip a ganner's wings, they beat their heads open on the nearest hard object, rock or wall or whatever. A clipped ganner is a dead ganner.

The Admiral flipped over onto his back and lay naked to the sun. But his pile of magics was in easy reach. "Crazy world," he mumbled, "where even the birds are part fish." He tilted his head slightly to stare at me out of squinty eyes. "You want to stretch out, I can set up the tent easy enough."

"No, thanks." I was almost full; I hesitated, then pawed through the diminished pile of lilili.

"Hey, that's a color I've never seen."

I held it in my hand, a rich, vivid maroon, its skin velvet soft against my palm. "I like these, and they're not common."

He propped himself on one elbow, to see it better. I had already noted his somewhat greedy appetite, especially for new or unusual sensations.

"I'll give you half," I said and took a generous bite, leaving slightly more than the promised half, and handed it to him.

"Thanks."

"Test it first."

"No need, I tested some of the others. They're all off the same vines."

I made a grab for it, and chuckling, he shoved it toward his mouth. *"Test it, I said."* He froze, the lilili almost in his mouth, the juice dribbling over his fingers. I was ready to fight him for it, and he saw my determination.

"Fuss, fuss," he grumbled, but somehow, he seemed pleased. "All right, if you insist." He put the tiniest scrap into the tester, and the magic made a deep humming sound. He turned it so I could see the white light. "There now, satisfied—or did you just want it back?"

I leaned back, scratching casually against the rough trunk. "You Terrene are so messy when you're sick."

He took a bite, chewed, swallowed. "Did one of these make Neill sick?"

I frowned. "I can't remember. Lots of foods made him sick. He didn't have a magic like yours. He said, if he got sick, that was the price he had to pay." I hissed suddenly, remembering. "The only thing he wouldn't try was a Bacqua. He said everyone had to draw the line somewhere, and his was there."

"Umph." He was licking juice off his face. "What's a Bacqua?"

"A water-dweller, no skeleton, round and dark pink, lots of dangling, stinging arms, and you can see through them."

"Soft?"

"Yes. You have to cut the stingers off the arms, or they make you sick."

"Glad to hear there's something you can't eat, even if it's only jellyfish stingers. Does the rest taste good?"

"To a Delyen."

"Catch one then, and *I'll* give it a try. 'Kay?"

"Um. I think I would like the tent set up now. And

you'd better come under it, too. No use getting a sunstroke."

He grinned, and I knew what he was thinking. "It's too hot to do anything but sleep," I pointed out, adding, "It'll be cooler later." Both statements were true, so why had his grin widened? Did he really think he had tamed his ganner? The long scratches on my arms and legs I had gotten searching for the lilili itched; automatically I started to scratch and restrained myself with an effort. He saw my movement and offered a salve from his kit, but I refused. The scratches are harmless, and they stop itching fairly soon—if you don't scratch them.

"Now she tells me," he moaned. His own arms were covered with long red weals, evidence that he had been scratching vigorously. I didn't say anything. I had told him I could gather the fruit better alone, but he had insisted on coming along. Fire-fans, those delicate animals that live in colonies at the base of the lilili, their shells forming a broad lacy fan, are but one of the dangers of the reef, and a minor one at that.

(Oddly enough, he had been amazingly agile in the frondy labyrinth of the lilili. When I commented on it, he grinned and said simply, "My monkey ancestry." Then his lips pursed, and he stared at me speculatively for long heartbeats before saying, "Say, those funny seaweed trees whose tops stick out over the waves—do they ever come up onto the land?"

("Most usually," I replied. "This is a young grove, but barely started. Maychance its landward part has been torn away by a sea wave, or a great wind. A mature grove may cover a large part of an island, or even a whole island, or a very large grove can spread over a chain of islands, and grow high and thick enough that a climber in the upper fronds could not say if it were land or water at the base."

("*Ah-huh.*" He nodded to himself, as though I had answered a question he had not asked, as well as the one he had.)

It took no time at all to set up the tent. Like the boat that grew out of nothing, it was a tiny thing that fitted neatly into the hand. But when you pressed a scarlet spot on one edge, it began unfolding, until you had a large three-sided, black-and-gold-striped canopy. When you were through with it, a twist to a scarlet-patched corner made it fold itself back into a tiny lump again. Plastic with a double memory, he told me. At any rate, it kept off the heat of the sun, and we were soon stretched out asleep under it.

I knew something was wrong as soon as I woke up. I think it was the breathing, not deep and even, but ragged and gasping. Rough but not labored. I sat up, noting that the sun was low, and a cool, salt-tanged sea breeze was blowing. "Gorky Admiral? Lexi?"

Nothing. I touched his shoulder gently, then shook it harder. "Lexi, Lexi, what's wrong? Are you all right?" He had been sleeping on his side, his back turned to me. Hesitantly, I shook a little harder, and he flopped on his back, his arms sprawled crookedly, his eyes still shut. But he wasn't asleep, his breathing wasn't the slow even tones of sleep. I slowly turned up one eyelid.

It was truly amazing how much hate and fury could shoot out of one dark eye.

I smiled, very slowly, and sat up, crossing my legs so that I was most comfortable.

"You know, Lexi"—my tones were mock solicitous, but, oh, how I was relishing every syllable—"I do believe that you were foolish enough to scratch yourself on fire-fan, and then eat dark lilili. You know, I really do think that's your problem." I scratched luxuriously on a long score on my arm. "It's an odd thing, but fire-fan venom and dark lilili don't mix very well. I don't know why, but it's true. Not all the lilili, mind you, just the dark ones. Of course, lilili and fire-fans often grow together, so—they're each rather harmless alone, you see, but if you mix them . . . You do have a problem, don't you, Lexi, *darling?* Of course, you Terrene do have a saying, about turnabout being fair play." He was making a series of desperate whining noises; could he have talked, threats would have been pouring from him; but he couldn't. He was completely and totally paralyzed. Which is what happens to anyone who mixes fire-fan venom and dark lilili. Unless . . . "A pity you didn't eat the horn-shell, Lexi. I told you to, didn't I? The horn-shell undoes whatever the lilili does that makes the fire-fan venom so much worse." Definitely, there was threat in those breathy whimperings. "*I* ate the horn-shell, and very delicious I found it, too. And it is a protection against the lilili, as you didn't know. *Pity* you didn't know. Of course, it makes the fire-fan itch so much worse, but that's a small price to pay, wouldn't you agree, Lexi?" I hissed loudly. I hoped the thought of what he was going to do to me *later* was a solace to him, poor limited male. It was the only solace he was likely to have for quite some time. "Oh, that's right," I went on. I really shouldn't have, but I was owed some indulgence. "Your magic Terre tester told you not to eat the horn-shell, didn't it? Said it would make you sick, didn't it?" I hissed again. "That's a very ignorant magic, you know. I wouldn't trust it myself. But if you choose to, that's your choice, isn't it? You wouldn't have believed me if I'd told you to eat the horn-shell, would you? You could have; horn-shell won't make you sick if you eat it with dark lilili. They undo each other, you see. You don't get sick, and you don't get paralyzed from the fire-fan venom, either. You will know better, next time, won't you, Lexi?"

I got to my knees, which meant my head brushed the peak of the canopy, and pulled on my cloak. "The trouble with your magic, Lexi, is that you Terrene depend on it instead of using your heads. You've been here long enough to know that the reef dwellers who live together often have poisons that work together. But you didn't ask, and you depended on a magic that can't think . . . This is our world, Lexi, *ours*. Remember that." I gathered his magics together and dumped them into one of the net bags I had used to put the fruits of our diving in.

At the opening of the tent I hesitated and then came back. "You know, Lexi," I said, holding him very lightly at his most vulnerable point, "there are one or two things I ought to do before I leave." He stopped breathing. "You've been a very bad boy, and you should know by now what we do to bad boys." I pinched slightly. His chest heaved but no sound came out. "But without your magics, you've only one talent that I can see, minor though it is, and it would be a pity to spoil it. Besides . . ." Besides, you're not really a foe worthy of my blade. I could have done this any time, but you do have this talent; I flatter myself I've even improved it a trifle, and I enjoyed the holiday. "I could kill you," I went on, "but you should have hostage value." I pinched once more, hissing contentedly, backed slightly to get out from under the canopy, and stood up. "Be a good boy until I get back," I admonished. As if he had any choice!

Something flashed in his eyes then. There was threat, yes, but also, defeat, horror, hopelessness. A lot to read, perchance, in a pair of eyes. But I understood.

I had been there myself.

Perhaps, turnabout isn't always fair play.

I remembered, worse than the helplessness had been the not knowing.

"Lexi," I said gently, "the venom wears off. You don't even need to worry about whether or not I'll give you the antidote. There is no antidote, none is needed. Your paralysis will wear off naturally, but not," I smiled, "before I've carried out a few plans of my own. For now, Lexi, darling, you can—meditate."

I was trilling happily as I went down the rough rocks to the pebble beach. My plans were simple enough. All of Lexi's magics were going into the sea. Then I would take him to another island, just as I had taken Neill. And if his people offered enough—like perhaps the withdrawal of all Terrene permanently from Delyatam—I would even tell them where he was. If not, and I really didn't think I could win my war so easily, he would stay there indefinitely. He wouldn't starve, and it would do his character a great deal of good.

Chapter Twenty-three

MOTTO:

What news, what news, sweet laddie,
What news do you bring to me?
What news of my dearest sister,
From the furthest edge of the sea?

Dire news, dire news, brave lady,
Dire news do I bring to thee;
Dire news of mighty Leviathan,
And your sister from over the sea.

—*Ballad of the Bonny Laddie and the Lorn Lady*

We had sweetened our meal with an assortment of shelled creatures; among them had been a doublecurl. I searched the empty shell from our leftovers, cleaned it hastily at the sea edge, and blew long and loud over the water.

No answer; I blew again, and again.

I was almost desperate when I finally heard an answering hoot, faint and mournful. I swam out to meet, not the Tribe as I expected, but a single Cousin. She explained quickly, though I found it difficult to believe. The Tribe was being stalked—by Leviathan!

Now this is passing strange. Leviathan courses through our lives, Mistress of Death, a disastrous natural force conquering all unfortunate enough to lie in its path, formidable, unassailable by its size. But I had never heard of one deliberately *chasing* potential victims. No, Leviathan quarters our seas, eating all in its path, from tiny shrimp to the Cousins themselves. But it does not chase; it cannot. It simply eats, eats, eats its way through the waters, leaving sterility behind until the fertile sea replenishes.

But this one, were the Cousin not merely panicky (and small blame to her if she were!), had fastened herself on the Tribe like a (what was the story Neill had told, about a Terre goddess-messenger called a Fury, a Nemesis?) like the Wrath of the Goddess Herself.

The Cousins have long since evolved tactics, techniques, to avoid Leviathan. With warning, mature members of the Tribe can outswim Leviathan, but oldsters and younglings are not so fortunate. Without warning, without scent or a lucky click, a Tribe can be devastated.

But this Leviathan *harried* the Tribe.

I liked it not one whit.

Not merely because I had counted on the aid of the Tribe.

The Leviathan as mindless destroyer of the seas was plague enough; but what evil could an intelligent Leviathan accomplish.

I had to do something, and I had little enough margin of time to do it in.

We rode the Cousin to join the Tribe. Her fin was covered with a scabby growth and I padded it with a blanket. But somehow, though he was still paralyzed and could not speak, I did not think Lexi enjoyed his ride.

I had decided on a plan. I discussed it fully with the Matriarch of the Tribe. It was risky and dangerous, and would take most precise timing; but if it succeeded, this particular Leviathan would trouble us no longer.

When I was a youngling, we played together, as younglings will. One favorite game was a simple one called Chase. One player, the Catcher, ran or swam after the others. The first one she caught became the new Catcher. Normally, the game was only exercise, fun. But sometimes, if for some reason the younglings wished to punish the Catcher, or merely be cruel, as younglings can be, the Catcher would not change quickly, instead the Catcher-victim would be teased into frenzy. This would be done by the other players banding together, allowing the Catcher to chase one, and when that one began to tire, another would dash between the Catcher and the tiring one, luring her into chasing a fresh target.

Others would beckon, just out of reach. Confused, frustrated, furious, the luckless Catcher could be tormented into exhaustion.

Younglings are most often cruel to those who are different. I had played Catcher most futilely in my time.

The Tribe was going to play Chase with Leviathan. But the stakes in this game were the highest possible: Life—and Death.

I watched the game begin. I had never been so close to Leviathan before. She has a smell, faint but unmistakable, warm and rich, with just a hint of rot. Like a ripe lanna left a little too long in the sun.

I rode the Matriarch herself. I worried somewhat, because, intelligent as the Cousins are, they do not think in the same manner as we Delyene, and misunderstandings are always possible. One Cousin was overbold and I urged the Matriarch to order her away, but it was too late. She misjudged her margin of safety and paid the penalty. The Matriarch couldn't understand my anger. The Tribe was at stake, and such overboldness could someday endanger the Tribe; such a one was best spared.

She dropped me on the island I had chosen and I began to climb the cliff face. It was a hard climb, tricky in the dimming light. When I reached the top, I examined the lagoon within. Yes, it was as I remembered it. Huge, because it was formed when three islands grew together, slowly, speck by speck, as tiny animals built their shells and died. Shaped like a giant, smiling mouth enormous enough to contain Leviathan; and only one exit, a gash as though someone had drawn a blade through one lip near the corner. Except for that gash the walls were high, jagged. Yes, I thought it would do. I stood on the crest of the cliff and waved, the agreed signal. I heard the answering hoot. I worried my lip; time was getting painfully short. The light was fading fast.

Then I saw them. They must have been waiting. At first, from my height, they looked tiny, as though I could cover them with my hand. Then, rapidly, they got larger and larger.

There was no longer any doubt. The Leviathan was hunting the Tribe. From my aerie, helpless to aid or interfere, I watched. And then, it happened. Two of the

Tribe, just as it seemed as though they would be caught, flashed through the gap into the lagoon. And the Leviathan followed! A tight fit she was, but it was high tide, and she made it into the lagoon. She vanished around the curve, pursuing her victims.

"Now!" the Matriarch trumpeted. "Now!"

But the two Cousins were still inside!

And then I understood. They did not think I could do it, in time, if they escaped. The two Cousins within were sacrifices, deliberate, willing sacrifices. For the good of the Tribe. Best spared!

"Now, now!" the Matriarch hooted.

The death of the two within—or the Tribe without.

The gap was narrow, growing shallow as the tide went out. There were plenty of loose rocks on the peak. I began shoving them down, trying to make them roll down, to make them take as much of the face with them as possible.

Push, shove, *rumble.*

Crash, splash.

Time had no meaning, my hands grew slippery with blood or sweat. I had to finish, had to block the gap before she returned, the Empress of the seas. There was a shudder, a tremor, the whole cliff face seemed to be quivering. I flung myself backward, running, running. The whole face began to collapse under me. I slipped on rocks, on pebbles—falling.

I twisted outward. Falling! I tried to make a dive, tried not to think in that long fall of the rocks below. And then I hit.

Down, down, into the water.

Even deep under I could feel it, the rumble of falling earth.

The Tribe found me, carried me to the surface in triumph. Where there had been a gap, was now—nothing. The high cliff had broken off, had tumbled in. Instead of a jagged row of upthrusting teeth, with a gap, some of the teeth had fallen sideways, making a rock wall that rimmed the lagoon. All the way around.

I had caged Leviathan.

I had *conquered* Leviathan.

I was lightheaded with triumph. Until I remembered.

There was a greater menace than Leviathan on our world now. And I still wore his brand.

He was riding the messenger; I thought his eyes sought my wrist.

Was the paralysis wearing off? I told the Cousin to take him to another island and dump him. Above the tideline, I added hurriedly. Find a steep beach, and try not to break anything when you toss him. Face up and on sand.

I had to get the bracelet off. I had dumped all his magics well out to sea, and I didn't think he'd ever find them, but the sea can be as capricious as a male. Besides, I didn't know if he had been carrying whatever controlled the bracelet. If he had left it, at the Terre place . . .

I had spent most of the trip to the Cousins trying to pull it off. I pulled and pulled and pulled. I tried to wedge my heels behind it and push. It was too tight. My heels just slipped over it.

I tried to get one of the Cousins to help me. But a Cousin's arm is designed to tear meat from its shell: *big* chunks of meat from a big shell. When a Cousin wrapped one of her arms around mine and pulled, all I lost was strips of skin.

The cursed thing was too tight and too smooth and too thin to get any hold on.

I even worried a scale off the Cousin and tried to work it under the cursed thing. I wasn't *afraid* of Lexi, or the Terrene. Individually, person to person, they're nothing to worry about—but. Their *cursed* magics. I knew that their magics had led them to me, through a bracelet, once before. I couldn't know if I had pulled this one's teeth or not. The longer I wore the deadly thing, the more chance that a Terre magic would drop out of the sky and take me, helpless and furious, to wherever the Terrene chose.

If they didn't find Lexi, they would take it out on me.

And if they *did* find Lexi . . .

This time I picked my scale more carefully. I chose a long, thin one, triangular and razor-edged, like a broad knife blade. (I had often used Cousin scale blades; for some purposes, they are better than chipped flint or Terre metal.)

I sawed carelessly, frantically at the wristlet. It made no difference. I couldn't get the scale under it, and I couldn't even scratch its smooth dull surface.

I swung at the wristlet with all my strength—and the scale cracked in two. Blood flowed sluggishly from a long cut—but the wristlet was unmarred.

The Cousins surrounding the Matriarch were hooting softly. They are very sensitive.

All right, if there wasn't any other way, I was going to saw it off. With as much flesh as necessary. I picked up the largest piece of the scale, and pointed it under the wristlet. If it wouldn't go between the horror and my skin, then it would go under my skin.

Under my skin and through as much of my flesh as need be.

It was sharp enough.

Except it wouldn't go.

We use a tree sap sometimes, to hold things together, though there are those who feel that a properly fitted joint should hold without such. The sap makes a bond that cannot be broken. I didn't know how the wristlet had been put on. Lexi said, Put your hand in here, and I had; and when I drew it out, the wristlet was on it. But I had decided that there was some Terre form of sap beneath. I couldn't find a gap between metal and skin, I couldn't force my flesh away from the metal, I couldn't turn the thing around my wrist.

But now I knew it wasn't even that simple. I couldn't force the scale under the thing, even through my flesh.

I knew that I had very little time left. I wasn't fooled that Lexi and I had been truly alone, that his friends hadn't some Terre magic way of checking on us. I would have made such arrangements, I knew; surely Lexi had, too. No one, no matter how proud and arrogant and self-confident, goes along with a foe, alone, without making some arrangements for her own protection.

I was not, was not, going back.

A creature that will clip a ganner's wings is capable of *anything*.

I couldn't be sure that I had destroyed the magic that controlled the wristlet.

The sky was dark now, as dark as my thoughts.

So much for my grand plan, then, to use Lexi as a lever. Find me, and they'd find him. Find me . . .

There was only one thing left to do, and I did it.

The Cousins have no teeth. Instead the rim of their mouth is hard and sharp, edged like double blades. They feed by tearing the food into big chunks with their arms, biting off mouth-size hunks with their lips, and swallowing.

I tied a rope around my upper arm, positioned myself, and told the Matriarch I had something good for her, to bite down, *hard*.

I didn't know it would hurt so much.

Chapter Twenty-four

MOTTO:

She had not sailed a league, a league,
A league but barely three,
When she beheld her own true love,
Sailing by the lee.

—*Conventional transition verse,*
present in many ballads and sagas

I opened my eyes, blinking as the light hit them.

"Well, *hello,*" said a voice.

I was propped against something firm and warm, and some delicious sours juice dripped into my mouth.

I drifted into half-consciousness. Where . . . what . . .

I remembered . . . There had been pain, great pain, and weakness . . . and chill . . . thirst . . . and hunger . . . and, finally, blessed unconsciousness.

Mindless, hurt animal, I lay, the effort of swallowing almost enough to send me back into oblivion.

Until I saw a piece of face, and it somehow joggled memory; I gasped and stiffened, whimpering.

"Easy, Val, easy, girl, you made it. You're safe. You got away from him."

The voice was vaguely familiar. "Na-Neill?"

"Neill and nobody else but. You pulled it off, tawny-eyes. You're here, and I haven't seen hide nor hair of Gorky the Gross." His face came into focus, and I choked. The sea-blue, deep blue eyes were Neill's; but the lower part of his face was covered with a horrible growth. He frowned. "Val, what's . . ." I managed to point with my good hand.

"You—your face, Neill. Your *face.*"

"What?" His hand reached up.

"All co-covered!"

He burst out laughing. "Oh. That. That's your fault, Valorous Val. You didn't leave me a knife, and my depil wore off days ago. It's just my beard, hair growing, hair like I have on my head."

Well, I could see that his head fur had grown, it curled around his shoulders, sleek black sparked with silver. But the stuff on his face was reddish-brown covering his face in tufty patches. "It—it's not the same color," I managed to get out.

He understood, despite my weakness. "No, it sometimes isn't among us. Sometimes darker, sometimes lighter, or redder. I guess you haven't seen much of it. It's not fashionable right now, and a lot of the fellows have had it permanently removed. But suppose beards become "in" again? What's the bother of putting on depil-inhib once a month or so? Unless you get stranded somewhere and it wears off. Of course"—his mouth stretched into a grin—"they have their uses." He put his face gently against mine so that our lips barely touched. His fur was soft and scratchy against my cheeks. He moved his face slowly, gently, his mouth working against mine. Goddess, don't the Terre males think about anything but sex? Granted, it is the right and proper function of a male to act as a male; still, such unmasculine boldness!

After a (pleasant!) interval, he leaned back, smiling at me until, reluctantly, I smiled back. One of his eyes blinked in agreement, and he began squeezing more juice into my parched mouth, talking gaily, teasingly, deliberately distracting my attention, until my mood was lighter.

I waited until he left to examine my arm. What was left of it. I couldn't see the worst; he had wrapped the stub in what I realized must have been his kilt. To the good, I could see none of the angry orange streaks that heralded internal poisoning; the skin and somewhat wasted flesh I could see seemed healthy enough; and though I felt deathly weak, the chill had left me, and I knew that, in time, I would heal and regain my strength.

On the other hand—I had no other hand.

Never to race again.

Never embrace a male.

Never haul a net, wield shield and spear, knot a message, raise Cup and Blade on high during a Ceremony . . .

Never . . . never . . . *never* . . .

Ah, Goddess, have You room in Your Retinue for a crippled Servitor?

"Now stop that!" Neill stooped to enter the shelter, his arms full of fresh-picked fruit. "Stop it, I say!" The laced vines and leafy branches that formed the roof of the shelter made everything within appear green; even the air had a faint greenish tinge. But Neill's face was red, even under the brown and the growth he called beard. "Done is done," he went on. "Are you sorry you did it?"

"No," I whispered. "NO!" I repeated more firmly. It was the only price to pay, and I had paid it gladly. But how had Neill known that *I* had done it—I, myself, and not the Gorky Admiral?

He read my unspoken question in my eyes. "You've been sick, Val. Very sick. So sick I never thought I'd pull you through. But you did it, you pulled yourself through, girl. You must have a core of solid three-phase dural. But while you were sick, you—talked. Talked? Babbled, rather. Screamed. Threatened. Pleaded. You lived it over, again and again. The Admiral. That sadist Clem. All of it, over and over. You . . ." He took a deep breath. "I didn't want to listen. Even professional nosiness has its limits. But I didn't dare leave you. Not while you were so sick, delirious. Not while you needed care, not while you were sick enough to do anything, walk into the ocean, maybe, or off the cliff. And I must admit, fascination. With you, your thought processes. You're—something else, Val. But I sure paid the price for my mental Peeping-Tomism. Your picture of me . . ." He worried his lower lip between his teeth. "It's all wrong, Val. I—I do 'work' in the sense that I—well—I accomplish things." A flashing-teeth, predatory grin. "I'm not sure, madame judge-and-jury, that you'd appreciate all I've accomplished. Judge-and-jury isn't a bad term for me, either, come to think about it. But I won't lie to you, Val. There are worlds with grems like you waiting for me to show my face so they can tie a noose around my neck and pull it tight. And they'd have the legal right to do it—

only—" He paused. "You don't have laws on your world, Val, but you must have some equivalent. Something that —that guides your actions, your behavior. You're a grem, and a good one from what I hear, but you can't do it all yourself, you must have some guidelines."

I blinked slowly. "We have Customs, our Religion, Family Councils, the Canons, and the sagas and the ballads and—"

"Of course. And did you never, ever feel that something you did, all right and tight and according to precedent—was really *wrong*. Unjust. Inequitable."

I didn't say anything. In the first place, I felt as weak as though I had just emerged from a too-long Esta-fee, and in the second place—I could see where his argument was leading, and I didn't like it. Give every Delyen no bound to her actions but what her own judgment of "right" can provide, and you would have senseless anarchy. And yet—and yet . . .

"I *correct* things, Val." His voice was hard, stern. "And I'm not always too particular about who or what is in my way. And I take my cut for what I do, I'm not ashamed of that, either. I earn it." A rueful grin. "What I am ashamed of, sometimes, is taking money for my 'official' work. I have that, too, you know, and mighty handy I find it at times. I string words together, which gives me all the excuse I need for all the pokin' and pryin' I want to do. Getting paid for my word-stringing, that's the real crime. It's like getting paid for—" He paused, stared down at me, blinked one eye in a gesture I was too confused to interpret. "But that's my life, tawny-eyes, and I enjoy it. I go to a new world, and amuse myself, and if my money runs out before inspiration comes in . . ." He shrugged. "I can always get some kind of unskilled work; even on high-technie worlds, there are always openings. I'm free, Val, free, and that's the way I've always wanted it. I 'work' when I choose, and where I choose, and no responsibilities, even to myself. Speaking of responsibilities," he chuckled, "I almost forgot. Here we go." He propped me up and began squeezing more fruits into my mouth.

After a bit, he paused, frowned. "Does it—bother you, Val?" Silence. What *could* I say? "Knowing that I know, I mean," he went on.

I thought it over. I don't seem to have, can't really understand this Terre trait called modesty. I don't shove my body at others. (Ugh, pallid fishbelly skin!) But it's not modesty (as I understand modesty), rather consideration. There are more attractive things to look at, after all. But if it's hot and I don't have to worry about the sun, I'm as quick as anyone else to drape my kilt over my shoulders, so that the insignia shows, leaving my body cool and free. But this mental showing, this inner nudity —no, I didn't care for it.

I thought of something else. "Are you"—I searched for the Terretz word—"jealous of the Gorky Admiral?"

"Jealous? Jealous! I'd like to flay him and stake him out for the ants to feed on—if they could stomach him! But—jealous?" He snorted. "Never. Envious, p'raps. Of this *talent* you seem to think he has. Though"—he laid his finger alongside his nose—"I've enough masculine pride to believe, anything he can do, I can do better. No, Val. It's what he did to you. What he tried to do to you, except you wouldn't play." He stopped squeezing, stared down at the mashed pulp in his hands. "D'you think, if I tore the pulp with my fingers, you could swallow it, Val?"

I nodded, and he began to shred the pulp, ripping it with quick, angry jerks. Somehow I got the impression it wasn't fruit he was shredding, it was something else. Or someone else. He fed the bits to me, a tiny mouthful at a time; I swallowed slowly and cautiously.

Finally, he burst out, "Val, this band or wristlet or whatever you were so frantic to get off. What did it look like, do you remember?"

I wasn't likely to forget. "It was thin and tight, so tight I couldn't get my fingers or a blade edge under it. It was greenish-brown in color, smooth but not shiny, and it had runes incised on it," I put my fingers on his wrist. "It was so wide, from here to here."

"Runes?" He seemed puzzled. "Oh, yeah, I forgot. Illiterate." Louder, "Can you remember what those—ah—runes looked like, Val? Can you make me a copy?"

I was lying on rock and smoothed flat dirt. He uncovered a patch near my hand and gave me a short stick broken off from a branch above. When I had the runes copied down, as well as I could, he stared at them for long heartbeats, frowning. "Are you sure that's what they looked like, Val?"

"Yes, as well as I can draw them. That's them. I *know.*"

He pulled on his lower lip, still frowning, then struck his forehead with the heel of his hand. "Of course, I'm an idiot. You were seeing them upside down." He crawled around to where he could look at what I had drawn from beneath—and began cursing, calling the Gorky Admiral a lot of names I had never heard before. At last, still muttering, he crawled back. Carelessly—or was it deliberately?—he rubbed out my careful runes in passing. He squatted beside me, began shredding another fruit.

"That—that *bastard,*" he spit out suddenly. "That—that bastard!"

I always suspected no decent Family would adopt the Gorky Admiral.

Neill continued to mutter and grumble to himself, and now I knew what he was tearing instead of fruit.

"Neill? What is it, why are you so angry?"

"Val, you poor innocent. He Tagged you. That flaming bastard Tagged you."

"Tagged? You mean labeled?"

"Ha!" he snarled. "Label. Sort of. You Tag *animals,* Val. Or, rather, scientists do. If they have the government backing to afford the equipment."

"An—imals?" I couldn't quite take it in. And I didn't like it.

He moved his head up and down. "Animals. You want to find out what their migratory patterns are, or what kind of social groupings they form, or whatever else shriveled-soul technies think of. So you catch a bunch of whatever animal you're interested in, knock them out with an anesthetic, put a Tag on them—and let them go. But after that, they're *yours.* You can follow them, knock them out, and collect them, bring them in forcibly. Whatever you want."

I was too rage-choked to speak. I had known (or at least suspected) what the obscene thing *did,* but to be labeled an *animal.* The Terrene have a saying, about adding insult to injury.

Neill recovered first. "Tch, now, sleep, my Valkyrie,

my gallant girl. Sleep and grow stronger. When you're better, we'll figure out some way to—fix—him—good."

We Delyene have a Ceremony, reserved for those who have committed the most obscene of sacrilege against the Goddess; I would not grieve to see the Gorky Admiral assume the leading part in such a Ceremony.

Again he read my mind. "No, Val. Whatever you're thinking it's not bad enough, it's over too flaming quickly. Now, remember, girl, our advanced technology. Means we have advanced methods of punishment, too."

Punishment is a problem. It sometimes seems to me, that punishment is almost futile. People who are truly sorry for what they have done punish themselves far more acutely than anyone else can. And those who don't care . . .

I slept and ate and slept some more. I don't know how many days had passed when I asked Neill to explain what he had meant by advanced methods of punishment.

He laughed humorlessly. "Loss of rank for a starter. Nice public disgrace. And then—well, he has a choice. You see, a while back, some great white father decided that killing someone, no matter what crime he has committed, was cruel and unusual punishment. So, that's out. Instead he can have a brainwash, or solitary."

"Brainwash?" It was night, and Neill had carried me down to the beach, and I lay in the warm sand, the waves lapping over me.

"What it means is, the sweet little psychs probe your mind down to its bitter dregs and redo everything they don't approve of."

"Redo your mind? That's impossible, Neill." I splashed water over myself.

"Is it? You had a taste of it, Val, just a taste. Imagine what happened to you, going on and on, run by experts, people who know all the human weaknesses, who know where to keep piling on pressure until something gives. Gorky and that Clem were amateurs, Val, amateurs. Brainwashing psychs are professionals, with a dozen professional techniques. Which one they use depends on how basic a change they want to make. Sometimes they use physical means. I mean cut open the brain and play games with it, use a laser, say to reroute nerves or cut out certain memories. Or they put in a controller, something like your wristband, only infinitely more sophisticated, to make you do or say or even think what someone else wants. Or they use drugs, change your personality chemically. Or there are the so-called Pavlov techniques. Use nerve shock—pain—to alter the personality. Used on thieves and murderers and such. Lots of 'cures.' Make them relive their crimes and at the same time give them a massive nerve stim; incredibly painful, I understand. Do it often enough and the victim—sorry, patient!—can't even bear to think about whatever you're conditioning him against. Of course, he may not be able to think at all, after that kind of treatment, but, the good of society, you know. Or there's something called a personality cleaner; what it does is literally destroy memories. Use enough, and you have a child. A little more, and you have a grown baby, a blank page to be molded as you please." He grinned. "And that, Val my love, is a mixed metaphor, something I would never use professionally. The trouble is, psychs being the kind of mental Peeping Toms they are, nit-pickers, do-gooders—they just can't leave anything be. Once you're in their clutches, they poke and alter and twist and—Val, you O.K.? You did ask."

"Yes, I did." I believed it, too. I had had my taste, and had no desire for any further samples. But the—the arrogance of it. To remake someone else's soul. "You said a choice. What was the other? Solitare?"

"Solitary. I'd choose it, if I had to make the choice, though few do. At least with solitary, you have a chance. It's just what it sounds like. Solitary. You live alone, completely alone, for whatever term you're sentenced to. Usually one or more years. But when the Court says alone, it means *alone*. You're put in a little one-man sized warp, with an air-recycler and a food synthesizer —and they launch it into nothing. No, I take that back, I think you get microreaders if you ask for them. Anyway, they shoot the thing out, on a random course. When your time's up, a relay snaps, and a soss starts bleating, and they pick you up. If you haven't committed suicide from loneliness."

I shivered. I decided that simple death was a kindness compared to mental mutilation or this horror of "solitary."

"Once some lucky stiff got picked up by accident, before his soss went off. He was on a major space route, and a skipper spotted him and thought he was honest salvage. There was a publicity-hungry shyster among the passengers, and he conned the skipper into bringing the guy in. Then he filed suit for a parôle, on the ground that he had served a term of solitary. The prosecution argued that the term had been for a fixed time, and he hadn't served it. The lawyer argued that the worst of the sentence was the separation, the knowledge that you were alone, and that it was cruel to make his client go through the whole trauma twice. It got bucked up and down through the courts, until some judge finally ruled that he had served more than half his term, and quoted some precedent called time off for good behavior. I think he was influenced by a psych report on the poor guy. Anyway, now they launch them on random paths, but in areas far away from the normal trade routes."

He paused to catch his breath. I had so many words to ask about I couldn't even remember them all. I wasn't even sure I had the general picture, much less understood the specifics. "What's a warp?"

"Ahhhhhhh. Let's see. It's like—ah—like a little boat. Except, instead of traveling from island to island, it goes from planet to planet. You do know what a planet is, don't you?"

"Delyafam is a planet."

"Hmmmmmm. Wish I believed you understood what you were saying."

"Delyafam is here, where we Delyene live," I explained. "Other planets are elsewhere, like the ones the Terrene come from." How I wished they'd stayed there! "I can get to anywhere I wish on Delyafam, on my boat. Almost anywhere," I amended, thinking of the Dire Sea and the Forbidden Circle. "Delyafam is all one piece, that's why. But I can't go to other planets, because they're separate. You Terrene can, because you have magic boats that can sail on nothing."

He made a hissing sound through his teeth. "Wow, you do understand. I'm amazed, Val, I really am. Primitives—I'm sorry, but you people are primitive—usually don't have a strong enough, accurate enough world picture to understand the concept of planet. But you seem to."

Why should I not? I live by and on the sea; I've seen boats sinking below the horizon, or rising, topsail first, above it. It's the same everywhere. So I know that Delyafam must be bounded, must be everywhere curved, moreover, curved about the same. I don't have a word for the shape Delyafam must be, but if you took my head, and smoothed it out so that it curved evenly all around, and put water on it, that would be like a little copy of Delyafam. I don't know what keeps the water from dripping off, since the curve is outward like a gourd, not inward like a bowl; but I suspect it is the same Hand of the Goddess that makes a fruit drop to the ground when it slips from your hand. I do not think it coincidence that Anatra and Sunatra and even the flaming Eye of the Goddess appear round.

Why must lack of Terre magic be considered the same as ignorant or stupid? Even Neill makes that mistake with us. Primitive. Why do the Terrene assume that their brand of magic is the only way? We are an ancient people, with a long and honorable past. We have chosen our life style, perfected it bit by bit, slowly, over many generations, considering each change carefully and at length. *We* don't have to barge into other people's seas because we can't control our breeding!

So who is "primitive" and who "civilized"?

Will it even be enough to drive them from our seas—once? We cannot follow them to their worlds. We haven't their magic. We don't want it. But—can we defend ourselves without it? And, if we accept it, will we still be Delyene—after?

"Neill—is a warp like a little windowless room, all metal and artificial, or mayhap several rooms together with halls between, all enclosed, with magics all over the walls . . ."

"Holy flaming Armstrong, he didn't take you aboard a warp!"

"And if you go outside, you have to wear strange heavy clothing all over; you mustn't take it off, and there are too many stars and they look all wrong, and—"

"He took you out—in a *suit!*"

"I think he did call it a suit. He took me out so I'd

know I couldn't get myself back to Delyafam. It was—it was a place of *nothingness*, the Plain of Dread."

In the soft Sunatralight, his face was bleak, shadowed into strangeness. "No wonder you understand about planets. Lucky you didn't float away."

"No, we were held down, where he took me. Like Delyafam, only I felt lighter. And the ground was shiny and cold, even through the clothing . . ."

He whistled thinly. "Not space, then. An asteroid, or—cold? Or hot? No, you wouldn't know the difference through the suit. A military base, then, on a non-E planet. Armstrong, if there was only some way to pin this one on him! If only I hadn't lost my comm in that melee in your Temple . . ." His voice trailed away. I wondered which of his possessions was the "comm"? I had them all, in my rooms in the House of Equity. Our people are not thieves. All had been turned in to me or the Temple as soon as they were found. Some were a trifle damaged, of course. "He won't let me within a kilometer of the Consul," Neill was musing aloud, "he'll know you told me. If only—there, Val, love." His voice got brisker. "You just concentrate on getting better. Old Neill'll think of something. I haven't bucked the Establishment this long without learning a few tricks. We'll hang your brave, aphro-using Admiral as high as Haman!"

On the word of an ignorant primitive? Those who have no honor of their own can ill afford to trust the honor of others. But we Delyene have honor . . .

Chapter Twenty-five

MOTTO:

I might have had a royal Consort,
From an isle beyond the sea;
Yes, I might have had a Queen's Consort—
Were it not for the love of thee!

—*Song of Neill, origin Terrafam,*
author of original unknown

Neill was proved accurate in one important item: Anything Lexi could do, Neill could do better. It seemed that one Terre male, all by himself, could keep a Delye female happy. At least, a convalescent Delye female. I should have been most content.

The trouble was I wanted to *keep* him—and it just wasn't possible.

I knew it was time I went back, that my duties were waiting, that every day I delayed gave the Hypasha and the Merwencalla that much more leisure to hatch whatever evils they planned.

I told myself that I was still too weak to make the journey, that a message via the Cousins (who still checked on me periodically) could so easily go astray. The truth was—I was enjoying myself. Not just the pleasure of sex, though Neill's talents in that direction were simply fantastic. No, it was the—the companionship. The mental closeness. Since the Hypasha and I had drifted apart, I had had no true friend. I was close to the Elyavaneet, but such was not the same. Nor was the emotion I felt for Drax and my other boys at all similar.

Neill was friend as well as partner, a mental equal, a mind delectable to explore, a dear, loving comrade.

When I was young and hot and madly enthralled with Draxuus I, three things were enough: a strong body, a pretty face, a sweet personality.

I was not ready to give up the new delights of companionship.

Would I ever again be content with *boys?* Boys who could never grow into men?

We talked, ah, how we talked! Argued and discussed, and agreed, and drew lines and defended them and got pushed from behind them.

And each day that passed I was one day stronger, and the end was one day nearer.

One day I gathered my courage—and *asked.*

(Among my people it would not have taken such. A boy has plenty of signals to let a Delye know if he is dissatisfied or content, truly looking or merely being polite. Neill seemed content enough with me, but I knew better than to interpret his actions as though he were a Delye boy.)

We had been swimming, for pleasure and food, and our harvest was spread out on the sand between us. He cracked a two-shell and handed it to me, his eyes down, not meeting mine. "You know," he said, after a long, *long* pause, "I do believe I've just been proposed to. A first."

I said nothing, sitting quietly, the sweet animal in my hand.

"I wondered when you'd get bored with this island paradise of ours," he went on, "when you'd want a boy instead of a man."

"Neill, it's not that. and you know it. If the choice were mine, I'd stay, but I . . ."

"Have duties." We said it together. "I know, Val, love," he went on. "I'm being unfair. Eat your horrible, so you'll grow well and strong." He smiled, but his face was sour. "That's the trouble, right there. You are well now, or almost." We both looked at the stump. It didn't look so bad. With Neill's help, I had trimmed it with a sharp shell and covered the exposed bone with a pad of skin and flesh. I've seen worse. Just an arm that stops about halfway between elbow and where the wrist had been. "So you're ready to pull your life together."

I couldn't deny truth.

"The odd thing is," he went on, "I feel the same way. I

ought to want to stay here with you, to lotus-eat, no cares, no worries, no responsibilities, no garrote hanging over my neck—"

"Neill, if—"

"No. Nomad, yes. Adventurer, yes. Lotus-eater, even with as exquisite an Eve as you—sorry 'bout that, tawny-eyes. Back we go, and I'll take my chances with the Lord High Executioner."

But if I added Neill to my household, that would be the end of any threat. Any official threat, that is; my household might share my dangers.

"That isn't the question, Neill. We have to go back, there was never any doubt of that. But after we get back, what then?"

"I never thought, when I was growing up in that créche on Argus V, that one day I'd be asked to join a harem. How do you work it, Val? Do the 'boys' have regular assignments, or do you just go eeny, meeny, miney, mo?" On the "mo" his hand shot out, forefinger pointing at me like a poised spear. I blinked. "No, no thanks, Val, baby. I never could *work* to schedule."

I understood him well enough. Were our roles reversed, I too would find it unthinkable, unbearable, to await his favors, to be ever alert for his summons. He had told me, and the Gorky Admiral, too, had implied such, that the Terre males had their own households, unnatural as that appeared to me. I had known, all along, that he would not be pleased to take a minor place in *my* household; but I had told myself it wouldn't matter, that he would be grateful for the saving of his life, that he would learn to like— What a liar I was! Worst of all, to lie to one's self!

Yet I couldn't give him up.

"Neill." I forced myself to speak calmly, persuasively. "I meant you no insult. I just wanted us to be able to stay together. And I wanted—"

"—to protect you," I would have finished, but he didn't let me.

"Val, baby"—his voice was ice—"you visit me in my cell, in that wet dungeon of yours, and I won't kick you out. Especially"—he laid his finger along his nose and shut one eye—"if it's been a while. And if I'm a little reluctant, not enough conscious of the honor, you can always have one of those muscle-head bruisers of yours work me over a bit. Make me more—ah—amenable to the wishes of the high and mighty Noblelady."

It wasn't going to work. I hadn't wanted it that way, I wanted to continue as we had been—equals. Something I'd never imagined I'd meet, a male with the capacity to walk beside me, to meet and match me. Neill.

I blinked what certainly wasn't tears from my eyes, and realized that the discomfort I was feeling was not entirely emotional. "My skin."

"Oh, flaming—why didn't you say so?" He stood easily, picked up the woven vine net bag. "You too tired to walk, want to be carried?" And I knew that had been the signal. Yesterday, for the first time, I had walked both ways, on my own, along the steep path that led from beach to shelter. We moved slowly, he ready at any time to stop and allow me to rest, to pick me up and carry me the rest of the way. For the first time I realized how much I was beginning to resent my physical dependency. I could not like being the weaker, the one that needed to be cared for, coddled. I understood how Neill must have felt, after being independent much of his adult life, to be forced into imprisonment, dependency.

At least I could lighten his mind's burden in one respect. With any favor of the Goddess at all, the Elyavaneet could . . . Merciful Goddess, I have never told him about the Elyavaneet and Willis . . .

So what? He shrugged his shoulders when I finished. That poor bastard Willis got his instead of me. So what? I'll still need to be tried by your Council or judged by your Priestesses or whatever, won't I?

I tried to explain how discrediting the Merwencalla bettered his chances.

He snorted. "No hanging judge, you mean. But as long as it's sentence first and verdict afterward, what chance have I got?"

"Neill, you committed sacrilege! Don't you know that everyone who even touched you in that melee had to undergo Penance and Cleansing. I had to be Reconsecrated myself."

He whistled softly. "You really believe, don't you?"

"Yes."

'But all those other men were there. And I meant no disrespect."

"But they were all Cleansed, Bound to the Goddess—Neill! *Are* you Bound to Her? None of the Terrene ever asked for a Consecration, and those missionaries of theirs always talked about their Three-in-one or whatever She is, so we just assumed that they trod a different path . . ."

"Sorry, Val, I can't get off the hook so easily. I'm a devout agnostic."

Well, devout was promising, and whatever heresy or strange path agnostic was, perchance one of the Priestesses would be willing to guide his feet onto the Path. And if so, then . . . I had a sudden picture of Neill making his First Duty in the Gardens, and word spreading and all the Delyene in the area hurrying to the Gardens, and lining up . . . and poor Neill . . . I began to hiss.

"What's so funny?"

"I—there's a Ceremony—oh, Goddess, Neill, I could just see you—oh, Neill, I would have to make arrangements, oh, oh, oh . . ."

"You do have your own sense of humor, don't you, Val? Now I never thought an execution was that funny, myself. Especially mine."

I sobered. "Not an execution, Neill. I was thinking of your Temple Duty. If—would you be willing to listen to Instruction, Neill, if I can arrange it?"

"Instruction—in what?"

"In the Way, Neill. You said you were devout in your own belief, and if it should turn out to be our Way under another Name, you could be Instructed and Cleansed, and do a Penance . . ."

"You know, Val, it's a funny thing. I'm not sure I could turn hypocrite, even to save my neck from the strangler."

I persisted. "I'm only asking you to listen, Neill. Listen with an open heart. You're smart enough to understand, if you'd just listen, and then you'd *know* . . ."

"Val, love, every religious fanatic from the year one has thought that way about his faith. The Only Right Way." He laughed. " 'But there are nine and forty ways of constructing tribal lays, and every one of them is right.' "

"Well, of course. Neill, if you understand *that* . . ."

"Maybe I don't."

"There is only one Goddess, but every worshiper makes her own paean of praise."

He sputtered. "I told you, I'm a devout agnostic."

"Neill, I don't care what you call Her; the Priestess could guide your feet onto the Blessed Path. Just listen, that's all I ask, just listen."

"Val, love, one of you comes in the cell and talks, what choice have I?"

"Listen with your mind and heart as well as your ears."

"That I can't promise."

Stubborn, thick-skulled—male. But maychance the Elyavaneet herself would be able to spare the time; she is Thrice-purified, after all, and I could think of no one more persuasive, more understanding, more—

The Elyavaneet! Now why didn't I think of her before. The Elyavaneet . . .

"Hey-ee, watch it!" I hadn't been paying attention; I tripped over a rock. Neill tried to catch me, and we both sprawled on the rocky path.

"Neill, Neill, Neill, Neill!"

"Val, are you all ri—*Val!*"

If that path hadn't been so rocky and sharp, I'd have raped him on the spot.

He calmed me down a bit, which wasn't easy, and when I tried to tell him it all tumbled out together, I was so excited. But I finally made him understand.

"Join your friend's harem instead of yours. I will *not!*"

"Neill, she would be giving you Instruction. It would be more convenient for her if you were to join her household, that's all. You would be her—her guest, Neill. Her honored guest. For my sake, for the sake of our friendship. The Elyavaneet is very wise, and gracious, Neill. Knowing her is a—a *privilege.*"

"A privilege it may be, Val, love. But *I* choose. I choose. Besides," he chuckled, "I draw the line at little old ladies. However gracious they may be."

It was my turn to sputter, but finally—had I been learning a sense of humor from Neill?—I began to hiss instead. Poor Neill. If only he could see himself through a Delyen's eyes. The Elyavaneet would never. Her taste is impeccable. But if she did—oh, the lesson Neill would learn if she did.

"What's so flaming funny?"

I couldn't tell him. Instead I pushed myself into a seated position with my remaining hand and began to explain, slowly and logically, the advantages of a position in the Elyavaneet's household, saving the best for last. Official protection. Light duties. Instruction in the Way. All the cord he wanted.

"Whoa, there, Val. All the what?"

"Cord. You did say you strung words for your duty, didn't you? How can you string words without cord?"

"I didn't literally mean string, tawny-eyes. I—" He sat thoughtfully, staring at me. "Val, the Delyene are officially illiterate, did you know that? Do you know what illiterate means?"

I shook my head in the Terre fashion meaning "No."

"It means, no written-down language."

"What's written-down mean?"

"Not spoken. Put down on some permanent material, so that it can be left or sent, from one messenger to another. Something that can be kept, even though the original maker is dead."

"That's what you do, isn't it? Do you make your own words, like a bard, or are you a copyist? Even if you're just a copyist, you'll need cord."

He nodded. "So-oo. I was right. How do you send a message, Val, if it's too long or too complicated to trust to someone's memory?"

"The same way anyone else does. Any Delyen, that is. Knot a message onto some cords. Oh! I can't, now. It takes two hands."

He nodded again, a funny look on his face. "Does each knot stand for a word or a sound, Val?"

I stopped thinking about never being able to knot a message again and told him. Both, of course. Knots for common words, and knots for sounds to spell out uncommon ones.

"Suppose you wanted to make a fire?" was his next illogical question.

I couldn't help hissing. Make a fire? On hot, hot Delyafam?

He persisted. Fires do have their uses after all. Pottery.

Or to harden some types of wood. (Or to cook food, he inserted. But when I asked him what cooking meant, he persisted about the fire.)

So I started listing ways of getting or making fire. Just to humor him. A metal disk, polished. A fire already in punk. A piece of clear rock, its edges lined up just so, to make flame jump from the Eye of the Goddess. (That one bothered him, until I explained further and he nodded. Oh. Quartz to focus the sun's rays.) Two rocks of the right type, struck together. Two sticks—

"Enough, woman." He held up his hand. "Enough already. You know how to make fire. Val, your people are misclassified. I thought it was funny, that fine cloth you weave, and those ships of yours, so lovely and so perfectly designed. And your pottery, too—of course, you have to fire your pottery, you couldn't get those exquisite designs without— Oh, Val, love, Neill has his story. And what a story. Just the kind old plasmamouth, my editor, likes. Mismanagement. Bureaucratic flub-dubbery. Unless—I wonder—could it have been deliberate?"

I got us back to the main topic; with difficulty, as Neill continued to mutter to himself. Lots of cord, and—except he didn't need any cord, just the thing called a comm. Which he described eagerly to me. I had thought it was an amulet. I had it, but it was dented where someone had stepped on it. I decided not to tell him I had it; it may have lost its power when it was Purified. Why get his hopes up? He kept talking about his story, until I got so teeth-clenched mad I began to pound him on the chest.

"Neill, can't you see? I can't take you into *my* household, not the way we both would like; we'd have no peace, no peace at all. I can't just dismiss my boys, Neill, it would be too cruel. But *you* could be accepted into the Elyavaneet's household—for Instruction. You wouldn't be expected to serve her. Oh, maybe help serve at a banquet, say. Or—can you sing? Most of your time would be your own. And when I came to visit the Elyavaneet—and I do, often—*you* would be the one chosen to bring me my refreshments—you could be—"

For a minute he stared at me puzzled, then a whole assortment of emotions chased themselves across his face. And then he started laughing. "Oh, Val," he finally managed to choke out. "A snake in paradise. You've discovered how to eat your cake and have it, too. Congratulations, girl. You've just invented the double household, infidelity and adultery."

I didn't understand him. None of my boys would feel insulted if I allowed myself to be entertained elsewhere, if none of them were available. And I couldn't turn them out of my household, or worse, retain them but keep their sandals out of my private quarters. Boys have their pride, after all.

"All right, Neill. The cell, then. I'll—visit—you when I can. It won't be what it could have been, but I'll come. Until—"

"Until the Lord High Executioner."

"One way or the other, until your sacrilege is paid for."

"Unless I escape first." He grinned.

"Don't try, Neill," I warned him. "A lone Terren, with no magics for protection. This isn't the Enclave, Neill. I couldn't protect you. Besides, I told you, with the Merwencalla discredited, you might only be required Penance and Contrition. And then . . . you could go . . . wherever you wanted . . ."

His lip curled. "I'm a man, Val. A man."

"I know." I wouldn't have you any other way. Besides, we could be together—for a time—

He rubbed his cheek, soft with its strange growth, gently against mine. "Hey, love, I've a treat I've been saving. Now seems a good time."

I wasn't interested in treats. Except—*what* was he saying?

". . . fresh-water pool, I always feel so itchy in the ocean. And who knows, maybe we'll click, stranger things have happened, Val, and Ma Nature always has one more ace or two up her sleeve. I know you'd take good care of our kid, if we got lucky. We might be that lucky in that pool, hey, Val . . ."

He couldn't know, he couldn't!

But he did. He said it. ". . . don't know why you people feel you need fresh-water, but there it is, our own little private place. If you think you need one of your Priestesses to bless it, fine, we can wait . . ."

Oh, Goddess, he hadn't been going *in* to the Inner Holy, he'd been coming *out!*

He *KNEW!*

". . . can't really see you as the little mother, but I bet you'd make . . ."

Oh, Goddess, oh, Goddess, oh, Goddess!

Chapter Twenty-six

MOTTO:

This above all: to thine own self be true,
And it must follow, as the night the day,
You've none but yourself to blame when things
go wrong.

—*Sayings of Neill*

I killed him the day we planned to leave.

I killed him as quickly and skillfully as I had always promised myself I would, should it become necessity. He never knew, until he found himself walking down that misty path.

I killed him, and with him died my hopes, dreams, all that would make the remainder of my life sweet instead of bitter. I executed my defense against the Merwencalla, destroyed the influence of the Elyavaneet in Council. All these I strangled, one-handed.

A Delyen may not weep, but she may mourn.

Neill, if I could have given my life in place of yours, I would have, singing triumphantly as I trod my chosen path.

But you *knew*, and for the sake of my people, for the survival of the Delyene, you had to die. We can only breed in sweet-water. And what could one like the Gorky Admiral armored in his magics do with such a knowledge? To breed is to live. Such a simple little knowledge. It meant little to you, so little; you thought it was just Ritual that we concealed the sweet-water pools so, shrouded them in mystery and ceremony. Didn't you know how rare, how very rare true sweet-water is on Delyafam?

You never complained about the water, but you ate a lot of juices, didn't you? Ah, my Delyafam, where the rain runs off the impenetrable rock, and only the highest-born rivers and springs can conquer the salt tide. And many of those high places on the new-risen isles, the deathcones, with their burning, flowing rock, and their water that eats away flesh. Is it true that Terrene can breed anywhere, water fresh or bitter, even in air? I can't decide whether to envy or pity them. For us, only sweet-water will do. Once, so the stories tell, the land was different, higher and broader, the climate not so hot, and many lakes were sweet. Now the land is innumerable islands, and the tiny pools of sweet-water are rare, so rare. So we are painfully vulnerable. And you had to die, Neill. Oh, Neill, I wish I could die, too. But I can't. I have—do I hear your deep chuckle?—duties. But when those duties are done . . .

I couldn't give his body to the seas, as I knew I should. Somehow the thought of teeth tearing at it, of scavengers fighting over the bits . . . I hadn't realized that I had such weakness inside myself. But I had.

I found instead, a cleft in the rock face, and dragged his poor husk there. I pushed it in as best I could, one-handed, and shoved stones down on top of it until it was covered, buried so deeply that neither sharp-toothed ganner nor land-crawling scavenger would be able to get to him. Oh, I knew the sea would eat away the land, as he always does, and reclaim his prize. But that wouldn't be for long years. By then Neill would have returned to the land, gone into the land, become one with the land. Then Neill could go into the sea, from whence we all came and to which we all return . . .

I could almost hear his mocking voice. *No Viking funeral in a blazing boat?*

I'm sorry, Neill. I haven't a boat. If I did, I'd have given you a proper Farewell. And I'm sorry you didn't get to ride the Cousins, you were so looking forward to that. But I couldn't risk taking you back to Swiftfaring. There are Terrene there. And one careless word . . .

But I said all the prayers I could remember, and some of my own, too. Goddess, take good care of this, your servant. Goddess, this was a man. A man.

"His life was gentle, and the elements
So mix'd in him that Nature might stand up
And say to all the world, 'This was a man!' "

Neill told me that once; unknowing he spoke his own epitaph.

Farewell, Neill.

Before I left, I carefully removed all evidences of habitation. I had my reasons.

The Tribe had moved on, of course. They cannot stay too long in any one area, their need for food is too great. But ever since they had brought me, half-crazed with pain and illness, to this island, one or two scouts had remained nearby. I would not have to swim to Swiftfaring.

The Cousin dropped me off within easy swim of the beach where I had been captured by Clem. I had considered the cave where the *Eater* was stashed, but the *Eater* was far too conspicuous. The Cousin hooted mournfully as I pulled myself up onto the beach. I was somewhat puzzled. The Cousins were not above co-operating with the Delyene, for a specific purpose. Say, driving a school of plunny into our nets, in return for a share of the catch. But I seemed to have acquired my own personal Tribe. She promised that a scout would visit this beach every high tide when Anatra was full, to see if there was anything I wanted. I smiled to myself. Such might be useful.

I was lucky. I found my cloak, carefully folded and placed well above the high tide mark. Lucky, that is, that it was found before the tide managed to reclaim it from where I dropped it on the sand. No doubt the finder muttered a complaint or two about the unknown owner's carelessness, before putting it safely away for my return. Twice lucky. Had one of the Terrene spotted it, no doubt they would have taken it with them, as they had my tow, to make it appear I had left of my own accord. As for the magic lightweight cloak the Admiral had given me, it had been lost in my long dive into the sea. I regretted not its loss.

Not so my own dear *useful* Delye cloak. With that, and a fruit juice that stained the skin orange, I would dare Swiftfaring. Not in the sunlight, when sharp eyes would see through the stain, and the sun burn through it, but at night I would be safe enough.

I wanted Neill's amulet—and a few other items.

Neill's possessions had all been placed in a small storage room near my sleeping chamber. I knelt beside the chest of woven reed and began sorting through it, taking each item out separately and shaking it, looking for items concealed in the folds. I was so absorbed I didn't hear sandaled feet in the trod-flat hallway.

"Who are you?" a voice snapped. "What are you doing in private quarters?"

I rose and turned—and relaxed. Yassu, my chief boy next to Draxuus, stood in the entrance, blade naked in his hand. It was dark in that room, because I hadn't roused the glow-animals. But it was not so dark that he couldn't see my crestless female head and female body as the cloak swirled open with my movements.

"Madam?" There was question in his voice. I was wearing no kilt for him to identify insignia, but it was still hot enough for that not to be unusual. "Have you concerns with the Kimassu Lady?" he asked. "She is on Retreat. May I be of service?"

"Yes, Yassu, you can."

"Mistress! Mistress, oh, *mistress!*" He almost spitted me on the blade, forgetting that it was in his hand. A most satisfactory reunion, marred only by his shock when he saw my missing hand. I laughed and told him a Terren had bitten it off. Not such a stretching of the truth at that.

Yassu had news for me; he thought I'd be pleased. The Hypasha had been Chosen. My stunned silence told him that I had not received the news as gladly as he had expected. Dear sweet lad, he hastened to assure me that my turn would surely be next. Poor innocent. He knew only that the Hypasha and I had once been friends. But it wasn't jealousy or envy that silenced me, or even rage at the Choosing of my friend-turned-enemy; it was worry. If the Merwencalla had been properly discredited, why then was the Hypasha Chosen? Surely, even if I could not be considered, there were others who could have been so honored. But after a bit I saw how this too could be turned to my advantage, and when Yassu heard me hissing, he was much relieved.

I felt bold enough then to enter my own rooms. Yassu

had gone to execute my orders, though some of them puzzled him greatly. I sat quietly on my bench, my eyes roaming unseeing over race banners, game trophies, mementos of past feats, past friendships—past loves. It would not be easy to choose, as I must, what to take with me.

But, ah, it was good to feel a proper blade at my side again.

One last task. I sat with the amulet in my hand and cursed myself because I had not thought to learn from Neill the proper rituals. It would not matter, in truth, whether Neill had his "last story" or not. But I wanted him to have it. I owed him at least the effort. I began playing with the amulet, dandling it through my fingers, stroking it. Then, because I could think of naught else to do, I spoke to it.

And—it answered me.

After that it was simple.

The amulet seemed most upset when I told it Neill was dead. It should have known; it was *his* amulet, after all.

But once it had gotten over its distress, it asked a great many questions, which I answered as patiently and completely as I could. The one fact I—withheld—was the precise manner of Neill's death. I said merely that he had committed sacrilege, and been condemned, and that I myself had seen to it that his body was given proper Farewell.

The amulet said it had always known that Neill would get himself into something he couldn't talk his way out of someday.

Oddly enough, I had to take several deep breaths before I could agree.

The amulet went on, asking me other questions, until suddenly—and this I have no explanation for, it began arguing with itself. I could barely follow the quick Terretz. And, believe this or not, I know only what I heard, it argued in more than one voice!

Then suddenly it stopped, and the voice I thought of as "my editor, old plasmamouth" spoke. "You're a native of this world, aren't you?"

"Yes, Amulet."

"Turn the comm so that you face the viz in the center."

The "viz" had to be the jewel. The other side of the amulet was smooth, except for some runes. The amulet continued to argue with itself, in low mutters, including, ". . . another of his jokes and not a word for weeks . . ."

I gradually realized what they were thinking. They thought I was a—it pains me to say it!—Terren. A Delyen does look (from a *distance!*) much like a shaven Terren, a mistake that can never be made with a Hardyen. There was one way to fix that. I hooked the chain about my stump and gave the amulet a good, close look at my hand, with its smooth, nailess, three-jointed fingers with suction discs below the surface.

Neill said, I told the amulet, that the Delyene were classified as Level Two and that was wrong, and Neill had thought it might be deliberate.

"I believe that, girlie; you speak mighty good Terran for a Level Two."

"I am the Kimassu Lady."

"Humph. Kimassu, do you know why—"

"Kimassu *Lady.*"

"Kimassu Lady, do you know why Neill thought you weren't Level Two?"

It seemed foolishness, but I told it about knotted messages, and the fire we used so seldom. And it asked more questions, so I talked about our boats so carefully crafted that we needed no binder to hold together a dozen-dozen-dozen pieces of reed and wood (and then I had to explain who we counted, which caused more commotion), and our tapestries and songs and history that went back a dozen-dozen-dozen generations to the First Empress (blessed be her memory!) and beyond. I told about the animals we trained from the sea to live on our walls to give light, and the shallows plants we had cross-bred, and cultivated, to give us food. And a little about our way of worshiping the Goddess (may She reign ever mercifully!).

The amulet chortled and congratulated itself and Neill and asked me questions and I answered them.

I even told it about Lexi, but it didn't want to hear. Happens too often to be news, it said.

I was sickened—*happens too often!* But I dropped it, only to have the whole subject come up when the amulet asked casually how I had lost my hand. So I told it, and it was the amulet's turn to be sickened. But it was the only way I could get the band *off*. So I told it again about the Gorky Admiral, and this time it listened and asked questions.

Yassu returned just as I was getting too husky-voiced to talk much longer; he said he had carried out all my orders. I told the amulet I would speak more with it later, gathered my chosen items and gave them to Yassu to carry, took one final look around the room—

The banner that showed that I had twice won the Three-isle Race.

My hand stretched toward it.

But I knew that I had twice been crowned with twined lilili leaves and deepgreen.

I left without another backward glance.

I began my recruiting for my army with my own dear boys, gathered by Yassu.

My speech was short and simple. I had a blood debt to pay, I said, and the Council would never approve of my paying it—against a Terren. I could feel them all staring at my stump resting against my side. I was going to devote the rest of my life, I said, to Vendetta. Any of them, I stated clearly, who chose to follow me in my compulsion could expect to be proclaimed outlaw, Dread, any blade's meat. I told them that the Elyavaneet Noblelady would care for any boy of mine who could not follow me, wholeheartedly, with an easy mind and a clear conscience. I warned that a life of Dread would be short and hard. I reminded them that blood debt and Vendetta breed more blood debt and Vendetta. I would understand, I said, if no one wished to follow me; I would make provision.

I only asked that those who stayed behind swear not to reveal aught I had told them, until my plans were matured.

The last was unnecessary. They were all eager to come. And though I had planned to refuse Jerbon (if he offered) because he was getting old, and Toddee and Plolto because they were overyoung, I saw that I had not true choice. None of them could endure being left out.

I had six days until the Hypasha's Dedication. Sometimes I wished I were two people; or better yet, a dozen. But it was make haste slowly, or all would be demolished before it could be properly begun.

My own dear lads weren't enough. I needed more than guards and fisherfolk; I would need, looking into the future, joiners and netmenders and those skilled in simples, blade-edgers, and . . . The list grew and grew. And each recruit more and more dangerous, more and more the chance that someone would say the wrong thing at the wrong time. I spoke to each potential recruit myself, in dark corners on the docks, in odd storerooms, even—how could I have been so bold—in the Sacred Courts, when we should both have been muchly otherwise occupied.

I was determined that the Elyavaneet should not be accused of complicity, so I took greatest care to avoid her and all her household. All for naught. She was ill, gravely ill, deathly ill; none of those who tended her thought she would arise again from her sickness.

In a way, I was glad, for now she could never be hurt by what I planned. Her successor as Speaker for Morningstar was the Hollydora Noblelady, a stolid stubborn Delyen that the Merwencalla would lead about by a string. If only I had been older; but I wasn't. And I would never Speak for Morningstar now.

I saw the Hypasha again, though she didn't see me. I was disguised (I was becoming rather skillful in that direction) in a guard's cloak and some stain. She was being Purified, and she looked sleek and full and confident. Poor Hypasha, I thought. If she only knew.

I had a great argument with the amulet. It didn't want to be left behind. It raved about half a story and kept begging me for Neill's sake. I told it logically that even if it was Neill's magic, the Terre masters were entirely too skilled with magics; and I was never, ever going to give them another chance at me, if I could help it. It kept arguing that it was scrambled, whatever that was. I had meant to bury it, as I had buried its master. Instead I hid it.

What I intended was simple. I wanted two things:

vengeance against the Terrene; and protection for my people. I thought I knew how to manage both. My people couldn't be blamed for my misdoings if I were outlaw, Dread, hunted by them. So I was going to do something so outrageous, so terrible, so unthinkable, so obscene, that the Council would have no choice but to proclaim me Dread.

First I would establish myself as outlaw; then—let the Terrene beware!

Poor Hypasha!

None too soon, I was ready to face the Council.

Chapter Twenty-seven

MOTTO:

And if the Soul can fling the husk away,
And naked on the sands of Heaven play,
Were not a shame, were not a shame you say,
In this clay carcass crippled long to stay.

—Song of Neill, original attributed to
Dwardfizgerrol Lady Bard, of Terrafam

Looking back now, over a span of many cycles, I can see how incredibly lucky I was, though at the time I thought it the result of meticulous planning and acute knowledge of those with whom I dealt. But now I know that it was the Hand of She Who Reigneth, though what Her ultimate purpose, I cannot judge.

I only knew that when I ripped the hood from my face and strode into the Circle, scant heartbeats before the signal that would have borne the Hypasha into her place there, I had the headiest feeling that I was standing, not in the Circle, confronting the leaders of my people, but astride Delyafam itself.

The Thrice-blessed conducting the Ceremony recognized me, of course.

"Why come you here, Kimassu Lady, to interrupt our most sacred endeavors?"

I made her an obeisance with such a swagger, such flourish, that it was an insult by itself.

They had recovered a trifle from the shock of seeing me where I should never be, and I could see the anger—and, yes, fear—growing in their faces.

"I bear a Petition, one that needs must be presented before the full Council." Indeed, it *was* the full Council, for there sat the Hollydora on the Elyavaneet's dais, and my beloved Noblelady yet breathed! I added an extra measure of fury for this insult to my Noblelady.

"Kimassu Lady." It was the aged, elegant Cahdiwaggu speaking, green-eyed peacemaker. "You know Custom. The complete Council must attend a Dedication." Incredibly she had read my mind (or the anger in my eyes as I gazed at the Hollydora), in this at least; and I knew her for the danger she was.

"I had not heard," I said silkily, "of the giant sea wave that wiped out great numbers to make this Dedication necessary so precipitously. Perchance it was a plague? Nay, then." I held up my hand to cut off the flurry of excuses. "I hold no grievance, against that which brings you together so timely for my purposes. I would present before you a Petition."

Again their voices beat against me. Against all Custom! Present your Petition at a regular Council meeting. Next Official meeting. Place it on—Approval of—Through your Family Speaker—How dared you interrupt—(A mutter, whose origin I could not fathom: Should have been *culled* . . .)

Senile old men!

I hurled the knife so that it cut the Circle when it landed, pointing straight at the Merwencalla, its crimson tassels fluttering from its rapid flight.

The voices stopped, except for a massed indrawing of breath; they *knew*. In confusion, they rose; or sank, trembling, in their stations. Even the glow-animals massed on the walls seemed dimmed. That I had dared to bring a Blade—and *such* a Blade—

I had to admire my enemy, the Merwencalla, then. She straightened in her chair, but that was the only sign she gave. She glanced about at those sitting or standing, frothing in rage or pinched and bitter; and there was total silence.

She couldn't ask, that would have been against Custom. I knew that the Hypasha, beyond the Curtain, would be wondering at the delay; why had the conch shells not sounded for her entrance. She'd find out soon enough.

I let the silence stretch out, until it seemed as though all the world were silent, as though time had stopped.

And when I could contain myself no longer, I swirled

the cape back and raised my mutilated arm high. "I call Blood Vengeance," I shouted, my voice echoing strangely, "against the Terrene! I call Vendetta. I call the Line of Dread. I call . . ."

Now this is the strangest part, but I had been counting on it. The Merwencalla *wanted* an excuse to set the Line of Dread about the Terrene, desired it to the innermost fiber of her being, had been searching for a valid excuse for cycles, lining up support. But—she could not accept that excuse from *me*. She couldn't, though it was her dearest wish, served to her on a crystal platter. I was she who had humiliated her. I had outmaneuvered her. I caused her loss of face, lack of influence; only Elyavaneet's illness had enabled her to cling to her high position by her fingertips. And now I was destroying her one chance to save face: the Hypasha's Dedication.

I made matters no easier for her or the rest of them. I was fiery, rebellious, demanding. I set the Council against itself. I flamed in the vortex of my own hurricane. I have never felt so *alive*, before or since. I was cloud-walker, earth-shaker, sea-drainer, temple-destroyer. I tore a world asunder that day, and whether the new world that rose from its ruins will be better or worse, I cannot say. I shall not live to see the end of my work, though I have seen its beginning.

They could not agree, and I harried them, as the fleet harries a school of plunnies into the nets. I harried them into my net, though it did not seem so to them. I demanded, they quarreled, vacillated *refused*. Their fire rose to match mine. Their pride, their dignity—the habit of command?—what could they do but deny me? And my fury turned against them.

The Shield of each Family was displayed behind each dais below the banner, lovingly polished, brave with enamel. My blade was hard scale, not metal, but—a step, a grasp, a throw—it rang valiantly against the Swordshine's Shield.

My voice rang, too, in the sudden stillness. "Honorlost Council, I cry Vendetta against you all!"

The Merwencalla was pale with fury. "I proclaim the Line of Dread around she who was the Kimassu Lady. The Blade that drinks her blood will be high-honored."

I *laughed!* It echoed off the high-arched walls and

through the dome-roofed passages. "Old *men.* Honor-lost cripples! Go sit in the sun and dream of past glories! Here I stand, come one, come all! Or—cry you a champion, be she not afeared to meet me, blade to blade."

I was staring at the Merwencalla, challenging. For a moment I thought she would pick it up. I wanted her to, I reveled in the thought. I was a sudden reversion back to our primitive ancestors. I didn't need a blade, I would tear her throat out with my teeth and drink her heart's blood. Klandu, we name it, that old berserker fury that sometimes overcomes our more civilized self to turn us into a mindless killing animal. I was on the brink, and she sensed it—and broke.

"Guards! *Guards!* To the Council Chamber! GUARDS!"

I hissed, but only to myself. Aloud, I cursed them all as honor-lost cowards.

The Hypasha and the guards, a dozen picked males, brightly accoutered, arrived together. Poor 'Paysha. Her wrath was immeasurable. The Dedication was ruined. I couldn't control myself. But instead of Klandu, that crimson, drowning flood of emotion, I hissed myself silly, until I was leaning on a guard because I couldn't stand upright. And the louder I hissed, the worse the turmoil, and more furious the Hypasha became, to say naught of the Merwencalla and the remainder of the Council. They were still arguing (the Hollydora and the Cahdiwaggu abstaining) whether I should simply be executed at the next dawn or saved for a full Ceremony in the Sacred Presence Hall (and *how* the Council can argue!) when the Hypasha controlled herself enough to seek permission to have me taken away and held until a decision could be reached. The Merwencalla gave her gracious consent, promising the Hypasha (the rest of the Council eagerly concurring) that the Dedication would be repeated on the very next auspicious day; the augurers would be set to divining immediately to determine that and—a fierce glare at me to imply what else the augurers would determine, and the quicker, the better.

I stood, swaying, limp and wrung dry, making no protest, while one of the guards untied the shield from my baldric, and apologetically patted me over for weapons.

'Paysha marched us out. Poor 'Paysha. I don't believe I ever saw anyone even half so furious. I could feel pity. Her Dedication, which should have been the supreme moment of her life, destroyed, worse, *sullied*.

At the door to the cell (a Council cell; not bad as cells go), she spat through gritted teeth, "Kimassu, may your anima freeze, may you shiver in the outer dark, may you—"

I couldn't help myself; I doubled over with laughter.

"All . . . right." She drew herself to her full height (such as it was). She was still wearing her ceremonial robes. "I am going"—she bit the words out in short hard phrases—"to petition the Merwencalla Noblelady . . . that you be executed in Viansploor . . ."

"How unworthy I am of this honor," I said.

"And I be permitted to officiate! I'll see you beg for mercy, *beg*, Kimassu!" Hands and lips trembling, she stared at me. Then suddenly, my old friend, the Hypasha, barracksmate, chum. "How *could* you, Kimassu?" I almost weakened, but then: "Were you that jealous, Kimassu; you must know that *you* could never be . . ."

That did it. "Are you sure," I cooed, my voice sweet with solicitude, "that you don't wish to practice somewhat, Hypasha? After all, it takes more than natural talent and enthusiasm to make a good Viansploor—last—properly." I smiled, showing my teeth. "I'll be glad to give you some pointers."

She literally chattered in her rage. With an effort, "I don't want to *weaken* you."

A hit, a definite hit. I decided to end the farce. "Have you ever noticed, 'Paysha, how alike guards look? One tends to notice the insignia on the kilt and not the face . . ."

I hadn't allowed Draxuus in the Council Chamber, he was just a bit too conspicuous, his beautiful face too memorable. But now he stood proudly at the forefront of his fellows; she recognized him first, and then looked, really looked, at the others. "Kimassu, what means this?"

I smiled. "The Council is still arguing. But I reject their authority. While they argue, I'm going to act."

"They wouldn't dare touch me, not one of them!"

My smile broadened. 'Paysha showed lack of imagination. As if *she* were the only stake at risk! "They wouldn't; but I would," I told her genially, my eyes locked with hers. At the same time, I held out my hand, palm up, and felt a hard, shivering with rage shell placed in it. I slapped 'Paysha without looking down, my target, a curve of bared shoulder, chosen in advance. She felt a blow, glanced down, but wasn't quick enough to pick off the stinger. I wasn't bitten since I had slapped and immediately jerked away, a technique I had practiced assiduously with harmless crawlers.

She didn't even have time to scream.

"Quick, catch her!" They did, with a ginger care for the angry azure-and-jet stinger. Drax knocked it off with his knife hilt and crushed it under his sandal.

"All ready?" I asked Draxuus.

"Yes, mistress."

"Then let's go. Careful with her, now." I knew they would be without my saying. 'Paysha was a Lady, and it would be some while, if indeed ever, that these boys lost their awe of a Lady. It was to be one of my most difficult problems.

If I say so myself, it was a neat plan, cleverly executed. There were two major fleets and an assortment of odd ships in the harbor, their crews ashore eager to take part in the celebrations following a successful Dedication. We took every one, without a blow struck.

The Hypasha recovered consciousness, trussed helpless, and stowed in a protected but fish-stinking cargo net. For two days more she refused to speak to me or to the boy who fed her, but on the third day's nooning, she could no longer contain her curiosity. "Well, Kimassu?"

"Well, Hypasha?"

She was seated on a low hummock, her hands tied before her, her feet hobbled with a long rope, the rope looped up between her bound wrists. A boy squatted and fed her patiently. "What do you intend?"

"Many things. For *you*—you needn't fear. You've hostage value, 'Paysha. I might be able to trade your tender hide for a pardon—but only if it surrounds your breathing body. So, for now . . ." I let my voice trail off, finishing the half-truth that was worse than a lie.

"I see." But her eyes were narrow with suspicion.

"I doubt," I added, for good measure, "if the Council will be willing to bargain for damaged cargo, so . . ." I spread my arms wide. "You've little to fear, 'Paysha."

"I don't fear you, Kimassu." A pause. "I don't understand you, either."

"That isn't necessary." I tried to keep my voice expressionless.

"No, but . . ." Her voice trailed off. "This isn't like you, Kimassu; I just can't see . . ."

Only three people would have known me well enough to realize that. Neill was dead, and the Elyavaneet dying; and as for the Hypasha—she would not long be a threat.

I forced her to eat Skensa, the one thing that will dull our sense of direction. "A precaution, only," I told her. "If you should escape . . ." She was blindfolded or stowed in a covered net by night and day. But otherwise, she was treated with care and solicitude, her every need anticipated. Except one. The Hypasha had been Purified a full cycle before her Dedication was scheduled. And 'Paysha was a sexually normal Delyen. I watched for subtle signs (which rapidly became not so subtle) and bided my time.

Meanwhile I planned and established bases and rendezvous points; I set up tasks and duties and watched for signs of likely lieutenants. I organized and . . . waited.

The hrex spawned, and the water was thick with wriggling, snapped-off hindparts, full to bursting with eggs and sperm. Our ship (I had renamed him the *Wave-eater II*) had separated from the main fleet, and we gathered to fill our bellies to surfeit. Delicious as they are, hrex don't dry, so it was take what you can eat—and eat it. Despite our care, and the festival spirit that the hrex season engenders, 'Paysha had lost weight; she looked drawn and nervous.

I put it to her bluntly. The boys would be honored to please her, BUT . . . And I would be glad to let them, BUT . . . I wanted her word of honor: None of the boys to be hurt, in any manner, before, during, or after, no matter what her fury or frenzy or disappointment or whatever; and no escape attempt, before or during or after, until I gave the word.

"Aren't you tired of those ropes?" I coaxed. "The hrex'll be spawning for days. We can leave most of the boys here, they deserve a little holiday. You and I and a few picked lads'll take the dinghy for a joy-sail, like old times, 'Paysha . . ."

"And if I say no?"

I tried a bluff. "I'll go alone, and the closest you get to a *boy* is when he feeds you."

"I won't give you my parole!"

"Wait until the Council gets around to buying you back, then."

She cursed; I was firm.

She gave in. The boys lined up on the beach, giggling and jostling each other for position. There were a scattering of lumpen females among the crew (mostly passed-overs, but some merely young), so no one would be left out of the celebration. (One of the lumpen had a great deal of potential. She had been passed over because, in her early barrackshood, a strange growth had developed in her throat, so that she spoke painfully and almost unintelligibly. But impeded speech, I had discovered, was not impeded body or mind. I had plans for her, the Minyat, but I was in no hurry. I had been tempted to take her with us; but I decided to leave her in charge. She was overyoung, anyway; her turn would come. I assured her, in great detail. Her turn would come.)

So we sailed off into the cool of early evening, the boys pleasurably excited, and the Hypasha—impatient wasn't the word! She couldn't understand what was wrong with the beach, but I never liked group activity; besides, I knew this sweet little island nearby with—*everything*—

She was so hot by the time we reached the pool, that it didn't matter that it was a tight fit for two couples. Nor did she notice, until it was far, far too late, that the water was sweet, not the tiniest touch bitter.

Her curses turned both air and water crimson; but the damage was done.

Finally she calmed down enough to ask why.

I shrugged.

She looked at me then. "Goddess, you, too! Why?"

I drew a deep breath. "Because it needs must be so, 'Paysha. Would you hear me tell why? And listen, with heart and mind?"

She snorted. But when I held out a hand to draw her out of the pool, she came. "We'll be back shortly," I told Drax and the other boys. "Amuse yourselves as you wish until we return."

"Prepare yourselves," 'Paysha added, and they dissolved in happy laughter.

There was an ache deep in my stump and I absently rubbed it as we strolled along in the Anatra-lit darkness.

"Did a Terren bite your hand off?" she asked.

I hissed loudly. "Someone's been talking behind my back. No, I'll get to that in a minute. Tell me, truly, 'Paysha, what do you fear?"

"I? Nothing!"

"Fear's not quite the right word, then. What are you wary of, what do you treat with respect, what worries you—"

"You!"

" 'Paysha, in all seriousness. What?"

"I don't follow you."

"Sea wave, hurricane, blade's edge, greenrock, slaytail—"

"If you mean, what do I think could kill me, all you named and more besides."

"What about whatever could kill the Delyene?"

"Nothing. Any of those you named could kill some Delyene; nothing can kill all of us."

"Not even the Terrene?"

"Pah. Stories to make younglings quake in their barracks. The Terrene are few and weak, honorless posturers."

"There are many," I disagreed, "and their magics make them mighty."

"Pah."

"Would you believe a Delyen could conquer Leviathan herself, alone and weaponless?"

She laughed and clapped me on the back. "Oh, now, Kimassu, tell another!"

"I killed a Leviathan, some days agone," I told her soberly. "I alone, with my mind and knowledge of our Delyafam." Her mouth dropped open, so I told her about it. In the end she was but half-convinced. "Even Leviathan can be destroyed," I repeated over and over. "And if Leviathan, why not the Delyene?"

I could feel her turning away from me, hardening herself against my arguments. "There are worse things than physical death, 'Paysha." I glanced down at my stump. "Much worse."

"Tell me." Her eyes had followed mine.

"The Terrene have magics far beyond what they have shown us. One of them wanted to keep me, wanted to subject my will to his, wanted to . . ."

"His? A male?"

"A male. He put a wristlet on me, 'Paysha, and it made me do what *he* wished."

Her eyes were wide and unbelieving.

"It's truth, 'Paysha. I was like a puppet on the end of a stick. And he held the stick. If I struggled against the stick, the wristlet hurt me, and when I tried to run away, it made me unconscious. So, I got rid of it the only way I could. Hand and all. I'm nobody's play toy, but that's what we'd all be, all the Delyene, if the Terrene have their way. You know, I used to wonder how they regarded us; I knew they scorned us because we haven't their magics, thought of us as lesser beings, as we regard lumpen, or even our boys. But it's worse than that; we're animals to them, plunny for their nets, daggerteeth to be wary of, useful for a variety of purposes we can't even conceive of. They don't recognize the Goddess, or any higher power, just themselves. And if they're not stopped they'll destroy us, as a people, as a race. Unless they fear us. Unless it's convenient, or uneconomic. They've got to be stopped. And I'm going to try. I and the army you and I started breeding just now."

"An army? What is that?"

"A large number of beings dedicated to fighting for a single cause," I told her.

"What do you call what you have now? How large a number do you need, that you would commit this ultimate defiance against the leaders of the Delyene?"

"Because," I explained patiently, "these that I have, these boys and lumpen, they're following me for the adventure of it, or because they're personally loyal to me. They're good enough followers, but I need people who can do more. Who can do what must be done. Like, for example, with you tied up and me not near, I worry. You might order one of these to release you, and he would. They're trained to obey, they're trained not to think, they're . . ."

"Boys can't think! And as for lumpen . . ."

"I wonder. Raise them to think that they can, to rely on themselves, to be independent; and we'll see."

"You're mad. Totally mad."

I shrugged. "Or sane in a mad world. Who knows. But in my madness I will build. And what I build will—I hope and pray—save us from being crushed under the heel of the Terrene. Or at least buy us a little time. Or, maychance"—I smiled at her—"when the Terrene do crush us, my little band, they'll do it so viciously as to goad the Council into action. Who knows? However it comes out, 'Paysha, I *will* fight."

There was a long stillness. "I'll let you go, back to the Council, 'Paysha; when nothing *they* can do will stop me."

But she didn't go, of course. By her own choice. She had heard too much of my story, the details dragged out of me at odd times and places. They were hard, those first years, even with 'Paysha's willing help. I led raids, my own people, as well as the Terrene. I was outlaw, and remained so. But I was more. I made Delyafam *unprofitable,* in a dozen different ways. I harried and I nibbled. They set a price on my head, the Council, and then the Terrene, and then both together. I hissed happily; the higher the price, the more successful I was.

(One of those Terrene who set the price was Lexi. I sent a boat to pick him up, but I was wary of Terre magics, and the boat was small and filled with new recruits only. And following it, secretly, swimming in the water, a couple of trusted scouts. The scouts told me of the trap set on that isle, the capture of the hapless recruits. Oh, I made Lexi and the Terrene pay dearly for those innocents, that I did!)

But I did more than lead bloody raids. I set up bases, permanent bases, and I raised, to my own ideas, that first generation. I trained lieutenants, and I raised more sprats, until those I had trained were raising the sprats' sprats . . .

I age slowly, as my people do, and I have been lucky in my battles; but I think I am at the end of my path now, though I am still young for a Delyen. I have watched the Hardyene I brought with me age and die, so that there are now left of that original faithful band but a few lumpen—not lumpen, never lumpen any more, but Delyene!

It is not age that is my downfall, nor yet any of the wounds I brought back from our raids. But deep inside the stump that is my gift from the Gorky Admiral an infection has grown. Twice now, they have held me down and carved off putrid flesh. It is necessary again.

He is coming, my chief lieutenant, child of that first begetting of 'Paysha (May your breath be sweet upon her, Goddess!) and I. Somehow, though we mixed broods, as is Custom. I have always been sure this one was mine. I have always been most careful never to show partiality, but somehow this one, strangely, this male one, has always been my favorite.

His eyes are soft with intelligence, compassion; he is tall, strong, vital—intelligent. He says nothing, merely holds out a hand to assist me from my perch. I look away across the sea; almost I imagine I can see across the waters to another isle, another cliff, another time. I take his hand.

"I'm coming, Neillsson."

Can miracles happen? In some lights his eyes seem blue.